KATE HEWITT
THE
GIRL
FROM
BERLIN

bookouture

Published by Bookouture in 2021

An imprint of Storyfire Ltd.
Carmelite House
50 Victoria Embankment
London EC4Y 0DZ

www.bookouture.com

ISBN: 978-1-83888-800-8
eBook ISBN: 978-1-83888-799-5

This book is a work of fiction. Names, characters, businesses,
organizations, places and events other than those clearly in the
public domain, are either the product of the author's imagination
or are used fictitiously. Any resemblance to actual persons, living or
dead, events or locales is entirely coincidental.

To Cliff, whose ideas and expertise—and willingness to listen (and let me exist in the 1930s for several months)—helped me immeasurably to write this novel. I love you!

PROLOGUE

"Open the door, *Fraulein*."

There are three of them, crowding the narrow hall that smells of drains and decay and death. The older one who spoke is looking at her with a weary sort of indifference, which is somehow worse than if he'd been either angrily threatening or deadly quiet. He knows she is cornered, helpless. The other two seem just as bored; one scratches his stubbly cheek, his battered rifle pointing at her at a forty-five-degree angle. If he shoots her, it will be in the kneecap, except she doesn't think he is going to shoot her.

She swallows. Stays silent. And she doesn't move. She is not deceiving herself that she can keep these three soldiers here forever, or even for five minutes. But if she can stall them for just a few seconds... if she can give the others enough time to get away, to find some sort of escape, at least from this.

"Open the door, *Fraulein. Jetzt.*" Now. She hears a bit of temper in his voice, but not much. Not enough. She stays where she is.

The soldier who spoke sighs, as if he is a schoolteacher and she is a recalcitrant pupil in need of no more than a slapped hand. She is a fly he cannot be bothered to swat. He says something to the other, she can't hear what, a guttural command that feels inevitable. Her heart begins to thud. She can guess what happens next, and she is ready for it.

It feels as if every dark and uncertain moment up until now has been preparing her for this—from that first faint twinge of doubt she'd felt when staring up at the stadium in all of its Olympic glory to the terrible, leaden knowledge lodged inside her nearly nine years later, when she'd surveyed the sweep of broken bodies strewn over that once-hallowed ground. All of it, every single labored breath and agonizing choice, had been preparing her for the penance she can finally make, for she knows she has so much to atone for.

Have they got away?

The second soldier, the one who received the command, hefts his rifle to his shoulder, so it is aiming at her heart. She hears a click and she closes her eyes, her body pressed against the door, as she waits for whatever comes next, knowing she will accept it. She will embrace it, because perhaps then she can be forgiven.

That is the last thing she lets herself remember.

CHAPTER ONE

Berlin, August 1936

It was meant to be perfect, and yet it rained. Liesel Scholz craned her neck to look out her bedroom window at the dank sky that bore down on the city like an unwholesome blanket, turning everything to gray, the Grunewald forest on the edge of Berlin shrouded in tendrils of damp fog. A few fat raindrops spattered onto the pavement of Koenigsallee below, a rather dismal harbinger for the magnificent proceedings that were to unfurl today, in the Reich's most triumphant occasion to date. It was the opening of the Olympics, meant to be the finest display of Aryan superiority and strength the waiting world had ever seen.

"The weather dares to disobey the Führer," her father remarked lightly as he poked his head through the doorway of her bedroom. "But, more importantly, what do you think of my new suit?"

Liesel turned from the window, planting her hands on her hips as she made a show of inspecting her father's single-breasted suit, cut, as always, in the latest style. "It's quite... bright," she remarked a bit dubiously, for the pattern was of bright green check, far from the usual sober browns, blacks, and grays that most men wore these days. "But you look very handsome as always." With his tall, lean physique, sandy hair and hazel eyes so often full of humor, her father cut a debonaire and slightly louche figure, especially compared to the stern, stodgy types Liesel saw so often now—the Hitler Youth boys with their razor-straight partings and bright, steely eyes, or their corpulent fathers, with their glossily bald heads and ruddy, sweating faces.

Otto Scholz was nothing like either of those unlovely specimens, and for that, as much as the attention he showered on her so easily and so happily, she loved him.

He chuckled now as he gazed down at his outfit with a wry look of acknowledgment. "Ah, yes, so it is, but I want to be noticed today. There will be many important people around us, Lieseling," he explained, using the pet name he'd made up for her when she was small, a play on *liebling*—or darling—and one Liesel pretended to think was babyish but secretly still loved.

"Why am I not allowed to be noticed, then?" she returned with a half-mock pout.

A faint frown creased her father's forehead as she dared to touch on that one forbidden subject—her mother. Ilse Scholz had, despite her own penchant for high fashion and French perfume, insisted Liesel wear a plain dark skirt and white blouse with a pair of obnoxiously sturdy shoes. In such a staid outfit she looked even younger than her fourteen years.

"*You* do not need to make an impression," Ilse had told her with a pointed look at her husband. Otto had simply smiled, ignoring the jibe, if it had indeed been one.

Liesel couldn't tell if it had been or not; she so rarely could, when it came to her parents and their complex relationship. She believed her father adored her mother with an unreserved wholeheartedness, something that annoyed her on occasion as she loved being the center of his gentle and teasing affection, and too often she wasn't.

As for her mother... Ilse Scholz, a cool, dark-haired beauty who could have once graced Berlin's finest concert halls as a pianist if she'd chosen to do so, seemed too remote and withdrawn for that sort of intensity of emotion; her distant gaze often skimmed over everyone, including her husband, never resting or settling, but always drifting on, to an unknown place it seemed as if she'd rather be.

At least Liesel would not have to deal with her mother's cool disapproval today. Ilse had refused to come to the Opening Ceremony even though Otto had procured tickets to one of the VIP loges in the stadium, thanks to his position at IG Farben, one of Germany's largest chemical manufacturers.

"I have no need to see such ostentatious displays," Ilse had stated coolly, "and the excitement and crowds would be far too much for Friedrich."

Liesel's younger brother, at six years old, had a poor constitution and a weak chest, in addition to a slightly twisted left foot thanks to a difficult birth. "He needed an extra tug," Otto liked to say—and as a result he was hopelessly coddled, and, Liesel thought, rather spoiled by her parents, and sometimes even by her. She couldn't help but feel sorry for poor little Friedy, with his thick spectacles and his owlish stare, his dreamy ways and his hesitant, limping walk.

Perhaps because of his infirmities, or maybe because of the many miscarriages that had preceded his birth, and the children who had never come after, Liesel sometimes felt as if there was a river of loss running through the empty center of their home, although her parents never spoke of such things, or even acknowledged they existed.

Still, she saw it in the way her mother often went to bed in the middle of the afternoon, and how her father acted as if this were a perfectly normal thing to do. She felt it in the distance that had always yawned between her and her mother, especially as she'd grown older. Was it because her mother was afraid to love her? Or was she simply too weary from all the losses that she couldn't summon the energy for affection? Whatever the reason, it had bred in Liesel a deep, simmering resentment, as well as a silent disdain. Her father did not have such troubles. Why did her mother have to be so weak?

In any case, her mother did not seem to have those same troubles with Friedrich. Certainly, she refused him nothing, except perhaps to attend the Ceremony today, which he'd wanted to desperately, as he was an enthusiastic devotee of the Führer, listening to his speeches on the wireless with a grave intensity that belied his few years.

Ilse had promised him an ice cream at Café Kranzler on the Kurfurstendamm instead, which Liesel thought quite a poor second choice. Still, she was glad Friedrich wasn't going. It would just be her and her father, the way she liked it.

"Don't fuss about your clothes," Otto told her now with another one of his easy smiles. "I can't bear your frowns, and in any case, there's far too much to be excited about today. Are you almost ready?"

"Yes, I am." Liesel glanced at her reflection briefly, grimacing at the schoolgirl clothes her mother had insisted upon. She almost looked as if she were wearing the uniform of the *Bund Deutscher Mädel*, the girls' branch of the Hitler Youth and an organization she had no desire to join, although nearly every girl in her year had since turning fourteen, spending two afternoons a week, as well as most Saturdays, in such appropriate activities as learning childcare and homecraft, distributing leaflets or running races.

Liesel thought the girls were all ridiculous, going into faints over the Führer and being so pompous about their parades and their stupid gymnastics. She'd refused to join the *Jungmädel* for younger girls when she'd been ten, mainly because she thought this little show of spirit pleased her father, and he hadn't even bothered to ask her about the BDM when she'd turned fourteen in February, thank goodness.

"Not every Nazi has to goosestep," she'd heard him say lightly to her mother on more than one occasion, a remark to which her mother never replied, but which Liesel had always remembered.

Now, as they headed out to the car waiting on Koenigsallee, Liesel felt excitement bubble up inside her, irrepressible and infectious. The whole city would be out today. All of Berlin had been scrubbed to a ferocious shine for its many important and international visitors, every bit of it gleaming with a hard, unyielding brightness, despite the rain.

Her family had only moved to Berlin from Frankfurt back in February, for her father had been promoted to running a factory and laboratory in Schkopau, which he traveled to at least once a week, spending the rest of his time at the laboratory in Berlin. Liesel didn't understand much of it; she did know that despite being from Berlin originally, her mother had not wanted to leave Frankfurt.

"There is nothing good to come of being in Berlin," she'd declared to Otto in a grim, final-sounding tone, when he'd announced the move at dinner one evening.

"Ah, but, Ilse," Otto had exclaimed as lightly as ever, "what about the cafés and the cabarets?"

"You know as well as I do the cabarets play nothing but German marching music these days."

"The cafés then," Otto had insisted with a smile. "The coffee will be better, at least."

"These days it's difficult to find anything but ersatz."

Otto had thrown up his hands in a parody of defeat. "Very well," he'd intoned gloomily. "There is nothing whatsoever that is good about Berlin. Not even the house on Koenigsallee that is twice as big as this one, or the chauffeured car we shall be able to use, or the beauty of the Tiergarten or Grunewald…"

A flicker of a smile had touched her mother's mouth and then died, but she had not made any reply.

Now, as they drove toward the Olympic Stadium in the newly constructed Reichssportfeld built for this year's Games, Liesel felt as if she were about to ascend onto a stage, as if the whole city were putting on a performance, a collective breath held before the show was to begin, and for a few moments she could imagine she was its star.

It was as if there was a crackling excitement in the air, an electric hum that traveled along her veins and ignited her heart as she gazed at the crowds heading to the stadium on foot: families with picnic baskets, children skipping ahead, smiling soldiers of the *Schutzstaffel* enjoying the spectacle and yet still smart in their black uniforms—a streaming surge of humanity intent on celebration. Today was important; today *she* was somebody important.

"Look how clean the city is," Otto remarked as the car headed up Douglasstrasse toward the Reichssportfeld. "Not a begging gypsy in sight."

"Who cares about gypsies?" Liesel returned, and Otto chucked her under the chin.

"Not you, apparently."

"Of course I don't." She never even thought about them, dirty begging creatures on street corners. She turned back to the window, her nose nearly pressed to the glass. The car continued to crawl forward in the traffic and people on bicycles weaved in and out, everyone heading toward the stadium.

"I doubt you'll see anyone important walking or cycling," Otto remarked dryly. "Anyone who is anyone will be coming in a chauffeured car as we are."

"I just want to *see*," Liesel answered. She didn't actually care about the so-called important people—Goebbels or Göring, Himmler or Hess, or even Hitler himself—the members of the Nazi elite who so many adulated, as celebrities bored Liesel; they looked too severe, and when they could have spoken, they often shouted instead. Who cared for their fury? She was not interested in them.

Besides, her father didn't seem to actually *like* any of the Nazi officials, although he never said as much, and he'd been a

Party member for three years. Liesel had long ago noticed how a wry, slightly mocking edge entered his voice whenever he spoke about Hitler or the men who surrounded him. That was good enough for her. If her father didn't like the Nazis, if he found them ridiculous, with their strutting and their shouting, then she would feel the same.

She did, however, like being a part of things, especially on a day like today, when the whole world felt electric and alive, and she was right in the middle of it.

Their car pulled up to the magnificent Olympic Stadium, a huge, oval amphitheater—modeled on the Colosseum of ancient Rome—that could seat over one hundred thousand people. Today it would be crammed full of both spectators and competitors, as athletes from many countries processed through the stadium, dipping their flags to Hitler's straight-armed salute while the crowd roared their unabashed approval and the world watched, for the Games were to be televised for the first time in history.

Liesel followed her father into the stadium, doing her best to adopt his worldly, insouciant air as he flashed his papers and slipped through a cordoned-off area guarded by a stern-looking SS officer, to a wide tunnel that led to the VIP loges.

They really were important, she thought with a thrill as they traversed the grand concourse bedecked with scarlet and black swastika flags, her father smiling and waving to anyone he recognized, while Liesel kept her chin up, her head held high, as if she were a grand lady rather than a girl in school clothes. At least she could pretend.

The sheer size of the stadium, already filling up with people, took her breath away, although she tried to look unimpressed by its magnitude. It seemed as if all of Berlin would be there to see the momentous events, crammed into its towering rows of seats, eagerly awaiting the spectacle.

Their seats, however, were something of a disappointment; although they were indeed in one of the VIP loges, it was far from those reserved for the top Nazi officials by Hitler's viewing platform, and instead was a third of the way down the length of the stadium, on the side. Still, they would have a good view of the athletes as they processed, and that would surely be more interesting than watching a bunch of Nazis complete an endless round of fervent *Sieg Heils*.

"I'd rather see Jesse Owens than Joseph Goebbels," she told her father with a pert look, and he smiled faintly before pressing a finger to his lips.

"A sensible approach, I'm sure, although not one I'd discuss with our present company." He nodded toward a couple that were making their way to their loge—an overweight man with pomaded hair and a Party pin on his lapel, and his unsmiling wife in a gray skirt and matching belted jacket, both cut in a severe style. "Herr Wolff, Frau Wolff," Otto said as he sent his arm out in the straight salute that had become essential to the most basic pleasantry. "Heil Hitler."

"Heil Hitler," Herr Wolff replied, and Liesel had to dodge out of the way as his arm shot out like an iron. She looked at him and his sour-faced wife with undisguised resentment; if she had been hoping for interesting or amenable companions for the afternoon, she knew now she was to be disappointed.

Still, the sheer spectacle of the event was enough to keep her entertained; the ceremony began with a flyover of the massive Hindenburg, the Olympic flag with its five colorful circles streaming behind it, and then Hitler entered the stadium through the Marathon steps, sober-faced, high-ranking Nazi officials flanking him. He paused to accept flowers from a little girl before ascending the platform, as the orchestra burst into a rousing rendition of Wagner's *March of Homage*.

As the officials filed onto the viewing platform, Liesel felt a reluctant flicker of fascination she hadn't expected, simply because they were clearly so *important*. What must it feel like, to have half the world staring at you in such awe? To have that much attention and power, and to know it full well, to consider it your right and your due?

As the orchestra struck up *Deutschland über Alles*, Liesel glanced at her father; she saw he was merely mouthing the words as he studied the men on the platform, his hands in his trouser pockets, a slight frown creasing his features as his gaze moved slowly over each one.

A few minutes earlier, when Hitler had ascended the platform, the crowds had gone wild, as they always did; Liesel had had to suppress the urge to clap her hands over her ears as the *Sieg Heils* roared over the stadium in a wave of nearly demented exultation. Next to her, Herr Wolff's face had adopted a frenzied look, his eyes bulging as spittle flew from his mouth.

"I have never understood the need to deify such a petty little man," Liesel had once heard her father say, late one evening, when he'd thought she'd been in bed but she'd crept down the stairs to listen to her parents talk in low voices over glasses of cognac. "And I've heard he has bad breath *and* terrible gas."

"Otto, really." Her mother had laughed, a rich, throaty sound Liesel normally never heard. "The adoring crowds won't know such things."

"And if they did? I wonder…" Her father's voice had been a mixture of amusement and sobriety. "Could the Third Reich be felled by the power of halitosis?"

Now, in the huge stadium, Liesel was as close to Hitler as she'd ever been, close enough to see the shock of glossy dark hair that flopped over his forehead, the ruthlessly trimmed moustache that seemed to her so small and so silly; the stern look in his eyes that somehow, despite her own determination to somehow feel superior to the leader of her country, made her straighten her spine.

His eyes, she saw, really were as blue and penetrating as the colored portrait that adorned so many sitting rooms, including their own.

The cheering and the frenzied *Sieg Heils* continued as the parade of nations began, each country processing in front of Hitler while his arm remained as unbending as an iron rod, his expression unflinching and severe.

Liesel was fascinated by the seemingly never-ending parade of smartly dressed athletes preceded by their country's flag, all of them walking in time and most unsmiling as they saluted the men on the viewing platform.

"It is convenient," Otto remarked *sotto voce*, "that the Olympic salute so closely resembles that of the Nazi party."

Liesel glanced at him uncertainly. "There is an Olympic salute?"

"Indeed." He nodded toward the team from Canada now marching past the viewing platform, arms straight out. "They are not, in fact, *heiling* Hitler, whatever he and his cronies may prefer to believe," he told her in a murmur only she could hear.

The large team from the United States, Liesel noticed, did not offer Hitler any salute, but rather removed their straw boaters and placed their hands over their hearts. As they passed by the platform, their flag did not dip.

"Ah, the symbolic gesture," her father murmured, his lids half-lowered. "So powerful. So pointless."

Finally the team from Germany, as the host country, came out last, and although Liesel had not thought it possible, the crowd's roaring grew louder, fiercer, their fists raised or their arms shot out, so it seemed to her as if there was something almost angry about their joy.

"The German people have waited a long time to be feted in such a way," her father explained to her quietly, answering her silent question as he so often seemed able to do.

When the athletes had all assembled, the last runner of the torch relay, a concept that had been introduced only this year, emerged from the tunnel and did a graceful circuit of the stadium before lighting a cauldron at the top of the stadium that would burn for the entire Games. There was something both noble and inspiring about the single figure with his torch held aloft, so Liesel felt a stirring inside her, a sense of purpose as well as being part of something greater. She glanced around at the exultant crowd, feeling united with them in a way she hadn't expected.

Then the president of the German Olympic Committee made a speech that Liesel did not bother listening to, instead studying the athletes assembled in the stadium like soldiers of the world, many in colorful ensembles from their home countries, and then Hitler himself stepped forward, causing the wild crowd to fall silent in an expectant, reverent hush.

"I proclaim open the Olympic Games of Berlin, celebrating the Eleventh Olympiad of the modern era," he stated, and the cheers and *Sieg Heils* began again in earnest as twenty-five thousand pigeons were released into the air and a cannon went off with a boom that made Liesel jump.

"I fear the pigeons have been startled," her father remarked with a nod to the flock of birds that had risen up over the stadium; it took Liesel a moment to realize the frightened birds' droppings were splattering all over the stadium, much to the rueful dismay of all the athletes assembled below. "How unfortunate," he continued in a low, laughing voice, "that our Führer did not consider the matter more closely." He turned to the loge's other occupants with a ready smile. "Herr Wolff, how did you enjoy the day's festivities? Quite a remarkable show, don't you think? I can hardly wait until the competitions begin."

"Germany will excel, of course," Herr Wolff said, bristling, and Otto smiled faintly in return.

"Of course."

Later, as they walked out of the stadium amidst the stream of humanity, Liesel, still caught up in the exultant emotion of the day, asked her father rather suddenly, "Vati, why don't you like Hitler?"

Her father's expression remained relaxed even as his gaze darted quickly around at the people walking near them. "Who says I don't like him? Why, I don't know him. But if he came to tea, I daresay I would be very pleased. I'd certainly serve him some cake. I hear he has as much a fondness for it as he does a dislike of meat."

Liesel smiled at that as she persisted with her point. "Yes, yes, but you know what I mean."

"I wonder if *you* know what you mean," Otto returned. "Or are you merely parroting things you've heard while crouching behind doorways or on stairs?" His smiling yet shrewd gaze pinned her in place for a moment before he caught sight of someone walking ahead of them. "Herr Ambros. Were the ceremonies not magnificent? Have you met my daughter, Liesel?"

Liesel waited silently while her father exchanged pleasantries with his work colleague; she heard them talking about Schkopau, although she could not follow the conversation.

"Your father has friends in high places," Ambros told her with a smile that did not reach his eyes, and Liesel glanced at her father uncertainly, not sure how to reply. She did not know much about her father's work, only that he was a chemist and he liked to call himself an inventor. He'd done something with pesticides when she was small, but she didn't know what.

Finally they were walking again and once more she had his attention.

"Why did Herr Ambros say you had friends in high places?"

"Because I am ambitious, which is no bad thing."

"You still haven't answered my question about Hitler."

"I believe I did, and you surely won't get another answer from me," Otto returned lightly before a slight frown came over his features as he gave her a more serious look. "Liesel, at your age you must know the impropriety of such questions, especially in a place like this." He nodded to the crowded space all around them—the concourse bedecked by dozens of large swastika banners, the children waving flags, a couple of SS officers laughing and tossing a ball between them on a stretch of grass nearby.

"But you don't care about such things," Liesel answered in surprise. "You never have." Which was why she didn't either. The preening girls with their absurd adoration of Hitler, the teachers who lectured about race science as if it was something obvious and elemental, the fussy men who had been standing on the platform and even the brownshirts she saw marching on the streets... all of it was to be disdained, if quietly. Privately. "You've always acted as if you don't care about any of them," she insisted.

"I believe your opinion of me is far too elevated," her father replied a bit shortly. "I care as much as the next man. The Führer is the leader of my country. Naturally, I must respect and obey him, especially if I am to get on in this world."

They walked in silence for a few moments; Liesel felt strangely disappointed by her father's strait-laced answer. It had almost felt as if he were scolding her, and for what? Parroting his own opinions? Was he allowed to tease, and she wasn't?

She'd liked it, she realized, when she and her father had been complicit in their disdain for the Nazis, even if she knew better than to say as much to anyone else. She liked the feeling of being different together, a little bit superior and smug to the crowd that followed so blindly the leaders that were so earnest and so very dull. She did not want to be like everyone else, and she certainly didn't want her father to be.

"I can tell I have not lived up to your lofty expectations," Otto remarked wryly as they reached the street. "And for that I am, of course, sorry. But I am not a rebel, Liesel, and neither, I think, are you. It's easy to make smart comments, less so to actually *do* something." He let out a quiet sigh as he gave a small shake of his head. "As Goethe says, 'To think is easy. To act is hard.'"

"And what would you do, if you could do something?" Liesel asked. She wasn't entirely sure what her father meant, although she knew he loved to quote his beloved Goethe. He'd read her both parts of Goethe's *Faust* as bedtime stories, and she'd memorized passages herself, just to please and impress him.

"Obey my Führer, like I said," he answered after a moment, his voice sounding strangely heavy. "And protect and care for my family, as any good father would do. That is all I can hope for in this world, all I aspire to."

Yet he'd said he was ambitious. Liesel opened her mouth to make some protesting reply, but her father silenced her, touching her arm as he nodded toward a fleet of buses lined up at the side of the stadium, waiting to take the athletes back to the Olympic Village some twenty miles away. "Do you see the brackets on the top of those buses?" he asked her, and Liesel gazed at the buses blankly.

"Yes…"

"That's where the machine guns will go," he said softly. He sounded both sorrowful and impressed. "Ingenious, is it not? Right there in plain view of the whole world, as we celebrate a strong and peaceful nation. And the gliders that are so gracefully arcing over the stadium on this happy day?" He tilted his head upwards, a faint smile on his face as he regarded the display above them, the gliders as slender and lovely as birds. "Attach a motor to one and it becomes a fighter plane."

Liesel lowered her head to stare at him in confusion. Why was he talking about guns and planes, on today of all days? "What are you saying, Vati?"

"We are a peace-loving nation determined to rearm ourselves, my Lieseling," he replied with a small smile. They started walking again, toward the waiting car. "And like it or not, that is how I will make our fortune."

CHAPTER TWO

It lay on her bed, indicting her with its ugliness: a white middy blouse with the wretched emblem on its sleeve, a navy skirt, a black tie, sturdy marching shoes. Liesel hated it all.

"What *is* this?" she demanded of her mother as she stormed downstairs, holding the blouse aloft as if it were a dirty rag.

Ilse was sitting in the dining room with its dark, heavy furniture, the velvet curtains drawn against the summer sunshine. She was still in her silk dressing gown, even though it was after four o'clock in the afternoon, and there was a half-drunk glass of schnapps on the table, as well as a pack of French cigarettes Liesel knew could only have been procured on the black market. Whenever her father brought them home, he made a game of her mother having to find them, checking all his pockets in smiling exasperation while Ilse laughingly searched for them.

Last night, her parents had attended another party, this one celebrating the end of the Olympic Games and hosted by the eminent Joseph and Magda Goebbels, on Peacock Island in the Wannsee. At breakfast, her father had regaled her and Friedrich with tales of the three thousand guests, the three orchestras, the "aisle of honor" of female dancers with blazing torches that guests processed through, and, of course, the endless Rhineland champagne and requisite fireworks.

Liesel had been entranced by it all. Only two days before, her parents had gone to Hermann and Emmy Göring's even grander party on the lawns of the new Ministry of Aviation building, which had included a recreated eighteenth-century village guests could walk through and a carousel they could ride.

"Even Herr Reich Minister Göring went on the merry-go-round," her father had told her with a laugh. "He became quite, quite breathless." Everyone knew Göring was rather fat, as well as ridiculously flamboyant. The image of him on a carousel had made Liesel laugh.

But she was not laughing now. "Why was there a BDM uniform on my bed?" she flung at her mother in accusation, shaking the blouse for dramatic effect.

Ilse tapped a cigarette out of its box and lit it with the silver lighter engraved with her initials that Otto had given her as an anniversary present years before. She took a long drag, her eyes fluttering closed, before she opened them to stare at her daughter with a steely sort of indifference. "Because you are going to wear it, of course."

"But why?"

"Liesel, you are being pedantic. Because you are going to join the *Bund Deutscher Mädel*, naturally. Don't act stupid when you most certainly are not."

Liesel's chest puffed out as she clenched her hands into impotent fists while her mother sat there and smoked. "But I don't want to join the BDM. You know that."

"Sadly, we all must do things we would rather not in these strange and unfortunate times," Ilse replied as she tapped her cigarette on the side of the ashtray and watched the ash fall off with more interest than Liesel felt she'd shown her. "Why don't you try it on and see how it fits?"

Liesel stared at her incredulously. Even for her mother, this level of indifference was hurtful, a realization that only made her angrier.

She'd refused long ago to let herself be hurt by her mother, by how very bored she seemed by either Liesel's anxieties or her successes. If Liesel won the essay prize at school, her mother just shrugged. If she fell out with a friend, her mother only sighed.

"Why do you want me to join the BDM?" Liesel asked now.

"*I* do?" Ilse glanced up at her, her thin, highly arched eyebrows raised. "What funny notions you have. It is not I who wish it, Liesel, but I know you will have trouble believing that."

"It's not Vati," Liesel returned after a startled pause. "He wouldn't."

"Wouldn't he?" Ilse held her daughter's gaze coolly before dropping it with a shrug. "In any case, soon it will be compulsory to join. You'll have no choice. Better to do it now, when you do." She took another drag of her cigarette. "Or at least that is what your father says."

Liesel stared at her for a moment, anger and hurt and disbelief coursing through her in a hot, acid rush of emotion. *Vati wouldn't*, she wanted to say again, but didn't, because she knew it would only incur her mother's weary disdain. But surely—*surely*—he wouldn't? Her father made fun of the relentless propaganda of the Nazis, in his gentle, wry way. He might have said he'd obey the Führer because he had to, but he wouldn't make her join a ridiculous marching club that spouted nonsense about Jews and gypsies. Not that Liesel really knew any of either, but it was all so absurd. Any thinking person knew Jews didn't have horns on their heads, for heaven's sake, no matter what the newsreel at the cinema might declare.

Her father thought the Nazis' relentless rhetoric against the Jews ridiculous; on occasion, he'd read out passages from her rewritten textbooks, laughing out loud at their absurdities. "Race science," he would proclaim, shaking his head. "How did we not know about this when we were in school, Ilse? And look! Such helpful pictures to aid our youth in identifying a Jew. What about Aryans with big noses? What sort of trouble might they be in now, all because of their proboscises?" He'd toss the book aside with a shake of his head and a twist of his lips, and Liesel felt vindicated because she hated the new textbooks. She did not want to win the essay prize any longer, not when the subject was *How Hitler Has Saved our Fatherland* or *Five Ways the Jews Have Attempted To Ruin Germany*.

No, her father wouldn't want her to join the BDM. Even if he was a Nazi himself, it was only in name. He didn't actually *believe* any of it, and neither did she. He'd quoted Goethe when he'd seen the SA marching down Unter den Linden; Hitler had the thousand lovely linden trees lining the grand boulevard cut down and replaced with Nazi flags. "There is nothing more frightful as ignorance in action," Otto had quoted softly as they'd watched the parade. Why would he want her to be part of that?

"I don't want to join," she told her mother, knowing she sounded petulant yet unable to help it, and her mother met her gaze again, this time with a surprising spark of emotion in her dark eyes.

"Why don't you?"

"Why?" Liesel stared at her uncertainly, unsettled by this sudden interest. "Because I just don't."

"Yes, but why?" Ilse smiled faintly, although the fiery spark remained in her eyes. "What do you not like about the BDM, my little Liesel?"

"It's boring and I don't like races. Or crafts or cooking. Or going on and on about Hitler," she flung at her mother, proud of all her reasons. Ilse, however, looked unimpressed.

"Oh? And why don't you like going on and on about Hitler?" she asked as she tapped her cigarette once more against the rim of the ashtray. "What is it about him that you dislike so much, I wonder?"

Liesel hesitated, for the truth was, she didn't actually know, at least not exactly. Her teachers couldn't praise him enough, and her fellow pupils—at least most of them—expressed a similar sort of ecstasy when it came to their revered leader. Her father might have gently mocked him, but she couldn't remember him ever speaking out specifically about any of his policies. Like him, she thought the rot about the Jews was nonsense, but she hadn't considered the matter more than that.

And Liesel was honest enough to admit that sometimes, when she listened to Hitler speak so passionately on the radio or from the loudspeakers lashed to lampposts, blasted through all of Berlin, she felt a strange stirring in her breast, a sense of patriotism she couldn't keep herself from feeling, although some nebulous instinct, gleaned from her father, made her try.

"He's far too angry," she answered after a moment. "About everything. And I don't believe all the things he says about the Jews." One of her teachers had insisted that Jews were closer to rats than humans. It was so ridiculous as to be laughable, and yet her fellow pupils seemed to take it seriously.

The only Jew Liesel had ever known was a former pupil from Frankfurt, Elsa Weiss, who had stolen the history prize from right under her nose. When she'd left the school three years ago, Liesel had been rather glad; now she would be the one to win all the prizes. Besides, if the Jews kept to themselves, it was no real bother to her, although she didn't think anyone needed to be so very *angry* about it all.

"Ah," her mother said, as if disappointed in the answer she'd expected Liesel to give.

"Everyone is so silly about him," Liesel continued, her voice rising. "With their *Sieg Heils* and their songs and their—their slavish devotion." It was a phrase she'd heard her father use. "And some of the girls in my class keep a photograph of him under their pillow and kiss it before they go to bed."

"So it is not Hitler you dislike," Ilse remarked, "but everyone's attitude toward him."

Liesel could not tell anything from her mother's level tone. "I… I suppose," she said, although she wasn't sure if that was entirely true. She didn't like Hitler, but as her father had so lightly said, she didn't actually *know* him. Would she serve him cake if he came to the house, as her father had joked? Probably.

"Very well, then, there is no problem," her mother continued as she stubbed out her cigarette in the heavy crystal ashtray. "You do not need to exhibit such an attitude yourself when you join, which I know you will want to do, as your father wishes it so much." Her mother gave her a faint smile that didn't reach her eyes. "It shall all work out, you see?" There was a bitterness to her words that Liesel didn't understand.

"He doesn't wish it," she insisted. She could not believe it of her father; it felt like a betrayal.

"Ask him yourself then," Ilse said, and once again she sounded bored. "He will tell you the truth. He always does." She rose from the sofa. "That is one good thing about him, I suppose. Now I have to go dress. We have yet another interminable party to attend this evening."

Knowing she would get nothing more from her mother, Liesel flounced upstairs and flung herself on her bed, hurling the blouse and skirt and shoes into the corner of her room. The shoes, at least, made a satisfyingly loud thud as they hit the floor.

She let out a growling sigh of discontent as she stared at the ceiling. When her father came home, she would ask him. Somehow he would explain everything so it made sense. And she wouldn't have to join the wretched BDM and pretend to fawn over the Führer with all the other girls in her school.

"Why don't you want to join the BDM?"

Liesel turned her head to see Friedrich standing in the doorway, holding a little tin airplane aloft—a model of the *Messerschmitt Bf 109* that had won the Luftwaffe's design competition last year. Its prototype had been debuted at the Berlin Olympics, to much fanfare. He gazed at her unblinkingly from behind his thick spectacles, his twisted foot hidden behind his good one, as it often was.

"Go away, Friedy," she said irritably. "You wouldn't understand."

"But why don't you?" he pressed. He moved his arm in a graceful arc, watching his little tin plane as it flew through the still, drowsy air of an August afternoon. "All the girls do."

"I just don't."

"Well, I do," Friedrich told her with cheerful conviction. "I can't wait."

"To join the BDM?" Liesel jeered wearily, and Friedrich gave her a look of patient condescension.

"No, the *Jungvolk*, of course," he said. "Silly Liesel."

Liesel rolled over so her back was to him, hoping he would go away, but he didn't. She could hear him humming softly under his breath as he flew his little plane about. After a few minutes, she rolled back over to face him.

"Why do you want to join the *Jungvolk*, Friedy?" she asked, thinking of her mother's similar question to her. He was already a member of *Pimpf*, the group for boys aged six to ten, although Ilse usually kept him from going, claiming his health was too delicate for boisterous meetings or hikes through the woods.

Friedrich blinked her slowly into focus as he looked up from his plane. "Because they give you a knife," he answered, as if it were obvious.

Liesel sighed and rolled back over. After ten minutes or so, she heard her brother pad back to his bedroom.

She didn't know how long she lay there, staring at the ceiling, as the house settled softly all around her with its quiet, familiar noises—Friedy humming in his room, her mother playing a few discordant notes on the piano before launching into the melancholy sound of Mahler's *Ich bin der welt abhanden gekommen*—'I am lost to the world.' It was her mother's favorite piece, banned by the Nazis, not that she cared. She played it whenever she was sad, which, to Liesel, seemed like most of the time.

Eventually she heard the sound of her father's car pulling up to the front of the house—he was driven to work every day in the city, although at least once a week he traveled to the factory he now supervised, in Schkopau. The light slam of the car door, his quick steps on the stairs, and then the snick and click of the front door opening and closing.

"Ilse? *Perle?*"

Liesel listened to the low murmur of her mother's voice answering back, and then her father's reply, although she couldn't make out any of the words. She tensed with an almost gleeful anticipation of her father coming up the stairs and confronting her; he would apologize for her distress, and he would tease her, and somehow he would explain everything so she understood and agreed. He *would*.

But he didn't come.

A full hour passed as the shadows lengthened across the room and in the distance Liesel heard the clatter of pots from the kitchen as their cook and housekeeper, Gerda, began preparing the evening meal, usually just bread and soup, before going home for the evening. Sometimes her daughter Rosa came after school and did her homework in the kitchen while her mother worked, although Liesel had never bothered to speak much to either of them. Although her father had said they could have live-in help in their big house in Berlin, her mother had refused it.

"I don't want people watching me all the time," she'd said, and Otto had sighed.

"They're servants, Ilse—"

"Servants are the worst."

Her mother had refused to be moved, and so they made do with Gerda, as well as a maid who came in several times a week to do the laundry.

The clanking of Gerda's pots died down, and still Liesel lay unmoving on her bed. Waiting.

Finally her father came.

She heard his quick steps on the stairs, and then the creak of the loose floorboard outside her bedroom. After a few seconds, he pushed her door open a little wider and then stepped inside her room. Liesel kept staring at the ceiling, rigid with determination.

"Uh-oh." Liesel glanced at him out of the corner of her eye to see him shake his head sorrowfully at the sight of the crumpled blouse and skirt she'd left on the floor. "Your poor uniform. Surely it doesn't deserve to be treated so badly, simple garment that it is."

"Is it true?" Liesel demanded, her voice hoarse after having been silent for so long.

"Is what true? Is the sky blue? Is Berlin the most sophisticated city in the world? Is my daughter the grumpiest girl I know?"

"*Vati.*"

He sat on the edge of the bed, his eyes crinkling at the corners as he smiled sadly at her. "Your mutti said you were not best pleased."

"You knew I didn't want to join the BDM," Liesel burst out.

Her father did not reply.

"You don't even like Hitler," she added defiantly. "You think he's a petty little man! I heard you say so!"

For a second, her father's face darkened and then he shook his head. "If I said such a thing, Liesel, it was not for your or anyone else's ears, and it is certainly unwise to repeat such a sentiment now. Even you should realize that."

Liesel stared at him in disappointed confusion. "You're not *scared…*"

"I am cautious, just as you should be." He sat back, crossing one knee neatly over the other. "When you are in school and your teacher is telling you things you know to be absurd, you do not tell her so, do you?"

"No," she answered after a pause.

"And when everyone says '*Sieg Heil*' at the start of class, you do not fold your arms and pout instead?"

"No," Liesel said again, rolling her eyes. "Of course not."

"No. Of course not." Otto nodded as if she'd given a very clever answer. "Because there are rules. And there are more rules now than there ever were before, which some people think is wonderful news and others think is rather unfortunate. Either way, the rules must be obeyed."

"But you're an adult," Liesel stated after a moment. "You don't have to obey silly rules in a school."

"No, but there are just as many rules for grownups as there are for children, if not more," he told her seriously before his expression lightened once more. "So many rules!" He tapped his head, rolling his eyes dramatically, making Liesel want to smile even though she knew he was treating her like a child, not a young woman of fourteen. "It's so difficult for me to remember them all," he finished, "but I do my best, and I trust you will as well."

Liesel was silent, absorbing what he'd said even as she resisted the truth of it. Her father, she'd always thought, was somehow above the rules, whatever they were. He laughed at them and stayed true to his conscience, just as she wanted to do.

"I sense some very deep thoughts," he remarked after a moment.

Liesel scooted up on her bed, leaning back against the pillows as she folded her arms and gave him a level look. "What does any of this have to do with me joining the BDM?"

"Nothing and everything," he replied, looking the most serious that he had since he'd first come into her room. "Your mother told you it will become a rule, that you must join, if you are Aryan. I have it directly from a trusted source. And if you wait until then to join, well…" Otto shrugged and spread his hands. "It looks suspicious, like you never really wanted to."

"But I *didn't*."

He sighed. "I know that, Lieseling, but it would make life difficult for you, as well as for me, if you did not join."

"You mean you'd get a nasty letter in the post, or someone would come to the door to tell me to join." She spoke scoffingly; it did not seem to her like something to be scared about—a fussy warden banging on about duty to the Führer. You just listened and nodded until they went away. They'd come already several times, going on about a drive for scrap metal, or, back in March, collecting for Winter Relief. It was all just words.

Her father pressed his lips together. "Yes, a letter in the post, that would be the start," he agreed. "But *only* the start, for then they would write your name down somewhere, in some nasty little book, and trust me, Liesel, it's better not to have your name in such a book."

Liesel frowned as she took in his sober expression, yet still with the same humorous glint in his eyes. "There's no book," she said, and her father let out a strange, sad little laugh.

"There are far too many of them, I fear, with too many names in them. Can you not trust me in this?"

I did trust you, Liesel almost said, but then didn't. She didn't even understand why she felt so betrayed by this one small act; her feelings were too tangled to sort out. Would it be so terrible to join the BDM? No, probably not. A few hours a week, preening and parading and being lectured to. Most likely it would simply feel like more school, and there were some fun things that the BDM did—camping trips and special days out. Last spring, they had gone canoeing, and Liesel had felt a treacherous flicker of envy, to see the girls lined up in their coats, their hair in plaits, their faces shining with excitement. They'd talked of nothing else for a whole week after.

Still, the very fact of her attending when she didn't want to—when she didn't even think her father wanted her to, not really—made her feel uneasy.

"Jews don't have horns under their hair," she said abruptly, and Otto raised his eyebrows, a small smile flitting across his face before disappearing.

"No. They don't."

"That's what they say, though. Fraulein Schmidt, who teaches Race Science, says it."

"Just because you listen to someone doesn't mean you have to believe them."

"Then why listen to them?"

He sighed. "Admittedly, a fair point, but this is the world we live in, Liesel, whether we like it or not."

"And do you like it like this?" she asked.

Her father did not reply for a moment, and Liesel had the sense that she'd asked a far more serious question than she'd realized.

"There are some things I like, and some things I do not," he answered slowly. "Which, I'm afraid, is what most of life is like. A series of compromises. So," he smiled at her as he patted her knee, "you will do this one small thing for me, even though you don't want to? And you know that I know that you don't?"

Liesel hesitated, scanning his face for something beneath the crinkled eyes, the small smile, yet she had the strange feeling that there was a deliberate blankness beneath the face that was so familiar, the face she loved, as if an invisible shutter had come down, hiding his true feelings from view, whatever they were. The realization felt like a loss.

"This one thing," she repeated, like a warning, and her father nodded.

"Yes. One thing. One thing only, I promise."

Slowly Liesel nodded back. Yes, she could do this one, small thing, for her Vati. Really, it was not so much. Yet as her father patted her knee once more and rose from the bed, the matter happily resolved, she felt strangely flat, and worse, disappointed.

She'd thought her father was above such fear-fueled pandering; she'd thought he was, if not quite a rebel, then at least a free thinker. Didn't he quote Goethe about freedom of thought? *"Niemand ist mehr Sklave, als der sich für frei hält, ohne es zu sein."* None are more hopelessly enslaved than those who falsely believe they are free.

How could they be free, if her father felt compelled to make her join the BDM, because it somehow made things easier for him at work? Although how it did, Liesel couldn't even begin to understand.

What would be next? For, as her father left the room, Liesel feared with a twinge of unease in her gut that this was not the end of the matter, but rather the beginning.

CHAPTER THREE

Frankfurt, November 1945

Frankfurt, like much of Germany after the war ended, was a city of ruins. Even though he'd seen the newsreels, and had the reports of airstrikes and bomb damage cross his desk back in DC on a daily basis—fifteen thousand bombs once dropped on a single night—Captain Sam Houghton was not prepared for the stench and gloom that hung over the city in a fog of devastation when he arrived in November of 1945.

He gazed silently out the window of the car as he was driven from the Rhein-Main Air Base to the Supreme Allied Command in the old IG Farben building, a behemoth of a structure that had deliberately been left unscathed during the endless air raids on the city. Streets of crumbled buildings, with protruding beams like giant matchsticks and endless piles of broken rubble, sometimes as high as the first floor of those that were still standing, slid by in a depressing reel as he watched.

The driver, Bennett, a second lieutenant who was speckled with acne and was chewing gum with a loud snapping sound, glanced over his shoulder as he nodded toward Liebfrauenkirche, a Gothic-style church that had had its roof blown off, its empty, arched windows reminding Sam of a medieval ruin, the interior filled to the rafters with broken rubble. "We got 'em good, didn't we, sir?"

There was satisfaction in the soldier's tone, along with a strange sort of pleading—perhaps a need, Sam mused, to be validated, after all the atrocities of war.

He smiled faintly as he gave his reply. "So we did."

He did not know what else to say. For nearly four years, since the United States had entered the war, Sam had spent his time behind a desk in Washington, carrying out background checks on military personnel who needed to be cleared for access to classified information.

In 1942, he'd only just completed his basic training before being recruited to the newly formed Counterintelligence Corps, or CIC. But instead of being sent out as a spy, he'd cooled his heels as an analyst. This was the first time he'd ever been in Europe, and he felt every inch of his inexperience, as if "greenhorn" was tattooed across his unlined forehead.

He was thirty-two years old and he did not feel remotely prepared for the task now assigned to him—to facilitate the reconstruction and, more importantly, the denazification, of a devastated post-war Germany. Before the war, he'd been a chemistry teacher; it was his degree in chemistry that had had him seconded to Frankfurt, along with the fact that most of the CIC operatives who had come over on D-Day now wanted to go home. The US Army was desperate for men to facilitate post-war operations; Congress had even considered reinstituting the draft, although that had soon been summarily dismissed. Americans, both soldiers and civilians, had had enough.

Having spent the war behind a desk, Sam had felt he hadn't had enough though. In fact he'd barely had anything. And so he was here, to sit behind another desk after the fighting had finished. At least he would be useful. Hopefully.

Bemused, he watched a street urchin in a motley and ragged assortment of clothes—a patched coat far too big for him, a pair of men's dress shoes and a woman's summer straw hat—dart into the street, heedless of the traffic. With a muttered curse, Bennett slammed on the brakes.

Sam craned his neck to see what the ragamuffin had wanted; the child, its face gaunt and soot-stained, had crouched down to retrieve a quarter-inch smoking butt of a cigarette an American soldier had carelessly dropped.

Leaning back against the seat, Sam closed his eyes. The car moved on, Bennett navigating the craters that pockmarked the street, some several feet deep. When Sam opened his eyes, he saw a hotel that had had its front destroyed, to reveal a series of bedrooms that made him feel as if he were looking upon some absurd dollhouse or perhaps a stage, but the play was long finished.

Worse than the devastation of the buildings, he realized, was that of the people. Germany was a country of the utterly, unbearably defeated. Sam's gaze skated away from a woman wearing a moth-eaten fur coat, a long string of pearls, and an entirely vacant expression as she staggered down the sidewalk, going nowhere. Two children pulled a wheelbarrow full of a random and useless assortment of junk—a dented pot, a broken clock, an old boot. No doubt they would sell it all on the black market for a potato or two; people were desperate and starving, especially the children who roamed the city in packs, like wild dogs, and just as feral.

"Almost there, sir," Bennett called back cheerfully. They had been driving down Reuterweg to Gruneberg Platz, where the IG Farben building stood like a citadel to modernity: six huge, spare wings and hundreds of blank-looking windows; it was, Sam had been told, the largest office building in Europe. Dwight Eisenhower now had his office in the building, and so would Sam.

Bennett pulled up to the front of the building, and after thanking him, Sam got out with his single kit bag. He'd been told to report directly to his CO, Major James Pitt, as soon as he arrived. Although he had never met the man, he'd done a bit of digging and learned that he'd been with the 45th Infantry, having fought the entire war, from North Africa to Sicily, to France and then into Germany itself.

After Germany had surrendered, Pitt had been transferred to CIC and Sam doubted he held a high view of pencil-pushers like him who'd sat the war out from behind a desk. Squaring his shoulders, he started forward.

After showing his identification to the various soldiers on duty, he was taken up in one of the peculiar paternoster elevators, open carriages that never stopped moving so you had to step smartly out onto the floor of your choosing, to the Major's office in the CIC Operation Center.

A pretty blonde secretary with a thick German accent, weary eyes, and heavy pancake makeup greeted him with a tentative smile and, a few minutes later, he was ushered into the Major's office, a spacious room with a cheap wooden desk, a couple of chairs and a few filing cabinets. The man standing behind the desk was stocky and severe, with a bullish, ruddy face that was currently sporting a scowl. Sam tried for a smile as he saluted.

"Captain Sam Houghton, sir, reporting for duty."

"As you were." Major Pitt gave him a long, squint-eyed look. "Just arrived, have you? What do you think to this beautiful city and its fair inhabitants?" There was a slight sneer to his tone that Sam did his best to take in his stride.

"They look like they're in need of our help, sir." As soon as he said the words, he realized they were the wrong ones.

"*In need of our help*?" Pitt repeated scornfully. "That's where you're wrong, Captain. They're in need of our *discipline*. Do you know how many Germans were affiliated with a Nazi organization during the war?"

"Around forty-four million, I believe, sir."

Pitt's mouth tightened; Sam realized he should have pretended to be ignorant of that particular statistic. He was a greenhorn, and

Pitt wanted him to know it. He already felt he did, but perhaps not well enough.

"That's right, Captain, and yet how many Germans admit to belonging to one today? Not a dickey bird." He shook his head, his expression one of hard-eyed contempt. "They're all miraculously innocent, of course. Not one of them wanted Adolf to come into power. Amazing that he did, really, considering all this *reluctance*." He paused, and Sam chose to stay silent. He had a feeling Major Pitt was not looking for a reply. "It's going to be your job to ferret them out, Houghton. One by one. You've got an office on the internal desk and a guidebook to interpreting the *fragebogen*—you know what that is?"

"The questionnaire given to all German adults who wish to gain employment," Sam answered and again he received a thin-lipped look. Soon Pitt was going to think he was being a smart-ass.

"That's right. Your job is to go through them all and then pick out the ones that seem suspicious. I was told you were good at analysis."

"I try, sir." He'd been commended for his diligence back in DC, but this was a different game entirely. He'd been involved in clearance, but he'd never had to catch people out.

"It's too bad you don't speak German, of course." Pitt snorted. "A CIC operative who doesn't speak the language is a bit of a liability, wouldn't you say?"

Sam doubted Pitt spoke fluent German. Most of the CIC operatives who did had already gone home, and the other ones were in the field. The desk agents did their best with the crash course in German they'd had during training and the help of interpreters. "I speak a little, sir."

"Well, you'll have a secretary to help you. First, Sergeant Belmont has selected a few girls for you to interview. You can get to that tomorrow. For now, you can rest and wash up—you'll be staying at a hotel until your accommodation can be sorted. Belmont will show you the way. Any questions?"

"These *fragebogen*..." Sam said slowly, reluctant to push back against Pitt so soon. "I thought I was here because of my chemistry degree? To help identify Nazi scientists who could be useful...?" He didn't know much about his brief, but he'd been told that, at least.

"You'll get to that in time, Captain," Pitt replied irritably. "For now we need you on the questionnaires. We've got a hell of a lot of them to go through."

"Yes, sir." What else could he say? If Pitt wanted him to cool his heels for a while, perhaps to let it sink in that he was indeed a greenhorn, there wasn't much Sam could do about it.

Pitt nodded slowly; it was not, Sam felt, a dismissal, and so he stayed where he stood. "I'm not keen on you administrators swaggering in here," Pitt told him, "thinking you know how it all works when you've only seen the war from a newspaper on the other side of the Atlantic." Sam swallowed and said nothing. "You have no idea what these people have done. What they're capable of. No damned clue. I suppose you've seen the pictures of the camps?"

"Yes, sir." The news had started trickling back to Intelligence in January of '45, the stories of the terrible death camps the Nazis had been so desperate to hide. Sam had stared with a muted horror at the grainy black-and-white photos of stacks of bodies and the living skeletons who gazed into the camera with dazed, unfocused expressions. It had been so hard to imagine the reality, looking at pictures that seemed too terrible to be true, and yet they were.

"I was there when we liberated Dachau," Pitt told him grimly. "And let me tell you, the pictures don't do it justice. You can't imagine. You can't *know*."

"No, sir," Sam said quietly. He agreed with Pitt, even if he didn't particularly like the way he was telling him, as if he were a father talking to a naughty and rather stupid child.

"And let me tell you, people who are capable of that… you can't trust them. Can't like them. I may have a pretty blonde Hilda as a secretary, but that's the extent of it. Do you know what I mean, Captain?"

"I—I think so, sir." Sam was well aware of the no-fraternization policy that had been gradually loosened over the last few months; first with GIs giving chocolate bars to hungry German kids, and then smiles to the elderly, and then cigarettes to *frauleins*—and some *fraus*—in exchange for their amorous attentions. It wasn't encouraged or approved of, but it was now generally allowed. They had to learn to live together somehow, after all.

"Good." Pitt gave him a terse nod. "Dismissed."

Out in the corridor, Sam waited for Sergeant Belmont to give him the address of his digs as various officers, secretaries, and soldiers hurried by, everyone seeming to be going somewhere important.

Finally, Belmont, a saturnine-looking man in his twenties with slicked back hair and a ready, if rather sardonic, smile, approached him. "Sorry for the wait. I've had the most ridiculous German, a Herr Huber, going all red in the face and insisting he has 'very important information.'" Belmont rolled his eyes as he put on a rather atrocious German accent.

"And does he?" Sam asked, to which he received another eye-roll.

"Doubtful. You wouldn't believe the number of desperate informants we get here—they'll say anything for a cigarette or a bar of soap. It's the very devil trying to find out if they've given us a fact or a damned fairy tale."

"And what about this Huber?" Sam asked as he fell into step with the younger officer. Belmont was his inferior in rank and yet clearly he knew so much more than he did. Although Sam wasn't sure he cared for the man's dismissive attitude, he knew he needed to learn.

"The man says he has fifty tons of paperwork for us. Fifty tons! As if we want to sort through all that. It would be like a needle in a dozen haystacks, trying to find anything remotely useful. Apparently he ran some sort of paper mill. The Nazis dumped a bunch of paperwork on him at the end of the war."

Despite Belmont's scornful attitude, Sam felt a flicker of interest. If the Nazis had dumped it, they surely must have wanted to dispose of some sort of evidence. "What sort of paperwork?" he pressed.

Belmont gave him a narrowed look before he shrugged and tapped a cigarette out of the crumpled packet in his breast pocket. "By all means, ask him yourself. He'll probably be back here tomorrow, demanding to see someone important. God knows what he wants for all that trash. A bottle of whiskey and a hundred cigarettes?" Belmont let out a dry laugh and lit his own cigarette.

Sam didn't reply, although he'd already decided to approach Herr Huber if he saw him. If the man was so insistent, surely he could be listened to. Besides, he had to start somewhere. That was as good a place as any.

"Major Pitt mentioned I'm staying at a hotel?" he asked, and Belmont nodded.

"Yes, well, it's more of a little boarding house. It's around the corner, on Wolfgangstrasse. But don't worry, you won't be there for long. Everyone here gets the most incredible digs—you'll be in a mansion with your own cook, maid, and driver before too long."

"A mansion?" Sam tried to look interested rather than blank. He hadn't heard anything about accommodation, so he had no idea what to expect, but it definitely hadn't been a mansion.

"Yes, everyone gets one. All those bigwig Nazis have been turfed out of their homes, of course. Plus you get all their liquor." Belmont laughed. "And whatever else you feel like helping yourself to."

Sam chose not to reply. He had a feeling he would be staying silent for a good while as he learned these new and unfamiliar ropes.

"Listen," Belmont said, "why don't you come out for a drink with us tonight? Then you can see what it's really about. Forget the Nazis. You've got to meet some German girls."

"A drink would be nice," Sam answered noncommittally, and seeming pleased, Belmont made the arrangements before giving him directions to the boarding house on Wolfgangstrasse.

Less than an hour later, Sam was in his room, having unpacked his bag and had a wash with a scant amount of tepid water. He stood by the window overlooking the street, which was half gentrified townhouses in shades of ochre and russet, half rubble and ruin. A few children were loitering in a half-collapsed doorway across the street, wearing a combination of rags and oversized adult clothing, looking gaunt-faced and shifty.

Bennett, his driver, had told him to be wary of pickpockets. Sam couldn't blame the kids for trying to get what they could; the ones he'd seen looked as if they were, quite literally, starving, their cheeks hollowed out, their ribs visible beneath their shirts. And the GIs he'd observed, swaggering about, smelling of Aqua Velva and cigarette smoke, were brimming with good health and money. Sam would have considered it a dangerous mix, but from what he'd experienced of the Germans so far, they were absolutely desperate to please the Americans, however they could.

The landlady's thirteen-year-old son had insisted on carrying his kit bag, even though Sam had said he could do it himself. When he'd asked if there was coffee, she had apologized piteously that she only had a bitter mix of chicory and acorns. Sam had said that would be fine, but he found the stuff undrinkable and had had to choke down a cup while the woman had looked on, beseeching and anxious.

Now he lit a cigarette and gazed at the street below, wondering how he should navigate this bizarre new world. Pitt seemed as if he was determined to dislike him, and Sam suspected he would be buried underneath an avalanche of pointless paperwork, with or without Herr Huber's fifty tons of the stuff. Never mind that back in Washington he'd been told he was needed to help identify chemists who could be useful to American interests; Pitt seemed as if he would prefer him wasting time. Belmont seemed friendly, but Sam felt cautious; the man had a bit too light of a touch. He acted as if he were at one continuous party, everything for his enjoyment, but perhaps that was how most of the CIC operatives acted these days. The war was over, after all, and soldiers wanted to have fun. They'd earned their right to relax.

And what of the Germans? The no-fraternization rules may have been eased, and Sam supposed he'd be hiring a German secretary, along with whatever other staff he was supposed to need, but was it possible to successfully consort with the enemy? The idea made him uneasy in a way he couldn't yet articulate.

He knew well enough that Germany hadn't been liberated or even defeated; the country had been annihilated. The US Army's brief was to completely destroy 'Nazi policy and Prussian militarism.' The British, French, and Soviets who had, along with the US, carved up the country like a Christmas turkey, had a similar MO. So how, Sam wondered as he stared silently down at the rubble-filled street, the children now scrabbling for some piece of trash in the dirt, was he supposed to get along in this brave new world?

The war was over, and it felt like the rules he'd learned by heart no longer applied. He had yet to learn if any new ones had taken their place.

CHAPTER FOUR

Berlin, 1936

When Liesel came into school in her BDM uniform for the first time, the other girls crowded around her, clucking and preening like a gaggle of admiring geese, all of them so surprisingly and stupidly pleased she'd finally joined their exalted ranks.

Liesel stood silently in their center, both bemused and treacherously gratified to be the unexpected object of their fawning attention, for she had not made many friends since moving to Berlin back in February. In fact, she had never been very good at making friends; she didn't see the point of the gossipy groups of girls who clustered together in the schoolyard and talked about such silly things—boys and sweets and, of course, their precious Führer. She could not make herself join in with their twittering, even though part of her knew it would be beneficial to do so, for the alternative was, and always had been, loneliness—something she had become well used to, and had learned even to enjoy.

She forced a smile as they surrounded her and exclaimed over her uniform and her hair, which she'd put in the requisite two braids, because some spiky, contrary part of herself had decided if she was going to be part of the BDM, then she would play the role properly, to the hilt.

Her father, when she'd come down for breakfast, had given her a rueful nod of approval, the look on his face communicating as clearly as if he'd said it out loud that he didn't particularly like the arrangement, but he understood its necessity. Liesel still wasn't sure if she really did.

Several weeks after the uniform had appeared on her bed, she still nourished a hard little seed of resentment of, and worse, a disappointment in, her father for his desire to have her join the BDM. She wanted her father to thumb his nose at the Nazis, if only in his own sitting room. She wanted to thumb along with him.

In any case, the first BDM meeting, as much as Liesel had both dreaded and disdained it, was almost disappointing in its staid dullness. They practiced singing several patriotic songs from the *Wir Mädel Singen* songbook for a proposed concert at Christmas, and then listened to a stuffy lecture on the importance of thrift in cookery. Afterward, there was apple cake, and their leader, Fraulein Abicht, warmly welcomed her as a new member and said she could take her oath at the next meeting. All in all, Liesel felt she had nothing to complain about, nothing she could mock to her father to show how ridiculous it all was, and the lack annoyed her.

As they left the school and headed out into the crisp autumnal evening, twilight already stealing over the city in a violet cloak, several girls linked arms with Liesel, propelling her along with them and shocking her with the unexpected intimacy. The girl on her right, Eva, smiled at her conspiratorially.

"You're one of us now."

After a second's startled pause, Liesel found herself smiling back; once, she might have considered those words a taunt, or even a threat, but as the three of them walked down the pavement with their arms still linked, she decided it felt more like a promise. It was quite nice, she realized, to walk together like this, to feel a part of things, even if she didn't particularly like the things she was part of.

She said goodbye to her new friends as she turned onto Koenigsallee, the night drawing in darkly, and the air possessing a damp chill that rolled off the Havel even though it was only September. She wasn't usually out this late, and Liesel quickened her step as she headed toward home. The street was empty, save for an old man on the other side who shuffled by with his head tucked low, his steps painstakingly slow, his back bent.

Usually Liesel wouldn't have paid any attention to such a person, nothing but a boring old man in shabby clothes, but some prickle of awareness had her watching him out of the corner of her eye as she headed down the street. She saw that a few SS officers were walking the other way, toward him, looking like shadows in their black uniforms, peaked caps, and high boots; she could see the silver *Totenkopf*, or death's heads, on their collars, the medals seeming to possess an otherworldly glow in the gathering dusk.

They were young and blond and handsome, and if it hadn't been dark, if the man across the street hadn't stiffened instinctively, Liesel might have admired their athletic forms, their vitality and sense of purpose. But, alone in the dark, she had a perception of menace from them that she hadn't experienced before, and she tensed in shock as one of them, a faint, jeering smile on his face, shot out a hand and flipped the old man's cap off his head, onto the ground. The man stopped where he stood, his bare head with its sparse white hair still bent as he gazed down at his rumpled cap on the ground. The men stood and watched, all of them silent and still, the moment taut and expectant.

It was no more than a schoolboy's prank, and yet the very air felt charged with something far more dangerous, an ugly expectancy that Liesel didn't understand but still felt and feared.

She'd seen SS in the street before, of course, many times, or the brown-shirted SA, either marching in formation or sometimes striding with purpose. Once, when she'd been with her mother, shopping in the Ku'damm, she'd seen a couple of brownshirts hurrying a wretched-looking person along the pavement and her mother had grabbed her arm and pulled her along. "Don't look," she'd said under her breath and Liesel had obeyed, because she hadn't liked the look of naked fear on the stranger's face.

Another time she'd seen the *Hitlerjugend*—or HJ—boys chasing a Jew, a little boy of seven or eight, but the boy had got away and the HJs had moved on, laughing and jostling each other.

Neither of those experiences had done more than brush at her conscience; they'd given her a moment of disquiet, nothing more. This time felt different. Liesel saw something cruel and hard and determined in the faces of the SS and she had an urge to cry out, as well as a terror to stay silent. She remained where she stood, frozen in time and space, as the soldier who had yanked off the cap pushed the man's shoulder.

"Pick it up, old man." The SS officer almost sounded friendly, but with a menace underneath the words that made Liesel draw her breath in slowly and then hold it for one long, taut moment.

Slowly, the old man reached for his cap with trembling fingers, and in the next instant another one of the SS had kicked his feet out from under him, so he went sprawling, hard on his knees, his palms and cheek hitting the pavement.

"*Bitte…*" she heard the man say, his voice feeble and beseeching, as another officer kicked him hard in the stomach. Liesel jerked back as if she'd been hit herself, shocked by the sheer pointless violence of the act.

She knew she should look away, keep walking and hurry home, but some horrified impulse kept her rooted to the spot, shocked and disbelieving, as the SS watched the old man lying on the stones, gasping for breath, with a disinterested sort of cruelty, as if he were a specimen rather than a man.

"Pick up your cap," the first officer said, and now there was a sound of steel in his voice.

With trembling fingers, still gasping and retching from the kick to his stomach, the old man reached for his cap and jammed it onto his head. The officer gave a nod of jeering approval and another kicked the man again, lighter this time, like a warning, or perhaps just a reminder.

They started to walk away, and as they did, the first officer caught her eye. Liesel stood transfixed as he grinned and winked at her. She stared back, horrified, shaking with fear, while the three men sauntered off. The old man was still wheezing on the street, clutching his ribs. Should she go help him? Of course she should.

Liesel hesitated, caught between doing what she knew had to be the right thing and a deeper desire to run straight home. She started to cross the street toward him, and a taxi horn blared. She jumped back. When the taxi had passed, the old man had got to his knees. Liesel ran for home. She didn't stop until she'd reached her house on Koenigsallee, her breath coming in ragged pants as she threw open the door so hard it banged on its hinges.

"Mutti!" she called, the whimper of a child caught in a nightmare. "Mutti!"

Her mother came hurrying down the stairs, dressed in navy silk and pearls for an evening out, her hair done in a neat roll, a look of fear on her face. "Liesel, *mein Gott*, what is it? What has happened?" She took her by the shoulders, inspecting her as if for scrapes or bruises.

Liesel simply shook her head, her body shaking, her teeth chattering, as her mother came and put her pale, slender arms around her. She didn't know why she'd called for her rather than her adored father, but as she breathed in the scent of her mother's French perfume—the orange blossom and jasmine of *Je Reviens*—and pressed her cheek against the smooth, cool silk of her dress, she was glad she did.

"You saw something," her mother said quietly, her arms still around her, and Liesel managed to get out jerkily,

"The SS. They… they beat up an old man. They knocked his cap off and then they kicked him in the stomach."

Ilse's arms tensed around her for a brief second. "Is that all?"

Liesel jerked out of her mother's embrace. "Is that *all?* He didn't do anything, Mutti!"

"Well, I know that," she stated coolly. "But trust me, it could have been worse." She paused. "Did they see you?"

"One of them *winked* at me." Liesel could not keep a shudder from going through her at the memory. The SS had looked so careless, so *happy*. How?

Ilse nodded and turned away. Liesel watched miserably as she reached for a cigarette from a silver box on the hall table and lit it, a preoccupied look on her face. She wished she was still holding her.

"Why did they do it?" Liesel asked, even though she knew her mother would not be able to give her an answer.

Ilse shrugged, a quick, jerky movement as she paced the hall, her heels clicking on the marble with sharp taps. "Who knows. Because they can?"

"But he wasn't doing anything wrong."

"Do you think he needed to be, to be treated like that?" The question was flung at her like a challenge.

"I... I don't know," Liesel said slowly. "I suppose I thought... I thought he must. Soldiers wouldn't... they have to be fair." As she said the words, she realized how childish they sounded, and yet she still wanted to believe in reasons why, ones that made sense and were just. It was the foundation of all her beliefs, of her knowledge of the world, gleaned from Sundays in church and her father's quotations of Goethe, a simple and innate sense of how things ought to be.

Ilse let out a sound of derision, a snort of laughter that held no humor. "If only that was the world we lived in, my dear, but it is not." She stubbed her cigarette out, half-smoked, just as the front door opened and her father came into the house.

"Ah, but what's going on here?" His mouth was curved into the faint half-smile he so often wore, but it morphed into a frown as he took off his hat and hung it up. "Liesel? Have you been crying?"

Liesel touched her cheeks; she hadn't even realized she'd been crying until she felt the sticky tracks of her tears.

"Surely the BDM wasn't *that* bad," Otto joked, a wrinkle of concern making a deep crease in his forehead.

"She saw a man being beaten in the street," her mother explained, a harshness to her voice that Liesel didn't recognize. In the dark blue dress, with the pearls against her throat, her mother's body seemed cold and angular now, and she looked at her husband as if she disliked him.

Otto held his wife's gaze for a long moment; Liesel felt as if a silent communication were passing between them, but she had no idea what it meant. "Was he a Jew?" he finally asked.

Ilse gazed at him for a second more before she looked away.

"Probably," she replied with a shrug.

"Well, then."

Liesel glanced between her two parents—her mother's pressed lips, her father's dismissive tone. She felt confused, but also treacherously relieved. *He was a Jew.* Stupidly, she hadn't even considered that when she'd watched the man being beaten. And yet... he hadn't been *doing* anything.

"We need to be at the Ambroses in an hour," Otto said as he started up the stairs.

"I'm ready now," Ilse told him, and walked into the dining room.

Neither of them looked at Liesel; the conversation, such as it had been, was over. She listened to the clink of crystal as her mother poured herself a drink, and then the creak of the floorboards as her father went into his bedroom, the door closing softly behind him. Still she stood in the hall, her heart thudding, her eyes dry.

He was a Jew. That made a difference, she told herself, even though she wasn't quite sure how. The Jews were blamed for everything, from the war to the loss of jobs to the country's descent into degeneracy during the years of the Weimar Republic. Most people Liesel knew disliked them, some virulently, others with a weary, tolerant indifference. She didn't feel anything in particular about them, because she had only known Elsa, and only to compete with for top of the class prizes.

And yet… in her mind's eye, she saw that old man shuffling down the street, feeble and alone, bothering no one. She realized that although she had laughed at the absurdities taught in her textbook or shouted by Hitler and his cronies, she hadn't translated them into steel-toed boots into stomachs. She let out a choked sound and her mother came to stand in the doorway of the dining room, her glass of schnapps held aloft.

"Get used to it," she said with some sympathy, but only a little.

"Don't you care?"

Her mother laughed, a hard sound. "You'll soon learn not to, especially when you realize you didn't care all that much in the first place."

Liesel didn't know whether her mother was talking about her or herself. Without replying, she walked past her back to the kitchen, where Gerda was slicing a loaf of rye bread for supper. Friedrich was sitting at the table, nibbling on the end of a cold sausage, and Gerda's daughter, Rosa, was sitting opposite, doing her homework. She looked up when Liesel came into the room, her eyes dark and watchful. Even though the girl was only about ten, something about her always made Liesel feel a bit hesitant, as if she was being inspected and coming up a bit short. As a result, she struggled not to dislike her, and she chose not to speak to her.

"You'll spoil your supper, Friedy," Liesel told her brother, and he shrugged happily, content with his bit of bratwurst.

Gerda looked up with a quick, nervous smile. "You had a good day at school?"

"It was all right." Liesel wasn't about to tell the housekeeper what she'd seen, although she had a burning desire to talk about it with *somebody*. She gazed at Gerda, in her plain dress and apron, moving around the kitchen with quick, brisk movements. She was a small, brown-haired woman who said very little; she'd been hired when they'd first moved to Berlin, but Liesel had hardly ever spoken to her.

She glanced next at Rosa, who had turned back to her homework, her thick blonde hair in two fat plaits down her back, like every good German girl. Watching them both, Liesel realized how little she knew them—this family who were bound up with hers, coming to her house nearly every day. What would Gerda have thought of the SS beating up that man—the crumpled cap, the kick to the stomach? Perhaps she wouldn't have minded. Perhaps she would have been pleased. And what about Rosa? What did she think about it all?

"Are you in the *Jungmädel*?" she asked abruptly, and Rosa looked up from her homework while Gerda stilled, a tension tautening the air that Liesel didn't understand but still felt. A look of something almost like scorn flashed across Rosa's features and Gerda came to stand behind her, her hands on her daughter's shoulders.

"No, *Fraulein* Scholz," she said quietly. "My Rosa is not in the *Jungmädel*."

"Why not?" Liesel asked, aware she was sounding a bit belligerent, or worse, petulant. "You're ten, aren't you?"

"Rosa turned ten in the summer," Gerda said, and Liesel heard a tremble in her voice. "But she will not join the *Jungmädel*."

Liesel stared at them both, feeling as if she were missing something, but not sure what it was. "Gerda," she asked suddenly, "do you like Hitler?"

Gerda stiffened, her hands tensing on her daughter's shoulders while Rosa made a sound that could only be derision. "He is our Führer," Gerda said after a moment, her voice wavering.

"Yes, yes, but do you *like* him?" Liesel pressed. "Do you think he's… he's a good leader?" She knew it was pointless to ask. What did it matter what Gerda thought of Hitler? And what did she expect the housekeeper of all people to say? No one said anything against Hitler. Liesel had known that, and yet she hadn't really *known* it, not until today. Not until she'd watched those boots sink into flesh, the *glee* on those men's faces…

"He's very good," Gerda said as she turned away to arrange some slices of sausage on a plate. "He is a very good leader." She sounded like a child reciting a catechism.

Liesel didn't believe her, but she didn't know what she herself believed anymore, never mind Gerda, and, in any case, she knew she wouldn't press. So she simply sighed and reached for a slice of sausage, popping it into her mouth while Friedrich grinned at her.

Rosa shot her a dark look from under her lashes, and Liesel found herself glaring back. Why did the girl have to act so superior, so angry? She was only a housekeeper's daughter, after all.

Gerda went into the dining room to set the table, and Liesel leaned against the sink, scuffing one shoe irritably against the floor. She felt restless, the need to *do* something making her twitch.

"Do *you* like Hitler?" Rosa asked. Her voice was quiet and yet strong; Liesel had never heard her speak before, except to answer her mother in monosyllables.

She glanced at the girl in assessment, and discovered she was looking back in much the same way, both of them taking the measure of the other, and neither seeming particularly impressed. "And what if I did?" she asked.

Rosa shrugged. "Why did you ask, then?"

"I like Hitler," Friedy piped up as he swallowed his last bit of sausage. "My teacher says he was sent to us from God."

Rosa made another soft snort of derision, the kind of sound no one made anymore in regard to their revered leader, not even her father. She looked away quickly from Liesel's narrowed gaze, and no one said anything as Gerda bustled back into the room.

"Rosa?" Her voice was sharp as she looked between Liesel and Friedrich, sensing something. "We must go. It is late."

Liesel remained silent as Rosa gathered up her things and reached for her coat. The whole conversation, such as it had been, had left her feeling more confused and restless than ever. Rosa seemed more knowledgeable than she was, with a worldly air that Liesel herself did not possess. It had annoyed her even as she hungered to know more, to finally understand. Yet what if there was no understanding?

After Gerda and Rosa left, she and Friedrich ate their supper in the kitchen, while her parents finished getting ready for their party, kissing them goodbye before leaving in a scented cloud of perfume and aftershave.

There had been so many parties since the Olympics, it seemed—an endless round of cocktails and dinners with people from her father's work, chemists and company directors and occasionally Nazi officers. Her father would joke about how important it was—"it's my civic duty, Lieseling, to drink champagne"—but Liesel didn't understand why this would be. Why was her father, who had been a mid-ranking chemist in an enormous company back in Frankfurt, suddenly so important in Berlin? Was it because of his ambition, or his friends in high places, as Herr Ambros had said? She supposed it didn't really matter, but it made her uneasy, along with everything else. After seeing those SS officers kick an old man, the world felt like a very uncertain place.

She wished her parents weren't going out tonight; she felt a childish need for protection, to feel safe and comforted in a way that being alone with Friedrich in this big, empty house would most certainly not be. The house on Koenigsallee was at least three times as big as their narrow townhouse back in Frankfurt, with cavernous rooms and creaky stairs and a long, cobwebby crawl space under the eaves on the top floor that Friedrich loved to play in but Liesel hated.

She told herself it wasn't as if she were in any danger; the SS would hardly come marching into the house and, anyway, they weren't after the likes of her. *He was a Jew.*

"Who is a Jew?" Friedrich asked as he dabbed at a crumb on his plate and then licked his finger. Liesel realized she'd said her last thought—*he was a Jew*—out loud.

"No one, Friedy."

"If you see one, you should run away," he told her seriously, licking more crumbs from his fingers. "They might hurt you, you know."

Liesel gazed at him wearily. "I don't know any Jews," she said after a moment. "And neither do you."

"But if I saw one," Friedy said thoughtfully as he dabbed at the last crumb on his plate, "I'd be scared. Wouldn't you?"

"No, I wouldn't." Briefly Liesel thought of Elsa; she hadn't been scared of her, but neither had she particularly liked her. "Why do you think you'd be scared of one?" she asked her little brother.

"Because they're bad and they'll hurt you." He spoke so simply, so utterly assured of the simple, stark truth of his words. It was there blazing in his face, in the clarity in his hazel eyes, his earnest look. All of it suddenly made Liesel feel rather unbearably sad. He was only six. How could he be so certain?

She propped her chin in her hand as she gazed back at him. "Do you think you'd recognize a Jew, if you saw one?"

"Yes, look, I'll show you." Friedrich scrambled off his chair and went to fetch a book from his schoolbag by the door.

Liesel waited, her chin still in her hand, as her gaze moved disconsolately around the kitchen, with its floor of worn black and white tiles and its blackened range, the deep stone sink.

Gerda had left everything neat and tidy, and with the curtains drawn against the dark night it could have felt cozy, but it didn't. Liesel was lonely and scared and so very tired, and she wished her parents hadn't left her here alone with Friedy. She was acting like a baby, she thought crossly, yet she couldn't keep herself from it.

"See," Friedrich said, and thrust a book into her hands.

"*Trau keinem Fuchs auf grüner Heid und keinem Jud auf seinem Eid,*" Liesel read slowly. Trust no fox on his green heath, and no Jew on his oath. What a title! She only just kept from rolling her eyes as she studied the cover, which showed a sly-looking fox next to a man, presumably a Jew, with a ridiculously big nose and ears, a horrible, leering caricature that was undoubtedly meant to terrify children.

She flipped open the book, frowning at the absurd illustrations of Jews who looked more like gorillas than humans—stooped-over creatures with long arms and big hands, hooked noses and hairy skin. She scanned the rhyming text, her frown deepening into dislike at all of the absurd, sweeping statements: Jews worked for the devil and could never be trusted. They were a pest like a fox; they were a curse that could be caught. Children should be scared of them and never, ever speak to them. The Jew was a greedy thief; the Jew was an evil doctor who would kill his patients. The Jew could be identified by his big nose, his hunched position, his Jew-sounding name, although some Jews "were sneaky" and had good, German-sounding names.

Liesel closed the book in disgust. "Friedy, this stuff is ridiculous rubbish. Surely you can see that?"

He shook his head slowly as he stared at her unblinkingly. "It's true. My teacher says so. Doesn't yours?"

Liesel shrugged the question away. Yes, her teachers said as much, although not in such an obvious and pedantic fashion. Somehow, seeing it written in rhyme in a children's book with colorful illustrations and flowery script made her realize all the more how completely absurd it was, and worse, how dangerous. *He was a Jew*. So what?

"Friedy, have you ever seen someone who looks like the Jew in that book? Maybe in the zoo, but not on the street."

Friedy brightened with interest. "Are there Jews in the zoo?"

"No, of course not, I meant like a gorilla!" She rolled her eyes, exasperated now as well as alarmed, but still wanting him to understand. "Jews don't really look like that, Friedy. They look like you or me. There was a girl in my class back in Frankfurt who was Jewish. Elsa. She had blonde hair and blue eyes. She was pretty."

For a second, Liesel felt a flash of regret for those old days; she didn't think she'd been unkind to Elsa, but she hadn't been particularly nice to her, either. They had always been in competition with each other, and more often than not Elsa had won. Where was she now? Liesel hadn't even considered where she might have gone, once she'd left the school, when the educational reforms had come in.

She remembered how, in the weeks before Elsa had left, she'd had to sit at the back of the class. She hadn't been called on by the new teacher, who had often proclaimed how dirty and stupid and immoral Jews were. Why hadn't she been bothered by that? Liesel wondered now. Why hadn't she felt indignant on Elsa's behalf? She'd only been eleven, but surely that wasn't an excuse. She simply remembered being pleased that with Elsa gone she would be the one to win the prizes. The knowledge shamed her now.

"Jews really do look just like us, Friedy," she stated firmly. "You might pass one in the street and not even know."

Friedrich glanced down at his book. "They must be good at disguises," he said after a moment. "So they can look like us and trick us."

"And have you ever been tricked by one?" Liesel demanded. It infuriated her that her brother was being taught to hate something he neither knew nor understood, and worse, not even to question it, no matter how preposterous it seemed. She thought of her father's quoting—*there is nothing more frightful than ignorance in action*—and she understood the sentiment much more now.

"No, I haven't been tricked," Friedy told her patiently, "because I'd run away if I saw one."

Liesel sighed and rose from the table. There was no point talking to Friedy about it, she realized. He was so terribly earnest, and so very little. But the very fact of that book made her angry; surely books were meant to tell the truth. They were meant to educate; they needed to be logical and based in fact. That was important; it was how anyone was able to make sense of the world.

Besides, she reasoned, even if people disliked the Jews, they didn't have to tell lies about them. *But then why would you hate them?*

With a clatter, Liesel dumped their plates into the sink for Gerda to clean in the morning. She pressed her fingers against her temples and closed her eyes, hating the questions that surfaced in her mind of their own accord, like bubbles floating up from the deep, waiting to be burst.

She didn't want to have to think about the Jews. She didn't want to have to be unsettled, to wonder, to fear, and yet already she sensed there would be no going back. She could not unsee that man on the street, the wink the SS gave her, the hard kick to the stomach, for no reason at all…

"Friedy, go get your pajamas on and brush your teeth."

"But it's early—"

"I don't care. I'll read you a story before bed. A proper one." And nothing about sly foxes or untrustworthy Jews.

Much later, after a restless few hours trying to focus on her own novel, Liesel finally fell asleep, only to wake suddenly, her eyes straining into the darkness, before she saw the orange tip of a cigarette and smelled the comfortingly familiar scent of her father's 4711 eau de cologne.

"You're awake." Otto's voice was gentle and disembodied in the darkness.

"You woke me up," Liesel answered without rancor. She felt only relief that her father was there. His presence, even though he was barely visible in the darkness, was a great comfort. He smelled of whiskey and cigarettes and aftershave, and when he moved, she heard the soft snick of his evening dress.

"So I did. I'm sorry. I was worried about you. I thought you might be angry with me."

Liesel was silent for a moment, absorbing his words and their implication. She realized she *was* angry, at least a little, but more than that, she was afraid. "Don't you care," she asked eventually, "that people are being beaten up for no good reason?"

"You don't know the reason, Liesel."

"You think there was one?"

"There might have been."

She stared into the darkness, her eyes straining to see, but there was only blackness, and the glowing tip of her father's cigarette, like a tiny beacon. "Do you think he deserved to be treated like that, then?" she asked.

A long silence and then her father said quietly, "I don't think anyone deserves to be treated like that, not even the Jews."

The sorrow in his tone broke something apart inside her, something she'd been trying to hold together all evening, ever since she'd first seen that man. "He was so old, Vati." Her voice trembled. "And they kicked him so hard."

Her father didn't say anything, but he leaned forward and put one large, warm hand on top of her head. Liesel closed her eyes, but a tear dribbled out anyway. "I'm sorry you had to see that."

"Why?" she whispered, an ache in her voice. "Why do they do that? Why do they hate the Jews so much?"

Her father sighed. "Sometimes people need someone to hate."

Did they? Liesel had never thought so before, and yet, as she considered the matter, she recognized the truth of it. Why did the girls at school pick on the ones who were different—the girl who wore glasses, or had a stammer, or was fat? Why did Liesel herself look at Rosa, whom she'd barely spoken to, and feel dislike for her seeming smugness? It was wrong, she knew that, and yet it *was*. Whether it was a cruel jibe in the schoolyard or tripping an old man in the street, all of it came from the same source of hate—yet why? Why did they have to be so, so hate-filled? "Why the Jews?" she asked.

"Because they have a lot of money, perhaps." Liesel felt rather than saw her father shrug as he took his hand away from her head and sat back. "You have to understand, Liesel, after the war... it was very difficult. Germany was utterly crushed. No one had any money... any food... our Reichsmarks were useless. You needed a wheelbarrowful just to buy a loaf of bread, and you'd better have bought it in the morning, for by evening it would have cost twice as much."

Liesel had heard such things before; her father had fought in the war, ending it as Hauptmann Scholz, and although he didn't like to talk about it, she had heard him say, without any of his usual lightness, that war was hell, and if anyone said otherwise they were telling a boldfaced lie.

"But what does any of that have to do with the Jews?"

"They have always had money. They control—or they used to—many of the banks. They seemed to prosper while everyone else failed. I'm not saying it was right, or even that it made sense, but it made people angry. Life was so hard, and they needed someone to be angry with. The Jews were an easy target, I suppose."

"But that man…" Liesel said slowly. "He didn't have any money. He wasn't doing anything. He was just walking down the street."

"You don't know the story behind that man, Liesel," her father returned a bit sharply. "And when you don't know all the facts, it's best not to think about it. Best to forget that it happened."

That was, Liesel thought, something her father wouldn't normally say. It certainly didn't align with his precious Goethe. In any case, she couldn't *stop* thinking about it. All night long she'd pictured that crumpled body, the trembling fingers putting the cap back on his head while the soldiers watched so sneeringly. She saw it every time she closed her eyes. She feared she always would.

"Do you hate the Jews?" she asked, and her father didn't answer for a long time.

"No," he said at last. "Of course I don't. But I love my country. I don't agree with everything Hitler says, far from it, but I do see the good he is doing, despite all the bad. Germany is strong again, Liesel. People have jobs and money and food. Everyone is happy."

"The Jews aren't happy—"

"Perhaps that is the price we have to pay."

Except they weren't the ones paying it.

Liesel closed her eyes, not wanting to think about it, just as her father had advised. It felt too complicated, too fraught, with the possibility of too much pain. And she feared that if she did think about it too much, the desolation she felt would be overwhelming. Besides, she reminded herself yet again, she didn't know any Jews anyway. Not since Elsa.

"I know it may sound harsh," her father said. "And I'm sorry for it. I would rather there were no laws against the Jews, and certainly no hatred. But as you grow older you will come to realize that life is a series of compromises, as I told you before. You have to go to the *Bund Deutscher Mädel*, and at the end of the day, a government has to do what is best for the most people who benefit from its leadership." He paused, reaching across to caress her cheek for a moment. "All right, Lieseling?" he asked softly, and Liesel could not make herself reply. She did not feel it was all right at all, and yet she wanted it to be.

She had so many more questions, but she didn't feel brave enough to voice them out loud. Worse, she realized as her father kissed her forehead and then quietly left her room, she feared she didn't want to hear his answers.

CHAPTER FIVE

Berlin, May 1937

As the dreary months of winter passed, Liesel felt as if she was finally opening her eyes to a world that felt horrible and strange yet was one, she realized more and more, that had been there all along. It was a world she both feared and disliked.

After that awful evening walking home from her first BDM meeting back in September, she began to notice things she'd been oblivious to before—happily so, and she wished, sometimes desperately, that she could be so again. She longed to be blithely indifferent to the changes being wreaked on the landscape of her life and her country; she wanted once again to be interested only in school and books and trips with her father to Haus Vaterland, the pleasure palace on Potsdamer Platz—all the childlike concerns that now felt so simple and small. The trouble with opening one's eyes, she realized, was it became very difficult to close them again.

The posters that papered many of the shops on the Ku'damm which she'd once skimmed over, uninterested, she now stopped and studied like a detective looking for clues. She read about '*Das Judische Komplott*'—the Jewish Conspiracy—and '*Das Weltpest*'—the universal plague. She noticed the signs on park benches—Only for Jews!—and the yellow stars on Jewish shops, meant to keep Aryans from entering.

And she saw the SS everywhere—their black uniforms, the gleaming death's heads, the great coats billowing out like bat wings. Most of them were young and blond and handsome, and before she might have admired the dashing figures they cut as they sauntered down the street, but now the mere sight of them gave her a sense of revulsion, a dawning terror as she recognized the power they wielded so carelessly and cruelly.

Even so, she could not keep from watching them out of the corner of her eye, waiting for them to spring on some unsuspecting soul, to have it happen again, just as it had with the old man and his cap.

One afternoon in May, she and her mother were shopping for a new pair of party shoes at Wertheim Kaufhaus on Leipziger Platz, Europe's largest department store chain, its Berlin store boasting two glass-ceiling atriums and nearly a hundred elevators. Her parents were hosting a dinner party in a few evenings' time, and Liesel was to make an appearance before they sat down to their meal. The prospect was both exciting and terrifying, although she knew her mother felt only displeasure at the prospect.

Liesel had crouched on the stairs listening to her parents arguing in the sitting room a few weeks before.

"I don't want those men in my house."

"Ilse, *perle*, you know I have to."

"You *don't*, Otto. That is where we have always disagreed."

Her father had sighed, a long, drawn-out sound. "This again? Are you serious?"

"You don't have to go as far as you do."

"That's where you're wrong. I'm not going far enough."

"Then maybe…" Her mother had trailed off with a sigh, and Liesel had heard the clink of her glass being refilled, not for the first time.

"This will pass, Ilse, you know it will." Her father's voice was both earnest and cajoling. Liesel could imagine him putting his hands on her mother's shoulders, kissing the back of her neck as he often did, especially when he wanted to appease her. She could picture her mother starting to soften, reluctantly, but still. "He just wants their money. When he has it, he'll be satisfied. I know it's not fair, but it's the way it is. If we can just endure…"

"And what about everyone else? Will they be satisfied?" Her mother's voice had sounded defeated. Liesel heard the tap of her heels as she moved away from her father.

"I cannot answer for all of Germany," he'd replied, and now he'd seemed sorrowful. "You know I wish it wasn't so."

"There is wishing and then there is doing."

"Ilse, it is a few men from my department. That is all. No officers, no SS. Just a few chemists, a few administrators. They'll drink our champagne and eat our lobster and that will be that."

"You know that's not true. Since we came to Berlin it has been nothing but parties."

"And are parties so very bad?" Her father was trying to sound teasing but her mother wasn't amused.

"When they are filled with Nazis, yes, they are."

"Ilse, I am a Nazi."

"Don't remind me," her mother had answered bitterly. Then, her voice softening, "You're not like them, Otto. I swear you're not."

"Of course I'm not!" The sound of movement; Liesel had imagined her mother enfolded in her father's long arms. "And I never will be. I promise you, it's just a party. For work. Because I have to."

A silence, and then a sigh, the sound of surrender. "And what of Gerda?"

"She can stay in the kitchen. We'll hire a girl to serve." Her mother did not reply and her father had added, almost casually, "I would like Liesel and Friedrich to greet our guests before we sit down to the meal. They will say hello, nothing more, I promise. Just to show their support."

"No." Her mother's refusal was immediate and absolute.

"It will look strange if they do not. Goebbels always has his little tribe come down at a party, you know that. How many is it now? Three? Four?"

"Four," Ilse had snapped, "the youngest is only a few months old, and I don't *care*. The last woman I want to be like is Magda Goebbels."

"And I'm not asking you to be anything like her. She is a frumpy hausfrau while you are a beautiful, beguiling woman." The caressing note in her father's voice had made Liesel blush, even from the stairs.

A long silence while she waited tensely. Once she'd longed to be the center of the attention, the prima donna on the stage, but Liesel knew already that she did not want to be at this party. She did not want to be paraded in front of Nazis, even if they were just chemists and administrators. She wanted nothing more than to hide in the shadows, her head down, unnoticed by this uncertain and dangerous world.

"Liesel can come down," her mother had said at last. "Friedy will not."

"Ilse—"

"He's too young."

"He's seven—"

"*No*, Otto. No."

Her father had sighed again. "Very well," he'd said.

Now, as Liesel followed her mother into one of Wertheim Kaufhaus' many elevators, she decided to take the opportunity to ask her mother some of the questions that had been buzzing in her mind like bees, ever since that night in September. Even now, six months later, she still saw that the pathetic, crumpled form of that man when she closed her eyes. She had not dared to talk to her father about it, but her mother, she hoped, might be slightly more willing.

"Why can't we shop in Jewish stores?" she asked once they were alone, soaring upwards, her mother inspecting her lipstick in the mirror of her compact.

Ilse raised her gaze from her tiny reflection to give Liesel a coolly amused look. "We're shopping in one right now."

"What?" Liesel stared at her blankly. "We are?"

"The Wertheim family are Jewish, although they're desperately trying not to be. They've put the store into Ursula Wertheim's name because she's the only one who could possibly be considered Aryan. It won't be enough, though, just wait and see." Ilse snapped her compact shut and stepped out of the elevator, and Liesel followed.

"Why won't it be enough?" she asked as her mother approached the counter, and she gave Liesel a sharp, quelling look before turning to the unctuously smiling saleswoman.

"I am looking for a pair of party shoes for my daughter, black, made of good leather."

Liesel knew better than to ask any more questions then, but she was not willing to drop the matter entirely. She had a burning desire now to have her questions answered, to have things make *sense,* and she realized, with a sense akin to grief, that her mother might have more truthful responses than her father.

She waited until the afternoon of the dinner party, when she found her mother in the sitting room, playing her favorite, melancholy piece by Mahler. She was still in her dressing gown, a cigarette smoldering in the ashtray on top of the piano, her hair in curlers.

"Shouldn't you get ready soon?" Liesel asked uncertainly. The house was full of flowers and crystal, and Gerda had spent the entire day in the kitchen, preparing the food—turtle soup, stuffed pigeon, lobster salad.

Ilse simply shrugged and kept playing, the music rippling from the piano like water.

"You know Mahler is banned," Liesel stated, her voice turning a bit strident. "Aren't you worried that someone might say something?"

She had learned, in her six months in the BDM, how many people "said something." Every week, she was asked, and even encouraged, to report on any "unpatriotic activities" committed by her parents or her neighbors. Asked so unobtrusively, and mixed in with the lessons on cookery and childcare, the gymnastics training and the coat drives and collections for Winter Relief, it was easy to simply dismiss it as one more seemingly innocuous aspect of the organization.

But then Liesel remembered how her father had spoken of names in nasty books, and a few months ago, one of her classmates, Irma, had told, with gleeful zest, how her neighbor had been taken away in the middle of the night, only a few days after she'd reported her for complaining about the "Guns not Butter" policy that had been introduced in the last year. Liesel had been silently horrified by the story; the other girls had been smugly satisfied, a job—and justice—done.

Fortunately she'd learned, in those difficult months, how to hide her reactions. At the second meeting, she'd said her oath to Hitler—*I promise always to do my duty in the Hitler Youth, in love and loyalty to the Führer*—in firm, ringing tones and she'd sung along to the rousing lyrics of their patriotic songs—*Onward, onward, fanfares are joyfully blaring. Onward, onward, youth must be fearless and daring. Germany, your light shines true, even if we die for you*, without flinching. She'd run the races—coming in near to last, as she'd never been particularly athletic—and she'd listened to how bearing children for the Führer would be her greatest privilege in life, and she'd even kept her face expressionless when her friends had whispered how they'd like to have Hitler's baby.

"You know how it's done, don't you?" Marianne, one of the older girls with a wide mouth and a sly, knowing manner, had said to her later. "You know the boy puts his thing right inside you?"

"Of course I know that," Liesel had snapped, although she did only vaguely, and Marianne had just laughed.

"Don't mind her," Eva, her closest friend from the first BDM meeting, had said. "She just likes to be shocking. My sister says she's far too fast. She lets the HJ boys do anything to her."

Liesel had not known how to reply. She'd heard the taunts of the HJ boys as they'd watched the BDM girls march in parades— "It's the *Bubi Druck Mich*!" they might say—"Squeeze me, laddie"—or "The *Bedarfsartikel Deutscher Manner*!"—"Requisite for German Males." The Leagues of German Mattresses was another. Liesel did her best not to respond to any of the jeering fake acronyms, just as she tried not to let the endless, angry Nazi rhetoric seep into her skull, infect her pores, so she had no choice but to breathe it out like some noxious gas.

It was difficult, though, more difficult than she wanted it to be, when it came at her endlessly, from every direction—the newsreels before the films at the cinema, the signs on the shops, the loudspeakers blaring from every street corner. It was in her textbooks and on the radio and even in the board games and books sold in the shops—*Juden Raus!* was the latest, a game where the goal was to round up all the Jews and drum them out of town.

It would, Liesel thought more than once, be so much *easier* simply to go along with it. To smile and nod, to listen and agree… to let herself simply believe, instead of always fighting silently against the relentless tide that was seemingly carrying everyone else along with it on its smug, self-righteous waves.

It would be so wonderfully simple, to let herself be stirred by the parades, the posturing, the rousing speech Himmler had given to all the BDM girls in Berlin, crowded into a hall that smelled of stale sweat and damp wool while he raised a fist and told them

Hitler needed "a generation of girls that are healthy in body and mind, sure and decisive, proudly and confidently going forward." She wanted to cheer along with all the others, instead of giving a half-hearted response, just to keep from suspicion. She wanted to let herself be carried away—and yet she couldn't.

She couldn't sing along to the music that raised her blood and made her proud of her country—or at least made her *want* to be proud of it—to feel the ferocity everyone exhibited that sometimes seemed angry, but other times just looked like joy. She was forbidden it all, by her own moral compass, and sometimes it made her despair; it always made her feel alone.

Now she felt a sudden, inexplicable surge of fury at her mother, looking so indifferent and even bored as she played her beloved, banned Mahler, without a care in the world, without any of the torment or struggle Liesel felt every day.

"You shouldn't be playing that Jew music," she snapped, and Ilse stopped playing, her hands resting on the ivory keys as she raised her thin eyebrows, her expression cool and slightly mocking.

"Is it happening already?" she asked. "Are they turning you into a little Nazi?"

"What if Gerda says something?" Liesel demanded, ignoring the question.

Her mother's mouth curved in something like a smile. "Gerda? I don't think so."

"Why not?"

Ilse played a few more notes. "Because Gerda," she said after a moment, her voice quiet, "is a Jew."

"What?" Liesel goggled at her. "But…"

"Did you think you'd be able to tell?" Her mother sounded amused, and somehow that made Liesel furious.

"Still, you—you shouldn't play it. The windows are open. Someone in the street might hear."

Ilse let out a dry little laugh. "I doubt any of those ardent Nazis will even recognize Mahler. They know nothing but marching music." She played another few melancholy bars before turning back to her daughter. "Are you worried for me, Liesel?"

"No," Liesel retorted, angered, as she ever was, by her mother's disinterested mockery. "But you know I could report you." She didn't know why she said it; she knew she never would do such a thing.

Ilse, however, stopped playing and gave her a look of such visceral animosity that Liesel took a step back, shocked at the horrible force of her feeling. "Go ahead," she said, and her voice was low and venomous, a savage challenge. "Do it."

"I wouldn't," Liesel protested weakly, and then, quite suddenly, she felt as if she could cry. Her eyes filled with tears and she dashed them away, angry at her own betraying weakness. "I didn't mean it, Mutti. You know I didn't."

The fire in her mother's eyes died and she slumped over the piano, her piercing moment of fury spent. "*Mein Gott*," she whispered. "What are they doing to us? To our children?"

Heartened by this moment of empathy, Liesel burst out, "I don't like it, Mutti. I don't like any of it."

Slowly, Ilse straightened. "No? All you have to do is march and sing." She rose from the piano to light a fresh cigarette from the smoldering end of the last one. "Really, Liesel, not much is being asked of you."

"And what is being asked of you?" Liesel retorted. She thought of the dinner party in just a few hours. "All you have to do is drink champagne and eat lobster."

Ilse smiled mirthlessly and drew hard on her cigarette. "We're a fortunate pair then, aren't we?"

"You know, we don't even know any Jews," Liesel blurted, and her mother raised her eyebrows. "Besides Gerda, I mean." She still couldn't quite believe their *housekeeper* was Jewish. And Rosa, as well! What did she have to be so superior about, then? As soon as she had the thought, Liesel was ashamed of it, and yet it still simmered inside her, born out of resentment.

"Don't we?" Ilse asked as she blew out smoke.

"Who else, then? The only one I knew was Elsa, back in Frankfurt."

"Ah, yes, and she was smarter than you, as I recall."

Liesel did her best not to let that burn. "Who else?" she repeated.

"They're not always easy to recognize, you know," her mother said, and once again she sounded amused. "Not like in those wretched posters, with horns like a devil."

"I know that." Liesel flushed in humiliation. Of *course* she knew that, and yet in an unwelcome flash of insight, she realized she'd been acting as if she didn't. As if she could spot a Jew from across the street, as if she would recognize him from one of the awful pictures in one of Friedy's horrible books. Why should she have known Gerda or Rosa was Jewish? Why should it make any difference to how she felt about either of them?

Ilse regarded her thoughtfully for a moment as she smoked. "This house was owned by Jews, you know," she said at last.

Once more Liesel goggled at her. "It was?"

"Did you think they lived in caves or sewers? Hid in the hills? Yes, Liesel, it was owned by a chemist, just like your dear Vati. He had to go to America, as did your father's closest colleague and good friend, Herr Stern. Do you remember him? He used to come over for dinner, with his wife and son. Hans."

Vaguely, Liesel recalled a weedy-looking boy with a sulky mouth. He'd played a lot of chess. "I think so…"

Ilse's mouth twisted. "Abraham Stern won a Nobel Prize, and they still didn't want him."

Liesel shook her head slowly, her mind spinning. "Who didn't?"

"IG Farben. The company is doing its best to Aryanize, to present itself to Hitler as a perfect, shining specimen, worthy of his regard and attention." Her voice was hard and mocking.

"Why…?"

"So they can make money, of course. Isn't that what this is all about? That's what your father says, anyway." Ilse stubbed out her cigarette. "The trouble is, the longer this goes on, the less I believe him."

"Vati is no Nazi," Liesel stated. She'd said it enough in the disquiet of her own mind; she had to believe it. The alternative was unthinkable.

"No," her mother agreed after a moment. "He isn't, despite being a loyal Party member for these four years past." She sighed, a slow, weary release of breath that seemed to come from the depths of her being. "But, do you know, I'm starting to think that makes it worse."

Three hours later, Liesel stood at the top of the stairs in the dress her father had chosen for her to wear, a frock of white organdie with a satin sash. With her hair in the requested braids and her ankle socks and patent leather party shoes, she looked, she thought, like an overgrown child rather than a young woman of fifteen.

"I wish I could go downstairs," Friedrich said as he came to the top of the stairs, wearing his pajamas and holding his battered Steiff teddy bear that he'd carried everywhere since he was a toddler.

"I don't." Now that the moment was here, Liesel's heart was thudding in her chest and her palms were damp with nerves. From downstairs, she could hear the low-throated chuckles of men, the simpering murmurs of the women, the clink of crystal and the snick of matches being struck; there was a gray-blue fug of cigarette smoke hovering over the hallway, and even from the top of the stairs the smell was overwhelming. Never mind that Hitler was said to hate smoking of any kind; here everyone was happy to light up with abandon.

"But you'll meet ever so many important people," Friedrich said longingly.

"I don't care about them." Liesel's mind had been circling on itself ever since her mother had told her about IG Farben wanting to "Aryanize" itself. What had happened to all the Jews they'd fired? Had they all gone to America? What about her father's closest colleague, Herr Stern? Did he miss him? Why had he never told her he was friends with a Jew? How could he agree that a price must be paid, when he'd been *friends* with one? Maybe many? She didn't understand. She wasn't sure she wanted to.

"Liesel, my Lieseling." Her father stood at the bottom of the stairs, resplendent in his dinner jacket, his sandy hair slicked back from his smiling face. He held a champagne glass in one hand, a cigarette in the other. "Come meet my associates. Reich Minister Göring is particularly interested to meet you."

"*Reich Minister…*" Liesel stared at her father in shock as his words penetrated her fear-fogged mind. Hermann Göring was the second most important man of the Reich, and he was in their *house?* Belatedly, she saw the steely warning in her father's eyes and she felt a wave of nausea roll through her, cramping her stomach. "You told Mutti that there wouldn't be any Nazi officers here tonight," she whispered accusingly, and her father's hand clamped down hard on her arm, making her wince.

"Yes, it is a pleasant surprise," he said in a carrying voice. "A very pleasant surprise indeed, to have the Reich Minister drop by my little gathering." Still holding her by the arm, he led her into the drawing room, where a dozen people congregated—men in dinner jackets and women in evening gowns, as glamorous a crowd as might be seen in Paris or London, all satins and silks and cigarette smoke.

The room seemed to swim before Liesel's gaze as she took in the well-dressed group, most of them smiling at her benevolently. She bobbed some sort of ridiculous curtsey and forced a greeting through her numb lips. "Heil Hitler."

"Heil Hitler," came the happy chorus back, and then a man cleared his throat meaningfully. Reich Minister Göring. Liesel saw him standing in the back of the room. He was wearing a heavily decorated military uniform that strained over his substantial paunch, a cigar clamped between his stubby fingers. Her father gave her a little nudge between her shoulder blades and she took a few faltering steps toward him.

"What a lovely specimen of our youth!" Göring declared as he lifted one beringed hand to beckon her forward. "Come here, child, and let me look at you."

On watery legs, Liesel took another step forward. There was a buzzing in her ears, and the room seemed to tilt and slide as she kept her gaze on the Reich Minister, who was smiling at her in tolerant approval. This was the man who was said to have the most power in the country, save for Hitler himself. The man in charge of the Ministry of Aviation, the man who was said to hate Jews with a viciousness that his current benevolence belied.

"You have quite a clever father, do you know that?" Göring said.

Liesel swallowed and bobbed her head. "Yes, sir."

"Do you know what he has done that is so clever?"

Liesel glanced at her father, who was smiling in his easy way, but with lines of tension bracketing his eyes, his body taut and alert. "He says he is an inventor," she hazarded. She did not actually know precisely what her father did, besides work in chemistry, something with pesticides, although that was years ago now.

Göring let out a big boom of laughter, so loud that Liesel nearly jumped. "Yes, indeed, he is quite the inventor! He has made a sort of rubber. Do you know where rubber comes from?"

Liesel's mind both raced and blanked. "From rubber trees?"

"What a clever young girl you are. As clever as your father almost. Yes, from rubber trees, all the way in Brazil." The Reich Minister's expression hardened for a brief moment. "And you must know that Brazil is far away from Germany."

"It's in South America."

"Indeed. And so your clever father has helped to invent a synthetic rubber, made from oil rather than trees. The Americans might have their neoprene, but we have good Buna rubber!" He let out a hearty laugh that still held a hard edge. "You know what we need rubber for?"

Liesel, who had always loved showing off her knowledge, wanted only for this wretched interview to end. "Bicycles?" she guessed a bit desperately. "And cars?"

"Yes, and planes, and ships, and tanks, and so many other things. So it's very, very good that we can make it ourselves, all thanks to your father and men like him." With a benevolent look, Göring gestured to the room full of chemists and their wives, who smiled and nodded back.

Liesel realized she was dismissed, and mumbling some sort of goodbye, she stepped back.

"Good girl, Lieseling, upstairs with you now," her father murmured as he took her into the hallway. "That wasn't so bad, was it?" He gave her one of his old, lilting smiles, but Liesel still felt too panicked to return it.

"Why was he talking about planes and tanks?" she whispered, and her father just shook his head.

"Upstairs with you now," he said, and gave her a little push. Liesel needed no further urging.

A sudden burst of laughter came from the sitting room, sounding like gunfire. Her heart was still hammering in her chest as she turned and watched her father stride back into the sitting room, an easy smile on his face as he responded to something someone had said, and another round of laughter erupted from the room.

Planes and ships and tanks. It was just as he'd said nearly a year ago, when he'd pointed out the buses with their brackets, the gliders that, with a twist and a pop, could become fighter planes. Germany was going to war, and her father, it seemed, was intent on paving the way. It was rather hard now, she realized with bitter despondency, to believe he wasn't a Nazi, or even that he didn't like being one. As she listened to him entertain his guests, she had a terrible suspicion that he was enjoying the experience very much indeed.

CHAPTER SIX

Frankfurt, October 1945

Sam's office was filled with paper. Major Pitt had, without a shred of humor, dumped at least ten thousand *fragebogen*, stuffed into dozens of cardboard boxes, into the small, already cramped space. There was barely enough room for him to sit behind the desk that had been carelessly shoved to one side.

It was not a good start to the already trying day. Sam had woken up late, his head thick and heavy from a night of too much drinking. Yesterday evening he had entered the dim and cramped bar where he was to meet Sergeant Belmont and his friends with the full intention not to have more than a single stein of beer, but somehow, in the ensuing events, he'd found himself matching the sergeant drink for drink, until he could barely stumble back to the hotel and his own rather lumpy bed.

Perhaps it had been the atmosphere of the place, with its rickety chairs, loud music and desperate laughter, the Americans lounging back in their seats, masters of the world, and the German girls, with beetroot lipstick and hollowed-out cheeks, sitting on their laps and acting as if they were having the most fabulous time.

"You're off duty, soldier," Belmont had told him with a slightly mocking laugh when he'd arrived, for Sam was the only American wearing his uniform.

He'd smiled tightly and ordered a beer.

"You can get whatever you want here," Belmont assured him. "Whiskey, cognac… whatever you like. It's all for the taking." He'd pulled a German girl onto his lap, wrapping his arm around her waist in a way Sam found far too familiar. "Isn't that right, *lieben*?"

The girl had smiled and snuggled closer, but Sam thought he saw a dazed, distant look in her eyes that he recognized; it was the same look he'd seen in the eyes of the children across the street from his hotel, or the woman staggering along in the fur coat. This was Germany's *stunde null*, or zero hour, the end of the Reich, but not yet the beginning of anything else.

When the war had ended nearly six months ago, Sam knew, eighty percent of Germany's infrastructure had been damaged or destroyed; in Berlin, the water, gas, and electricity supplies had all been rendered unusable. Hundreds of thousands, if not millions, of people were homeless, and worse, they were starving. With the German ration cards no longer accepted, and food having been scarce for years, most Germans now struggled to find any at all.

The occupying powers had agreed on a rationing system, but because of the difficulty with supply, Sam knew the Americans' ration was, in practice, only a thousand calories per person, the Soviets' even less. The official policy for the American occupation, as outlined in the Joint Chiefs of Staff directive, was to "take no steps looking toward the economic rehabilitation of Germany or designed to maintain or strengthen the German economy."

With that in mind, Sam wondered how on earth the Germans were going to get their country up and running, never mind actually back again. And meanwhile, he discovered as he'd sunk another stein of beer, the GIs were raking it in. A friend of Belmont's whose name Sam didn't want to remember had explained how he could, for a mere fifty cents, buy ten packets of cigarettes a week from the army PX and sell them on the German black market for a hundred bucks. He'd boasted that he'd already sent ten thousand dollars back home, and was hoping soon to buy a restaurant in Berlin.

"Don't look so sour," Belmont had told him when Sam had drunk another beer, having stayed mostly silent for the whole evening. "And don't feel sorry for them. They deserve everything they've gotten, you know, and more."

Sam had thought of the child snatching the cigarette butt from the cratered street. "Do they?"

"They're *Nazis*," Belmont had reminded him, his tone surprisingly sharp. "And if you think they didn't realize what was going on, think again. Oh, they'll tell you they had no idea, they thought the Jews were being taken somewhere east, to a new city or something, some damned utopia." Belmont had let out a hard laugh. "Trust me, they knew. They saw them rounded up in cattle cars or shot in the street. In the five months since the war has ended, we've chased down at least a thousand Nazis right here in Frankfurt. They're bastards, Houghton, every single one of them. They're not even sorry."

Sam had lit a cigarette and said nothing. He couldn't disagree with Belmont, at least not entirely, and yet neither could he see how exploiting the strained and overburdened system was helping anyone, Germans or Americans. In any case, the Nazis were finished; the Soviets were the threat now, according to the powers that be. That was why he was here, to find the useful Nazi chemists and learn what they knew, that would help in the war against the USSR. In any case, it surely behooved them to get Germany on its feet, turn it into a civilized nation again, rather than keep them choking in a stranglehold.

Belmont had eventually left the bar with the girl who had been on his lap, and Sam had stumbled home soon after, feeling sick both to his stomach and at heart. As he'd lay in his bed, his head spinning from too much alcohol, he'd half-wished he was back home, when everything had seemed so much simpler and less jaded.

When he'd closed his eyes, he could imagine he was in his family home on the Main Line, Philadelphia's genteel suburbs, with his mother coming into the house, smelling of roses and telling him he needed to eat more. His kid sister Nancy would beg him for a game of tennis but laughingly ask him not to win.

Or he could imagine he was back in his apartment in Philadelphia, where he'd taught chemistry; he'd pictured himself in the local bar, going out for a drink with friends, or simply sitting in his own living room with the windows open to the autumn night air, listening to the street traffic and reading the editorials in *The Philadelphia Inquirer*.

But he wasn't in either of those places; he was lying on a hard bed in a small room in a devastated city, and he had no idea if he'd be able, or even allowed, to do what he came here to do, or even how he felt about any of it. Eventually, his stomach and mind still churning, he fell asleep.

That morning he'd come downstairs to the landlady of the boarding house, a gray-haired hausfrau with a fluttering, nervous manner, asking him if he wanted any breakfast. Knowing it would be both sparse and unable to be spared, and that he could get scrambled eggs and bacon at the PX's canteen, Sam had declined. As he'd made to leave, his gaze had flitted to a noticeably bare square above the mantelpiece in the small, worn sitting room, the wallpaper brighter than that all around it. He'd glanced at the woman, who looked strangely terrified, and he realized the bare spot had to have been where the requisite portrait of Hitler hung.

"Are... are you sure you do not wish breakfast?" the woman had stammered, and Sam shook his head before leaving the house.

As he'd walked to the IG Farben building, the day cool and cloudy, dead leaves scuttling down the cratered street, he'd wondered whether the stammering hausfrau had been a Nazi. Then he'd wondered what that even meant. She obviously hadn't been in the SS or the Gestapo; most likely she hadn't been one of the *aufseherin*, or female guards, at one of the terrible concentration camps, either. But had she liked Hitler? Had she supported the Nuremberg Laws, the ghettoes, the camps? Had her son who had carried his kit bag marched with the HJ, had she cheered at *Kristallnacht*, as Sam had read many Berliners had done? Or had she been sickened by it all? It was impossible to know.

When he'd looked at all the desperate, defeated people around him, he felt pity mixed with a faint revulsion, but neither disgust nor hatred, as much as men like Belmont wanted him to. But if he'd come here six months ago, Sam had reasoned, or certainly six years, he surely would have felt differently. The people who scuttled by him now with bowed heads and slumped shoulders might have been swaggering and smug back then, high and mighty and hate-filled. It was simply so hard to imagine now, with their world in ruins all around him.

And yet he had to imagine it, for the sake of his job, and the ten thousand questionnaires currently in his office. Sam suspected Major Pitt was fobbing him, a useless greenhorn, off with so many pedantic forms, but they were all he had, and he intended to do his job as well as he could. If he could find out who was a real Nazi and who wasn't from the answers to the one hundred and thirty-one questions on each questionnaire, then he would do it.

He'd just pulled the first box toward him when a knock sounded on his door. Before he could bid anyone to enter, Sergeant Belmont sashayed in, holding a sheaf of papers, his eyes bloodshot, no doubt from the night before.

"Looks as if you'll be kept busy," he remarked with a rather smirking smile as he glanced around at all the boxes. "Fortunately I've brought help. Your first *fraulein* is here for her interview."

"Already?" Sam recalled that Major Pitt had mentioned interviews for a German-speaking secretary, but he hadn't realized they would take place practically the moment he arrived.

"They're eager," Belmont said cheerfully, and he somehow managed to make it sound lewd. Sam was starting to realize he disliked the man. Actively. "Here's her *fragebogen*." He handed over the six-page booklet, nodding to all the boxes surrounding him, "Don't lose it among all these."

"I won't," Sam said shortly. "Thank you, Sergeant."

Belmont merely raised his eyebrows, seeming amused by Sam's rather obvious attempt to put him in his place. "There's two more after her," he told him as he turned to leave. "And don't worry, I picked the pretty ones. That's a requisite here at HQ."

Sam did not reply. He started to flick through the questionnaire, but he had only read through the first questions on height and eye color when another, softer knock sounded at the door.

"Enter," Sam called, and then, as an afterthought, "*Tragen Sie ein.*" He realized belatedly he didn't know if he had the conjugation or even the word right.

It didn't matter; the woman entered anyway, closing the door softly behind her. Her hair was dark and arranged in a neat roll, and her eyes were a mossy hazel, glinting, for a second, with something close to humor.

"I speak English," she said, in a gently accented voice. "That is why I am here, yes?"

"Right." Sam let out an embarrassed laugh and retreated to stand behind his desk. He glanced at the questionnaire again. "You are Miss Anna Vogel?"

"Yes." She came to stand in front of his desk, inching her way around all the boxes, her chin tilted at a resolute angle. There was nothing haughty about her, but rather something quiet and strong and contained, a woman determined to be in control of herself.

"Please sit down, Miss Vogel," Sam said, only to realize there wasn't a chair.

A faint smile touched her mouth as he lurched forward to liberate a chair from all the boxes. He felt, quite suddenly, young and gangly, and rather ridiculously inept.

As he removed a stack of boxes from the one other chair in the room, he caught her gaze, and saw she was smiling faintly. Kindly, he thought, and he smiled back in wry acknowledgement. "There we are."

"Thank you, Captain." She sat down, crossing her ankles neatly in front of her, her hands folded in her lap. She wore a plain dress of navy serge, belted at the waist. It had clearly seen better days, the material shiny and worn at the shoulders and hips, but she looked well in it, her figure trim, her bearing graceful. Quickly, Sam looked down at the questionnaire, the German words swimming before his eyes for a few endless seconds.

"Tell me about yourself," he said at last.

"What is it you wish to know?" Her voice was quiet and measured, friendly enough but with a hint of caution. She did not want to give anything away unnecessarily, Sam suspected. No German did.

He surveyed her thoughtfully, conscious that here right in front of him was a person who had survived the war, who had taken part in it, in some way or other. She wouldn't be here if she'd been deemed a major, or even lesser, offender, but could she have been a follower? A *Mitlaufer*, or fellow traveler, as they were called, sympathetic but silent when it came to National Socialism and its inherent evils.

"Where are you from?" he asked.

"Essen."

"You have come a long way, then." She inclined her head in acknowledgment. "What brought you to Frankfurt?"

"I had an aunt here, but I discovered she had died in the bombing." A slight shrug of her slender shoulders. "And I wish to work."

"The rest of your family?"

"My parents are dead." She spoke tonelessly.

"I'm sorry."

Another inclination of her head; her eyes were watchful.

"Where did you learn English so well?"

A hesitation, slight yet telling. "My mother liked American films," she answered after a moment, choosing her words with care. "She taught me."

"You know it rather well, considering." He hadn't meant to sound suspicious, but he saw a slight blush rise to her cheeks as if he'd accused her of something.

"It seemed useful, to know it. My father wished it, as well. He made sure we had English lessons."

"We?"

"I meant me. I was their only child." For a second she looked flustered, but then her features ordered themselves again. She took a deep breath and let it out slowly.

She was nervous, Sam realized, underneath that sense of containment. Why?

"How did your parents die?" he asked.

"A bomb in 1943." She spoke flatly, without inflection, staring straight at him, with an almost cold look in her eyes.

Sam had the strange urge to apologize for the question, but he didn't. He held her gaze, and after a second hers softened and she looked down.

"I thought you would ask me about my typing speed," she remarked quietly, but with the barest hint of humor.

Sam braced one hip against his desk. "Very well. What is your typing speed?"

She looked up, and now her eyes glinted, inviting him to share the joke. "I don't know."

He laughed softly, and was gratified to see her smile, if only just. A flicker of attraction he immediately did his best to suppress went through him. "That isn't a problem, as I don't actually have a typewriter for you to use."

"Ah, well." She shrugged slender shoulders. "That is good, I suppose?"

"I suppose." A pause that stretched into a silence, and then Sam needlessly cleared his throat. "As you might be aware, I am not fluent in German. I can speak and understand a little, but I will need your help in translating these forms." He gestured to the boxes around him. "In order that I may analyze the answers."

She nodded once, and Sam raised his eyebrows, feeling a sudden need to get some further response from her, something that gave away who she'd once been.

"My brief is to determine who among all these were Nazi supporters, so they can be brought to prosecution."

Another nod. She kept her unblinking gaze on him, her face as still and smooth as if it had been made from porcelain.

"Naturally, you have already been vetted, to get this far in the interview process." At least, he hoped so. Judging from Belmont's casual manner and the general laid-back attitude among the CIC—Major Pitt excluded perhaps—it seemed as if military service had turned into one long party that bordered on chaos. "But I trust you have no loyalty to National Socialism?" It was, he knew, a ridiculous question, demanding only one answer, and yet he needed to ask it. He wanted to see her face as she replied.

"None." Her voice was calm yet flat, and although her expression didn't change, she pressed her lips together after answering, as if to keep herself from saying anything more. He sensed an intensity from her, but he did not know its source.

"What was your father's profession?" he asked suddenly, and she answered without missing a beat.

"He owned a hardware store."

"Your mother?"

"*Hausfrau*. Housewife," she corrected herself quickly, blushing slightly again.

"And you? Were you a student?" He didn't think she could be more than twenty-five or twenty-six.

"I worked in my father's store."

"For the whole war?"

"Yes."

"What about your National Labor Service?"

She looked disconcerted for a brief moment, and then she answered, "Not then. Then I—I worked on a farm near Cologne for six months."

"A farm? What kind of crop?"

"Potatoes," she said, after a second's pause. Still she didn't blink.

She was lying, Sam realized, about something. He'd learned enough during his intelligence training about interrogation techniques and reading signals to know that her unblinking stare, her unnatural stillness, could well be an indication of dishonesty. Yet about what? Potatoes? It didn't make sense.

"Did you enjoy it?" he asked, and for a second her brows knitted together in confusion.

"There was enough to eat," she said after a moment. She sounded less certain, and for the first time, her gaze moved away from his. She shifted in her seat, clasping her hands more tightly together.

"I'm glad to hear it. From what I have seen so far, food is the rarest commodity in all of Germany." She looked back at him, her gaze watchful, and he asked abruptly, "Do you have a place to stay in Frankfurt?"

She nodded. "Yes, the Housing Authority has given me a room in Heimatsiedlung."

"Very well, I shall let you know my decision in due course. Thank you for coming in." He rose from his seat and so did she, as graceful as ever, that small smile twitching at her lips, making him want to smile, as well. It was as if she knew what he was thinking, although, in truth, he didn't know what he was thinking himself, except perhaps that she was very beautiful.

"Thank you, Captain."

He nodded, feeling ill at ease once more, wondering what she'd been lying about. He supposed most Germans were lying about something, desperate to hide anything that kept them from work, from food, from survival. Perhaps she'd been in the League of German Girls, or had gone to a Nuremberg rally, or hidden a photograph of Hitler under her pillow.

If he read through all one hundred and thirty-one questions on her form, he'd no doubt find something that hinted at her being questionable. He wasn't sure he wanted to; he realized he was going to hire her, whether she was lying or not, and that knowledge brought both pleasure and a frisson of doubt.

Was he, like Belmont, being guided by his baser instincts? Anna Vogel was undoubtedly lovely, and yet it wasn't her looks that attracted him but that sense of quiet containment, like a deep river flowing right through the room, a stillness that fascinated him and made him want to know more.

"Good day, Miss Vogel," he said, and with the faintest of smiles, she nodded and turned to leave. As she did so, Sam caught sight of her shoes—a beat-up pair of men's brogues with fraying laces, the worn-through soles lined with cardboard. "You'll need new shoes," he said abruptly, and for a second, a look of something almost like scorn crossed her face before it vanished.

"I will try to find a pair," she replied, and again Sam felt the need to apologize. Again he didn't. The official policy, he knew, was still not to give Germans anything—not a clothing coupon, not a stick of chewing gum, and certainly not a pair of shoes. "Goodbye, Captain Houghton," she said, and then she was gone.

The other two women he interviewed, Sam soon discovered, were not nearly as interesting or qualified as Anna Vogel. One, a peroxide blonde with a breathy laugh and a forward manner, he discounted immediately; the other, an angular woman with dark eyes and strong brows, had lamentable English. Belmont had indeed picked the pretty girls.

Sam spent the rest of the day laboriously going through a box of the *fragebogen*, trying to decipher the German, realizing how much he needed an interpreter. He had already written Miss Vogel a letter offering her the position and instructing her to start on Monday. As far as he was concerned, it couldn't come soon enough.

By the end of the day, Sam felt he'd spent most of it rather pointlessly; he'd listened to Major Pitt bellowing at someone or other about something that had clearly gone wrong, and he'd heard footsteps running down the corridor once, clearly on some urgent mission. Meanwhile, he felt forgotten, left to molder under a pile of paperwork nobody seemed to care about, never mind that these bloody questionnaires were meant to be so very important. What about his all-important brief to find the scientists? It seemed, in the shambolic mess that currently was CIC, to have been forgotten.

He left at five, having declined a second night of drinks with Belmont, and headed downstairs, nimbly stepping onto one of the constantly moving elevators. Pitt had informed him he could move into his new accommodation, a villa in Bergen-Enkheim on the shores of Riedteich, a small lake, the next day. Sam felt both curious and apprehensive about the prospect.

He was just about to leave the building when he noticed a balding, red-faced man standing by the doors, looking agitated. Sam slowed his step.

"Herr Huber?" he guessed.

"*Ja, ja*," the man said in surprise, lurching forward in his excitement, looking for a second as if he would clasp both of Sam's hands in his before he jerked them back. "You wish to speak?"

"Do you know any English?"

"A little."

Sam nodded. "I have heard you have paperwork you wish the US Army to see?"

"*Ja*! Much papers. Trucks and trucks of papers." Huber flung his arms wide as if to indicate the sheer, vast quantity of the papers in his possession.

Sam thought of the stacks of boxes of questionnaires up in his office. No wonder Belmont had dismissed the man and his endless amount of almost certainly useless papers. Still, he persevered.

"What kind of papers? Where did they come from?"

"The trucks—they brought them. They said to burn, all must burn, but I did not."

"They…" Sam stared at the man, with his florid face and his shabby suit, his manner so earnest. "You mean the Nazis? They wanted to burn all of these papers?"

"*Ja*. They said they must be destroyed. They are… the facts… of people. Party people."

Sam's interest deepened. "You mean a record of members of the Nazi Party?" If that was the case, Huber's tons of paperwork could be invaluable. "Can you show me an example? Did you bring any with you?"

"*Ja*, here."

From his pocket, he thrust a yellow card at Sam; he took it, his gaze scanning it quickly. It was a record of Nazi party membership— *Nationalsozialistische Deutsche Arbeiterpartei*—with a name, photograph, and date when the membership had started. Such information was, indeed, invaluable, incalculably so. If they got their hands on all these, the boxes of questionnaires upstairs would become virtually obsolete. There would be no need to analyze answers to the many pointless questions, when the truth of Nazi allegiance would be written right there on the membership cards.

"How many of these do you have?" Sam asked.

"How many?" Huber repeated, blowing out his cheeks. "Many, many. Trucks and trucks. Many tons."

He might have a record of every Nazi on file, Sam realized with a thrill of wonder. "Stay here," he instructed Huber. "No, on second thought, come upstairs with me."

As he led Huber up to Major Pitt, Sam thanked whatever instinct had guided him to Huber... even as he realized he very well might have made an enemy of Sergeant Belmont in the process. At least now he would be able to do his job—and find the Nazis hiding in plain sight.

CHAPTER SEVEN

Berlin, November 1938

The Grinzinger Heuriger in Haus Vaterland, the pleasure palace on Potsdamer Platz, was buzzing with people intent on an enjoyable afternoon out, even though it was only a Wednesday. A replica of a Viennese café and wine bar, and the only venue in Berlin allowed to serve authentic *Sachertorte*, it had been a favorite place for Liesel to go with her father, back when she'd been young and silly and entranced by all the sights and sounds around her of the vast and varied pleasure palace.

Now she restlessly pushed the crumbs of the rich chocolate cake around with her fork; she had little appetite for anything these days, and she wished her father had not asked her to go out with him. He hadn't in months, maybe even a year.

When she looked back, Liesel thought the evening eighteen months ago, when she'd met Reich Minister Göring, had proved to be a turning point, at least in her own mind, and there could be no going back. Her father *was* a Nazi, whether he considered himself one or not. Whether she wanted him to be one or not. And somehow, she realized then, she had to determine how to live with that information, day by painstaking day, without becoming one herself.

The morning after the party, Liesel had come downstairs to a sea of half-empty champagne glasses and overflowing ashtrays, a stale smell of perfume and cigarette smoke still lingering in the air. Gerda was picking her way among all the mess, clearing up as quietly as she could. For a second, Liesel saw a look of such naked despair on the woman's face, she had an urge to comfort her, even embrace her. Gerda had looked up quickly, her expression clearing as she gave Liesel a tentative smile, although her eyes remained dark and shadowed.

"Good party."

Liesel had found she could not reply. She was picturing Göring standing in the corner of the room, as he had been the night before, waving his cigar around as he'd told her about her clever, clever father who was going to help them build all the planes and tanks and guns. And what of Gerda? She could not possibly think it had been a good party, confined as she had been to the kitchen, meant to be hidden from sight from the people who hated her and anyone like her.

Liesel had gone into the kitchen for some breakfast, coming up short when she saw Rosa standing at the sink, washing dishes. The girl gave her an uncertain look, a flicker of vulnerability in her eyes before she quickly turned back to the dishes.

"Why are you here?" Liesel had asked, a bit rudely.

"Helping my mother to clean up after your party."

"It wasn't my party," Liesel snapped. She didn't know why she was so angry, only that she was, and somehow Rosa, with her angry eyes and proud bearing, bore the brunt of it.

"It certainly wasn't mine," Rosa answered, and turned back to the sink.

Liesel watched her for a moment, guilt warring with that old anger at the girl's seeming superiority. "I know that you're Jewish," she said at last, and Rosa had stiffened before turning around, the fear in her eyes quickly veiled by a challenge.

"And what of it?"

"I don't mind," Liesel told her. "I'm not like that. It doesn't bother me."

Rosa's lip curled. "Oh, really? How magnanimous of you."

She had turned back to the dishes and Liesel stared at her back, annoyed by her tone that had seemed sarcastic, and also because she didn't know what magnanimous meant, although she could guess. "I was trying to be nice," she said with as much dignity as she could muster, and Rosa nodded, her expression turning resigned.

"I know."

"Rosa, there is no need to chatter so," Gerda said sharply as she came into the kitchen. "I apologize for my daughter, Fraulein Scholz."

"There's no need," Liesel had said, thinking she was being generous, but Rosa merely pressed her lips together and looked away. Liesel realized she could hardly blame the girl for hating her in that moment. She hated herself, for being so arrogant as to assure her she didn't *mind* that she was Jewish, as well as for being unable to keep from feeling smugly self-righteous as she'd waved aside Gerda's apology. For a moment she saw herself as Rosa must see her—arrogant, ignorant, self-righteous and unyielding, and abruptly she had turned and walked out of the room. Jew or not, she did not need, or want, a housekeeper's daughter putting her in her place.

Her mother did not come down all that morning; in fact, ever since that evening, Ilse had retreated even more to her bedroom, only coming out for meals or the ever-pressing social occasions. Her father seemed to spend as much time swilling cocktails with Party officials as he did making his synthetic rubber in Schkopau, and her mother went along reluctantly, as beautiful and lifeless as a statue at his side.

"Why do you go with him, if you hate it so much?" Liesel had dared to ask her once. Ilse was sitting at her dressing table, dusting her face with Elizabeth Arden powder. The scent of it drifted through the room, a ghostly reminder of happier days.

She had met Liesel's challenging gaze in the mirror and shrugged. "What else am I supposed to do?"

"You could refuse to attend."

"And jeopardize your father's standing among all his friends?" Her mother's voice was weary rather than mocking.

"Why not?"

"I wonder if you even know what that would mean." Ilse had put down the powder puff as she gazed at her reflection straight on. The powder had collected in the papery creases of her face, and Liesel had thought she suddenly looked old. She was forty-three. "No, I will continue to stand by your father's side like a good little mannequin, at least for now. He asks little enough of me, as it is."

Her father, Liesel noticed, ignored his wife's pronounced listlessness. He was as jaunty and joking as ever, but even so, Liesel saw the strain around his eyes, the way his smile dropped as soon as he thought no one was looking. She felt the unspoken tension in her parents' relationship as well as their own, and she suspected he did, too; his jokes often fell flat, and she no longer had any ability to banter, no desire to impress. When she looked at him, she felt a wave of sadness, a stab of hurt. She did not want to ask him any questions about anything, because she did not want to know.

Meanwhile, the Reich marched inexorably on—more and more "undesirables" were rounded up and sent away; more than once, Liesel had seen a crowd of shabby-looking people herded down the street, looking dazed and frightened, as brown-shirted members of the SA prodded them on.

More and more parades and rallies proclaimed German superiority; in March, Germany had marched, unheeded, into Austria, in what was seen to be a joyous reunification, welcomed by all, the triumphant Anschluss, a war of flowers.

Only last month, German troops had occupied the Sude-tenland with barely a murmur from any other country. Liesel had dutifully marched in a Hitler Youth parade to celebrate the reclaiming of Germany's borders, sick at heart, a smile on her face. She found it all unbearable now—the rallies, the rhetoric, the shouting, the hatred. She could barely tolerate the more innocuous aspects—the lectures on cookery and health, the gymnastics, the camping and canoeing—that she'd once thought of as a silver lining to the whole wretched endeavor. Now all of it felt tainted, terrible, and she was counting down the days until she could finally leave the BDM, until she finished school.

And yet she continued—the marches, the parades, the races, the lectures—just as her mother did with the parties and outings, because she did not know what else she could do. If she quit, it would be remarked upon; she—and indeed her whole family—could be in trouble, and for what? So she didn't have to listen to a lecture she didn't believe in anyway?

The words all washed over her, a babble of ignorance and hatred she tried not to let penetrate her mind or taint her soul, and yet sometimes it felt so very difficult. No matter how Liesel tried to resist it all, at least in the privacy of her own mind, trying to keep her thoughts both separate and sacred, she still felt powerless, swept along in a tide of feeling, trying only not to drown in the unholy sentiments swirling all around her. How long would it last? How far would it go? At the end of every endless BDM meeting, she gave a little sigh of relief. *Another day done.* And yet she feared it would never end. The world would never change back to the way it had been, or move onto something better. Something saner. It would always be like this… or worse.

Was she no more than a coward, she often wondered, silenced simply by fear? Were there other girls like her, at least one or two? Or what about the men and women she saw hurrying in the street, heads down, wanting only not to be noticed?

Perhaps she was a coward. She certainly felt afraid all the time, a cramping in her belly that never went away, even though she wasn't entirely sure what she was afraid of. But more than fear, she felt utterly, hopelessly helpless. How could she stop the relentless march of the Reich? How could she change anything, even one person's mind?

She'd tried, a little, with Friedrich, early on; she'd told him to stop reading the horrid books from school and she'd made a list of all the famous Jews through history, not that he'd heard of many of them.

"Albert Einstein, Felix Mendelssohn, Heinrich Heine…"

He'd looked at her blankly. He was only seven, after all, and yet still Liesel had persisted.

"I didn't know they were Jews at first, Friedy. They look and act just like us, truly. They've done amazing things with science and music and books—"

Friedrich shook his head, his expression becoming uncharacteristically obdurate. "I told you before, they're good at tricking people. You're *wrong*, Liesel. You're very wrong."

It had been her mother who had wearily told her to stop. "He'll report you," she had said one afternoon last winter when Liesel had been pointing to the pictures in one of Friedy's books and trying to explain their ridiculous fallacy. He'd become angry and thrown the book at her before running out of the room.

"He'll think he's doing the right thing," Ilse told her. "He won't even realize what it means, but the Gestapo will come in the middle of the night and take you away. Me, too, no doubt." She had shrugged, as if it was of little importance. "Maybe even your father, although perhaps his work will keep him safe, who knows. He seems to think it will."

Liesel's mouth had dried as the book had slipped from her fingers onto the floor. "They wouldn't," she said, stooping to pick it up. The lurid cover seemed to mock her and she turned it face down on the table. "They wouldn't," she said again, more forcefully this time. "Not for us."

She still couldn't let herself believe that such things could happen to *her*, to her family. They were different from the raggedy crowds on the street, the old man with his cap whose crumpled body she still saw when she closed her eyes. They were different even from the neighbor Irma had reported, from the man who ran the corner shop who had suddenly disappeared, with no explanation, and everyone acted as if he'd never even existed. They *had* to be different.

She might resist, but it was a point of pride, of honor, rather than anything else; *she* was safe. Her family was safe. All along, Liesel had believed that, and yet in that moment she wondered why she'd been so naïve.

"Open your eyes, Liesel," her mother had snapped, her voice turning grating and harsh, her eyes suddenly seeming wild as she thrust her face close to Liesel's. "They'll do it to anyone. Everyone. No one is safe. And if you think you are, because you are Aryan or your father is someone important, you are still living in a dreamland, where things like justice and equality matter to these people. They don't. Not now. Not here." She lit one cigarette from the tip of the other as she nodded toward the doorway Friedrich had run through. "They're too powerful, and he's too young. He believes everything they say, including not to trust or even to love your parents. They burrow into their brains, they drip-feed their poison, every second of every day." Her mouth had twisted. "And the worst part is, he *wants* to join. He *wants* to be a part of it all. He will learn to hate us, and he won't even mind."

For a second her mother had looked as if she might cry, but then her expression had hardened and she'd sucked viciously on the end of her cigarette. "The best thing you can do," she had said with another nod to the door, "is to apologize to him. Tell him you didn't mean it."

Liesel had stared at her, appalled. "I won't—"

"You have to. If you want to take a stand somewhere, Liesel, then take it, by all means. God knows, I wish I had the strength to. But don't do it over your little brother's pointless book. Make a bigger difference than *that*, for heaven's sake."

And so Liesel had gone upstairs to find Friedrich sitting on the windowsill of his bedroom, his arms folded, his face dark with a self-righteous anger. He was so small and slight, with his crooked foot hidden behind the straight one, his eyes flashing fire. She'd never seen him look so furious.

"Friedy…"

"You're *wrong*. Why are you telling such lies? You're a *liar*, Liesel."

Liesel had drawn a quick, steadying breath as she took the brunt of his anger like a punch to her gut. "I was mistaken, Friedy," she had said, the words sounding stilted and forced. "I'm sorry."

"You lied."

"No, no, it was only a mistake." Her hand had fluttered uselessly at her side as a sudden, very real terror clutched at her for the first time. Her mother was right: Friedrich could report her to his *Pimpf* leader or even his teacher; they were all ardent Nazis now, practically frothing at the mouth in their fervor. The Gestapo could come. She could almost hear the knock on the door, see herself bolting up in bed, her father's sleepy voice turning panicked… *it could happen.*

There was no reason, no reason at all, to think it couldn't, not to them, not to anyone. "Please forgive me," she had told Friedrich, a note of sincerity in her voice that was almost entirely motivated by fear. She was a coward after all, it seemed. "I really didn't mean it. I won't say it again, I promise."

A crafty look had come over his face then that chilled her far more than his childish anger. He was only seven, but he seemed so much older in that moment, so much more knowing. Was this what schooling had done to him, his afternoons with the *Pimpf?* "No," he had agreed slowly, a note of satisfaction in his voice that made Liesel's hand itch to slap him, although, of course, she never would, for many reasons. "You won't."

And so she hadn't. For the last year and a half, she'd kept utterly silent; she had not said anything to Friedy, or her father, or the other girls at school. She walked quickly down the street, her head bent low; she listened attentively in every BDM lecture; she dutifully answered her math problems: *The Jews are aliens in Germany. In 1933, there were 66,000,000 people living in Germany. Of this total, 499,862 were Jewish. What is the percentage of aliens in Germany?*

She did it all without complaint, without resistance, even as she felt as if she were howling inside—howling with fury, with fear, with impotence. Now, in the happy hum of the Haus Vaterland, the latest travesty, from only this morning, compelled her to speak, or at least not to eat.

"Not hungry today?" Otto said with a little smile as he nodded toward her untouched cake. "Perhaps we should have gone to the Wild West Bar. You could have practiced your English. Your lessons are coming on nicely, I hear."

Liesel could not summon a smile in response. The Haus Vaterland offered, in addition to the heuriger, an American restaurant, a Turkish café, a Bavarian beer hall, a Japanese teahouse, and a Spanish bodega, as well as a cinema and ballroom, all of which had once enchanted and thrilled her.

"It's all the same now, really," she replied as she put her fork down. The *Horst Wessel* song was booming from every speaker in the place, no matter what the ambiance of the venue was meant to be.

"Is that what is bothering you?" Otto asked, refusing to pretend to misunderstand. "The music?"

Liesel took a deep breath. She'd done her best not to ask her father any questions in the last year, because she knew she did not want to know the answers. Now she did. "Why did you fire Gerda this morning?"

"Ah." He sat back in his seat and crossed one leg neatly over the other. He was dressed in as dapper an ensemble as ever, wearing a checked suit with padded shoulders and peak lapels, although admittedly the pattern was less vibrant in color than it had been a few years ago. "I did not realize you had such an affection for our housekeeper."

"She was a member of our household for over two years."

"Even so, she was a servant," he replied mildly. "I did not see you speak to her very much."

"She is a good woman, Father." Liesel met his rueful gaze with a steely one of her own. "And what about her daughter Rosa?"

"What about her?"

"What will they do, without gainful employment?" Gerda, Liesel knew, was a widow, the only provider for her daughter. Over the last year and a half, Liesel had not become friends with Rosa, although she had tried, if only a little. She still disliked the girl's innate sense of superiority, although more and more she understood it, and suspected Rosa hid her fear and powerlessness behind it. Still, talking to Rosa made her dislike herself, and that was worse than disliking the girl. Their few conversations over the days and months had been tense if not actually unfriendly, often ending in reluctant compromise, if Gerda didn't put a stop to any interaction first. Even so, Liesel did not wish any ill to come to either Rosa or her mother, and certainly not thanks to her father's machinations.

"So why did you?" Liesel asked.

Otto was silent for a moment, swinging one leg. "You know Gerda is a Jew?"

"Yes. What of it?"

Her father sighed, a look of disappointment flashing across his face at her question, as if she were being petulant on purpose. Perhaps she was. "Liesel, you know why."

"Are the people at your work really going to care if your housekeeper is Jewish?" she demanded in a low voice. "How are they even going to know?"

"You'd be surprised what they make their business to know. I have to be careful. If it makes you feel better, I gave Gerda a glowing reference and six months' salary. I am not *trying* to be cruel, you know." He leaned across the table, covering her hand with his own as he gave her a sorrowful smile. "Please don't hate me, Liesel, for the way the world is."

"I don't understand why you go along with it all," Liesel returned, dropping her gaze to her discarded cake. She wanted to pull her hand away from her father's, even as she fought an urge to rush into his arms like a child, press her cheek against his chest and close her eyes to the world. She wanted to have him tease, and be able to laugh in response. She was so very *tired* of this endless, impotent anger she felt, yet she could not lay it down. "I don't understand why you have to."

"If I didn't, I would lose my job."

"Would that be so very bad?"

"You might think it would," he replied, a hint of wryness in his tone, "when we had no money, no house, no opportunity for you or Friedrich to go to school."

"I don't even like school anymore." And she would be finished this year, anyway. Once, she would have hoped to go to university, but not now, not under the Reich, when so much felt uncertain or fraught. In any case, girls were discouraged from university, and the subjects they were encouraged to study didn't interest Liesel. She didn't know what she would do; the future felt utterly unknowable, and perhaps it was better that way.

"And no opportunity for me to find another position," Otto finished quietly. "Anywhere. They would make sure of that. Liesel, I have told you before I don't like everything that is happening now. I doubt anyone does, not even Hitler himself. But this is the world we live in. I have to make the best of it. I don't want something even worse to happen to you, or to any of us, because I decided to show an ill-thought spark of defiance."

Liesel looked up then, a ferocity blazing in her expression and her voice that she usually didn't let anyone see, and certainly not her father. "'It is the strange fate of man, that even in the greatest of evils, the fear of the worst continues to haunt him.'"

Otto smiled. "Ah, Goethe. I think you love him as much as I do."

"Do you really?" Liesel demanded. "Because you don't act as if you do."

He sighed. "Sadly, I fear I cannot afford to in these times."

"Yes, you *fear*." She shook her head and pulled her hand away from his. "I thought you were above all that, Vati."

"I have said before, you think too highly of me."

"I don't anymore."

He looked pained for a second, and Liesel almost took the words back. Then his expression ironed out into implacability and he nodded slowly. "Then perhaps it is time for me to tell you what I must ask of you now, although indeed I hope it will not be too onerous. Perhaps it will even be a pleasure."

Yet it didn't sound as if it would be a pleasure, with his voice heavy with both regret and decision, and a tremor of fear went through her. So this was why he'd invited her to Haus Vaterland on a Wednesday afternoon; he had some request to put to her, something he knew she would resist, if not outright refuse. She put her hands in her lap. "What is it?"

"It is a social occasion, quite an important one. Normally your mother would attend with me, but she doesn't like to leave Friedrich."

"And she doesn't want to rub elbows with *Nazis*," Liesel retorted before she could think better of it.

"*Liesel*." Otto leaned forward, looking angry for the first time since they'd sat down, his face flushing as his gaze darted around the busy café.

Liesel realized she'd been goading him all afternoon, but she didn't care. She felt wild inside, desperate to do damage, to make something *matter*, even if it hurt.

"Don't be imprudent, please," he entreated quietly. "Speaking so in a public place such as this. It accomplishes so little, and it could threaten so much." He took a careful breath as Liesel forced herself to look calm. She knew he was right, even if she didn't like it. Spouting off about Nazis in a café would serve no purpose. "I have been invited to a shooting party at Carinhall in a few weeks' time, for the weekend. I'd like you to accompany me there."

Liesel stared at him blankly for a few seconds, unable to make sense of such an incredible request. She'd known her father was acquainted with some high-ranking Nazis, but only in a professional capacity; they graced him with their presence on occasion, and he allowed it, for work. She hadn't realized he was as important, as entrenched, as this, to secure such a coveted invitation to a very select party. "Carinhall…"

"The weekend house of Generalfeldmarschall Göring, yes."

Göring had been promoted last February, Liesel knew, to the highest military rank. Her mouth dried as she continued to stare, absorbing her father's words. "Why me…?"

"Because if I go alone, it will raise questions about my family's loyalty, and as I said, your mother does not wish to leave Friedrich alone for an entire weekend."

"I could take care of him."

Otto shrugged; it was obvious that her mother was reluctant to attend not because of Friedy, but because of Göring. She despised him, Liesel knew, and his vicious hatred of Jews, hidden beneath his friendly, flamboyant manner that many Germans adored.

"And is that why you are going?" she asked. "So you don't raise questions?"

"Essentially, yes. The Generalfeldmarschall is very interested in my work, which can be of quite a sensitive nature. I have to be careful, Liesel. No one can question my loyalty."

"You mean the synthetic rubber, for the planes and the tanks."

Otto flinched, an expression of annoyance at her imprudence in mentioning specifics. "Among other things."

"What other things?"

He shrugged, impatient now, a little restless as he recrossed his legs and glanced once more around the restaurant. "The work I used to do with pesticides, and similar matters. I can hardly explain it all to you now, and you wouldn't understand it anyway. It could be fun, you know, Liesel. There will be other young people there, I am sure, and you are almost seventeen now. Almost a lady. You will be allowed to have dinner with us, attend the party in the evening, have a sip of champagne?" He raised his eyebrows enticingly, but Liesel did not feel tempted in the least.

"The last time I saw the Reichsminister," she reminded him shortly, "you dressed me up like a six-year-old in organdie and satin."

"That seemed wisest, then," Otto returned. "I wanted you to be seen as a child."

Liesel's stomach cramped. "And now you don't?"

"Now I wish you to be seen as the lovely young woman you are. All I am asking is for you to attend a party, to eat good food and even drink a little champagne. Nothing too taxing, I promise you." He raised his hand to summon the waiter, his expression hardening a little. "And now, since you seem determined not to eat your cake, I will ask for the bill."

CHAPTER EIGHT

By the time Liesel and her father left Haus Vaterland, it was darkening to dusk, the sky a steel gray and the wind whipping the bare branches of the trees along the street as they walked down Leipziger Strasse, toward the waiting car. They were only a few hundred meters from Göring's Ministry of Aviation, with its imposing neoclassical façade of limestone and marble, built on the monstrously gigantic scale of Hitler's new vision for Berlin.

As they crossed the street, Liesel looked away with a shudder. To think she was going to go to the man's weekend house, a shooting party of all things... She could scarcely take it in, and yet she knew, with a leaden sense of inevitability, that it would happen. Just as with everything else, she did not know how to resist, or even if she possessed either the courage or the will to do so.

And, she realized sadly, as her father kindly took her arm to help her into the car, she loved him. She loved his light laugh, the wry tone, the way he listened so intently and considered her questions so seriously. Even now, knowing he had to be a Nazi more than in name, she found ways to excuse him. To exonerate him. She wondered if that would ever stop, and shivered inwardly to think of what might cause it to.

As they sped back toward Grunewald in the oncoming twilight, Liesel noticed crowds gathering on street corners and outside shops; even in the car, she sensed an expectant menace about them. Then she glimpsed a couple of SA with smug smiles milling about as a boy wearing the brown of a Hitler Youth uniform hurled a bottle through the plate-glass window of a Jewish-owned shop while a crowd watched and cheered. Liesel gasped out loud.

"What are they doing—"

Otto glanced out the car window, his expression tightening as he saw the commotion and heard the cheering before the car sped past. "Causing trouble, it would seem."

"But why…" Even as the words escaped her, the question she couldn't help but keep asking, Liesel knew why. *Because they could*, just as her mother had said.

A cold, numbing horror stole through her as she witnessed similar scenes all the way back home—broken windows, jeering crowds, dawdling SA or, worse, ones who were rounding people up, herding them into vans, with doors slamming closed on faces pale with terror, heads bloodied by beating.

It felt as if the city was splintering along its seams; as if the very fabric of society was being rent in two. The foundation that had held everything together was crumbling to dust. She watched, utterly appalled, as several HJ boys whipped a woman down the street; her shoulders were hunched under their blows, her face haggard with misery and despair. She was holding the hand of a small child who cowered against her, trying to avoid the blows.

At the back of the crowd, another woman also held her toddler, up above her head so the chubby child could view the grim spectacle, a look of delight on the mother's face as she shouted her approval. Liesel thought she might be sick.

"Don't look, Liesel," her father said quietly. "Just don't look."

"Is that your only answer? Don't look? Don't *see*?" The words felt as if they were ripped from her too-tight throat and she felt a sudden, visceral hatred for the man she'd always adored, the father she'd thought she'd always love. "How can you not? How can you let this happen all around you, and not *do* anything?"

Otto glanced at the stony-faced driver before hissing in a low voice, "I don't like it, of course I don't. But what can I do?"

"What can any of us do?" Liesel exclaimed wildly. "We could say 'enough.' We could help that poor woman—" She nodded toward the woman she'd just seen staggering down the street, whipped along by the HJ. Her stomach cramped again and she clamped one hand to her mouth, unsure whether she was going to vomit or sob. She felt sick, utterly sick, both to her stomach and in her heart. "None of this can be right," she whispered. "This shouldn't be happening." She shook her head slowly, as if she could deny the reality of all that was being enacted around her, but she knew she couldn't.

It had been terrible enough seeing those SS officers kick an old man lying in the street. It was even worse to watch the crowds taking part, to register the vicious joy on their faces as they watched shops being destroyed, livelihoods being trampled, people being beaten.

Her father had told her people needed someone to hate, and while she still didn't understand *why*, she now believed him utterly. She glanced at yet another smashed window, this one of a dress shop. The dresses, all silks and satins, on the mannequins had been slashed to shreds. She let out a little whimper of despair.

"It's one evening," Otto stated as he looked away from the window and its grim sights. "When people are letting their tempers get the better of them. It's not pleasant, I know, but occasionally people need to—"

"Not *pleasant*?" Liesel repeated disbelievingly. "Is that all you can say?"

Her father simply shook his head and closed his eyes, leaning his head back against the seat.

Liesel turned back to the window, determined not to ignore the evil devastation being enacted all around them, but the car had pulled into Hagenstrasse, the street where Heinrich Himmler lived, and all was calm and untroubled, not an SA in sight, the curtains on every window drawn tightly across, making Liesel think of her father's closed eyes. *Just don't look.*

Neither of them spoke until they were back at the house on Koenigsallee, but Liesel had seen more than enough. Her stomach was roiling, her heart like a stone inside her. As they climbed out of the car, the acrid smell of smoke filled the air, and the sky held an eerie, orange glow—from fire, Liesel realized.

"The synagogue on Fasanenstrasse is burning," Otto stated quietly, and Liesel turned to give him a sharp look.

"How do you know?"

"What else could make a blaze that would light the whole sky? If they are breaking into the shops, they are most likely burning the synagogues as well."

"All of them?"

He shrugged and Liesel looked up at the livid sky, shreds of gray cloud skating across the orange. It looked surreal and unholy, and as she stood there in the stillness of the chilly evening, she realized she could not hear the clang of any fire engines.

"Come inside," Otto said and reached for her arm, but she shook him off as she hurried into the house.

Her mother was, as she so often was, closeted in her bedroom; Friedy was in the kitchen with their new housekeeper, Helga, a stolid-looking woman with a face like a boiled pudding.

"Liesel," Otto called plaintively as he shut and locked the door behind him, but she ignored him as she went upstairs. She meant only to go into her bedroom and close the door against her father and the world, but at the last minute she went to her parents' room instead, wrenching open the door with a sudden, satisfying viciousness, glad when it swung back to hit the wall with a crack.

Her mother was lying under a heap of rumpled bedclothes, her face to the window, her back to Liesel. She didn't so much as stir as Liesel came into the room, although she must have heard the sound of the door being practically wrenched off its hinges.

"Do you know what's happening out there?" Liesel demanded in a raw voice.

"They are burning the city." Ilse sounded lifeless.

"They are burning the synagogues," Liesel corrected. "And breaking the windows of all the Jewish shops. I saw a woman being whipped down the street by boys only a little older than Friedy."

Ilse drew a shuddering breath, her back still to Liesel. "What do you want me to do about it?"

Liesel stared at her in impotent fury, her heart thudding, her fists bunched. She wanted to fight, but she didn't know how. "I want you to *care*!" she exclaimed. "You don't like the Nazis, I know you don't. You won't go to their parties, and so now I have to."

"What?" Slowly, Ilse sat up in bed to stare at Liesel, her hair in dark tangles about her pale face, puffy from both sleep and drink. "What do you mean?"

"Father asked me to accompany him to Carinhall in a few weeks, for a shooting party. And, meanwhile, the city burns and Jews are treated worse than dogs, and no one else in this house even *cares*." She shook her head as she bit at her lips; she felt as if she could pull her hair out by the handfuls, or run screaming into the street, *something*, anything to alleviate this feeling of frenzied helplessness, to *act* rather than to simply think or to say. "How can you live with yourself, Mutti?" she demanded.

With a mirthless smile, Ilse gestured to herself—her stained nightgown, her tangled hair. "Do you call this living?"

"Then do something," Liesel begged. "Anything—"

"What?" she demanded. "You want me to run to Newman's piano store and ask them to stop smashing those precious instruments? They wouldn't stop, not for a second, and then they'd turn on me, on your father, and on you, Liesel—*you*! Not to mention

Friedy. *Friedy...*" She let out a choked sound that was close to a moan. "I can't, Liesel, I can't. For all your sakes, as much as my own, if not more. There's no point, anyway. It wouldn't help. It wouldn't change things. Nothing will."

Liesel opened her mouth to reply, not even knowing what she could say, because hadn't she thought the same thing? How could a single person stem a tide, a flood? They'd simply be pulled under, like everybody else. Then a hammering at the front door silenced her before she spoke. She and her mother exchanged a quick, panicked look before Liesel practically flew downstairs.

"Liesel, don't—" Ilse called, but she was already unbolting and then flinging open the door. She had no idea who would be standing there—a despairing shopkeeper, a smug stormtrooper? Göring himself? But it was none of these; it was her old housekeeper, Gerda, fired only that morning, with her arm around Rosa, whose blonde hair looked as if it had been hacked off with a pair of garden shears, in some parts so close that Liesel could see her blood-flecked scalp.

"Please," Gerda said quietly. There was a streak of blood on her cheek and a bruise forming on her temple. "Can you help?"

Liesel hesitated for a fraction of a second, and even that tiny pause shamed her. This was Gerda, *Rosa*, people she had accused her father of not helping. "Yes..." she began, only to hear her father draw a startled breath from behind her.

"Gerda..."

"Will you let them in?" Liesel demanded in a hard voice, and her father made a choking sound, whether of outrage or reluctance, Liesel couldn't tell.

"Yes, of course I will," he said, his voice tight with either anger or fear. Perhaps both. "Gerda, please. Come in."

The housekeeper hurried inside and Liesel closed the door, glancing at the empty street with sudden panic. What if someone had seen Gerda come there, seen her usher the housekeeper inside? Would she be reported? Would she be dragged out of the house, whipped down the street like that poor woman, for helping a Jew? She knew it was perfectly possible, and the thought terrified her utterly. She understood her father's reluctance; she even felt it. Quickly, she slid the bolt across.

"Gerda, dear God, what happened?" Otto asked as he shepherded her and Rosa back into the kitchen.

Helga looked up from the soup she was stirring, slack-jawed, eyes wide and bulging.

"Helga, you are dismissed for the evening," Otto told her tersely. "We shall see you in the morning. Take care in the streets. It is a troubled night."

"Gerda!" Friedrich exclaimed, looking delighted for the span of a second, before he took in their injuries. "What has happened?"

"Friedy, go upstairs."

"But—"

"Upstairs," Otto snapped. "Now."

Helga hurried to gather her belongings, casting Gerda and Rosa a darkly suspicious look that made Liesel's mouth dry; Friedrich simply looked sulky as he sloped upstairs.

When they'd gone, Otto turned to Gerda. "What happened?" he asked quietly. Their former housekeeper swayed where she stood; she looked as if she might collapse right then and there. "Sit down, please," he said, and pulled out a chair.

Gerda guided Rosa into it, and then sank into the one adjacent.

"We need warm water and iodine," Liesel said, and then, realizing there was no one else to do it, she went to the sink to fill the kettle.

"I met Rosa at her school and we were walking home when the trouble started," Gerda told them quietly. "Some HJ boys followed us from school. When they'd caught up to us, they grabbed Rosa." She drew a shattered breath and Liesel focused on lighting the stove, needing to do something practical. To help, if only in this small way.

After a few seconds, Gerda resumed.

"They knocked us both around a bit and I thought—I prayed—that would be the end of it. Then one of them took out his HJ knife and said 'the Jew can't have Aryan hair.'" Bitterness spiked the words that she'd remembered. "They did their best to shave her head."

"I'm so sorry…" Otto said, looking stricken, as helpless as Liesel felt.

"Even then I hoped it would be the end of it, that they would just leave us alone. But some others had joined, a few SA, even some housewives! Everyone was laughing at us, *enjoying* it. It seemed to them like the… like the most marvelous game." Gerda let out a strangled sob before she pressed one trembling fist to her mouth. "I knew we had to get away before things got worse. They were like hounds that had scented blood. They wouldn't stop until it was spilled all over the street."

In the horrified silence that followed, the kettle began to whistle and Liesel poured the water into a basin. Her father looked haggard, his eyes hooded as Gerda put her arms around her daughter. No one spoke. Liesel brought the basin to the table and was about to dip a dishtowel into the warm water when her mother appeared in the doorway, her dressing gown belted around her waist.

"Let me," she said, a command, and she reached for the rag. Liesel gave it to her silently, stepping aside as her mother crouched in front of Rosa and gently began to dab at her wounds, each touch of the cloth seeming to Liesel like a seeking of forgiveness, an offering of atonement. Rosa closed her eyes.

"You managed to get away," Otto stated after a moment. Liesel couldn't tell anything from his tone.

Gerda drew another shuddering breath. "Yes, we ran. Some of the boys continued to chase us. I was so afraid of what they might do. And so we came here, because I knew… Herr Scholz, I knew you were a good man." Her voice wavered as she gave him a pleading look, and Liesel saw her father's mouth compress.

"I don't know about that," he said quietly.

"They will stay," Ilse stated in a hard voice as she wiped a streak of blood away from Rosa's cheek. The girl, her face pale, her eyes closed, had not said a word since she'd come into the house. There was no anger in her now, no sneering sense of superiority that Liesel had always resented. She looked defeated, small, younger than her twelve years.

"Yes," Otto agreed heavily. "They will stay. At least until it is safe."

The next hour felt surreal. Outside, the city burned and shattered, and here in the house on Koenigsallee, a grim, silent calm prevailed. Ilse finished seeing to Rosa and Gerda's injuries, and Liesel ladled out soup and sliced bread. She kept shooting glances at Rosa, wanting to say something, but she didn't know what. An apology, perhaps, for resenting her, yet such a childish sentiment surely served no purpose now, when Rosa's body and spirit were both so battered. In any case, Rosa barely looked at her; she seemed to exist in a haunted world of her own, her face blank, her eyes staring.

They all ate together in the kitchen rather than the dining room, something that Friedy asked about but no one answered. Afterward, Gerda and Rosa helped clean up the meal and then Gerda said with dignity, gathering her coat around her, "We won't trouble you any further, Herr Scholz."

Otto looked as if he wished to agree and send them both on their way into the dark night, the sky still livid, the city still being rent by destruction, but Ilse gave him a hard look.

"You'll stay until morning," she stated, a command rather than an invitation. "It will be safer by then. You can leave before Helga arrives."

Gerda glanced at Otto, who gave a short nod. "Thank you, Frau Scholz," she whispered.

"Liesel, show Rosa up to your bedroom," Ilse instructed. "She can borrow one of your nightgowns."

Rosa had not spoken during the meal, and she remained silent as Liesel took her upstairs. She gave the girl a sideways glance, wanting again to say something—*anything*—but having no idea what kind of words could bridge such a moment.

"I'm sorry for what happened to you," she finally said, and Rosa glanced at her, her gaze focusing on her with a ghostly hint of her old sharpness, like armor she was desperately trying to assemble.

"Are you?" She sounded weary, even lifeless, and Liesel struggled not to cringe in shame.

"Yes, I am. I know we haven't… we haven't been friends, but I would never wish something like this on anyone, ever." Suddenly her eyes were filled with tears, to her own horror. What did *she* have to cry about, compared to Rosa? "Is that so very… magnanimous… of me? I don't mean it like that. I just don't know what to do. The whole world is on fire, and I—I don't even have a bucket."

Rosa took a step closer to her, her eyes glittering with a sudden, desperate ferocity. "*My* world is on fire," she stated. "*My* world has burned to the ground. You are just watching."

"We took you in tonight," Liesel said helplessly, blinking back the tears that felt shameful.

"*That* is magnanimous of you," Rosa stated flatly. "Thank you for the nightgown."

She turned away, and in silence Liesel led her to the guestroom she would share with Gerda. She felt angry, as well as ashamed, offended by Rosa's lack of gratitude even as she recognized it for what it surely was—barely disguised fear, a terrified helplessness at the burning world around them. How could she blame her for such a response?

Once Rosa and Gerda were settled in their room, Liesel paused in the hallway, straining to listen to the low voices of her parents downstairs.

"If this gets out, Ilse…"

"She was your *housekeeper*, Otto. Surely even the most devoted Nazi will understand you wanting to help a former employee."

"Some will, some won't, and the trouble is, I have no idea which is which," her father returned sharply. "You don't realize the risk—"

"Oh, but I do," Ilse said softly, her voice like steel. "I always have, just as you have. Why do you think I haven't done anything before now?"

CHAPTER NINE

Frankfurt, November 1945

Sam sat at the head of the long table in the elegant dining room of his new home and gazed rather bemusedly at the heavy, dark oil portraits hanging on the walls. He wondered who they were of—frowning ancestors or famous Germans? Or perhaps just random strangers whose portraits the former occupant of this house—a devoted Nazi who had been a minor executive at IG Farben—had picked up at a charity shop? He didn't particularly like the look of them, anyway.

"Your dinner, Captain Houghton." Annika, the white-haired hausfrau who was now his cook and housekeeper, scuttled into the room with a tray, her every movement an apology.

"Thank you, Frau Weber."

She bobbed a hurried, abject curtsey and Sam suppressed a sigh. He did not enjoy this pathetic kowtowing, yet he recognized he could not keep his staff, along with so many other Germans, from performing it. Since moving into the villa in Bergen-Enkheim over a week ago, he'd suffered it as pleasantly as possible, even though it always made him feel like gritting his teeth.

The villa itself was lovely, lovelier even than the home he'd grown up in back on the Main Line. Made of white stucco with gardens rolling down to the Main River, the Riedteich just visible in the distance, it had a drawing room, dining room, study, library, and five bedrooms above, in addition to the kitchen and servants' quarters. It felt like an absurd and even offensive amount of space for one man, particularly when many Germans were squeezed into shabby, dilapidated apartment buildings, often several families sharing a single dwelling, like Anna Vogel was.

Sam had suggested to Major Pitt that he didn't need such extensive quarters, and his superior had looked at him with a mixture of disbelief and scorn.

"Enjoy it, Captain, and stop trying to be such a martyr."

Sam had remained silent, knowing there was no point discussing the matter any further. He had been in Frankfurt now for two weeks and he was realizing more and more that he was an outlier in the CIC, with his disinclination to fraternize with Germans, especially the women, and yet at the same time his desire to treat them all as fundamentally decent human beings, at least until proved otherwise.

In his two weeks of working through the boxes of *fragebogen*, he hadn't done much proving, something Pitt had noted sourly.

"We're here to *find* the Nazis, Houghton, not pat them all on the head."

Pitt had, at least, been pleased by Sam's discovery of Herr Huber's treasure trove of index cards, although after his initial exultation, Sam had not heard anything further, and he had been relegated back to sorting through the questionnaires as if the record of NSDAP membership didn't exist—or his brief to investigate chemists, for that matter. The sheer waste of it all annoyed him; surely it would make more sense to cross-reference the questionnaires with the membership records, but when he'd suggested such a thing, Pitt had given him a forbidding look and told him "it's all under control."

The result of the whole endeavor was, unfortunately, that Sam was still buried under paperwork with no sign of his orders changing, and, in addition, he'd incurred the surly dislike of Sergeant Belmont, who no longer invited him out for drinks.

Sam would have given such outings a miss anyway, but he didn't appreciate being the object of someone's enmity, especially someone like Belmont, who he suspected could be quite nasty when he chose to.

Now he glanced down at his dinner—steak and potatoes, courtesy of the US Army—and tried to summon an appetite. He usually left at least a third of his food on his plate, because he knew Frau Weber would scrape it carefully into a bag to take home to her family.

His housekeeper, along with his driver and gardener, had been waiting at the house when he'd arrived, all of them looking both eager and terrified. The driver, a man named Krause, had explained in halting English that they had been employed by the previous resident, and had been instructed to stay on for whomever from the US Army took his place. Sam had decided not to question the veracity of this version of events; he could afford to pay them, and he knew they needed jobs. Everyone in CIC had German staff, from housekeepers to cooks to chauffeurs. One major even had a butler.

Sighing wearily, Sam took a few bites of steak before pushing it away and lighting a cigarette. All around him, the house echoed with an eerie sort of silence, like a pulse, or the ticking of a bomb. As beautiful as it was, Sam disliked the grand rooms, the dark furniture, the muddy oil paintings with their faces scowling down at him, haughty and stern. All of it felt suffocating.

After a few moments, Frau Weber crept in, looking timid, and Sam waved to his plate.

"I'm finished, Frau Weber. *Ich habe fertig.*"

A fleeting smile, no more than a twitch, passed her lips before she ducked her head and took the tray. Sam realized he must have misspoken—his German, despite his earlier knowledge and steady tuition since he'd been here, was really quite mediocre.

He rose from the table and wandered toward the drawing room, with its horsehair sofas and velvet curtains framing French windows that led out to a terrace and the gardens, now cloaked in frost and darkness.

He stood at the windows, gazing out at the chilly night as he smoked. His thoughts drifted, as he found they often did, to his enigmatic secretary. Anna Vogel had been working for him for over a week and yet he wasn't sure he knew her any better than he had at that first interview, although he still suspected she was lying about something.

Last Monday morning she had shown up in the same dark dress she'd worn before; she'd replaced the men's brogues with a pair of well-worn but serviceable heels of black leather with a thin strap around the ankle.

"You managed to find some shoes," he'd said in far too jolly a voice, and she'd given him a narrowed look that made him feel ashamed. He wondered what she'd had to sell to procure them, or had she stolen them? He didn't know and he didn't ask.

Anna had gotten to work right away, transcribing the answers written on the questionnaires one form at a time in small, neat handwriting; Sam had not been able to locate a typewriter for her yet, although he'd put in a request.

"Then you will finally know my typing speed," she'd said with a small smile when he'd told her, and he'd found himself grinning back. These brief glimpses of humor, of the woman she must once have been, before the war, intrigued him and had him longing for more.

Mostly, though, they worked in silence. As Sam had gone through the questionnaire answers himself, he'd experienced a welter of irritation, impatience, and wearied defeat—a tangle of feeling he was becoming familiar with. Some of the questions were utterly, insultingly absurd—*Did you ever play with toy sol-*

diers?—while others barely touched on the depth of involvement even an ordinary German might have had—*Did you ever hope for a German victory?* Who wouldn't have hoped, when the bombing raids and firestorms went on and on? And yet what German, trying desperately to be cleared for work, would answer truthfully?

Anna's face, as smooth and clear as a block of ivory, and just as uninformative, so often gave nothing away. Sam suspected she must have had a great deal of practice in controlling and hiding her emotions, to transcribe answer after answer without so much as a flicker.

He'd tried, gently at first, to cause some sort of reaction, akin to tossing a stone into a millpond to see the ripples, but hardly any ever came.

On the first day, he'd explained the process of denazification to her, going through the five levels of classification.

"I am working to determine what level of involvement these individuals had. The lowest is *Entlastete*—the exonerated. I don't know how many of those we'll find." He'd already found too many, according to Pitt, but he felt an urge to see Anna's reaction to his remarks. There was nothing.

"Then there is *Mitlaufer*, or fellow travelers. People who supported National Socialism, but not actively." Those individuals would most likely get a fine, or a potential temporary restriction on employment. "But it's the next two levels I'm really interested in—the *Minderbelastete*, or less incriminated, and the *Belastete*, who are the activists, militants, and profiteers." Sam had paused, watching her face, but Anna had simply gazed back at him, unmoved, almost serene.

"You said five levels," she had said after a moment when the silence had seemed to hum between them. "You only spoke four."

"Spoke of," Sam had corrected, and she had blushed. He had corrected her because it was official policy, but he actually liked her hesitations and malapropisms, the little things that made her more approachable. The calm he found so fascinating also intimidated him. "And yes, there is one more. *Hauptschuldige*—major offenders. Many of those are already found, or else they're dead."

Many high-ranking Nazis had killed themselves in the last days of the war—Hitler, of course, as well as Goebbels, Himmler, Bormann, Decker, and many others. Robert Ley, the head of the German Labor Front, had hung himself in prison at Nuremberg only last week. The trials were set to start shortly.

"I see," Anna had said quietly, and looked down at the questionnaire she was in the middle of transcribing. Her expression had remained composed, but Sam had sensed something powerful from her that he couldn't quite discern. Sorrow? Grief? No, those were too simplistic. Whatever she felt, it was tangled up with something else, as well, and made him think of the German concept of *Weltschmerz*, a weary, complicated melancholy feeling at the state of the world, or so he'd read in his book of German philosophy.

"You must have known some of the *Belastete*," he'd remarked, "back in Essen."

She had looked up, a sudden, fierce light blazing in her eyes for no more than a second, before her expression cleared, turning determined. "We all did, Captain Houghton. It was impossible not to."

"What happened to them?"

She had shrugged. "They disappeared. Ran away when they knew it was the end. They were cowards, you see." Her lips had tightened and something flashed across her face again, a lightning streak of emotion that was gone before Sam was even sure he'd seen it.

"I'm sorry," he'd said quietly. "Do these questions distress you?"

"The war is over," Anna had replied, which was really no answer at all.

"That is an answer worthy of a *Gretchenfrage*," Sam had dared to tease, another term from the book he'd been reading.

To his surprise, Anna's face had lit up.

"You know *Faust*?" she had asked eagerly.

"No, actually, I don't." He had smiled at her, abashed. "I only read the term in a book." And he wasn't even sure he'd used it correctly.

"It is from *Faust*, when Gretchen asks him what he thinks of religion." The interest in her face had leached out, like light from an autumn afternoon, replaced by sorrow. "A difficult question for the man who sold his soul to the devil."

"I'm afraid I don't know much German literature," Sam had replied, an apology. "I was a chemistry teacher before all this."

"Chemistry," Anna had repeated slowly. "Will you be involved with the search for scientists?"

"You know about that?" Sam had asked, startled, although he realized he shouldn't be. CIC, for all its being about cloak-and-dagger work, seemed to have remarkably few secrets.

She had shrugged, although her gaze remained intent. "I heard about it from someone at a bar."

Sam had realized he didn't like to think of Anna as one of those *frauleins* at a bar, sitting on someone's lap, tucking carelessly offered cigarettes into her handbag to sell later. "I'm meant to be," he'd told her, "but right now I'm cooling my heels until I get further orders."

She had frowned quizzically. "Cooling your heels?"

"It's an expression," he had explained with a small smile. "Waiting pointlessly."

"Ah, I see. Thank you." She had glanced down at the pile of questionnaires on her desk. "Do you think this is pointless?"

"Sometimes I wonder," he'd admitted.

"People must answer for their crimes," she had stated, surprising him.

"Yes," he'd answered after a moment. "I suppose the question is how many."

"Enough," she had replied flatly, and they had both got back to work.

Now, as he stared out at the night-shrouded gardens, Sam realized he was thinking about Anna Vogel because he was lonely. He hadn't made any real friends in CIC, and it seemed impossible to form any kind of genuine relationship with a German. He missed his family, his teacher friends in Philadelphia, even Helen, the girlfriend he'd broken up with before the war. He missed having a *life*.

He wondered if he should head out to one of the bars that Sergeant Belmont frequented. Have a drink, find a girl, if just to talk to. His preoccupation with Anna Vogel was unhelpful and distracted him from his job. And yet, still he wondered. She fascinated him, with her quietness, her sudden blazing moments of emotion, the glimpses of humor that made him feel as if he could come to know her. He knew that was a dangerous, as well as a fruitless, notion. Anna Vogel did not give anything away lightly.

Yet he was still wondering the next morning, as, outside, rain steadily fell, streaking down the windows, and Anna came into the office twenty minutes later, breathless and bedraggled.

"I'm sorry… the trams… they did not run."

Sam nodded his understanding, for he knew the tram lines had been completely destroyed by the end of the war, first by the Allied bombing in 1944 of all the central depots, and then by the blowing up of the lines by the Wehrmacht in the very last panic-fueled days of the war. Only two lines were currently up and running, and doing so unreliably.

"Don't worry," he said. "Take your time."

"Thank you, Captain." She gave him a brief smile and he watched out of the corner of his eye as Anna took off her coat, a shabby man's overcoat that was far too big for her, and hung it up on the coat stand in the corner of the room. She was wearing a gray dress today; she only had two, and she alternated between them. She always wore the shoes with the ankle strap, the leather worn thin but polished.

He glanced back at the papers on his desk as she fixed her hair and then turned to her own desk, set up on the far side of the room, with a purposeful air. In just over two weeks, Sam had managed to go through two hundred questionnaires. Of those, he'd flagged up just twelve to be passed to Major Pitt. What his superior would do with them, Sam didn't know; would they be used in interviews or interrogations, or simply put away in a dusty filing cabinet somewhere? He had no idea, and the futility of his work made him want to ground his teeth in frustration. He suspected he was being treated like a toddler, given busy work to do so he could be kept out of the way, at least until they decided to use him for the purpose he'd come for. When he'd dared to ask Pitt about it again, his commanding officer had given him a fulminating look.

"Just do your job, Captain. Surely that shouldn't be too hard for a desk jockey like you."

Rain fell steadily all day, the view of the city obscured by a dense, dank fog. Somewhere in the distance, someone was drilling, another hammering; these attempts to repair the broken city seeming futile when so much was wrecked. Yet, Sam acknowledged as he pulled another questionnaire toward him, you had to start somewhere. One at a time, brick by brick, question by question, the city would be rebuilt, its society restored. Or so he hoped. He did not like to think of what the alternatives might be for Germany, or for its desperate citizens.

At noon, he rose to go to lunch; Anna always had a sandwich at her desk, something dire-looking, made of black bread and a thin layer of meat paste. Today, Sam hesitated, feeling sorry for her, as well as something more. Her hair was still damp from this morning's rain.

"Do you want to have lunch out?" he asked. "There's a little restaurant off Gruneberg Platz that's not too bad. It does schnitzel with noodles, and not much else." Even for the Americans and their money, German restaurants only had so much they could offer.

Anna eyed him for a second, as blank-faced as ever, and then she gave a brief nod. "Thank you. That is very kind."

Sam did his best to suppress the thrill of excitement her acceptance caused him, and they headed out into the rain.

"You said you were here to find the scientists," Anna said once they were seated at a small table in the back of the restaurant, waiting for their lunch. "When will that be?"

"I don't know. When Major Pitt decides to humor me, I suppose." At Anna's quizzical look, he explained, a bit reluctantly, "I didn't fight in the war. I stayed back in the States, doing paperwork. He holds it against me."

She cocked her head, her gaze sweeping slowly over him. "Was that your choice?"

"No, those were my orders, but, to be honest with you, I didn't mind. I wasn't desperate to get my hands on a gun." A familiar guilt soured his insides. Did his reluctance make him a coward? He still wasn't sure.

"And you do not know if you should be blamed for following orders," Anna stated, skewering him with her quiet perception.

Sam looked down at the table. "I guess not," he said after a moment.

To his surprise, Anna reached across and touched his hand, barely more than a brush, and yet it electrified him. "I do not know either," she said sadly.

They spent the rest of the afternoon working in a silence that felt, at least to Sam, companionable, and at five o'clock he rose from his desk, dreading another evening in the cavernous, mausoleum-like villa he would have to call home for who knew how long. It was still raining heavily, and before he'd even thought it through properly, Sam heard himself saying, "The trams most likely still aren't running, and it's as wet as the dickens out there. Let me drive you home."

Anna, in the process of putting on her coat, looked up, startled. First lunch, now this. Did it seem like too much to her? "Thank you, but I—"

"I have a driver," Sam explained. "It's no trouble." Even if Heimatsiedlung was in the opposite direction from Bergen-Enkheim. "Please," he added. "How else will you get home? It must be three or four miles. You'll be drenched."

Still she hesitated, staring at him with dark eyes and a pale face, before she finally nodded, the movement seeming somehow resigned. "Thank you, Captain Houghton."

In the quiet intimacy of the car, Sam began to regret his decision. Anna had scooted to the far side of the seat, her handbag clutched in her lap, her face turned toward the window, nothing about her inviting conversation or the sense of companionship he'd felt before.

Surprise had flickered across Krause's face when he'd seen the car's other occupant, but he hadn't said a word. He never did. They rode in silence through the darkened, rain-lashed streets; the weather had deterred the usual ragamuffins and street urchins who crowded by HQ, desperate for whatever cigarette butts or chocolate bars they could scrounge off the military personnel coming and going.

Sam struggled to think of something innocuous to say, but he came up with nothing. Why did Anna look so tense? They'd had a nice time at lunch, hadn't they? Her reaction made him feel guilty, and he didn't like it. Even so, he was conscious—too conscious—of her skirt spreading out on the seat, the rise and fall of her chest. When he shifted his position, his elbow brushed hers and she moved away. Every time she blinked, her dark lashes swept against her pale cheeks. Sam turned to look out his window, the rain streaking steadily down the pane, as the car bumped along the cratered road.

After fifteen endless minutes, Krause pulled the car up to a depressing block of apartments, four or five stories high, small-windowed, the façade cracked and peeling. Dingy courtyards and stretches of overgrown grass separated one block from the next and only added to the feel of neglect and despair. Sam saw shadowy figures loitering under the dripping eaves of various buildings, and as Anna opened her door, he opened his.

"I'll see you up."

Anna looked as if she were about to protest, but then she remained silent. Her shoulders rounded, slumping in resignation, or perhaps just in response to the sloughing rain. "Thank you, Captain," she murmured rather dutifully.

As they headed through the downpour, Sam took her arm; Anna tensed but did not resist. He felt as if he were doing everything wrong, and he didn't understand it. Surely he was just being kind? A gentleman? Why did she seem to resist so much, even as she said nothing?

She fumbled with the front door, its lock broken, and Sam followed her up a set of narrow, rickety stairs, their footsteps echoing through the empty hallway that smelled of old cooking oil and drains, until Anna reached a door at the end of a narrow corridor, turning around quickly to face him.

"This is where I live." She pressed back against the door, her eyes wide as she looked up at him, waiting, *willing* him to leave.

Sam stood there, feeling entirely disconcerted as he realized in that moment he had been acting in a rather ridiculously naïve manner; he had accompanied Anna into the building as a gentlemanly gesture, yet she clearly thought he was after something more, like so many other GIs, and just as clearly the prospect terrified her.

And yet wasn't he, at least a little? Not like Belmont, with his self-assured swagger, but *something*. With a jolt, Sam realized he hadn't actually been that naïve, after all. He'd been hoping, without actually articulating it to himself, that Anna might invite him in for a drink, a chat, maybe... maybe it would have led naturally to something more. Even now, with her looking so desperate and scared, he could picture an alternative scene—a glass of schnapps in her room, Anna turning to him with a cautious smile. He imagined himself stepping closer as her smile turned expectant, sleepy... He gave himself a hard mental shake as a terrible sense of shame scalded him. How could he be thinking like that, even for a moment? And it was clear in Anna's face that she knew he had.

"Goodnight, Miss Vogel," he said stiffly. "*Gute Nacht.*"

Shock blazed across Anna's face, along with relief, both undisguised, shaming him all the more.

"*Gute nacht,*" she whispered, and with stiff, quick steps, Sam turned around and walked back down the corridor. As he headed toward the stairs, he heard Anna open the door of her apartment, and then the unmistakable sound of a bolt being slid in place.

CHAPTER TEN

December 1938

The forest of Schorfheide was an endless, boggy stretch of tall, slender pines shrouded in fog, marching like soldiers to an unseen horizon. A sparse, hardened, icy crust of snow speckled the ground, possessing none of the pleasing, pillowy softness of a proper snowfall.

As the car moved slowly down the narrow track toward Carinhall, Göring's impressive hunting estate, Liesel pulled her fur coat more tightly around her and tried not to shiver in the near-arctic air. Next to her, her father looked all around him with alert interest, as if the gloomy forest was the most enthralling thing he'd ever seen. Although he hadn't said as much, Liesel suspected he was looking forward to rubbing elbows with high-ranking Nazis for a weekend of parties and shooting. She could not say the same.

It was three weeks since the night that had become known as *Kristallnacht* had been wrought upon the country—the Night of Broken Glass. Although there were no official reports of the devastation, and Hitler had made a speech just twenty-four hours later without mentioning it at all, Liesel had been able to see the terrible aftermath for herself—broken windows, wrecked shops, homes, hospitals, and synagogues, glass and rubble littering the streets, and, worst of all, Jews hurrying past with their heads down, trying to make themselves invisible. There had been whispers and rumors of arrests, beatings, even deaths. Liesel remembered seeing the woman whipped down the street, the pale-faced people herded into vans, and she believed every whisper, knew it as truth.

The evil, beating heart of the Nazi Party had been exposed in all its bloody, raw reality, and for that, at least, she could be glad. Now, surely, no one could hide behind excuses and explanations that it wasn't that bad, or it was just about the money, or soon it would stop. Now no one could pretend not to see, not to know exactly what was happening and how terrible it was.

And yet, somehow, her father still did. The next morning, with an apologetic but firm farewell, he'd sent Gerda and Rosa on their way before breakfast, while her mother, distant and blank-faced, drank coffee alone in the dining room, and Liesel watched on helplessly. Rosa gave her one burning glance as she'd left, and she'd seen something pleading and desperate in that gaze that had made her feel both ashamed and yearning.

I want to help, she had longed to say, and yet she didn't. The words, burning in her chest, had bottled in her throat. She wondered if she would ever see Rosa again.

Her father went whistling to work, while Liesel chose to stay home from school. She could not face her ranting teachers or indifferent peers after the previous night. Her mother did not so much as remark upon her decision; she had played the piano all morning—the slow, haunting strains of Mahler's Symphony No. 5 drifting through the house, while Liesel had paced her own room, longing to do something, anything. *Why* did she have to be so powerless? What could she do?

At lunchtime, she had finally gone outside herself, to walk down the Ku'damm and see the changed, broken world for herself. She had watched as Jewish shopkeepers swept up broken glass, their heads bowed; when she met a man's gaze, he looked away quickly.

As the days passed, she discovered that something had changed between her and her mother, who no longer stayed in her bedroom, but rather played the piano endlessly, with frantic determination, as if every stroke of her fingers on the keys counted for something, and perhaps it did.

There had emerged, since *Kristallnacht*, a silent solidarity between them that needed no words, even as her father came into the house with a determined spring in his step, kissed Ilse's cheek and tickled Friedy. Liesel did her best to avoid him, without seeing to do so, but she suspected her father noticed and chose not to say anything.

Something had changed in the city of Berlin, as well. The rabid glee Liesel had seen on the faces of so many on that terrible night had been replaced by a silent, cringing sort of shame, like partygoers who had indulged too much the night before and now had to face the new day, embarrassed, exhausted, and bloated by their regrettable excesses. It was as if everyone had decided, without saying a word, that the Nazis' relentless persecution of the Jews had perhaps gone on long enough, after all, and should be at least a little curtailed.

Liesel saw it in her BDM meetings, when several girls exchanged eye-rolls as Fraulein Abicht railed about "the Jewish problem"; she felt it in the streets, when people passing by shattered windows frowned in disapproval at the mess of broken glass, or shook their heads in dismay at yet another *"Achtung Juden"* sign that had been plastered to a window or hoarding.

And yet such displays weren't nearly enough; they didn't amount to anything, Liesel realized, not really. In fact, they were worse than nothing, for in the days after *Kristallnacht*, the Jewish community was fined a billion marks by Göring himself for the damage inflicted upon them, and Jewish pupils were officially excluded from non-Jewish schools. Curfews were imposed upon all Jews, and only yesterday they had been banned from most public places. No one had protested any of it. Despite the grimaces and the eye-rolls, no one had said a word.

Her father had even attempted to justify these actions, albeit in a half-hearted, shamefaced sort of way, but with a determination in his voice that Liesel had come to recognize. He would make her see his point of view, for he did not like even her silent disapproval.

"In some ways it is better, Lieseling," he had said, his hands held palms out in appeal, the ghost of a sympathetic smile crinkling his tired features. They were standing in the sitting room, waiting for Helga to announce dinner.

Ilse had not come down, and Friedy was in the kitchen, as he often was, trying to snatch whatever titbits he could before the meal. Her father had stood by the fireplace, pushing his hands into the pockets of his trousers as he rocked back on his heels. "At least now the Jews know where they stand. There is no more pretense. They can make preparations to leave the country, which will be far better for them."

Göring had said as much, in a speech he had made after the Anschluss—"*The Jew must understand one thing at once. He must get out!*"

"And where will they go?" Liesel had challenged. She wasn't so ignorant anymore; she knew that Jews were not allowed to take any money or possessions with them if they left Germany, and many countries, such as the United States, France, or England, were unwilling to accept a steady stream of beleaguered refugees.

She'd learned to read between the lines of the articles in the *Berliner Tageblatt*, the city's most liberal newspaper, kept in check yet still allowed circulation by the propaganda minister, Joseph Goebbels, in order to give the rest of the world the illusion that Germany had a free press.

"There are ways," her father had insisted. "I know, because I have seen it done."

"You mean your colleague Herr Stern."

"And others," he had replied evenly. "Yes. It can work, Liesel. The company did not kick them out into the street like beggars. They were given positions in America, transportation, houses. Some are doing even better there than they were here."

Liesel had hesitated, wishing she knew how much truth was in his words. Judging from the shadows she saw in his eyes, not every Jewish employee had received such an impressive promotion, and most fleeing now received nothing at all. "But it's still not right."

"I am not saying it is right or good or anything but reprehensible," he had returned, his voice rising. "But it *is*, Liesel, and we must live with it."

"And profit from it, as well," she had snapped. "As you do, quite handsomely."

For a second, her father's face had darkened with anger, and he yanked his hand out of his trouser pocket, half-raising it, almost as if he would slap her across the face, something he'd never done. Even to imagine it was laughable, absurd; she had kept his gaze without cringing, but it took effort.

"What I do," he had said in a low voice that throbbed with both pain and menace, "I do for the sake of this family. For the clothes on your back, and the food on your table, and the roof over your head. If you don't like it, you know how to leave." He had nodded meaningfully toward the front door, and Liesel had stared at him in shock. Was he actually *threatening* her?

"If I had a place to go to, then I would," she had retorted recklessly, even though she knew she didn't mean it. She could never leave her father, her family. *Friedy*. Her eyes had filled with tears and her father's fierce expression had collapsed.

"Oh, Liesel, Lieseling, why have we come to this?" he had entreated as he pulled her into a hug. She went stiffly, resting her cheek on the lapel of his jacket but not relaxing into his embrace. "I am sorry for speaking so," he had told her as he stroked her hair. "I know how difficult this is for you, and I hate it. If there was something I could do, I would." He had pulled back to gaze earnestly down into her face. "You know that, don't you? I helped Gerda and her daughter, after all. If I can do something to help, I do it, I promise. Liesel?" He had searched her face, looking for approbation, and, reluctantly, Liesel gave it.

"I know, Vati." How could she blame her father, when really, she was no better?

Here she was, after all, driving in her father's fine motorcar to a weekend party hosted by Göring himself. And while she wasn't looking forward to any part of it, she was still going.

Her father drummed his fingers against the leather armrest as the car emerged from the dense forest, a set of massive stone pillars looming in front of them like, Liesel thought, the gates to hell.

"Almost there," he said with an attempt at joviality. They had barely spoken since leaving Berlin over an hour ago.

Liesel drew a steadying breath, her heart starting to hammer as her nerveless fingers clutched at her coat and the car turned between the pillars, toward Carinhall.

She had heard much about the grand place since her father had accepted the Generalfeldmarschall's invitation. She knew it boasted a cage for Göring's tamed lions, and a hunting hall, and a large library. It had a swimming pool and a ballroom and a model train set that the former King of England had been photographed playing with, and, since the birth of Göring's daughter, Edda, in June, a miniature castle for his baby daughter to play in once she was able to toddle to it.

Her father had told her all this as if it would impress her and make her excited to attend the weekend party. None of it did, and neither did the expensive and very grownup dresses he'd ordered for her when he'd taken her on a shopping trip to the luxurious second floor of Berlin's biggest and most elegant department store, KaDeWe, taken over by the Nazis from the Jewish owner

Hermann Tietz five years ago. "What a beautiful young lady you look, Liesel," Otto had exclaimed, and Liesel had stared at her reflection—her strained face, the satin dress—and said nothing.

She did not know exactly what her father expected of her on this weekend. He had not given her any particulars, only insisted that she enjoy herself. Her mother, however, had given her far sager advice.

"You must be careful, Liesel," she'd said the night before, when she'd come to her room, right before Liesel had been going to bed. She had glanced at the open valise laid on the chaise by the window, filled with all of her lovely new clothes. "You must be very, very careful."

Liesel had studied her mother for a moment, noting the way she held one hand to her throat as she swallowed convulsively. She'd lost weight in the weeks since *Kristallnacht*, the bones of her hips and the wings of her shoulder blades jutting out from beneath the dark silk of her dressing gown. Liesel had begun to understand the struggle her mother faced every day, minute by minute. She wasn't indifferent, but rather helpless and despairing, just as Liesel herself was. Still, she resented her mother for abdicating her responsibility in accompanying her father to Carinhall.

She had given her mother a level look as she placed several folded handkerchiefs into the valise. "What do you mean, Mother?"

"I mean you are going right into the hornet's nest, Liesel. The lion's den." Ilse had smiled mirthlessly. "You know Göring keeps lions?"

"Father told me. I think he believed I would be impressed."

Ilse had sighed and sank onto the edge of the bed. "There will be very important men at this party, Liesel. You cannot lose your temper with them, or ask them inopportune questions. For heaven's sake, do not talk about the Jews." Liesel did not reply and her mother had sighed. "I'm sorry you're going, but it's better that it's you and not me. There is Friedy to consider, and I know I couldn't carry it off."

"I'm not sure I can." When Liesel thought of mingling with men like Göring and his colleagues and cronies, her stomach cramped so hard she winced.

"You must." Ilse's voice had come out both resigned and hard.

"I could refuse to go," Liesel had said, half-heartedly, because she knew she wouldn't. Yet *why* she wouldn't was not entirely clear to her—for her father's sake? For her own? *The clothes on your back and the food on your table…* yes, she cared about those, more than she liked to admit. She was afraid of taking a stand, afraid of what dark avenues it might lead her down, the dead-ends she would be forced to face. *To think is easy. To act is hard.*

"You could," her mother had agreed after a moment. "But would it be worth it? If you're going to make a stand, Liesel, as I told you before, make it count."

Liesel had gazed unseeingly out the window at the dark night. "I don't want to be complicit."

"You already are," Ilse had stated flatly. "We all are. There is nothing we can do about that."

"Look," Otto said, startling her out of her thoughts as the car emerged from the dense forest onto the sweeping expanse in front of the hunting lodge. "Isn't it magnificent?"

Carinhall was indeed magnificent—designed by the same architect as the Olympic Stadium, it was a grand edifice of white stucco with a wooden roof, and several large terraces overlooking the placid, icy waters of the Grossöllner See.

The car pulled up to the imposing front doors, and Liesel glanced at her father, who was smiling benignly while she fought an overwhelming terror. The usual niceties, and even speech itself, felt beyond her right now. She didn't think she could do this, after all. A whole weekend of exchanging pleasantries and rubbing elbows with a bunch of Nazis… Göring himself… Her legs were watery, her stomach hollowed out, her heart thudding.

"It'll be all right, Liesel. It's just a party, remember, that's all." Otto gave her a sideways, sympathetic glance as he reached over and squeezed her hand. "Trust me."

But that, Liesel thought numbly as she climbed out of the car, was the one thing she feared to do, even as she longed, with every fiber of her being, to be able to.

Several hours later, having been shown to her room, rested, washed and then dressed, Liesel was heading down the hunting lodge's main staircase to one of its impossibly grand reception rooms for drinks before dinner.

Although so far she had only murmured greetings to a handful of well-to-do guests, standing by her father's side, she quickly realized how ill-suited she was to such a gathering as this. Almost everyone was at least ten, if not twenty, years older than her, sophisticated and cynical, with a hard, glamorous edge that hinted at brutality—whether it was one of the smartly dressed Wehrmacht officers or the elegantly-clad woman wearing Schiaparelli or Chanel—designs she recognized from her mother's fashion magazines, despite the Führer's insistence on all women wearing only German designers. Those rules, along with so many others, clearly did not apply here, where Göring's decadent and extravagant excesses were on full display.

At nearly seventeen, Liesel knew she was half-child, half-woman, even in the elegant cocktail dress of dark green crepe de chine her father had bought her, with a silk rosette festooned to one shoulder. She could hardly be relegated to the nursery with Göring's baby daughter Edda, but neither did she belong among this crowd, and it only took a few moments circulating in one of the lodge's grand rooms, sipping champagne that tasted sour in her mouth, for her—and everyone else—to know it.

Her father had done his best to introduce her, proudly and lovingly, but Liesel hated being treated like some sort of pet accessory, a child to be patronized amidst all the elegant, worldly-wise adults.

"Oh how sweet," one woman, the wife of a Nazi officer who worked under Himmler, drawled with narrowed eyes. "But where is Ilse?"

Her father had his excuse ready; Friedrich had been poorly with a winter cold, and Ilse had wanted to stay to nurse him, as any good German woman of the Reich would. He did not say the last, but it was clearly implied. Looking around at all the lavishly dressed and made-up women, Liesel did not see many women modelled on the Reich's standards—modest, self-effacing women who focused only on *kinder, küche, and kirche*: children, kitchen, and church. She saw hard-eyed socialites who looked every bit as ambitious and ruthless as their male counterparts, and absolutely every one of them scared her. How on earth was she going to endure the evening, never mind the whole weekend?

After an interminable cocktail hour, she was relieved to go into dinner, a massive undertaking in the lodge's huge dining room, with five courses of different, bloody meats, some of which had been hunted and killed by Göring himself.

Liesel had been seated at one end of a long table, away from all the important people; her father, she saw with a plunging sensation, was only three seats down from Göring himself, and next to Heinrich Himmler, who looked disconcertingly incongruous in his black SS dress uniform, with his myopic blinking stare behind small, round glasses and his pale, pudgy face.

Her father had once joked that Himmler knew how to manage poultry better than people; he had run a chicken farm before he'd joined the Nazis and eventually been appointed to head the police. Liesel knew from the vicious quotes she read in the papers that Himmler was obsessed with purity of race. He had been quoted as saying about the Jews, "the more that die, the better." And now her father was chatting with him.

Liesel's stomach cramped at the sight. When had her father become so important, to be seated next to the highest-ranking officers in the room, some of the most dangerous men in the world, the men he'd once gently and sardonically mocked?

"Good evening, *fraulein*." A laughing voice on her left had her tensing instinctively.

Liesel turned to see a young man in the navy blue of the Luftwaffe dress uniform smiling at her, all sunny ease and cheerful bonhomie.

"Good evening," she managed back, although nerves were still swarming in her middle and she kept shooting glances toward her father, tensing all the more when she saw him throw his head back and laugh at something Himmler—*Himmler!*—had said. Her father had said he was a brainless brute only used to wringing necks. *What had happened?*

"May I have the pleasure of an introduction?" the man on her left asked, fair eyebrows raised, and Liesel flushed.

"My name is Liesel Scholz."

"Ah, you are Otto Scholz's daughter," her companion said knowingly. "Göring's wunderkind."

Liesel stared at him in surprise.

"He was given a prize of a hundred thousand marks for his part in making Buna rubber," he explained with a laugh. "Hitler awarded it himself. Didn't you know?"

For a second, Liesel's mind spun. That was a huge amount of money, but her father had never mentioned any such prize, at least not that she could recall, and yet... the move to Berlin. The big house.

She glanced away from the Luftwaffe officer, desperate to organize her scattered thoughts.

"Oh, that," she finally managed to say in what she hoped was a light tone. "That was years ago now."

"Yes, I suppose it was. But the Generalfeldmarschall still speaks highly of him, I know, and his team." The man gave a little shrug of acknowledgment of his insider information. "I only know because my uncle is a chemist with IG Farben, as well. He's quite envious. Your father seems to be the man of the hour. Something about mass production, I think. Isn't he in charge of a factory?"

Liesel managed a rather sick sort of a smile. "Yes, he runs the factory in Schkopau." The careless words of her companion had hammered home one unfortunate and undeniable truth—her father was, and always would be, utterly indebted to Göring, to the Nazis, to Hitler himself. She'd continued to turn a blind eye to it all, to hope desperately that her father was only going along with it because he had to, but the truth was that he'd courted this. He'd wanted it. He'd told her himself, after all, that he was ambitious. She just hadn't realized what it had meant. Her father, Liesel knew now without a doubt, was in far, far deeper than she'd ever realized or feared, and it seemed it was exactly where he wanted to be.

CHAPTER ELEVEN

"My name is Friedrich, by the way," the Luftwaffe officer said, interrupting Liesel's spinning thoughts. "But everyone calls me Fritz. Oberleutnant Fritz Burkhardt."

"You're a pilot." She tried to smile as she stated the obvious. Fritz Burkhardt was a handsome man who looked to be in his early twenties. He had an easy manner and a ready smile, as well as the blue eyes and blond hair that were considered so enviable, and even necessary, these days, despite the fact that some of the highest-ranking Nazis possessed neither.

"Yes, it runs in the family. Father, brother, another uncle. I was destined, or perhaps doomed." He smiled to indicate the joke; nothing in his clear, laughing gaze suggested he disliked being in the Luftwaffe.

"So your uncle the chemist broke the tradition?" Liesel joked back, a bit weakly.

"Sadly, yes, but he's doing important work, at least, as your father is." His smiled widened into a grin. "May I serve you some boar?"

Liesel glanced at the slivers of barely cooked meat running red with bloody juices and had absolutely no appetite at all. "Yes, thank you," she replied, for she could hardly refuse to eat.

Despite Fritz's easy manner, the evening looked to be interminable. Already her head throbbed and her cheeks ached from the effort of smiling. She did not want to look at her father, but she did anyway; he was leaning toward Himmler, to listen to what he said, a smile on his lips, his forehead creased. What could the head of the SS possibly have to say to her father? She didn't want to think of what it could be.

"Do you do much flying?" she asked Fritz, after he had served them both some of the boar. There were a dozen other dishes on the table near them—several other roasted meats, trembling jellies and vegetables swimming in heavy cream sauces. Liesel wasn't sure she could manage a mouthful of any of it.

"As much as I can. I'm testing planes now, rather than seeing any action. The more experienced pilots are going to Spain, of course."

"Yes." Liesel had read about the German involvement in the Spanish Civil War, although it was so outside of her everyday life that she didn't think about it very much, although, with a guilty pang, she wondered if she should. Yet one more thing to worry and feel helpless about. "Which sorts of planes are you testing?"

"I was up in a Messerschmitt Bf 109 the other day."

"My little brother has a toy one of those," Liesel told him. "His name is Friedrich too, but we call him Friedy." For a second, she pictured Friedy's slight form, his dark eyes, his knowing look, his dreaminess slowly but surely being replaced by an arrogance that had begun hardening his boyish features into a more malevolent cast. He was due to join the *Jungvolk* next year. What would happen then? What sort of boy—and then man—would he become, in this brave new world?

"It's a good flyer. I'd love to try one of the Junkers, though, for dive bombing. Do you know of Ernst Udet?"

Liesel nodded; she, like everyone else, knew of the handsome fighter pilot turned movie star, now in command of the Ministry of Aviation's development sector.

She and Fritz continued to chat about planes and flying, and somehow, through it all, Liesel managed to relax, at least a little. Fritz was easy company, and it was far more pleasant to listen to him enthuse about various planes without thinking about what those planes might be used for one day.

"Do you think there will be a war?" Liesel asked when they'd been served their fifth and final course. The question had continued to rise like a bubble in her consciousness all through the extravagant meal, despite her desire to push it down, and now it popped.

Fritz looked at her in surprise. "Of course there will be a war."

His easy assurance shocked her, even though she realized it shouldn't. Her father had been certain two years ago, when he'd pointed out the gliders and buses at the Olympics. Göring himself had told her as much, when he'd talked about what the synthetic rubber would be used for. And if that wasn't enough, every day fighter planes flew over the city and endless rows of soldiers marched through the streets. What was it all for, if not a war?

"It seems so strange," she said after a moment. "It has only been twenty years since the last one ended."

"I doubt you remember it," he replied with a smile, and Liesel returned a bit sharply, "And I doubt you do, either. You can't have been more than four or five at the time."

"Actually, I was three." He looked amused, and not at all offended by her sharp tone. "But surely you can see a war is inevitable, if the rest of Europe won't allow Germany to regain her borders? We were treated shamefully at the end of the last war. It's only right that we are able to take back what was stolen from us."

Fritz spoke with such conviction that Liesel could feel herself being swayed despite an innate sense of caution. She knew she *wanted* to be swayed, for what did she really know of such things? If the papers were to be believed, the invasion of Austria and the Sudetenland had been greeted with rejoicing and flowers rather than tears or recrimination. "My father spoke so despairingly of the war," she said slowly. "And all its terrible hardships."

"It will be different this time," Fritz pronounced with ringing confidence. "We are far more prepared and far better equipped. And, of course, we have the right on our side."

The right? Did they? Liesel was ashamed to realize how little she knew. Even reading the *Tageblatt*, she did not understand the complexities of Germany's demands for territory or *lebensraum* for its people. And what about the Jews? Where did they fit into all of this? She remembered her mother's warning and she knew she would not ask Fritz about that.

"Come, meet some of my friends," Fritz urged as they finished their dessert. "Enough of this talk of politics. I would much rather dance, wouldn't you?"

Liesel let herself be led away from the supper table to another grand reception room; Fritz had half a dozen friends, young Luftwaffe officers like himself, all with well-connected relatives that allowed them to snag the coveted invitation to Göring's country retreat.

The crowd's hard-edged ambition that Liesel had felt earlier had relaxed into something that seemed as if it could be even more dangerous—a reckless, drunken determination to enjoy oneself. Couples lounged on chaises and sofas, limbs languorously entwined, or danced sinuously, their bodies so close together Liesel could not tell one from the other. All of it was a far cry from Hitler's shrill demand for Aryan purity and female modesty, but then Hitler wasn't present, and Göring was known for his many excesses.

As she danced far more sedately with Fritz and then one of his friends, Liesel looked around for her father, but could not see him anywhere. She wondered where he was, and who he was with. Another woman? No, even now she believed her father still loved and adored her mother. No, she feared he was closeted with some high-ranking officials, Himmler, or perhaps even Göring himself. Plotting—yet about what? Ensnaring himself even more in this sticky, sinister web. And where did that leave her? Her mother? Friedy?

"Come outside," Fritz urged her after their last dance. "It's too hot in here."

Her mind spinning from the two glasses of champagne she'd drunk, as well as all the overwhelming events of the evening, Liesel followed Fritz out onto a terrace overlooking the Grossöll-ner See, now swathed in darkness. The air was sharp with cold and the scent of the pines that flanked the villa like silent sentinels. Although she could hear laughter and music from inside, the night felt still, a sense of tranquility hovering out of reach.

"Will you hunt tomorrow?" Fritz asked as they stood by the balustrade overlooking the lake.

Liesel shook her head rather firmly. "No. I don't shoot."

"It's just as well. Women shouldn't, really, and Hitler doesn't like it, anyway. You know he's a vegetarian?"

"I had heard as much, yes." Liesel marveled at how casually Fritz spoke about people who loomed larger than life in her mind—and in her nightmares.

"He's really rather squeamish, which is a bit ridiculous, considering." He withdrew a packet of cigarettes from his breast pocket and offered one to Liesel. Although she'd never smoked before, Liesel took one now. She felt the need for something to occupy her hands, her mind.

Smiling a little, as if he guessed her inexperience, Fritz stepped closer to strike the match to light her cigarette. Liesel breathed in the scent of his aftershave—not the familiar bitter lime of her father's cologne, but something dark and musky and not unpleasant.

As she inhaled, the cigarette lit and her lungs filled with smoke, sending her into a fit of coughing. Tears streamed from her eyes as she did her best to bring herself under control, while Fritz regarded her with sympathetic amusement.

"You don't smoke?"

"Not usually." Somehow, with a herculean effort, she managed to stop gasping and wheezing. Her chest ached and her eyes stung.

"Poor little Liesel." His voice was caressing. "Am I corrupting you?"

Alarm and something else—something warm and treacherous and molten—stole through at the sleepy look in his eyes that even an innocent such as herself could decipher.

"I'm not so easily corrupted," she replied unsteadily, and Fritz smiled.

"We'll see."

His head dipped, and for a thrilling, terrifying second, Liesel thought he might kiss her. She'd never been kissed before, and part of her knew she would not mind being kissed by Ober-leutnant Fritz Burkhardt. Part of her would welcome it… to feel something other than fear, to think pleasant things could still happen, girls could fall in love, men could flirt. Life could go on as it always had, as it always would, promising simple pleasures to those who contented themselves with such things.

But then a sound from the other end of the terrace had Fritz stepping smartly away, and in horror Liesel blinked the shadowy figures of her father and Generalfeldmarschall Göring into focus. Her father gave Burkhardt a swift, narrowed glance, but Göring was smiling with seeming benevolence. His face was even more florid than usual, his fat fingers heavily beringed—in the pale glare of moonlight, Liesel saw stones of red, yellow, green, blue.

"Well, well, stealing a kiss under the moonlight, Fritzy?" Göring gave an indulgent chuckle, while Fritz smiled in rueful acknowledgment.

Liesel stood frozen, hardly able to believe her companion for the evening was on such close terms with Göring himself, despite his earlier careless words. And what of her father? He and Göring had been talking privately out on the terrace. *About what?* She felt as if the pieces of her world were tilting and sliding, reframing a picture she did not want to take in. It had been there all along, and yet now she saw it with piercing and unwanted clarity.

"Ah, little Liesel," Göring said, turning his attention to her. His gaze swept over with a strange mixture of paternalism and lasciviousness. "Are you enjoying yourself, my dear?"

Liesel couldn't keep from glancing at her father and noting the warning in his smile. "Yes, Herr Reich Minister—Generalfeldmarschall," she replied, stumbling over his recently acquired title.

Göring let out a booming laugh, seeming to enjoy her blushes. "As you should!" He reached out one plump hand to chuck her under the chin as if she were a child.

Her father gave her another quick smile as he patted her shoulder. "Good girl," he said quietly, and the compliment, given at such a moment, made Liesel want to cry.

The two men moved back inside and she let out an unsteady breath as she flung her half-smoked cigarette into the lake.

"I didn't realize you were so well acquainted with the Generalfeldmarschall," she remarked when she trusted her tone to sound level, even light.

"He's my godfather," Fritz replied with a shrug. "My father flew with him in the *Jagdgeschwader*." At Liesel's blank look, he explained, a little loftily, "The Flying Circus in the war—part of the original Flying Corps."

"Oh, I see."

"We're not that close. Father only sees the Generalfeldmarschall once in a long while. But he likes to take an interest in all the young officers." He smiled and stepped closer, but the wary pleasure that had been stealing through Liesel's veins had turned frigid.

"It's freezing out here," she said with a half-mock shiver. "Let's go back inside."

Fritz merely smiled, a slow curling of his lips as his gaze moved thoughtfully over her. "As you wish," he said, and took her by the arm to lead her back into the party.

As they stepped through the doors, a bright flash blinded Liesel so she stumbled back and Fritz put his arm around her waist.

As Liesel blinked the world back into dazed focus, Heinrich Hoffmann, Hitler's personal photographer, gave them a bland smile. "A photograph for the Reich," he said, hefting his Leica, and then moved on.

CHAPTER TWELVE

Frankfurt, December 1945

The war crimes trials in Nuremberg had been going on for three weeks and Sam was still buried under endless questionnaires. The only sign that he was actually doing something productive was Major Pitt's occasional terse word of grudging approval when he flagged a form up, and it led—or at least Sam believed it did—to an interrogation or arrest. So far, amidst the thousands and thousands of arrests the US Army had made, Sam had been involved in a mere twenty-eight.

He had managed to procure a radio to bring into his office, and he listened to reports on the trials as he worked through the questionnaires, his heart stirring as he heard prosecutor Robert H. Jackson's opening statement, his voice ringing with conviction.

"The wrongs which we seek to condemn and punish have been so calculated, so malignant, and so devastating, that civilization cannot tolerate their being ignored, because it cannot survive their being repeated. That four great nations, flushed with victory and stung with injury, stay the hand of vengeance and voluntarily submit their captive enemies to the judgment of the law is one of the most significant tributes that Power has ever paid to Reason."

He didn't know how much Anna was able to understand of the proceedings, so far conducted in English, and as she worked at her desk, her face remained as passive and placid as a milk pudding, her head bent over the forms she was transcribing. They had not spoken of the evening when he'd driven her home, now nearly a month ago; Sam had tried, haltingly and awkwardly, to apologize the next morning, although for what he could not exactly articulate, and Anna had brushed his words aside with a briskness that had silenced Sam completely.

"There is nothing to apologize for," she'd said, turning back to her work, and Sam had not been able to think of a reply.

There had been one moment during the radio broadcasts when her almost calm composure had cracked just a little, in late November, when the prosecutor had shown a film of the concentration and prison camps footage taken by Allied forces back in the spring. They had listened to the narration in silence; Sam had stilled, his hands flat on his desk, as the matter-of-fact monotone of the narrator spoke of prisoners being shot by the SS as they ran toward their liberators; of dazed and starving men being herded into wooden buildings that were then doused with gasoline and set alight; of women forced into slave labor, beset by illness, starvation, and abuse, forced to work until they, quite literally, dropped. At the mention of slave labor, Anna's hand had slipped, and several questionnaires had fluttered to the ground. She had murmured her apology, her head bent and her face lowered, as she stooped to retrieve the papers.

In early December, everyone at CIC in Frankfurt was shown the film, and Sam got to see the images he'd heard about on the radio for himself. He sat in the darkened room with a few dozen others, the stark reality of the camps hammering relentlessly into him with every shocking image.

Even though he'd seen photographs before, the moving images, one after the other, held far more horrifying power in the undeniable reality and sheer size of it all—stacks of bodies, endless corpses, face after face in the agonies of death, body after body twisted and mangled and emaciated, all of it on a scale that boggled his mind and sickened his heart, done by people who were meant to be modern and civilized, above this sort of craven atrocity.

He watched in numb silence until the camera focused on the wrinkled, prune-like face of a female prisoner as she gave a broken-toothed smile for her liberators, and something in him twisted with a wrenching pain. He rose from his seat, excusing himself, and went to the hall outside to light a cigarette.

A few minutes later, Sergeant Belmont, with whom he was still on uncomfortable terms thanks to the whole Herr Huber episode, joined him.

"Not easy, is it?"

"No," Sam replied flatly. He did not want to talk of the film to Sergeant Belmont.

"You can see why they deserve everything they get."

"Yes, those twenty-four officers on trial, and anyone like them," Sam agreed.

Belmont raised his eyebrows. "But not the pretty secretaries, eh? Because they *must* be innocent."

Sam did his best not to flush; had the wretched sergeant managed to notice his interest in Anna, when he was doing his damnedest to hide it, even from himself? "You're the one dining and dancing with the pretty secretaries, not me," he replied.

Belmont shrugged. "Why shouldn't I have some fun?"

And pocket the proceeds, as well. Belmont was, like so many others, profiting off the black market, selling cigarettes for as much as fifty times their price.

Sam smoked and said nothing.

"Why do you care so much?" Belmont asked sourly. "You act like such a puritan, Houghton, but these people are complete savages."

Sam was tempted to berate the man for not addressing him by his higher rank, but he didn't. He'd come to realize that the rules were different here; Belmont had a credibility gained in the battlefield that Sam would never be able to earn.

"You honestly think they didn't know about that?" Belmont demanded as he flung his arm out toward the room where the film was still rolling. "You don't believe that they looked the other way because it was easier, safer, or maybe even because they liked what was happening? Nobody made much of a fuss when they herded the Jews into camps, or packed them into trains. They saw them off in cattle cars just fine, as far as I can reckon."

For a second, Belmont's face looked ugly, twisted with hate, and yet Sam could understand it. He knew the sergeant had risen up through the ranks as an enlisted soldier; he'd seen it all, just as Major Pitt had, helping to liberate thirty thousand prisoners at Dachau. Sam was the one who had to rely on photos and films, who drew pictures in his imagination and struggled to keep reminding himself that they were real. Those stacked bodies—each one had been a person with a heart and a soul, a sense of humor and a fear of pain. That prune-faced, broken-toothed woman had once been young, laughing, *normal*, instead of a stick-like crone, a tragic caricature, someone who didn't seem quite real. He had to remind himself of these facts, and yet they still remained difficult to comprehend.

"I'm sure some of them knew," he allowed. "They must have."

Belmont shook his head slowly. "And yet still you exonerate them?"

"I'm not exonerating anyone." Sam released a heavy, pent-up breath of frustration and weariness. "But we can't put the entire nation in prison."

"We can try," Belmont replied, and flicked his cigarette out the window. He glanced back at Sam as he started down the hall. "I'm Jewish, you know," he said in an offhand way, and kept walking.

Sam still felt a leaden heaviness inside as he returned to his office, where Anna was working quietly; none of the German secretaries had been invited to the screening.

She gave him a swift, searching look as he came in, and then looked back down. Sam walked to his desk, but instead of sitting down he stared out the window at the bleak winter's scene below.

Although the Allied powers had expected the cold winter months to result in the deaths of many starving Germans, and had dug the necessary burial pits in preparation, so far the weather had been mild. A damp, gray fog clung to Gruneberg Platz, a few dozen people huddled pathetically outside the gates of the IG Farben building, waiting for an American soldier to emerge. Whether they wanted an audience or just a few discarded cigarette butts Sam didn't know. He stood there silently for a few moments, trying to organize his shifting, seething thoughts. Finally he turned around.

"Did you know?" he asked Anna.

She looked up, instantly alert. "Did I know...?"

"The camps. The deaths." He waved an arm, gesturing toward where the film was being shown, then to the world outside, where bodies had been stacked like lumber or laid in lime pits. Many of the people who had survived were now in other camps, for displaced persons, their homes and lives wrecked beyond repair.

Anna kept his stare unblinkingly, but he saw how her whole body had gone tense, so that it was almost vibrating. The moment stretched between them, twanging like a tuning fork. Sam realized he was breathing hard and he tried to control it.

"Yes," she said after a moment, her voice toneless, her gaze steady. "I knew."

The breath rushed out of Sam; he hadn't expected the admission. For a second, he felt a strange sort of triumph that she'd actually confessed; it was replaced, with dizzying speed, by an overwhelming rage and even hatred, shocking him with its sudden strength. *She knew.* She'd known about the deaths, the murder, of thousands—*millions* of people. She'd known—and she'd done what, exactly?

"You knew," he repeated. He felt his hands curling into fists.

"Yes." She met his gaze unwaveringly; he could not see anything in her face—not regret, not shame, not guilt, not fear. All was bland. Indifferent, or was he imagining that? Surely he must be. He thought he knew her well enough, had believed she had finer feelings, a sensitivity, a kindness... Was it all wrong? False?

"How?" he demanded. "How did you find out about the camps?"

A pause as she continued to gaze at him steadily. "I saw them when I was in Poland."

He stared at her, nonplussed. "Poland? When were you in Poland?"

"It was... during my National Labor Service." She glanced away briefly, and he felt sure she was lying. "I was cleaning houses there, for the *lebensraum*. I... saw things."

"In Poland." He stared at her hard. "You said you were near Cologne for your national service, working on a farm." She didn't respond and he stated flatly, "You lied." He had been right. The potatoes *had* been a fabrication. But why?

Anna's gaze flickered with uncertainty for a moment, although she did not look away. "Yes," she finally said. "I did."

"Why?"

A tiny shrug, more like a twitch of her shoulders. "Because I was afraid."

"Of what? There's nothing wrong in completing your service in Poland." At least no more wrong than anything she would have had to do for such service—cleaning houses that had belonged to other people, farming fields that had been owned and worked by Ukrainians, assembling guns or bombs in an armaments factory... women all over Germany had done something to aid the war effort. Could they—should they—be blamed?

"There's something wrong in knowing," she replied, her gaze moving across his face as if searching for answers, testing him.

He thought he saw anger in her eyes, and he didn't understand it. "Isn't there?" she challenged. "Don't you blame me, simply for knowing? I blame myself."

His throat worked as he forced the word out. "Why?"

"Because I should have done something. And even if I'd done something, I should have done more." She was silent, one hand fluttering at her throat, her fingers seeming to seek something underneath her blouse before she let her hand fall away. "Don't you think so as well, Captain Houghton?"

"I... I don't know." Which was the disturbing truth. Did he blame her? Did he even have a right to be angry? What would he have done in her place?

"Nor do I," she replied quietly. "But I will always feel guilty."

He wanted to ask her what *things* she'd seen in Poland, how she'd felt when she'd seen them. An hour of grainy black-and-white footage had left him with a throbbing headache and an acid twisting in his gut. How had Anna reacted to seeing the real thing, in all of its horrifying devastation? Had she actually seen one of the camps, watched what had gone on there? What had she done with that knowledge?

"I can't imagine any of it," he confessed at last.

"No," she agreed, with a small, sad smile. "You can't."

They remained silent for a moment, the air between them crackling with unspoken things—tension and longing and regret.

Anna smiled at him again, fleetingly, and Sam found his anger had drained away, replaced with a deep, weary sorrow—and a yearning he wouldn't let himself name. Then Anna turned back to her work.

Sam felt no lighter or easier in his mind as he pulled out his chair and yanked a paper toward him, that restless longing surging through him, making his fingers twitch as he held the paper between them. The words swam before his eyes—the questions marching down the page in inky soldiers of black and white.

Have you ever been a member of the NSDAP? Yes. No. Dates.
Have you ever held any of the following positions in the NSDAP?
Reichsleiter. Gauleiter. Kreileiter. Ortsgruppenleiter.

He looked up and saw that Anna was bent over her type-writer; he had finally nabbed one for her a week ago. The steady click of the keys under her capable fingers was the only sound in the room.

"Were you a member of the Nazi Party?" he asked suddenly.

Anna looked up, her expression determinedly calm. "You know I would not be here if I was. And, in any case, women did not…" She paused, trying to think of the word. "Take part in…" Another pause as she struggled for the right word. "Such things. You must know that, as well, Captain."

"*Kinder, küche, kirche,*" Sam answered with a cynical twist of his lips.

Anna nodded. "Yes."

"Were you married, then?"

"No." Something flashed in her eyes, and then was quickly veiled. "Did you think I was?"

"How would I know?" He sounded almost belligerent.

"Surely, in all the time we've known each other, I would have spoken of my husband, if I'd had one." She sounded sad, and yet her words gave Sam a wary pleasure, for they implied a certain level of connection, of intimacy.

"What about a fiancé, then? Someone…" Surely there had been some man in her life, at some point.

She glanced down at her typewriter. "I used to see a pilot in the Luftwaffe."

Sam ignored the entirely unreasonable twinge of jealousy this reluctant admission caused. "What happened?"

"He died. But we'd… we'd stopped seeing each other before then, really."

"How come?"

A long silence while Anna seemed to retreat into herself, as if a reel of memories was running through her head and she was transfixed, watching it.

"He was a Nazi," she said finally. "A nice one. Mostly." She glanced at him, defiance and a faint humor both glinting in her eyes. "They did exist, you know."

"I'm sure they did." According to the questionnaires he had to sort through, Germany was full of them. "So, what happened? Before he died, I mean?"

She sighed and looked away. "I couldn't... It was complicated." Of course it was.

Sam snatched up another questionnaire. "It doesn't matter now, anyway." He shouldn't have been asking such questions, and yet she'd chosen to answer them.

He kept his gaze on the questionnaire in front of him, the type blurring before his eyes, as the silence strained between them.

"If you wish to know more about me, Captain Houghton," Anna said after a moment, her voice quiet, "it is all on my questionnaire."

"I never even looked at your questionnaire," Sam told her, and she drew her breath in.

"Why not?"

He glanced up at her and saw the heightened color in her cheeks, the flash of her eyes. They were both angry again, and he wasn't sure why. "Because I knew I was going to hire you anyway."

She pressed her lips together, and he couldn't tell if he had displeased or flattered her with his remark.

"It wasn't because you're pretty," he added, and knew instantly he should not have said such a thing.

Anna's expression veiled, like a cloud coming behind her eyes, and after a few taut seconds she turned back to her typewriter.

"I didn't mean it like that," he stated, and she just shook her head.

They worked in suffocated silence for the next hour, with the words on the page still swimming before Sam's eyes. He couldn't concentrate on anything; he kept seeing images from the film blazing through his brain, on the back of his lids, and then he'd picture Anna's face, so blank and unyielding. She'd had some sort of relationship with a Nazi; she'd said they were nice. *She knew.* He could not reconcile those things with what he knew about her, what he thought he knew about her.

"Captain Houghton." Her voice was soft, startling him out of his circling thoughts. "Yes?"

"I'm sorry."

He stared at her, his mouth dropping open as the restless anger that had been picking at him fell away. She looked so very sad. "What... what are you sorry for?"

"For all of it," she said simply. "All of it."

He made no reply, because he did not know what to say. He could not exonerate or absolve her, if that was what she was seeking. He didn't know if it was.

"Anna..." he began, only to be interrupted by a sharp tap at the door.

"Captain Houghton?"

Major Pitt's secretary—a woman named Johanna, not Hilda as he'd somewhat sneeringly told Sam on their first meeting—opened the door.

"Yes?"

"Major Pitt wishes to see you, sir. At once."

Sam glanced back at Anna, who gave him the faintest of smiles before she went back to her typewriter. Excusing himself, he walked swiftly out of the room, to his superior's office down the hall.

Major Pitt was standing behind his desk, looking as irritated as ever, and another officer stood by the window, hands in the pockets of his trousers, his stance, Sam thought, deceptively relaxed. There was a mildness to his expression that seemed deliberate, a loose-limbed ease to his position that somehow felt false.

"Captain Houghton, Major Lewis," Pitt introduced tersely.

Sam saluted, and the man waved a hand in acknowledgment. "Sir?" Sam asked.

"Major Lewis is here to discuss Operation Paperclip with you," Pitt said. He paused. "It's your time at last, Captain."

Sam's heart rate went up a notch as he glanced at the officer who was smiling at him in an amused way that felt slightly like a sneer. "Sir?"

Lewis took a step toward Sam, his expression so very genial. "You know you were seconded here because of your experience with chemistry?"

"Yes, I was told I would need it to help identify scientists who could be useful to the US Army."

"Indeed. You've heard of Operation Overcast, I presume?"

"To detain and potentially evacuate German physicists? Yes." He'd been told only the basics of the operation which had been directed by CIC, back when he'd been put forward to go to Frankfurt. All he knew was that at the end of the war, the U.S. government had been eager to locate and detain German scientists, in particular physicists and aeronautical engineers, "to assist in shortening the Japanese war and to aid post-war military research." He knew, only from hearsay, that several prominent men had been spirited back to the United States, along with their families, to become part of the once top-secret Manhattan Project. He'd presumed he'd been brought to Frankfurt because they wanted yet more scientists to aid them against the new enemy, the Soviet Union.

"Well, now it's Operation Paperclip," Lewis said easily. "We've already poached the physicists, thank goodness, but we're after some other scientists now. Engineers, experts in aeronautics, electronics, even architecture." His smile widened; he had very straight teeth. They almost looked as if they'd been filed. "This relates to you because, as I believe you've been told, there are a few chemists we are looking for, men who worked for IG Farben, in fact." He glanced around the room in bemusement, silently inviting Sam to imagine the office building when it had been full of German scientists and industrialists, and firmly controlled by the Nazi Party.

"Chemists," Sam repeated neutrally.

"Well, the thing is," Lewis said with a little laugh, "we're not too good on the science. We know Ambros, for example, helped to develop chemical weapons, including Sarin and soman, at a factory in Schkopau. But we don't know who else was involved, and if you look at the files explaining their work, it's just a whole lot of chemical symbols." He gave another laugh, spreading his hands with a shrug. "Beats me."

"Surely there are better informed chemists who could help you in this," Sam said, even though he was reluctant to admit as much. Part of him was eager to do something—anything—other than sifting through endless questionnaires, but he still couldn't keep from feeling cautious, even though he knew this was why he'd been seconded here. He had a BA in chemistry from Princeton, it was true, but surely PhDs were a dime a dozen among the CIC.

"We arrested Ambros back in June 1945," Lewis continued as if Sam hadn't spoken, "but he was whisked away by the French and they kept him. We'll get him back eventually, I'm sure, but in the meantime, we're after some others. And this is where you come in."

He paused meaningfully; Sam felt it like a fatherly rebuke for his seeming impatience.

"You're an analyst, and you know how to sift through a vast amount of information in a relatively short amount of time. So this is what we want you to do. Go through the questionnaires and find any scientists—chemists, in particular—who have filled them out. Then cross-check them with the Nazi Party files that are being consolidated."

"The files Herr Huber brought here?" The ones he had brought to the CIC's attention, he wanted to add, but did not.

"They're currently in Munich," Pitt interjected, silencing him with a swift look. "But they will be gathered together at the Berlin Document Center by the new year."

"When you have a list, we'll go through them together," Lewis said, as if he were suggesting a cozy lunch date. "After that we'll see what steps we can take. It might be we've already got some of these guys in custody and we don't even know what we're sitting on." He smiled toothily. "But if we don't have them, then we need to find the bastards."

"All right," Sam said slowly. It meant he would be poring over more questionnaires, but at least he felt he had a sense of purpose now. "And if you find these chemists, what will you do with them?" he asked, ignoring Pitt's look of indignation at the presumption of his question.

"Well, that all depends," Lewis said in his easy way, "On how useful they can be to us."

CHAPTER THIRTEEN

Berlin, September 1939

It had been a summer of parties. While Germany had tightened its relentless vise on its already beleaguered Jewish population, Liesel had, upon finishing school in June, found herself catapulted into a world of social events, concerts and cocktails and trips to the cinema. She'd met handsome Luftwaffe pilots and charming young SS officers, with their wheat-blond hair and dancing blue eyes, their determination to drink and dance and, for the moment, forget that war loomed large on the horizon.

It was a strange, surreal world, and if Liesel thought about it too much, she felt sick. Her solution, which she knew was no solution at all, was not to think about it and simply be, do, dance.

In the morning, she read the *Berliner Tageblatt* over cups of coffee—while the rest of Germany had to content themselves with ersatz made with chicory or acorns, her father regularly bought home precious packages of fragrant beans. Neither Liesel nor her mother asked how he procured them.

Then, in the evenings, she often went out—to parties and dances, drinks at bars or meals at cafés, often with Fritz Burkhardt and his friends, and sometimes, far more reluctantly, with her father.

It had all begun in June, when she'd finished with both school and the BDM, her father had come home one day announcing cheerfully that "a certain someone" had been asking about her at the Ministry of Aviation.

"You were at the Ministry of Aviation?" she'd repeated narrowly, and her father had smiled and shrugged.

"A business meeting. Don't you want to know who it was?"

"I can guess." Fritz Burkhardt had written her a few cheerfully scrawled postcards since the hunting party back in December, saying he hoped to see her in the summer.

Now that she was out of school and with no intention of attending university—a prospect greatly discouraged for good Aryan girls, who, according to the Führer, should be focusing on home and family—he seemed to have decided to intensify his pursuit. Liesel found she was both flattered and fearful, a tangle of contradictory feelings she had become used to over the last months, when nothing felt straightforward.

The shooting party at Carinhall had, according to her father, been a great success. On the Saturday, Liesel had stayed back for the actual hunt, watching an ebullient Göring, dressed in a rather ridiculous medieval hunting costume, complete with green leather vest and a large feather in his cap, set off in his role as Reich Master of the Hunt. They had returned triumphant, with several magnificent stags, bloody and dead, laid out for Göring's satisfied inspection.

That evening, there had been another banquet and party, and Fritz had kept close to her side. When he'd asked her onto the terrace again, he had stolen the kiss Göring had teased him about the night before; the brush of his cool lips on hers had been pleasant yet strangely numbing, and as they'd broken apart Fritz had given her a wry smile.

"That wasn't so bad, was it?" He must have known it was her first kiss.

Liesel had shrugged, uncertain. "I suppose not."

He'd laughed and led her back inside, undeterred by her seemingly lukewarm response.

In truth, Liesel hadn't known how to feel about Fritz's kiss, or anything else.

Back inside, Fritz had ushered her into a ring of Luftwaffe officers who had all seemed to want to get to know her, and their interest had been flattering, as well as something of a distraction. They were just young men, boys really, and none of them seemed to be fervent Nazis. Being with them felt easy—easier than anything else.

But then her father had strolled up to the group, along with Obergruppenführer Himmler, and Liesel's body had gone rigid. They'd all chatted easily as she'd tried to keep from so much as glancing at Himmler, the head of the entire SS. When Heinrich Hoffmann had snapped another photo of the group, she'd been blinded, blinking a foreign world back into focus.

It had almost seemed as if her life was happening to someone else, like a newsreel she was watching, everything blurry and black and white, the choices impossibly distant, even as she made them herself.

It continued to feel that way as the summer stretched on and she read the news and went to parties and chatted with pilots and soldiers who were drumming their heels or going through exercises, clearly waiting for something. The whole country felt like it was holding its breath as time marched relentlessly on and Germany prepared for war—war with Europe, and war against the Jews.

Since *Kristallnacht*, things had become more and more unbearable for Jews living in Germany. Almost every day it seemed as if a new law was being enforced—Jews could not own a business, practice law or medicine. They were required to sell all immovable property, stock, and businesses to non-Jews, usually at a shockingly low price. An immigration bureau had been set up in Berlin; Jews were desperate to leave, even if it meant forsaking their homes, livelihoods, savings, and heirlooms, which the Nazis were more than happy to take for themselves.

When her parents had attended Göring's famous Christmas ball, just a few weeks after the hunting weekend, her mother had remarked on all the new artwork the Generalfeldmarschall had acquired. Liesel would not have understood her acid tone even a few months ago; now she knew what her mother was really saying, that Göring, along with so many others, had stolen artwork that once hung in Jewish homes for his own walls.

Hitler even blamed the Jews for the possibility of a world war, proclaiming in a speech to the Reichstag in January that "if international Jewry should succeed in plunging the nations once more into a world war, the result will not be the Bolshevization of the earth and therefore the victory of Jewry, but the annihilation of the Jewish race in Europe."

Liesel had listened to the speech on the radio with her parents; her mother had been utterly silent and her father had given a hard laugh. "This," he had said, "despite the Wehrmacht mobilizing the most significant army in Europe, and Germans taking over all of Czechoslovakia in March."

It was one of his few criticisms against the government; the days of his lightly mocking jokes or wry asides had long gone.

Liesel had chosen, quite deliberately, not to speak any longer of politics to her father. She'd already been avoiding such dreaded conversations, but realization had crystallized inside her when they'd sped away from Carinhall, back in November.

"That went well, don't you think?" he had said jovially, rubbing his hands together in the icy interior of the car.

"Did it? You were quite chatty with the Generalfeldmarschall." She had tried to speak tonelessly but didn't quite manage it; the edge was there, or perhaps her father simply knew her too well.

"He is my superior, Liesel," he'd replied mildly. "Göring has been placed in charge of all the manufacture of synthetic rubber, as well as other useful materials. I must answer to him."

"Thousands answer to him, if not millions," Liesel had replied, "but few take a cigar with him on the terrace of Carinhall."

Otto had shrugged, a small smile playing about his lips. Liesel knew he liked the image of himself that she'd just presented—well-connected, socially confident, successful, Göring's chosen protégé. She had turned to stare out the window at the gloomy forest slipping by, endless rigidly straight pines standing in their just as unrelentingly straight lines. Even the forest was itself like a regiment, waiting for war.

"He has taken an interest in me," Otto had stated with another shrug. "It is good for us, Liesel."

"Is it?"

"You can't object to the Generalfeldmarschall," he had protested. "He's nothing like—" He'd glanced quickly at the driver. "He's fun, he's flamboyant, he enjoys nothing more than a party. What could you possibly object to in him?"

He also possessed a virulent hatred of Jews, Liesel knew, but she was too aware of the driver, his hands encased in black leather gloves resting on the wheel, his expression deliberately bland, to say anything. It was a dark day indeed, she had reflected, when you couldn't even trust your chauffeur. But that was the world they lived in now; you couldn't trust anyone—not the baker who sold you bread, nor the HJ boys who came rattling their boxes and asking for money for the Winter Relief. Not your neighbor, with whom you no longer exchanged pleasantries, and not even your little brother. At nine years old, Friedy had become, Liesel feared, a proper little Nazi, devoted to his Führer.

"And what about Himmler?" she had asked in a low voice. "You seemed quite cozy with him."

"It was business only," Otto had answered after a pause. "There are discussions about building a new factory."

"A new one? Where?"

He had shrugged, the movement evasive. "Out east. It isn't significant."

Yet the fact that he wouldn't tell her, and that he'd been talking to Himmler about it, suggested to Liesel that it was. Her father seemed intimately involved in every aspect of the Nazis' decisions, a fact that both frightened and bewildered her. She pictured him in his suit of bright green check at the Olympics, murmuring wry asides about Hitler, not important enough to be seated near the viewing platform, and she wondered how that gentle, laughing man had become a dedicated Nazi.

She feared there was nothing she or her mother could do to sway him, not, she acknowledged, that either of them ever tried.

As listless as ever, her mother's sudden bouts of manic energy were dedicated to the piano; and they usually preceded a dreaded social engagement, although over the winter and spring months, she attended those less and less. When Liesel finished school, her father began asking her along as a matter of course, rather than Ilse.

"Your mother has a sensitive nature," he'd explained, as if it were so very simple. "She finds all the parties and parades exhausting. Besides, you have fun, don't you? I seem to see a certain *Oberleutnant* by your side rather often."

While Liesel enjoyed Fritz's company well enough, she did not look forward to the rallies and parades that it had become necessary for her father to attend. It seemed as if there was one almost every week, a forceful display of the Reich's power. Yet she went along with him, mostly because she did not know what else to do. To refuse felt like the pointless courting of an unnecessary danger; as her mother had said, *if you're going to take a stand, make it count.* But Liesel wondered if she would ever find the moment—or the courage.

When her father did not require her presence, Liesel went out with Fritz and his set; she far preferred the lighthearted company of the dashing pilots to the scowling arrogance of most of the high-ranking officers with whom her father now rubbed elbows and smoked cigars.

The pilots talked of their planes like children talked of toys; they wanted to fly, not fight, and there was relatively little talk of hating Jews or gypsies or anyone else, which was a blessed, if somewhat guilty, relief. Not hearing it, Liesel knew, didn't mean it wasn't happening, but at least she didn't have to think about it so much.

As the cool, damp summer drew to a close, a new energy and tension seemed to vibrate through the whole city, as if the very air crackled with expectancy. It reminded Liesel a little of when she and her father had gone to the Opening Ceremony of the Olympics just over three years ago, when the whole country had been focused on celebration. She felt that same frantic, frenetic energy now, as if everyone was walking a little faster, looking a bit more alert.

It had started, she thought, in April, with *Führerwetter*, the enormous and magnificent celebration of Hitler's fiftieth birthday. The BDM were marching, which made Liesel thankful that, as she was almost finished school, she had managed to get out of it, citing duties to her father. Her mother had claimed a headache and stayed in bed; she'd also, much to Friedy's fury, insisted he was unable to march because of his twisted foot. "It would be too much for him," she'd proclaimed in a tone that brooked no argument. "He'll have to stay home."

As usual, her father had demurred to her mother when it came to Friedrich, even though her little brother had burst into angry wails when he'd learned he would not be able to see the magnificent parade.

"It will go on forever," Ilse had said sharply. "You know how much Hitler likes to show off. You can't stand for that long. It would make you ill."

Every house in the country was required to set out a swastika, and the city seemed ablaze with red and black as Liesel and her father had walked toward the newly constructed East-West Axis, from where they would view the parade in one of the VIP enclosures near Hitler's platform. Their seats, Liesel had discovered, were far closer to the platform than they'd been three years ago.

Otto had been uncharacteristically silent during the walk, viewing the rather frantic festivities with a faint smile tugging at his lips; he'd paused in front of a nearly ten-meter portrait of Hitler outside a publishing house and gave a little laugh.

"That's quite something, isn't it?" he'd asked Liesel, and for a second she'd felt as she used to, that they were in on a joke together, but then her father had walked on, a bland look on his face, and she had wondered if he meant what he'd said, if he'd actually been impressed by the monstrous picture. She didn't know anymore, and the realization had sent a pang of melancholy through her, a longing for the way things had once been between them, and she feared would never be again.

By the time they had arrived at their seats in the VIP enclosure, Liesel was already exhausted by all the *Sieg Heil*ing and steely smiling; Otto had glad-handed his way across several rows of prominent Nazi officers, and Liesel had had to murmur her own greetings to each one.

They'd even had to pose for a picture with Göring, taken by the ever-present Heinrich Hoffmann, wielding his trusty Leica like a weapon. Liesel had given the camera a bright, if pained, smile, before Göring had pinched her cheek rather hard and told her what a beautiful young woman she was.

They'd only just taken their seats when Hitler had emerged from his seven-liter Mercedes; with a regal nod, he had ascended to the throne-like chair, gilded with red plush, flanked by his officials, ambassadors, and attachés, including the newly appointed "Protector" of Bohemia and Moravia, or what had once been

Czechoslovakia. Liesel was close enough to see the sweat beading his forehead.

She had imagined, quite suddenly and vividly, taking a gun out of her purse and shooting him in the head. Never mind that she didn't have a gun and, even if she did, she was a terrible shot. Never mind even that she would be killed instantly, or worse, after being tortured, for doing it. It would still be worth it. *Make it count*, her mother had said. That certainly would, and yet she knew there was no way she could do such a thing. Still, she imagined it, longed for it, even as the inevitable sense of futility swamped her.

Finally the parade had begun, starting with a display of Germany's air force; Heinkel bombers and Messerschmitt fighters darkened the sky like a flock of overgrown, angry birds as everyone craned their necks upwards to take in the sight.

"Fritz is flying today, is he not?" her father had asked, and Liesel had merely nodded. She did not like to think of Fritz taking part in this ostentatious display of Germany's might, yet she knew he'd been looking forward to it for weeks.

After the air force came the regiments—an endless stream of infantry, marines, and paratroopers—followed by the motorized units, trucks, motorcycles, and the enormous Panzers. Then it was the turn of the artillery—howitzers, cannons, and anti-aircraft guns, on and on, the biggest display of war power in peacetime.

Liesel had ached with tiredness as the hours marched past along with the men and guns. By the time it had finished, they had been in their seats for nearly five hours, and there was a party at the Ministry of Aviation to attend afterward. The mood was jubilant, triumphant, and as they had left their seats, Liesel wondered how anyone could convince themselves that Germany was not a nation about to go to war.

By the first of September, that sense of jubilation had waned, and a new, tense uncertainty had taken its place. In many ways, life continued on as normal.

The day was mild, and Fritz had invited Liesel to a showing of the new film *The Merciful Lie* that evening at the UFA cinema on the Ku'damm. Yet still, the air crackled as if at least it knew, and wanted to give warning.

Liesel sat in the dining room, sipping coffee and scanning the newspaper headlines—more examples of "Polish outrages" that she didn't know whether to believe or not. Her mother was still upstairs, as she often was, and her father came into the room, rubbing his hands together in a way that suggested either purpose or anxiety, perhaps both.

Liesel glanced up at him. "Is everything all right, Father?" she asked coolly. "I thought you would have gone into work by now." He now spent two or three days a week at the factory in Schkopau, the rest of the time in Berlin, and he was usually gone by eight o'clock in the morning.

"Not today." Otto prowled around the room while Liesel watched, bemused and more than a little wary. "There is going to be an announcement on the radio. The Führer is making a speech."

Liesel tried to ignore the prickle of irritation hearing him call Hitler the Führer caused in her. Once he would have only used the title mockingly, but now he seemed sincere. It was just another small yet alarming way in which he'd changed.

"A speech? About what?" She glanced at the paper. "Poland?"

"Yes, I think so."

"You must know." As far as Liesel could tell, her father continued to have quite regular meetings with the Generalfeldmarschall. How much he knew about the government's inner workings she could not bear to consider.

"I can guess. As can you, no doubt." He gave her a quick, harried smile. "What do you think is going to happen, Liesel?"

There was a challenge in his tone that she hadn't heard in a long time, and it was one she was reluctant to take up. The last few months she'd been so determined not to think about anything—the plight of the Jews, Fritz's increasing attentions, the way her father had leaned in to murmur something to the Generalfeldmarschall at the party after the *Führerwetter*, both of them looking so serious. She had to block it all out because it felt like the only way to stay safe, to stay sane. If she let herself think, she'd have to start asking questions and finding answers, and Liesel knew she could not bear either. Not yet, and maybe not ever.

"I suppose," she answered slowly, "Hitler is going to invade Poland."

Otto let out a bark of humorless laughter as he threw himself into a chair. "Of course he is," he replied, an edge of irritation to his voice. "His endless forbearance has been sorely tested by the warmongering Poles, after all."

There could be no mistaking her father's sarcasm as he raked a hand through his hair before letting it fall dejectedly to his side. Liesel regarded him for a moment, nonplussed by this about-face.

"You cannot be surprised or even displeased," she remarked finally. "Everything you have been working on has been leading to war."

"That doesn't mean I have to like it." Otto let out an annoyed breath. "No one actually wants war, Liesel. I've told you before that it's hell. That hasn't changed. It never will."

"Then why," Liesel asked, genuinely mystified and growing angry, "have you been making Buna rubber? It's always been for guns and tanks and everything else. Göring said so himself. So did you."

"Because if we are going to have a war, I want us to win it," he snapped, and he rose from the table without having any breakfast.

A few minutes later, Friedy came down for breakfast, his chest puffed out with pride. He was wearing his brand new uniform; today was finally his first day in the *Jungvolk*.

Liesel took in his black shorts and crisp tan shirt, a black neckerchief tucked into his shirt and the white *Siegrune*, like two little lightning bolts, on a cloth badge sewn onto his left sleeve.

"Don't you look smart?" she said after a moment, and her brother puffed his thin chest out all the more.

"Thank you, Liesel."

Liesel's heart ached even as she smiled at her brother's seriousness. At ten years old, Friedrich was not much bigger than when he'd been six, and he was often beset by colds and coughs that wracked his thin frame to pieces. His twisted foot caused him to walk with a noticeable limp, so he had to drag one foot behind the other, and his eyes looked owlish and dreamy behind his thick spectacles. She sometimes worried that the other boys in the *Jungvolk* might bully him because of such seeming imperfections. He'd been protected in the *Pimpf*, mostly because Ilse had kept him from going much at all, and he'd never marched in a parade or gone on a hike.

But it was different now; her mother was less involved and Friedy was more determined. Besides, boys could just about get out of being in the *Pimpf*, but not the *Deutsche Jungvolk*. People would notice if he didn't attend, and draw dangerous conclusions. She just hoped he wasn't disappointed, or worse.

Her father came back into the dining room just as Friedy was finishing his breakfast; he did a double take at the sight of his son in uniform, but then gave a wide smile.

"Well, well, look at this handsome young DJ! I barely recognize you, my little soldier!"

Friedrich gave him a rather reproving look. "Don't joke, Father," he said with so much dignity that Liesel didn't know whether to smile or weep.

Her father nodded seriously, taking his rebuke in the same spirit it had been given, and as Friedy left for school, he gave him a most sober salute, which Friedy returned with an almost alarming level of gravity, while Helga beamed on, as proud as if Friedy were her own son.

As he marched out of the house, Liesel caught the tremble of her father's lips; for a second he looked as if he might cry. But then he turned to Liesel with a forced smile and a light clap of his hands.

"Ah, our little soldier off to his own little war," he said as he poured himself another cup of coffee. "Shall we sit in the drawing room? The speech is at ten o'clock."

And it was clear from his tone that her father knew more than the gist of what it would contain.

At five minutes to ten, the four of them were all ready and seated; Helga perched on the hardest chair, by the door, invited by Liesel's father and as ever eager to hear what her beloved Führer had to say. Ilse had drifted in only a few minutes before, still in her dressing gown, a cigarette dangling listlessly from her lips, her hair in a dark cloud about her face. She ignored them all, sinking onto one end of the sofa as if she were the only person in the room. Liesel sat in an armchair, her back ramrod straight, her hands clenched in her lap, as her father twiddled the radio dial before marching music blared out and she jumped at the noise.

A few seconds later, a voice came on, demanding that "those who are assembled rise and stand to greet the arrival of the Führer."

Helga lumbered determinedly to her feet and Ilse winced at the ensuing predictable cheers and applause, which died down as Göring introduced Hitler, and then he began his speech.

The words—delivered in an angry and emphatic rising cadence, nearly every sentence he uttered followed by a round of dutiful and determined *Sieg Heils*—washed over Liesel in a numbing tide. *No honorable great power would tolerate such a state of affairs… his love of peace and endless forbearance should be not mistaken for weakness or even cowardice…*

And then, finally, the stark truth, delivered with triumph rather than regret: "We have now been returning fire since five-forty-five a.m. Henceforth, bomb will be met with bomb. He who fights with poison gas shall be fought with poison gas. He who distances himself from the rules for a humane conduct of warfare can only expect us to take like steps. I will lead this struggle, whoever may be the adversary, until the security of the Reich and its rights may be assured."

As the *Sieg Heils* rang out yet again, no one spoke. Helga was quivering with emotion, although Liesel could not tell what it was. The housekeeper had lost a son in the last war, she knew, but she adored her Führer and she had no more sons to lose.

Ilse had smoked four cigarettes in the space of a few minutes, and was now staring rather vacantly out the window, at the peaceful garden and street that looked as if they belonged to an unchanged world, where war would never be so thoughtless as to impinge.

Liesel glanced at her father; she didn't think she'd ever seen him so serious. He looked almost as if he were grieving, his shoulders slumped, his gaze turned inward and his mouth turned down as he rubbed his chin.

"Now you will make your fortune," Liesel couldn't keep from saying flatly, and Otto looked up at her with blank eyes.

"At what price?" he asked quietly, and then, in the manner of someone reciting a dirge, he quoted softly from his beloved Goethe, "War is in truth a disease." He paused before the haggard lines of his face hardened with resolve and he quoted again, "You must either conquer and rule or serve and lose, suffer or triumph, be the anvil or the hammer." He glanced between the three of them—daughter, wife, and housekeeper—his eyes filled with defiance, his body still slumped with defeat. "And we, my *lieblings*, are the hammer."

CHAPTER FOURTEEN

Berlin, December 1939

It had been a long, strange autumn. After the momentous announcement on the first of September, and then Britain declaring war on Germany just two days later, Liesel had felt as if the very earth should shake, the planets move out of their alignment, the sky tear apart. Surely something should *change*.

Yet, for the most part, life seemed to go on as usual in Berlin, and indeed in all of the country—people went to work, heads bowed under a gloomy sky as they boarded a tram or a bus; they read newspapers and went to the cinema and, when the sun came out, strolled in the park.

There were changes, of course, and unwelcome ones at that— ration cards and nightly blackouts, with curtains drawn across every window, and air-raid sirens wailing through the small hours, although Berlin had not yet been bombed, and Göring had, in his usual bombastic way, certain no British plane could reach the capital, proclaimed to his Luftwaffe "if one enemy bomb falls on Berlin, you can call me Meyer."

Still, her father had arranged for their dank and damp cellar to be converted into a surprisingly cozy shelter, its beams reinforced with steel, its whitewashed walls lined with shelves. He'd brought in several beds, as well as a table and chairs, books and games and tins of food. They tramped down there dutifully every time the siren went, but mostly it was used only by Friedy, as a den to play in.

While cream cakes soon became a luxury most went without, and butter and coffee remained scarce, in general, even without the boxes of chocolates her father came home with every so often, the Scholzes' table was fairly well laid.

In fact in every facet of life, things had gone on with an unsettling amount of normality; if she didn't think about it—and she usually chose not to—Liesel would not have realized there was a war on.

In September, Fritz had been deployed to bombing missions over Poland, but when he had leave, he often came to call on Liesel, taking her out to the cinema or for a party with fellow Luftwaffe officers, all of them seeming to find the war enormous fun, as if dropping bombs was some sort of grand game of marbles. Liesel tried not to think about that, either.

As Christmas approached, a certain pall of gloom came over the city as the shortages of war become more readily apparent; Christmas trees were scarce, presents were almost impossible to buy, and there had been another, harder push for people to celebrate not Christmas but *Julfest*, a Nazi-created celebration of Germanic culture honoring "the fallen soldiers of the Fatherland." Even the Christmas carols had been rewritten so that "Silent Night" proclaimed *"Adolf Hitler is Germany's star, showing us greatness and glory afar."*

In the Scholz household, however, Christmas was in full, festive swing, with Otto bringing an enormous fir tree into the house just a few days before Christmas Day.

"Where on earth did you get it?" Liesel exclaimed and he gave a delighted smile.

"A present from the Generalfeldmarschall, from the forests of Carinhall."

"The Generalfeldmarschall must hold you in high esteem indeed, to provide you with a Christmas tree," Ilse remarked tartly, and Otto shrugged.

"Who am I to question my good fortune?"

"'Everyone holds his fortune in his own hands,' isn't that what your precious Goethe says?" Ilse retorted.

"To think you can quote him as well," Otto exclaimed, ignoring the barb. "I am so pleased."

Ilse turned away with a scowl, saying nothing. Liesel had become more and more aware of these little spats that burst from her parents like gunfire; her mother attacked and her father parried, as genial as ever. Liesel thought her mother seemed almost desperate to pick a fight, finding fault in everything, especially in her husband. Every gesture or word, no matter how seemingly innocuous, was a slight to her, and worse, an indictment. Even the Christmas tree could not be forgiven, and despite the ages-old tradition for the mother of the household to decorate it, Ilse refused to do so.

Liesel ended up decorating it, furtively, for her brother's sake. He was still young enough to want a proper Christmas, although he'd sulked about not celebrating *Julfest*, which was what his DJ leaders had been encouraging their members to do.

"We can remember our culture and the fallen soldiers while we celebrate Christmas," Liesel told him. "It doesn't really make that much difference."

"If it didn't, why would they change it?" Friedrich demanded, looking even sulkier. Liesel knew he was in a bad mood because it had been over three months since he'd joined the *Jungvolk*, and he was still not a fully-fledged member in possession of the long-coveted knife.

In order to become a full member, he had to pass a series of physical tests that had so far been quite impossible for him to do—run sixty meters in twelve seconds, and complete a day-and-a-half hike. Liesel feared he would never be able to complete such tasks, and what that meant for his membership she did not know.

Three days before Christmas, she was strolling down the Ku'damm looking rather fruitlessly for a gift for Friedy; she had thought of buying him a knife, but she knew he wanted to be given it by the DJ, not his sister. Then she'd considered purchasing a collection of fairy tales, but she had discovered they'd all been rewritten to Nazi dogmatic drivel. Even the wrapping paper, she'd seen, was covered in swastikas. She was feeling tired, footsore, and more than a bit exasperated when she caught a glimpse of blond hair from the corner of her eye—a usual enough occurrence—but familiarity breathed through her in a gust of memory and she realized at whom she was staring.

"Rosa!" she called and the girl stiffened before she quickened her step, her head down as she dodged through the Christmas crowd thronging the street. Liesel hurried after her, heedless of the curious stares she received from a few passers-by. "Rosa," she said again, breathlessly, as she caught up to the girl. "Rosa, please. It's me, Liesel. Liesel Scholz. Your mother was our housekeeper—"

Slowly, Rosa stopped and turned to her. Her face was tense, drawn in lines of deep suspicion and fear, tempered by a weary resignation that somehow seemed worse in someone so young. She could only be about thirteen. "I know who you are," she said quietly; there was no sullen superiority now.

"How are you?" Liesel asked. "And how is your mother? Are you keeping well?"

A flicker of the old contempt flickered across Rosa's face, and Liesel realized how ridiculous her question must sound. "I am fine, Fraulein Scholz."

"Please call me Liesel," she insisted. "And your mother?"

"She is fine."

"Can't we get a cup of coffee or something?" Liesel suggested a bit desperately. "I've been wondering how you've been after…

that night. I've been worried." Although Rosa's hair had grown back so it brushed her jawbone, her face was gaunt, her body scrawny underneath a shabby, patched coat.

At Liesel's suggestion of coffee, Rosa pressed her lips together. "That isn't possible, Fraulein." She glanced pointedly at a nearby café with the all too familiar *Juden Verboten* sign hanging in its steamy window. Liesel had got so used to seeing them in nearly every shop window that she'd almost forgotten they were there, or what they meant. Jews were not allowed in any sort of establishment these days, and Liesel blushed as she realized her thoughtless error.

"I'm sorry. I didn't think..."

"No," Rosa agreed tiredly, and Liesel experienced a rush of shame. She could not possibly begin to understand what Rosa endured, day after day. "Come back to my house, then," she urged. "It's not too far. We'll have coffee there. My mother will be so pleased to see you." That was if she had yet risen from bed.

Rosa hesitated, glancing left and right, a look of apprehension on her face. Then, quickly, she nodded. "All right. Yes. But will your father approve?"

"Of course he will," Liesel said with more confidence than she actually felt. At least, she acknowledged silently, her father wouldn't have to know about it. He was in Schkopau again, until Christmas Eve.

They walked back to the house on Koenigsallee without speaking, although Liesel longed to ask Rosa questions. She wanted to know how she really was, how Gerda really was, because she didn't think they could be at all fine. Perhaps there was some way she could help, although she could not imagine what it was.

Rosa glanced around cautiously as they stepped into the house. Liesel had only just taken off her coat when Helga came out of the drawing room brandishing a feather duster like a weapon.

"Fraulein Scholz?" Her gaze moved to Rosa and her heavy brows drew together.

"I'm just meeting up with an old friend," Liesel said quickly. Although she never talked of politics with the housekeeper, she knew well enough how devoted Helga was to the Führer. She'd listened to some of his speeches on the radio with tears of joy in her eyes, and she performed the *Hitlergruss* more than anyone else Liesel knew. "We'll be up in my room. We don't need anything." So much for coffee. Liesel realized now what an impossibility that was.

Giving the housekeeper what she hoped was a quelling look, she hurried upstairs with Rosa. In her bedroom, with the door firmly closed, Liesel breathed a sigh of relief.

Rosa walked slowly around with a strange look on her face, a mixture of wonder and resignation. She reached out and touched the ornately carved wooden frame of the cheval mirror standing in one corner. "I forgot how beautiful this room was."

With some embarrassment, Liesel looked around the room with uncomfortably new eyes, noting the mirror, the matching bureaus, the velvet armchair and chaise by the window, the wardrobe full of clothes.

"It's so good to see you," she said, to which Rosa gave an eloquent look of disbelief. It wasn't, Liesel knew, as if they'd been friends; most of their exchanges had possessed a veiled hostility, and yet she meant what she said. "I know we haven't always got along," she continued stiltedly. "To be honest, I often thought you looked down on me."

"I was only envious," Rosa replied quietly. "It seemed as if you had it so easy, and you didn't even realize." There was no venom in her words, no trace of the sharpness that had once been so evident. She only sounded resigned.

"Has it been very hard for you?" Liesel asked tentatively, and again contempt flashed across Rosa's face as with a scalding rush of shame, Liesel realized how idiotic her question was. Of course it had been hard. It had been as good as impossible. And yet she still could not imagine it. "I'm sorry, that was a foolish question. Of course it has been hard. It is just… I don't *know*, Rosa."

"Do you want to?" Rosa asked wearily, and Liesel looked away, acknowledging her own willful ignorance. No, she had not wanted to know these many long months. She'd done her best not to know, not to think, only to exist. It had seemed easier, and yet now she recognized how shameful that impulse was. Rosa, certainly, did not have the luxury of that choice.

"Yes, I do," she said staunchly, even though she trembled under Rosa's challenging gaze. The girl was four years younger than her, and yet she seemed decades older, a world of weary experience in her dark eyes. "Tell me. Please."

Rosa nodded and spread her hands. "What is it exactly you wish to know? My mother cannot find work, because no gentiles are allowed to employ her. She does what piecemeal sewing she can, but it is not enough. We are afraid to leave the apartment, for fear of being beaten, or worse. I have stopped going to school."

"But that's terrible…" Liesel shook her head slowly. She had known all the regulations, of course, but she hadn't let herself consider their impact, the day-to-day details that were both heartbreaking and harrowing. "I'm so sorry." The words were inadequate, useless, yet she had no others.

"You did not make the laws, Fraulein Scholz," Rosa said with the ghost of a smile. "I should not blame you for them, I know."

Liesel regarded her uncertainly. "Do you?"

Rosa sighed. "No, of course not. None of this is your fault, and in truth you and your family have been good to us. It's just… I am always angry. I can't help it. It is so unfair." Her voice trembled on the last words and she bit her lip as she looked away.

"Let me take your coat," Liesel suggested, longing to comfort this girl in whatever way she could. "We can sit for a while…"

Rosa shook her head, pulling the shabby garment more tightly around her. "No. I shouldn't stay long. Your housekeeper..."

"She's a stupid old woman—"

"And stupid old women can mean the arrest or even the death of a Jew," Rosa told her quietly. "I do not wish to be arrested because of either your housekeeper or your good intentions, as much as I appreciate the sentiment."

Liesel blinked, absorbing the matter-of-factness of that statement. "Surely you wouldn't be arrested just for visiting a friend," she protested feebly, even though Rosa had just explained how she might be. Even now, Liesel struggled to understand, to believe. She thought suddenly of the man on the street, his cap, the kick to the stomach, the look of sneering joy on the faces of the SS. She hadn't let herself think about any of that in years.

"I don't want to find out," Rosa said simply. "You'd be surprised what accusations they can drum up. I only came here because... because your family was kind, once, and I thank you for it. But I can't stay."

"Please, let me help you," Liesel said.

Rosa shrugged. "How?"

"I could give you some money..."

For a second, Rosa looked tempted; money, Liesel knew, had to be extraordinarily tight. She hurried to her bureau, riffling through the top drawer, looking for the small, ornate porcelain box where she kept some marks. "I have some right here..."

"No. No thank you." Rosa sounded reluctant yet firm. "I cannot risk such a thing. I could be accused of stealing it."

"I wouldn't—" Liesel began, shocked and hurt by the unspoken accusation.

Rosa shook her head. "No, but *they* would. Thank you, but I can't take your money, Fraulein. You can't help me." For a second, Rosa's lips trembled and she looked impossibly young, far too young to have endured the things she already had. And what more might she have to, as Hitler continued his relentless attacks on her people?

"Some food, then," Liesel suggested, for she knew Jews were given far fewer rations than other Germans, and could only queue for them at the end of the day, when there was barely anything left. She'd seen them, looking despondent, coming away with the heel of an old loaf or less.

Rosa shook her head. "Thank you, but no. Your housekeeper would wonder. No, it's better if I don't take anything. Safer."

Liesel stared at her helplessly, feeling entirely useless. She'd brought Rosa here, she realized, simply for her own sake. She'd wanted to do something to make herself feel better, never mind Rosa. The knowledge was utterly shaming. "How is your mother?" she asked finally. "Really?"

Rosa hunched one shoulder. "She is surviving. We all are. Just."

"Did you ever think of leaving Berlin?" Many Jews in the city had left Germany altogether, after *Kristallnacht*, but the doors to the world had closed on the first of September.

"We didn't have the money. Besides, my grandmother is here. She can't travel and my mother wouldn't leave her. So." She squared her shoulders in a gesture that looked heartbreakingly brave. Liesel knew Rosa was under no illusions of what the future might hold for her and her family. Things would only get worse.

"I'm so sorry," she said, knowing the words were no more than a sop. "I truly am, Rosa. I wish…" She bit her lip. "I wish I'd been kinder to you, back then. When your mother worked here. I should have been."

"You weren't unkind," Rosa replied. "And in any case, I'm sure I was annoying." She gave her the ghost of a smile that Liesel tried to return. "It doesn't matter now."

"I just wish there was something… anything… I could do."

Rosa let out a huff of humorless laughter. "So do I. It's like a nightmare I can't escape. My grandmother doesn't understand.

Her memory fails, and we have to always be reminding her about what the new laws are. There are more every day. I wonder, will there one day be a law that does not allow Jews to live?"

Liesel drew back, horrified by the notion. "Surely it wouldn't come to that..."

Rosa pressed her lips together as she shook her head. "I don't know what it will come to, then. Sometimes I feel as if I can't stand another second of it. As if I must scream or cry or claw at my skin. Anything to make it stop." She looked away, as if she regretted saying that much, and impulsively Liesel reached for a heavy, silver-backed hairbrush on her dressing table.

"Please, take this, at least. It's made of good silver. You should be able to sell it for something. And if anyone asks, you can say it is a family heirloom." Plenty of Jews were selling what heirlooms they had left, if only for pfennigs. She held the brush out, her gaze imploring. "Please. I must do something." As she said the words, she realized how true they were. She could not let Rosa leave without helping her in some way.

Rosa stared at her for a moment and then slowly took the brush. "*Danke*, Fraulein," she said quietly as she slid the brush into the pocket of her coat; it looked bulky, suspicious, and Liesel prayed she hadn't made things worse for her.

"I wish there was more I could do," she whispered.

"Perhaps one day there will be," Rosa replied. Liesel heard a hint of challenge in her voice, as well as a hesitation. "If my mother is willing to leave. One day... perhaps you could help." She gave Liesel a sudden, beseeching look. "I know your father is someone important. He could get us papers, perhaps. Find a way out of Berlin, or even Germany. I know it happens..."

"Yes..." At the mention of papers, Liesel's mouth had dried. Forging identification papers was a charge that would most likely land you in the Gestapo headquarters on Prinz-Albrecht-Strasse. Liesel didn't know much about what went on behind the thick walls of the massive, classical-fronted building, but she'd heard whispers of the interrogation and torture, and that was enough to terrify her. Would her father be willing to risk so much, or call in favors from high-ranking friends Liesel wasn't sure he even had the right to?

"Never mind," Rosa said quickly as she read the reluctance that Liesel knew had to be written on her face. "It's too much to ask. I know it is."

"No…" Liesel's voice trailed away. "I will ask my father," she promised Rosa, "if the time comes, when you are able to leave." Although what her father would say to such a request, she had no idea. He'd been willing to help his old housekeeper and her daughter after *Kristallnacht*, but with something as big as this? Already she could see him shaking his head, the genuine regret that would shadow his eyes. *If I could do it, Liesel, of course I would.* "I will try," she insisted as firmly as she could, but both she and Rose heard the betraying waver in her voice.

"I must go." Rosa patted the bulky lump in her coat. "Thank you, Fraulein."

"Please, call me Liesel," she implored again, meaning it even more this time. It seemed a foolish request now, when she didn't know if she'd ever see her again, but Liesel meant it all the same. "I'd like to think we are… friends, of a sort."

Rosa nodded slowly. "Liesel," she said, and then she nodded to the door. Liesel went to open it, listening for Helga. The housekeeper was in the dining room, humming "Exalted Night of the Clear Stars," one of the more popular *Julfest* carols.

"Let's go quietly," Liesel whispered, and they began to tiptoe down the hallway. They'd reached the top of the stairs when the door to her parents' bedroom opened and her mother stood there, wearing a rumpled dressing gown, her dark hair in a tangle about her face. She looked like some sort of bedeviled ghost. The smell rolling off her was of cigarette smoke and schnapps, and Liesel suspected she was drunk.

Her eyes widened and her mouth opened soundlessly as she caught sight of Rosa. "*Rosa...*"

Liesel pressed a finger to her lips. "Helga," she mouthed, and it occurred to her how utterly ludicrous it was, that all three of them were terrified of a flat-footed, potato-faced housekeeper who smelled of sauerkraut and spoke of Hitler as if he were both her father and her lover. But then, that was precisely why they were so terrified.

Ilse gave a slow nod of understanding, her eyes full of tears as she pressed her fingers to her lips and blew Rosa a boozy kiss. Rosa smiled back, the first time she'd done so since Liesel had caught sight of her on the Ku'damm, and they started down the stairs.

As Rosa slipped out the door into the wintry twilight, disappearing into the shadows, a shudder went through Liesel. Would she ever see her again? She had no idea what the future might hold for either of them in this turbulent, uncertain world. And in the midst of such terrible times, she acknowledged disconsolately, with all that was available to her, she had only managed to give her a hairbrush.

CHAPTER FIFTEEN

Frankfurt, December 1945

Christmas was going to be quiet. It had been over a week since Sam had met with Major Lewis and joined Operation Paperclip, and his mission had given him a much-needed sense of purpose to keep sifting through the paperwork that still surrounded his desk in dozens of cardboard boxes.

After he'd returned from Major Pitt's office, Anna had given him a silent look of enquiry, which Sam had hesitated to respond to. He was conscious of the tension, and even anger, that had pulsed uncomfortably between them before he'd left; he was also conscious of the delicate nature of his work, although he knew most CIC officers allowed their secretaries practically unlimited access to their classified files.

"We're looking for something in particular now," he had said a bit abruptly and she had merely waited for more, not saying a word. "I've been asked to be involved in a particular operation to identify scientists," he had explained. "And in particular chemists. It was what I came here for, and now it's finally happening."

Something had flared hotly in her eyes before her expression quickly became veiled once more. "Chemists?" she had repeated.

"Do you not know the word?" He had hesitated, racking his brains for the vocabulary. "*Chemiker.*"

"I know the word," she had replied. "But why only chemists?"

Sam had frowned, resenting the impertinence of the question, perhaps more than he should have. He had never before felt the need to put Anna in her place.

"It's the directive from above," he had replied shortly, and, with a nod, Anna had turned back to her typewriter. Sam had stared into space for a few moments and longed for a cigarette.

As the days had passed, the weather stayed mild and gloomy, with a damp fog shrouding the city in its unlovely mist. Sam had managed to identify the questionnaires of nineteen scientists he could cross-check with the Nazi Party files in Berlin; Anna had been particularly assiduous in her translations and Pitt had been grudgingly pleased with the result, while Major Lewis had been nowhere to be seen. Presumably he was out in the field, hunting down Nazis, or perhaps at Camp King, the interrogation center just outside of Frankfurt. Sam struggled not to feel as if he'd been forgotten yet again.

On the twenty-third of December, as he cleared his desk for a few days' holiday, he glanced at Anna, who was reaching for her coat and bag. They'd barely spoken in days save for the minimum required for work, and he felt—again—as if there was something he needed to apologize for, something unspoken he longed to say out loud to bridge the silence between them and yet he feared there were no words that would accomplish such a thing. She'd worked hard, at least, setting to her tasks with a determination that seemed almost personal in its focus.

"Have you any plans for Christmas?" he asked finally, and she turned to him with a small smile.

"Is it Christmas? Somehow I had almost forgotten." He realized she was joking, with the dark humor so particular to Germans, and he smiled back.

"Admittedly it is easy to do. Will you be able to… celebrate?" The question seemed incongruous when he thought of the life she must live, with no family, having only a room in a flat crowded with strangers, in a city that was not her own.

"One of the families in my flat has invited me to share their dinner." Anna paused. "But I do not wish to take away from what they have."

It was a depressing prospect—Anna alone on Christmas, with no tree, no presents, no family, unwilling to share a meal out of concern for those who would have to go without. And meanwhile he was swimming in space, alone in a five-bedroomed villa with an entire turkey to himself, should he want to purchase one at the PX.

"You could come to my house for Christmas dinner," Sam said suddenly, and Anna stilled in the way she often did when she was surprised but did not want to show it. "Just for dinner," he emphasized, and then stupidly flushed. Surely that had not needed to be said. "Bring a friend if you like." He did not even know if she had any friends. Anna still had not replied and Sam finished with a rather dismissive shrug. "If you want," he said as if he didn't care either way, when he knew very much that he did, and yet he was at pains to assure her, without stating it explicitly, that he wasn't like the others, that he didn't *expect* anything.

"That is very kind," Anna said at last, choosing each word with care. "You are very kind, Captain Houghton," she repeated, and Sam waited for her to refuse. "Thank you. I will come."

"You will?" He looked so surprised that she smiled, her whole face lighting up and reminding him quite unnecessarily just how pretty she was.

"Yes, I will. Are you surprised?" She clucked and shook her head. "You expected me to refuse."

He gave a self-conscious laugh. "Well, actually, yes."

Her smile dropped as she nodded soberly in agreement. "I almost did. I am not used to... enjoying things. If that does not sound too..." She paused, searching for the word. "Pitying."

"Self-pitying, you mean," Sam answered, "and no, it doesn't. I'm just glad you want to come. And that you think it's something you might enjoy."

For a second, her eyes were bright with mischief. "You think me too dour."

"Not at all," he said quickly. "I cannot imagine what you…" He decided not to go down that well-worn line of thought. "I'm just glad," he said simply.

"And so am I," she said, smiling. "Thank you for the invitation. I will bring a friend."

"Good," Sam said, a bit too robustly, in his eagerness not to seem disappointed by that prospect. "Good."

On Christmas Day, Sam stood by the drawing-room window and watched the silvery mist rise from the frost-tipped gardens like smoke as the clouds evaporated across a pale blue sky. It was as tranquil a scene as he could imagine, the stillness of the wintry morning broken only by the sound of Annika bustling in the kitchen, making preparations for Christmas dinner.

Sam had been reluctant to have her come in on the holiday, but she had insisted. "It is good," she'd told him in her hesitant, half-broken English, "to be busy." She had tapped her forehead. "To forget."

Sam knew her husband and two sons had all died in the war—the husband from a weak chest, the sons in battle midway through the war. She had much to forget.

Now, as he stood alone, he let his mind drift to his family in Bryn Mawr—his parents and his kid sister Nancy, who wasn't such a kid anymore, but an opinionated young woman who had graduated from Wellesley last spring. They would all be together; he could picture them so clearly in the living room at home, the big, bushy Christmas tree in the window, the smell of his mother's turkey roasting, the sound of Bing Crosby on the radio.

Two days ago, he'd received a parcel from his mother with a packet of shortbread she'd baked that was hopelessly stale and a pair of lumpily knit socks she'd made herself. *I know these are terrible,* she'd written in her long, newsy letter. *You know what a horrible knitter I am! But I wanted to show you I care.*

Those silly socks had brought a lump to his throat. Sam hadn't realized quite how alone he felt until he'd held them in his hands.

And now Anna was coming for dinner, and he had a horrible feeling he might embarrass himself, by acting as if there was some sort of connection between them, when really it was only a fabrication caused by his own loneliness. At least she was bringing a friend; hopefully that would keep him from saying, or worse, doing, something foolish.

By the time Anna and her friend were meant to arrive, fires were laid in both the dining and drawing rooms, and delicious, comforting smells of roast goose—there had been no turkeys, after all—as well as apple and sausage stuffing and cabbage and potato dumplings, which Annika had insisted no Christmas meal would be complete without, were wafting through the house.

Sam had insisted on sending his car for Anna, knowing public transportation would be patchy at best, and his stomach tightened in anticipation, and more than a little nerves, as it pulled up in front of the house.

He straightened his shoulders as he went to open the door, taking in the sight of Anna emerging from the car, followed by her friend, a slight blonde woman around her age.

"Merry Christmas," Sam called out in a jolly voice as he stood aside to let them in. "*Frohe Weihnachten.*"

Anna smiled faintly at that, but her friend simpered at him in a way Sam found alarming. He'd seen plenty of girls like her—faces heavily made up, a frightened yet avaricious gleam in their desperate eyes. He glanced at Anna, but she had turned away to take off her coat.

"Let me hang that up for you," he said, and allowed his hands to briefly brush her shoulders as he slipped the coat off. He moved away quickly.

"This is Margarete," Anna said as she gestured to her friend, who had slipped off her own coat and was holding it to Sam with a girlish smile. He sprang forward to take it. "She has a room in the same apartment as I do."

"Very good."

They all stood staring at each other for a few seconds before Sam sprang to attention once more.

"A drink?" he suggested and Margarete, who had been studying one of the gloomy oil portraits on the wall, turned to him with a wide smile.

"*Ja, bitte!*"

Sam glanced at Anna, who smiled and murmured, "She doesn't speak much English. Yes please to the drink, for both of us."

Sam led them both to the drawing room, where a fire was now crackling merrily. He went to the drinks table, where several crystal decanters belonging to the recent owner had been filled thanks to the PX—whiskey, rum, cognac.

He hesitated and Anna said softly, "Anything will be fine."

He poured them all cognac and handed the glasses around with a smile. "*Prost*," he said.

"*Prost*," Anna replied, and Margarete hefted her glass before downing it in one.

Instinctively, Sam glanced at Anna again; she smiled faintly and gave a little shrug, as if inviting him to share the joke, if there even was one.

As far as Christmas dinners went, Sam had certainly had better. Annika had outdone herself with her cooking, but Sam struggled to feel anything other than discomfort, between Anna's carefully veiled quiet and Margarete's brazen flirtatiousness. He had opened a bottle of wine for their meal and found he could not fill Margarete's glass fast enough. By the time dessert came—a raisin-studded stollen dusted with icing sugar—his temples were banded with tension and he'd opened a second bottle just so he could have some.

When they retired to the drawing room after the meal, Margarete half-collapsed onto a sofa and, while Sam stoked the fire simply to have something to do, fell asleep.

He turned around, taking in the sight of Margarete slumped against the velvet pillows with her mouth open, snoring gently. "Oh…" He didn't know whether to groan or laugh.

"You must excuse her," Anna said quietly. "She… had a difficult war."

Sam glanced at her warily. Surely every civilian in Germany had had a difficult war. "What does that mean, exactly?"

Anna made a fluttering motion with her fingers. "Her husband, father, brothers, all dead."

"I'm sorry."

"It is hard, when there is no one left." She looked away, taking a sip of the schnapps he'd poured earlier. She'd barely drunk all evening, unlike her friend.

"Whom did you lose, Anna?" Sam asked quietly.

She turned back to him, startled; he realized he'd never used her Christian name before. He held her gaze, willing her to see and accept his compassion, because in this moment that was all it was, simple and sincere. Behind him, the fire sparked and crackled as the logs settled on the grate.

"Everyone," she said after a long, expectant moment.

"And who is everyone?"

She hesitated. "My whole family."

"You said before you were an only child?"

Another hesitation; was she lying about even this? "Yes," she said at last, the word gusted out of her.

"I'm sorry."

She gave a shrug; such sentiments were, Sam knew, all too cheap.

Sam walked over to the sofa opposite her and sat down. They remained silent for a few minutes, the only sounds that of the fire and Margarete's snoring. Anna sat very still, her forest green dress almost the same color as the upholstery of the sofa she sat on.

"Your dress is very pretty," he said at last, and Anna's hand fluttered by the sweetheart neckline.

"Thank you. I had one like it, before the war. It feels like such a very long time ago."

"What was your life like, before the war?"

"Happy, although perhaps I did not think so at the time." She gave him a faint smile. "I was... how do I say..." She paused, her forehead crinkling as she tried to think of the elusive word.

"Unhappy?" Sam suggested, and she gave a little, impatient shake of her head. "Discontented?"

"Yes, perhaps that is it. Discontented. I always wished for things to be better."

"I suppose we're all like that, a bit."

"Yes, perhaps."

"Did you like working in your father's store?"

For a second she looked at him as if she didn't know what he was talking about, and then she nodded slowly. "The store. Yes." She took a sip of her schnapps. "What about you, Captain Houghton? What family have you left behind in America?"

"I have a kid sister, Nancy." Sam smiled at the thought of her. "She's twenty-two, which I find hard to remember. I keep thinking of her as about sixteen."

"Yes. We freeze people as we remember them." Anna smiled and nodded.

"She's always teasing me, telling me I shouldn't be so serious, that I need to get a girlfriend." He paused, realizing how that might sound, and he shifted in his seat. "I suppose I might, when I'm demobbed. Back in America, I mean, after all this. Then, I will. Hopefully."

"Yes." Anna hid her smile behind her glass, and Sam let out a sudden laugh.

"I'm making a fool of myself, aren't I?"

"No." But her smile had deepened, revealing a dimple. He realized how much he liked seeing her smile. He wanted to make her laugh.

"It's just… I don't want you to think… I know there's lots of guys who seem to think that German women…" He trailed off, embarrassed yet glad he'd at least said something, inarticulate and fumbling as it had been. He felt the need to set the record straight.

"Do not worry, Captain Houghton," Anna said. "I do not think that."

"But you did." If he hadn't that extra glass of wine, and the schnapps on top of it, he never would have said as much.

Anna's eyes widened but she said nothing.

"When I walked you to your door," Sam continued, determined, now, to have the truth. "You thought I'd ask to come in. That I'd… demand it, even."

She drew a breath and released it in a long, soft sigh. "I did wonder," she admitted. "It is only because… because there have been so many…" She trailed off, shaking her head, and Sam realized he didn't actually want her to finish that sentence.

"I thought about it," he confessed, holding her gaze, wondering if it was the alcohol or just the loneliness that had emboldened him to say as much. "But I wouldn't. Ever. Not if… not if you didn't want me to."

A flush touched her cheeks, painting them rosy, and her head was angled so he could see the curve of her shoulder, the soft, white skin of her neck. A few tendrils of hair curled on her nape.

"I'm sorry," Sam said eventually. "I shouldn't have said that." He downed the rest of his schnapps as misery took hold of his gut. He'd feared he was going to make a fool of himself today, and now he had.

"No. You do not need to be sorry." Anna glanced up at him, her cheeks even rosier. "In truth, Captain Houghton, if you had asked… I do not know how I would have answered."

Shock turned him speechless for a second. "But you seemed… you seemed frightened."

She gave a little shrug. "Even so. That I cannot help. But I know you are a good man. It… shines out of you."

Which made him sound like a saint, or maybe just a sop. "I'm no angel," he said, and she let out a little laugh.

"I meant it for good, yet you are offended."

He shrugged, smiling a bit shamefacedly. "The good guys don't usually get the girls, do they?"

"They should," Anna replied, her tone turning surprisingly fierce. "They should."

He paused, unsure whether to take the conversation any further. He had never expected her to admit to so much, and yet it left him wanting even more, restless with longing. "And if I did ask?" he finally said, his voice not quite steady. "One day?"

She gazed at him for a long moment, her expression conflicted, making Sam wish he hadn't pressed the point. When she spoke, her voice was soft and sad. "I am not…" She paused, her gaze still lowered. "I am not a good bet, Captain Houghton."

"A good bet?"

"That is the phrase?" She glanced up at him quickly, her dark eyes like liquid, before looking down again.

Sam shifted in his seat, his empty glass cradled between his hands. "It depends on what you mean."

"I am not… I am not a good woman to love." Her lips twisted. "Or even to…" She fluttered one hand. "You know."

Sam did his best not to flush—or to imagine *you know* in any sort of detail. "Why don't you think you are?" he asked.

Anna shook her head. "Too much… has happened."

He frowned. "You mean the war?"

"Yes, everything. I can't…" She blew out a breath, frustrated by her lack of language, and then she looked at him and shrugged. "I can't," she said simply, and Sam wondered what she meant. Couldn't love? Couldn't feel desire? Couldn't risk her heart? He wasn't about to ask her to clarify, and unfortunately, despite the conversation they'd just had, he didn't think it much mattered. She could not, and so he would not. "Besides," Anna said with an attempt at a smile, "there is a woman for you in America, yes?"

"No." Sam glanced down at his drink. "I mean, not yet."

"But you must be thirty, at least. You've had a…" She paused, a crinkle in her nose as she thought of the word, "girlfriend?"

"No. That is, I have," Sam said quickly, flushing again, feeling like a boy. "There was someone a long time ago."

"But…?" Anna's voice was soft.

"But it never went anywhere. I think she was expecting me to ask her to marry me, but I never did." He paused, rotating the glass between his palms as he remembered Helen. She was a geography teacher at a girls' school in Philadelphia; they'd met at various student concerts and plays, and when his friends had needed a fourth for bridge, he'd invited her. Somehow that had led to dinner, and then tennis, and then they were dating.

He'd liked her well enough; she'd been good company, with nice eyes and a warm laugh. Athletic rather than pretty. But as the years had run on, Helen had grown impatient and Sam had done his best to stick his head in the sand. When she'd forced a confrontation, he'd only felt relief, mingled with a little guilt, that he was finally able to say no.

"You broke her heart," Anna suggested with a small smile, and Sam shook his head.

"No, I think I just disappointed her a bit. We weren't…" He paused again, feeling embarrassed. "We didn't love each other. Not like…" Not the way he wanted to love a woman—to breathe her in, to hold her close, to feel like he could never get enough even as he was entirely, utterly complete. He was a foolish romantic, he supposed.

Anna seemed far more pragmatic. "There's still time for you to find someone."

"And for you, Anna." He leaned forward, earnest now. "Don't give up on your life just because of the war."

Anna stared at him for a moment, the ghost of a smile still curving her lips, although her eyes looked haunted, two dark, wide pools that held far too many secrets. "I think life has given up on me, Captain Houghton."

On the sofa, Margarete stirred with a snort-like snore, and dropping her gaze from his, Anna rose from her seat.

"It is getting late. We should go. I will wake Margarete."

Sam watched in a half-drunken stupor as she gently shook her friend by the shoulder and spoke softly in German. Margarete came awake with a fearful suddenness as she lurched upright, her blank expression one of complete terror, before her gaze focused on Sam and she gave him a winning smile. He could still see the fear lurking behind her eyes, and he felt sick. What did "a difficult war" mean, really?

Slowly he rose from the sofa; his body ached and his head throbbed. He longed to take Anna in his arms, simply to comfort her, all the while knowing he never would. She was as distant from him now as she'd ever been, and somehow breakable too. He thought if he touched her, she might shatter, and yet he knew her now better than ever.

I am not a good woman to love.

But what if he loved her anyway? He didn't, of course; he didn't know her well enough for that. And yet, his fascination—and his desire—was still strong.

"I've been meaning to tell you," he said as they walked toward the hall and he fetched their coats. "We'll be going to Berlin for a few days after the new year."

Anna turned to face him, her eyes widening. "Berlin? Why?"

"There are some documents there I need to cross-check with the *fragebogen*. Files of Nazi Party membership. So we can find out which scientists are the real Nazis."

Her hand fluttered by the neckline of her dress, just as it had when he'd told her it was pretty, her finger pressing into the hollow of her throat as if reminding herself of something, anchoring herself to an invisible touchstone. "And then what will you do?"

"That's not up to me to decide. Prosecute them, I hope." He frowned, taking in her wide eyes, her fingers still fluttering. "What is it?"

"Nothing." She dropped her hand and reached for her coat. When her gaze met his, it was as coolly composed as it ever had been. "Thank you for the lovely dinner, Captain."

CHAPTER SIXTEEN

Berlin, June 1940

Summer had finally arrived, with bright sunshine, wide blue skies, and warm teasing breezes—and the fall of France. Liesel stretched out on the grainy sand of the lido at Wannsee, watching as Fritz and a few of his friends tossed a ball between them a short distance away, their bodies tanned and muscular as they dodged between families sitting on blankets, heedless of the sand they kicked up.

The beach was full of Berliners desperate to soak up the sunshine and, for a few hours, forget the war. It had been a dark and dreary winter, as everyone tried to maintain a sense of normality, to keep the war on the fringes of their consciousness, even though it could be felt more and more each day.

As Germany had racked up more successes—Poland, then Denmark and Norway, and finally France—the cautious dark-eyed wariness of September gave way to a collective ebullient swagger. The victory in France had culminated with a three-day holiday and a raft of celebratory parades. All of it made Liesel tired, and glad for the break of a simple afternoon on the beach, with nothing to focus on but sun and sand and sky.

She tilted her face to the sun and closed her eyes, grateful for the moment of quiet, just as Fritz jogged over to where she was sitting, throwing himself down next to her with a careless shower of both water and sand.

"Hey," Liesel protested, holding up her hands against the spray, and in response, Fritz leaned over and gave her a lingering kiss.

He'd been doing that more and more lately; sometimes Liesel suspected that now that he was actually flying on missions he'd gained a cocksure confidence that had transferred to their fledgling relationship. For they *did* have a relationship, something that continued to surprise her, almost as if Liesel were not a willing participant in it, despite it being a year since he'd started taking her out.

"Fritz," she said, a bit reprovingly, as she glanced around at the families assembled on the beach—stern hausfraus in modest swimsuits, surrounded by their sedate blond children.

"What?" He leaned back on his elbows, laughing. His muscled chest glistened with water droplets and his blond hair was slicked back from his high, aristocratic forehead. "Who cares what a bunch of frumpy hausfraus think? Besides, that could be you one day." He nodded meaningfully toward a middle-aged woman nearby who looked rather grim-faced as she sliced a sausage for her children while they waited with wide-eyed patience, all seated cross-legged on a blanket.

"What?" Liesel let out a hard note of disbelieving laughter as she realized what he was implying. "I don't think so."

Fritz arched an eyebrow. "Don't you want to get married?"

"Not while there's a war on," Liesel replied firmly.

"And what about doing *your* duty for the Führer?" he added, waggling his eyebrows in a way that was meant to make her laugh but decidedly did not. "You could try for the gold Cross of Honor."

Liesel pressed her lips together and decided to say nothing. The Cross of Honor of the German Mother had been instituted last year, awarded to women who bore at least four children. The gold cross was for women who bore eight.

"Well?" Fritz demanded, now sounding slightly petulant.

"I don't think so," she said again, lighter this time, trying for a laugh, but Fritz's expression had turned serious and a little sulky.

"But you do want children, don't you?" he asked after a moment. "And marriage? One day?"

Liesel hesitated, caught completely by surprise at this sudden turn in the conversation. She had been stepping out with Fritz for a year, but she had not remotely thought about marriage. She rarely even thought of romance, despite the more frequent kisses. She didn't want to think of either, not in relation to Fritz.

He was a distraction, nothing more, a way to while away the time and not think of all the things that scared her. As for someone else, some hazy person in the distant future whom she might love and be loved by in return, right now it felt like a fairy tale, a dream to keep for the time when it was possible to think of such things. Perhaps one day it would be.

"I'm only eighteen," she finally said, with a little laugh.

"The Führer believes women should get married as soon as possible," Fritz replied. "Eighteen is practically on the shelf."

Liesel couldn't tell if he was being serious or not; she decided he had to be joking.

"And I suppose I must listen to the Führer on this rather personal matter," she teased, and for a second Fritz's face darkened.

"You shouldn't joke like that," he returned rather shortly, and Liesel stared at him in surprise.

She'd never spoken to Fritz against Hitler, or the war, or the fact that Jews were now being forced into ghettoes, although not yet in Berlin. She'd never breathed a word of the discontent and fear that constantly surged and seethed within her, impotent as it was. She hadn't told him how she hated Hitler, and the SS, and the cringing fear that lurked beneath the misplaced patriotic pride in every Berliner.

She'd said none of this, not even a whisper of it, and yet now he was looking at her with a faint frown settling between his fair brows, his lips thinned as if she'd displeased him and needed to be disciplined.

"I wasn't joking," she replied before she could think better of it, and Fritz's frown deepened, his lips a hard, flat line.

"Liesel, I'm serious."

"So am I." Her heart felt as if it were being squeezed in her chest.

They stared at each other for a moment and then, with an irritated sigh, Fritz stood up, yanking the blanket with a sharp tug so Liesel had to scramble off it or be dumped in the sand.

"We should get going. I have to be back at the base by six."

They walked in silence to the S-Bahn station at Nikolassee. Liesel knew she wasn't imagining the chill that had sprung up between them, although she could hardly believe it to be so. Why was light, laughing Fritz, who cared more for flying than fighting, now trying to pick one with her? And over the absurd *Mutterkreuz*! She would have laughed, save for the fear cramping her stomach.

Fritz was Göring's godson, yet another thing she tried not to think about. He didn't seem like a Nazi, and she always did her best to act as if he wasn't. Now she remembered.

"When will I see you again?" she asked as they walked into Nikolassee's neogothic station, with its arched windows and tall clock tower.

"I don't know." Fritz hunched one shoulder, his face turned away from her as he cupped his hand to light a cigarette. "I don't know when I next get leave."

Liesel stared at him for a moment, wanting to say something to dispel this sense of distance, yet also longing only to walk away. She didn't care enough about Fritz, she realized, to make an effort, but perhaps, for her own safety, she needed to.

"Maybe I will try for a bronze," she finally said, summoning a smile, but Fritz only frowned at her before striding toward the platform, leaving Liesel no choice but to follow.

*

By the time she reached Grunewald, with Fritz traveling on to the airbase at Gatow, Liesel was hot, sticky, and tired. The festive, party-like atmosphere of the city over the last few days had flattened into something gray and faded, as if reality were finally encroaching again. They were at war. No matter how many victories or triumphant parades there were, it could not be forgotten.

Fritz had not spoken to her once as the S-Bahn had rattled north, and he'd barely said goodbye when she'd got off at Berlin-Grunewald. Now, as she stepped into the dim interior of the house on Koenigsallee, she wondered if she should finish with Fritz altogether; she'd enjoyed his lighthearted company, but if he was going to get serious on her—in different sorts of ways—she wasn't sure he was worth the effort, or potentially the danger. Yet ending things might not be as straightforward as she'd like, especially if Fritz was suspicious of her loyalties. Besides, what else would she do with her time, her life? The days stretched in front of her, both empty and perilous.

As Liesel shed her light jacket, she heard the clatter of pots and pans from the kitchen as Helga made supper, and she noticed that the drawing-room curtains were closed, and most likely had been all day, because her mother hadn't yet decided to rise from bed.

Her father had been at the factory at Schkopau all week, and his absence meant that Ilse made even less of an effort than usual, often spending the whole day in bed, rising only to eat and sometimes not even that. Sometimes Liesel thought her mother intended to sleep away the entire war. Her father had been spending more and more time away, usually in Schkopau, although last week he'd gone to Poland. He hadn't said why, and Liesel hadn't asked.

With a weary sigh, she sifted through the pile of post that had been accumulating on the hall table in her father's absence, the usual mixture of propaganda leaflets and bills, only to pause when she came across a slim envelope addressed to her parents, and stamped with the address *Tiergartenstrasse 4, the Reich Committee for the Scientific Registering of Serious Hereditary and Congenital Illnesses.*

Liesel stared at the address blankly; she'd never heard of it, but, of course, there had to be hundreds of shadowy Reich committees controlling every aspect of life from behind the scenes, pulling puppet strings, watching and recording. Just looking at the stark, black typeface on the envelope gave her a chill of foreboding, and in one swift movement, she picked up the silver letter knife on the hall table and slit open the envelope.

> *This is to notify whomever it may concern that Friedrich Scholz, of 58 Koenigsallee, Berlin, child of Otto and Ilse Scholz, has been reported to the Reich Committee for the Scientific Registering of Serious Hereditary and Congenital Illnesses, and the matter is being referred to the relevant authorities who will take appropriate action.*

The words swam before Liesel's eyes as she struggled to take in their undoubtedly malevolent meaning. Relevant authorities? Appropriate action? *Friedy?* What could it possibly mean? Nothing good, she knew. No *referrals* of any sort ever boded well.

With trembling fingers, she stuffed the letter back into its envelope. She wouldn't panic. Whatever it was, her father would sort it out when he returned. As distasteful as it could be, having a father who hobnobbed with the likes of Göring had to have its uses.

"Liesel, look!"

Liesel shoved the letter under the pile of leaflets and bills as Friedy hurried down the stairs, dragging his twisted foot behind him. Was that why? she wondered numbly. A twisted foot was considered a hereditary disease needing referral to some godforsaken committee? If so, then Goebbels himself, with his built-up shoe and decided limp, ought to have received one of the wretched letters, and just like Friedy he should be waiting for the *appropriate action.*

Liesel pressed a hand to her mouth, although whether she was holding back a wild laugh or a desperate sob she didn't know.

"What is it, Friedy?" she asked after a few seconds, when she trusted her voice to sound normal. She had an urge to pull him into her arms, to squeeze him as tightly as she could until he squirmed away. She contented herself with merely brushing the dark hair out of his eyes; he ducked away impatiently from even that touch.

"I got my knife!"

"You did?" She knew Friedrich had been on probation with the *Jungvolk* since September, trying to complete the necessary and onerous tasks to gain full membership. Memorizing all four verses of the *Horst Wessel* song and answering questions about Hitler's life and the Nazi Party had been easy for him; running sixty meters in twelve seconds and completing a day-and-a-half hike had not.

"Yes, I got it today." He held it out to her like a reverent offering to a deity. "Isn't it beautiful?"

Liesel did not think the small knife with its black leather scabbard and diamond insignia was beautiful. It symbolized so much that was wrong with the Reich—the violence, the hatred, the blood, the indoctrination. But she knew she couldn't tell her brother any of that.

"It's lovely, Friedy. Well done. But..." She hesitated, not wanting to ask questions that would only make him angry. "How did you get it? You haven't completed the initiation exercises..."

"Oh, I did all that," he answered with a breezy nonchalance Liesel didn't trust. "It was easy, in the end."

"The day-and-a-half hike…"

"I told you, I did it."

He sounded irritable now, and Liesel decided not to press. She knew he couldn't have done the hike—he hadn't gone on any camping trips in months—but she was reluctant to agitate him when the reality of that awful letter was still pulsing through her.

"Well done, Friedy," she said, and allowed herself another caress of his hair before he jerked away. Friedy reverently slid the knife back into the scabbard.

They ate alone in the dining room; when Liesel had knocked on her mother's door, there had been no reply, but the stale smell of cigarette smoke and schnapps had lingered in the air like an ill-conceived perfume.

The house felt cavernous and empty, with her mother shut up in bed and her father absent, as well as Fritz's coolness to consider. After dinner, Liesel went into Friedrich's bedroom to see if he wanted her to read him a story, but with typical ten-year-old worldliness, he scorned the idea.

"I'm still going to kiss you goodnight," Liesel warned him before going downstairs to drift through the empty rooms. She played a few discordant notes on the piano that seemed to fall into the stillness of the room; despite her mother's ability, Liesel had never learned. She vaguely recalled lessons when she had only been six or so; to her mother's great exasperation, she'd deliberately slammed the lid on her fingers to keep from having to practice, and she wondered now why she'd been so stubborn and what happened to that strength of will she no longer seemed to possess.

As twilight settled on the city, Liesel drew the blackout curtains across the windows, shutting the world outside in a way that felt like both a comfort and suffocation. Denmark, Norway, now France. How long would it go on? How long would Hitler enjoy his victories? When the whole world was crushed beneath his merciless heel?

And what of the Jews? So many of them had left, a fact which brought her both relief and sorrow. At least then they were safe, and yet—to leave all your possessions, all your friends, the family who couldn't or wouldn't go with you…

Liesel shuddered at the thought. And yet that was surely better, *far* better, than the alternative. She had not heard from Rosa since she'd seen her at Christmas, although she often looked for her in the street. Would Rosa and her mother have to move into a ghetto one day? Where would it end?

The night was closing in and Liesel went upstairs to tuck Friedy in, pausing by her mother's door but hearing nothing. Friedy was already in bed when she came into his bedroom; he'd drawn the curtains and had a book of rewritten Norse folk tales on his lap that he wasn't reading.

"All right, Friedy?" Liesel asked lightly as she perched on the edge of his bed.

Slowly he closed the book and put it on his bedside table. His forehead was puckered into a frown as he drew in his knobbly knees. His chin drooped toward his chest and he let out a heavy sigh that seemed to come from the depths of his being.

"Friedy?" Liesel prompted gently.

"I wasn't given the knife." The words came out in a wretched whisper of confession.

Liesel regarded him quietly, unsure how to navigate this moment.

"How did you get it then?" she asked after a pause.

"Hans gave it to me. He had two, because his older brother doesn't use his anymore. He's joined the Wehrmacht." He bit his lip. "He shouldn't have, I know, and I can't even show anyone I have it, because everyone knows I haven't been initiated." His face seemed to collapse as he kicked his legs out, rumpling the bedsheets. "And I won't ever be, Liesel. I can't do that stupid race. I never will."

"Oh, Friedy." Her heart ached for him. Even though she'd rather he had nothing to do with the *Jungvolk*, she hated seeing him looking so sad, knowing he would never measure up.

This had to be why they'd received the letter from that awful committee. Someone in the DJ must have reported Friedy for not being able to do the sixty-meter sprint or the wretched hike. Yet what could it mean?

"Don't try to worry about it so much," she told him, even though she knew he would, and she would, as well. "There are so many other things in life besides being in the *Jungvolk*."

"There aren't," he retorted mutinously, and Liesel kissed his forehead. For once, Friedy did not squirm away.

How was it, she wondered as she left his bedroom, that a boy who was utterly devoted to the Führer, who *Sieg Heiled* when hearing him pontificate on the radio, who dreamed of possessing the DJ knife more than anything, could be turned away from the *Jungvolk* and his heart's desire, and for no good reason?

And what of the appropriate action that might be taken? Would he not be allowed to attend the DJ meetings? Or did that letter hint at something darker?

As with so many other things, Liesel was afraid to think. She longed for her father to return; as much as she hated his politics, she feared she needed them now.

CHAPTER SEVENTEEN

Berlin, June 1940

They came at night, just a few days after the letter, while her father was still in Schkopau. It was a sultry summer's evening, the humid air making everything feel sticky and damp, when Liesel opened the door to two strangers—a kindly-looking nurse who introduced herself as Frau West, and a serious-eyed but smiling doctor called Menzler. She thought they were there for yet another collection, perhaps for wounded soldiers, when Dr. Menzler spoke in a kindly but firm tone.

"You should have received a letter."

Liesel froze at the simply stated words. She knew what letter he meant, of course; it was right there on the hall table, still stuffed inside its crumpled envelope. She'd done her best to forget about it, at least until her father came home, but she hadn't. It had pulsed malevolently all the while, reminding her of her own ignorance, taunting her with its unknown threat. Now she stared at the Herr Doktor with his firm smile and hard eyes and felt an unknown terror seize her, turn her speechless.

Finally, her voice close to a croak, she managed, "Yes, but it must be a mistake. There's no one like that here."

"May we come in?" Menzler spoke as if she had not; he was already stepping across the threshold with firm purpose. Liesel had moved out of his way before she realized what she was doing.

"My father isn't home," she said, her voice sounding high and thin. "He manages a factory in Schkopau that is very important to the Reich. He is there on business."

Menzler gave her a tolerant smile, brushing aside her words like a fly that was not worth his notice. "Where is Friedrich Scholz?"

Liesel hid her shaking hands in her skirt. "What do you want with him? He's not ill."

"He is a very lucky boy, Fraulein," Frau West told her warmly. Her face was as round as an apple, with eyes like buttons. She looked kind, but Liesel knew not to trust her. "He has been selected for participation in a course of specialized treatment for children with hereditary conditions."

"But he doesn't have a hereditary condition," Liesel answered numbly. She hated how weak she sounded. Already she could feel the conversation slipping away from her, as desperate as she was to hold onto it. "He only has a twisted foot, from a difficult birth. That's all. It's not hereditary. It's barely noticeable." She thought of mentioning Goebbels' own twisted foot, but decided it would be better not to.

There was a hard knife's edge to Menzler's smile as he repeated, "Where is Friedrich?"

"I'm here." Friedy stood at the top of the stairs, one hand on the banister as he gazed down at them all. His shirt collar was crumpled, his shorts creased. He looked pitifully thin, hiding his twisted foot behind him, a look of wary confusion on his face at the sight of two strangers in their hall.

Menzler looked up, his shrewd gaze appraising Friedy in every last damaging detail—the foot, the thin chest, the myopic gaze. "Did you hear what Frau West said, Friedrich?" he asked, his voice turning as warm as the nurse's. "You are going to a special place to have treatment. You are a very fortunate boy. The Führer cares so much for you, he wants you to get better. Isn't that wonderful?"

"He does?" Friedy's face brightened unbearably. Liesel had to bite her lip to keep from crying out. "Will he fix my foot?"

"Oh, undoubtedly." Menzler sounded so sure, so *kind*, that for a second Liesel let herself doubt. It would be so much easier, so much better, to believe they meant what they said. Perhaps there were medicines, surgeries… why shouldn't they want to help Friedy, a devoted son of the Reich, the child of a prominent Nazi? It made *sense,* and yet…

"When do I go?" Friedy asked. He sounded like a child who had been promised a trip to the zoo, his voice high with childish excitement.

"Right now. We have a car waiting."

"Now?" His face flushed with pleasure. "Oh! I'll pack my things—"

"Friedy—" Liesel began, helplessly, for Menzler was already cutting across her, his voice smooth and assured.

"Oh, don't worry, Friedrich," he said. "There is nothing to pack. Everything you need will be at the hospital."

"You want me to go right now?" Friedy sounded as if he couldn't believe his luck, even as a flicker of uncertainty shadowed his eyes.

"Yes, right now. As I said, our car is waiting."

"I need to say goodbye to my Mutti—"

"Let us not trouble her," Menzler returned with a kindly smile. "Goodbyes are hard for muttis, aren't they? Your sister can tell her what has happened. Think how she will rejoice and thank the Führer, when you return."

Liesel's stomach clenched so hard, she thought she might be sick. "He's not going," she blurted.

"But Liesel, he *said*—"

"Be quiet, Friedy." Liesel's voice shook as she turned to Menzler, who was gazing at her with a mixture of impatience and disdain, both badly concealed by a tight smile. "He's not going," she repeated. She had to hold onto the doorway to steady herself, for her legs were trembling. "At least not until my father can approve. As I said, he is a very important person to the—"

"Assuredly. But I have an order here, to take Friedrich now." Menzler's voice had turned steely; all pretense of kindness had dropped like the flimsy mask it was. "I'm afraid you have no choice in this matter, Fraulein."

"You cannot take a child away from his family like this," Liesel insisted, futilely, because she knew they could. They could do anything they wanted. If she resisted, they could have her arrested. They could take *her* away, and not to a special hospital.

"He is going to a good place," Frau West assured her. "Don't be selfish in keeping him here with you. We must think of the good of the Reich."

"I want to go, Liesel," Friedy told her as he came down the stairs, dragging his twisted foot behind him, a detail that did not escape the notice of both Menzler and West, Liesel could tell. "I want to get better so I can join the *Jungvolk*." He laid one hand on her arm, looking up at her with a heartbreaking mixture of maturity and naivete. "Then I'll get my knife for keeps."

The next few moments seemed to happen in slow motion, or as if she were underwater, unable to speak or even breathe. Menzler opened the front door, and Friedy turned to him with a trusting smile.

"Will I need my coat?" he asked and Menzler smiled and shook his head.

"I don't think so. It's so warm."

Liesel watched with a dazed sense of unreality as Friedy skipped across the hallway and slipped his hand in Frau West's. She knew exactly what was going on in his innocent, untroubled little mind; he felt chosen at last, accepted and cared for, despite, or even because of his poor crooked foot, and she feared the terrible opposite was true. Would they lock him away somewhere?

Leave him in some hospital room to languish for the rest of the war? When would she see him again?

"You can't do this," she tried again, laying her hand on Menzler's arm. He glanced down at it as if it were something distasteful. "My father will be so angry," she insisted, her voice growing stronger with the desperate strength of her conviction. "He is an important man, a personal friend of the Generalfeldmarschall's—"

"I do not know your father," Menzler stated coolly, "but I know my orders. And as you can see, your brother is more than happy to accompany us."

"Don't fret, Liesel," Friedy insisted, that old irritableness creeping into his voice. "I'm not a baby."

"*Friedy*—"

"Good day, Fraulein Scholz."

The door had closed behind them before Liesel had even blinked. She stared at it in disbelief for a second; Menzler and his sidekick nurse hadn't been in the house for five minutes, and now her brother was *gone?*

Startled into action, Liesel wrenched open the front door and shouted her brother's name into the night, her throat raw with the panicked effort, as a car pulled away from the curb and then disappeared into the darkness.

For a few seconds she simply stood there, her mind spinning blankly. Then she ran upstairs to her parents' bedroom, pounding on the locked door until her mother finally stumbled over to open it.

"Liesel, for the love of—"

"They've taken Friedy."

Ilse's sleepy, befuddled expression cleared in an instant as she stared at Liesel in shock. "What?"

"A doctor and a nurse. There was a letter from some committee for hereditary diseases—it came a few days ago. I was waiting until Father got home, but then they came and they've taken him away in a car." The words poured out in a jumbled, half-hysterical rush; Liesel felt herself shaking.

Her mother stared at her for a long, suspended moment and then, to Liesel's shock, she slapped her across the face, hard enough to make her ears ring. Liesel raised one hand to her throbbing cheek; she had never been hit before in her life.

"How dare you," Ilse said in a low, deadly voice. "How dare you let them take my son?"

"How dare *I*...!" A sudden, terrible fury rose up in Liesel like a spitting, hissing viper. "How dare you blame *me*, when you've been in a drunken stupor for the last two years?"

As quickly as her rage came, it went; Liesel watched as her mother seemed to collapse in on herself, her head bowed, her shoulders shaking with sobs.

"We need to call Father," Liesel said. Her mind was clearing even as her body still shook. "As quickly as we can. There must be some way to get in touch with him. He can do something."

"He's at Schkopau. It's impossible."

"It's *Friedy*, Mutti. I don't know where they've taken him. They said a hospital somewhere. But they didn't even give an address!" With an icy, hollowed-out feeling, Liesel realized afresh just how terribly suspicious it had all been. There had been no papers to sign, no real information given. No hospital mentioned—nothing but a *special place*. And special places in the Reich were surely not where anyone wanted to go. How could she have let them take him? And yet how could she have not? "And they said he didn't need any clothes," she whispered, "not even a coat."

Ilse's face paled and then she straightened her shoulders, wiping the tears from her eyes before she headed to the hall telephone with grim purpose. "We'll find a way," she said. "We must."

It took over an hour, but they finally got a message through to Otto. Two hours later—the trip from Schkopau was usually just over—he was striding through the door, his face etched with lines of strain and anger.

"What are you talking about?" he demanded without preamble. "Who took him? Where? Why?"

Haltingly, Liesel explained about Dr. Menzler and Frau West; she showed him the letter from the Reich Committee for the Scientific Registering of Serious Hereditary and Congenital Illnesses, and all the while her father's face grew darker and darker with fury.

"This is a mistake," he said as he thrust the letter away from him. "This never should have happened."

"Do you know where they've taken him, Otto?" Ilse sounded like a frightened child. "Can you do something?"

"I'll find out." Without another word, he turned around and strode out of the house.

Liesel and her mother passed an endless night of agonized wondering; sleep was out of the question for either of them. Liesel made coffee from her father's precious beans and they sat in the drawing room, drinking it in silence, as the marble clock on the mantle marked the hours and eventually the sky lightened to a pearly gray, a chink of gloomy light glimpsed between the heavy blackout curtains.

Still there was no word. At seven in the morning, Helga came in with her usual cheer, shouting *Sieg Heil* to a stony-faced Ilse and an exhausted Liesel before, bemused by their lack of reaction, she headed into the kitchen, from where there emerged a loud, discontented clatter of a bucket and mop. Liesel knew the housekeeper had an affection for Friedy, but she could not bear to explain the situation to her now.

Ilse went to the window and looked out at the street; people were going to work, heads lowered against a damp summer sky.

"Where do you suppose they took him?" she asked tonelessly. It was the first time either of them had spoken in hours.

"They said a hospital, to help his foot."

"As if they want to help his foot." Ilse let out a sound that was half hard laugh, half moan of despair. She leaned forward to rest her head against the cool glass of the windowpane. "How could this happen to us?" she whispered. "We were meant to be safe. He *promised*."

Liesel did not bother to reply. They both knew that in this brave new world, no one was safe, not even Göring's pet scientist, his much-feted protégé. The realization was as absolute as it was terrifying.

At ten o'clock in the morning, Liesel rose to wash and dress, and advised her mother to do the same.

"We don't know what's going to happen. We might need to go somewhere, to fetch him. Or… answer questions." She had no idea what might be required of them, but she wanted to be prepared.

Ilse nodded wordlessly.

By half past ten they were both dressed, if in a rather uninspired collection of clothes, and back in the sitting room, waiting for Otto's return.

The day slipped by, hour by painstaking hour. Helga dusted around them, disgruntled by their presence; Liesel brought her mother some bread and cheese and bid her to eat, which she didn't.

At six, Helga went home, having left a meal in the kitchen that no one would bother with, and still they waited. Liesel's eyes itched with fatigue and her body felt jittery from lack of food and too much coffee, her muscles stiff from sitting for so long. Where was Friedy? Why had her father not sent word, at least?

Then, at seven o'clock in the evening, as the light was beginning to be leached from the sky, he came home. Ilse rose from the sofa at the sound of the door, her hands at her throat, her eyes dark pools of fear, as Otto came into the drawing room, his face haggard and gray with weariness—and something worse, something dark and terrible in their depths that made Liesel catch her breath. He was holding Friedrich's hand.

"Friedy!" Ilse cried, and fell to her knees in front of her son, her arms coming round his frail body.

Friedy gazed at her almost unseeingly, his thin shoulders slumped, his expression vacant. There was a smear of dirt on his cheek.

Liesel looked at her father, a silent question.

"It was an administrative error," he stated tonelessly. He turned away, taking off his hat to rake a hand through his hair that, Liesel saw, was more gray than brown. She had not noticed until that moment, just how old he was becoming. "Just an administrative error." He nodded toward Friedy without looking at him. "He needs food, and a bath, and bed." A shudder went through him and he shrugged off his coat, dumping it heedlessly on the sofa.

"I will see to him." Ilse tenderly took Friedrich by the hand and led him toward the kitchen. He went docilely; he hadn't spoken since he'd come into the house, and he didn't speak as he went with her into the kitchen.

Liesel glanced back at her father; he had his back to her, his head bowed, his hands braced on the mantelpiece, on either side of the clock that continued to tick on, relentlessly marking the hours. He looked like a man who was near to breaking, or worse, one who had already broken and did not know how to put himself together.

"What happened, Vati? Where was he?"

Her father simply shook his head.

"Please, tell me," she insisted, her voice rising to a high quaver. "I need to know. I was the one who spoke to them, who *let* them—"

"You couldn't have known, Liesel." There was a wealth of knowledge, of grief, in his voice. "No one could have known."

"Known *what?*"

Otto was silent for a long moment, his back still to her, his head bowed. "They took him to Schloss Hartheim," he said at last.

"Schloss Hartheim…" Liesel had never heard of the castle. "Where is that?"

"In Austria. About seven hours away."

Liesel's mind spun. "So far…"

"Fortunately I managed to arrive there only a few hours after Friedrich did." Another shudder went through him, a visceral response to the story he was relating. "Thank God, Thank *God* I did."

"Vati…"

"They kill them, Liesel." Her father spoke so quietly that she had to strain to hear the words, and even then she thought she must have misheard. "It isn't a castle," he continued, "Not anymore. It's a killing station. For disabled or congenitally ill children. Adults, too. They inject them with poison or gas them in sealed chambers, because they're deemed not worthy to live."

She stared at his hunched back, wanting to see his face, to gauge his tone, his expression, because his words couldn't possibly make any sense. Even in her worst moments of foreboding or fear, she had not thought of such a thing. To be hospitalized, yes, to be locked up for a time, perhaps… but to be *killed?* Murdered, in utter cold blood? A child?

She thought of Menzler's kindly smile. *You won't need your coat.*

"No…" she whispered.

"Yes. I saw it with my own eyes. They lie to the parents and say they are getting special treatment and then they are killed, because they are a blight on the Reich, with their imperfect bodies, their inferior minds." Her father's voice was flat, betraying nothing. "That is what happens."

"But Friedy…"

"When I came, they'd put him in a room. A cell, almost. There were others…" His voice broke and he shook his head. "I had to telephone the Generalfeldmarschall himself. If I hadn't been able to contact him…" He let out a shuddering breath. "I don't know what would have happened."

"They would have killed Friedy." The words fell from her lips like stones into the stillness. She realized she should not be surprised. She'd seen the newsreels before the films, emphasizing children who were fit and healthy and whole. The hunched shoulders of a dribbling cripple, the angry declaration about how many marks it took to care for someone like that. She'd let it all pass over her, she'd let herself not care, because Friedy wasn't like that. Except, according to the Reich, it seemed he was.

Her father didn't answer, and a helpless fury welled up in Liesel.

"These are the people you work for," she spat. "*This* is your precious party."

"The people I work for *saved* Friedy," Otto retorted, his voice dropping to a savage hiss. "If I hadn't been able to call on someone as highly ranked as Göring, your brother would have been killed."

"Killed by the people, the party, you serve! How can you do it?" The words tore at her throat, scraped it raw. "How can you serve them, when you know what they're capable of? *An administrative error.*" She spat the words in disgust. "We're talking about lives, children's lives. A castle, a killing station, *full* of administrative errors? Is that how you justify it to yourself?"

"I justify nothing!" Her father's voice came out in an anguished roar as he turned from the fireplace. "And I know it more than you do. I *saw* it, Liesel. I saw it with my own two eyes." He pressed one hand to his eyes as if he could blot out the memory. "And I can never not see it," he finished in something like a groan. "As much as I long to."

"Then stop working for them, Vati, please," Liesel begged. "They're stealing your soul, as surely as Mephistopheles stole Faust's!" Yet in Goethe's famous tale, Faust had willingly given it, thinking he knew the price of such a transaction, and would pay it gladly. Was her father the same, only to later realize the terrible, terrible cost? Could any of them realize how much this war, this world, would cost them all?

"I can't stop, Liesel." He dropped his hand from his eyes as he regarded her with weary yet intractable decision. "I can never stop."

"Why?"

He shook his head, and her frustration bubbled over into fury once more.

"You're a *coward!* You don't want to stop because you're afraid."

"Of course I'm afraid," he snapped. "As you should be. Do you think I could just walk away from my position? Do you think they'd let me?"

"Why shouldn't they?" Liesel countered. "If you just quit…"

Otto let out a hard, humorless laugh. "How can you be so naïve even now, Liesel? No one just *quits*. No one walks away. Not when you've been where I have. Not when you've seen what I've seen."

"What have you seen?" Her heart trembled within her as she braced herself for his answer, but her father just shook his head.

"I can't, Liesel. I can't. It's impossible. I'm both too important and not important enough. Not important at all." He sighed wearily. "The war won't last forever."

And what would happen after the war? A lifetime of this fear and uncertainty, this cruelty and violence? She couldn't bear the thought. "So you'd rather sell your soul?"

"You don't have to be so melodramatic." He took a deep, steadying breath. "I know terrible things are happening. This… this *committee* to kill children… it's evil. I know that. Of course

I do. Any sane person does! But I'm not part of anything evil, Liesel. I'm a chemist. I make *rubber*. That's all I do. I can't be responsible for everything the Nazis wreak on society. It's not fair to act as if I am."

Liesel stared at him for a long moment, taking in the haggard, careworn lines of his face, the rounded stoop to his shoulders. He'd aged a decade in the last year, and nearly as much in a single evening. He was only forty-seven, yet he looked like an old, broken man.

"You can be responsible for your own actions," she stated quietly. "You could refuse—"

"The cost would simply be too high," he cut across her. "Can't you see that? I would be killed—you and your mother would be sent to a camp. And what do you think would happen to Friedy?" He shook his head sorrowfully. "I wish it were another way."

He sounded so resigned that Liesel almost felt sorry for him. Then she remembered how, all along, her father had courted power—from his flashy suit at the Olympics to cigars at Carinhall. Her father had *wanted* this. He might feel powerless now, but he hadn't been then. Surely there was still some choice left to him?

"There must be a way you could leave," she insisted. "Claim ill health, or Mother's health, that you need to be at home for her. You could do *that,* surely. You just don't want to pay the price."

He blinked, a flash of hurt crossing his face. "Liesel, any way I tried to leave… it would mean my life."

Liesel lifted her chin. "'To think is easy, to act is hard.' You said that to me at the Olympics, before any of this had really begun. Is it too hard for you, Vati?"

"Do you *want* me to die?" He sounded incredulous as well as pained.

"No, but I want you to live with honor. You *could* quit. We could run away. The Jews are doing it. They forge papers, they are smuggled out even now—"

"With absolutely nothing to their names, and at great risk to their lives and to the lives of anyone who helps them! It isn't as if they can just get on a bus or train, Liesel."

"I would rather have nothing and be free of all this," Liesel cried. "This house is a prison, Vati! It's a *tomb*. Why can't you see that? Why can't you be willing to let it all go?"

"Everything I've worked for? My career, my reputation?"

"We could go to America. You always insisted we learn English! Why should we not use it? There must be many universities or companies that would be glad to have you." The idea suddenly seemed so wildly plausible—Liesel could practically see them tucked away in some leafy town in America, driving a big car, living in a house with a white picket fence like in the films, although they were so heavily censored these days that hardly any American films made it to German screens.

"You think they would gladly welcome a scientist who was a member of the Nazi Party?" Otto shook his head. "I don't think so."

"You could give them intelligence about your research. There must be so many things you know that they would want to learn—"

He recoiled at that. "And now you want me to commit treason?"

"Treason!" She stared at him in disbelief, only to realize with a cold, plunging sensation that he would never, ever leave, and it wasn't just fear that was keeping him there. It was patriotism as well as ambition. Even now, when his own son had been about to be killed by the government he served, her father could not abandon his party, his country, his career.

Something of what she felt must have been visible in her face for he gave a little, shamefaced smile. "I know I've disappointed you. For that I am sorry."

"For *that*? What about for the Jews being rounded up all over the country? What about for the children being killed as we speak—"

"Liesel." Wearily, he passed a hand over his eyes. "Please, can you not blame me for every single one of the country's woes?"

"We won't blame you," Ilse said from the doorway, her voice ringing out hard and flat, "but neither will we absolve you. It ends here, Otto."

He stared at her uncertainly, his forehead creased. "What ends here?"

"Our marriage," she declared flatly. "I won't support you any longer. I won't attend your parties. I won't stand by your side."

"You've hardly done that in over a year," Otto snapped, riled. "So I suppose it doesn't matter."

She kept his gaze. "I won't sleep in your bed."

He flinched as if she'd struck him. "Ilse…"

"It ends here. Tonight I am no longer your wife."

Liesel bit her lip as her father's eyes filled with anguish.

"You are speaking out of your hurt and fear. I understand that. Please, let's not argue now. Let's sleep, rest, and then consider what is best to do…"

"I am not going to change my mind." Liesel had never heard her mother sound so certain.

"It wasn't my fault," Otto whispered. "I didn't even know about this wretched committee, and it was I who saved him. If I hadn't called Göring…"

"Don't mention that man to me." Ilse turned away. "If you hadn't followed him like a dog with its master, we wouldn't be here. We would have left long ago, like I asked. Like I *begged*. We would have gone to England or to America, like you once said we would. Why did the children learn English, if not for that?" This was news to Liesel, and yet she realized she was not surprised that her mother had wanted such a thing, just as she had. "But you wanted to stay, for your own sake."

"For the sake of my country—"

"For the sake of your own ambition. You saw how you could rise here, with your Jewish colleagues and competitors out of the way. Abraham Stern was twice the chemist you've ever been." Otto flinched but said nothing. "This is not my Germany," Ilse stated, "and you are not my husband. I have nothing more to say to you." She turned and walked out of the room.

"Liesel…" Her father turned to her in pathetic, pleading appeal, his hands spread out in supplication, and Liesel stared at him helplessly. Even now, she loved him.

"I'm sorry, Vati," she whispered.

"Please don't hate me." He sounded broken and old, and it tore at her heart.

"I don't hate you," she said, but she wondered if she should.

CHAPTER EIGHTEEN

Frankfurt, January 1946

The black Mercedes sped down the autobahn, past low-lying fields glittering with frost under a bright blue sky. The mild weather of December had given way to a cold, hard January; the air seemed to spark with it, like flint on steel.

Sam glanced at Anna, who sat next to him, her gloved hands laced together in her lap, her face turned to the window so he could see the smooth, pale curve of her cheek, the fullness of her lips. *I am not an easy woman to love.*

The trouble was, he'd been thinking, since Christmas, that she was. Or at least she was an easy woman to become fascinated with, as he had been since he'd first met her, with her quiet beauty, her soft voice, that sense of containment and her cloak of sorrow. Sam had been thinking of her all week, even though he'd been trying not to. There hadn't been much else to occupy either his thoughts or time; he'd had several days' vacation from work, with nothing to do but think, read, or walk the marshy grasslands around Bergen-Enkheim.

At least now they were on their way to Berlin, with a folder full of names and a job to do. Sam was glad for the sense of purpose both gave him. He needed it. Perhaps Anna did, as well.

Major Lewis had made it clear before he'd left that his brief was simply to "find the scientists"; other agents and archivists would be sorting through the nearly fifty tons of material, much of it to provide evidence for the war trials that were continuing after a hiatus over the holidays.

Sometimes Sam wondered if his task was actually possible; even if he did "find the scientists," he was only finding their files. The men themselves could be anywhere—fled to South America, hiding in some remote village in Bavaria, or even hidden in plain sight.

"Leave that to the field agents," Lewis had told him with a patronizing smile when Sam had voiced the concern, before leaving for Berlin. "We just need the names and the photographs."

As they approached Berlin, with its flat, barren fields and marshy woodlands stretching out in every direction, Sam noticed that Anna had become tenser, her hands now clenched into fists in her lap, her alert gaze moving over the outskirts of the ruined city, the bombed-out buildings and cratered streets, the stark black and white sign declaring that "You Are Now Entering The American Sector. Carrying Weapons Off Duty Forbidden. Obey Traffic Rules."

While almost all of Germany had been bombed, Berlin had also been carved up like a Christmas goose, with the city itself divided into four districts—the Soviets had the most territory in the eastern part of the city, while the British, French, and Americans had divided the western districts between themselves.

"Have you ever been to Berlin before?" Sam asked as the car drove carefully down the potholed road toward Grunewald. They were staying in a small hotel on Hochsitzweg, a quiet, leafy street near the Document Center.

Anna hesitated and then replied, "Once or twice."

"Oh? Before the war, I suppose?" Essen had to be at least six hours from Berlin, not a quick trip in the best of times.

"Yes. Before the war." She turned even more toward the window, so he could not see her face at all, almost as if she wanted to hide from him.

Sam sat back, his gaze skating over the ruined buildings, the gray glint of the Wannsee visible in the distance before the car drove on through Zehlendorf, to the hotel in Grunewald, on the edge of the park.

It had taken nearly seven hours to travel to Berlin, thanks to the detours they'd had to take in the places where the autobahn had not yet been repaired from being bombed or deliberately destroyed, and Sam was more than ready to stretch his legs, have a wash and a meal.

"I've booked us for supper at Café Vaterland," he told Anna, and she stiffened all the more. "It's supposed to be a nice place." The restaurant, Sam knew, was at the precise point of all four sectors meeting, with doors to both the western and eastern sides. In a gesture of goodwill and determination to rebuild the city, it had reopened recently to much acclaim. "It was quite a place before the war, I heard," he continued. "With about a dozen different restaurants. Did you ever visit there?"

A pause before she spoke. "Once or twice." The same as before. She certainly wasn't giving anything away.

"That's something I would have liked to see. They had a Wild West Bar, I heard?"

She gave a brief nod, her face still averted. "I never ate in that one."

They were driving through leafy Grunewald now, a mix of rubbled ruins and beautiful old houses with classical fronts in a variety of colors and long, sashed windows. Sam could almost imagine what it must have been like, when Berlin had been a beautiful, cosmopolitan city, buzzing with energy and glamor, instead of the devastated wreck it was now, the pot-holed streets filled with Army Jeeps and commandeered Mercedes, gangs of civilians, mostly women, working on carting wheelbarrows of rubble away, and cranes positioned over the city like giant fingers pointing toward the darkening sky.

Sam had read that eighty percent of Berlin's city center had been destroyed; ruined buildings were now being demolished, while new ones were being put up, the old and the new jumbled together. It was a city that was beleaguered but also in transition, trying already to reinvent itself, desperate to be reborn amidst the endless ashes.

At the hotel, Sam checked in and then handed Anna her key, which she took with murmured thanks. Their rooms were next to each other in a narrow corridor, a fact that felt awkward as they both unlocked their doors, just a few feet from each other.

"I'll meet you downstairs in an hour?" Sam suggested. "Our reservation is at seven."

Anna merely nodded; she'd been even more silent than usual since they'd arrived, her dark gaze darting everywhere. Sam wished they could get back a hint of the camaraderie and teasing they'd once had, but it felt ephemeral, out of his reach.

In his small room, which was shabby but clean, Sam washed his face and then shaved with a small amount of tepid water; the city was experiencing shortages of electricity and water, with both being cut off on a regular basis.

He realized he was looking forward to dinner, just the two of them, more than he should have. He thought of their conversation at Christmas, about love and romance and *you know*, and his stomach clenched with an anticipation he guiltily tried to suppress. Anna should be off limits, never mind that at least half the CIC desk agents were most likely sleeping with their secretaries. Sam didn't want to be like them. He wouldn't be. And yet he knew he was tempted, more so than ever, now that he knew Anna had been tempted, at least a little, as well.

She was already waiting for him when he headed downstairs. He'd chosen to wear his uniform, although many agents donned casual dress whenever they could, as if their posting was nothing more than an extended vacation, their military status an afterthought.

Anna was wearing a plain white blouse and dark green skirt, and she'd left her hair loose about her shoulders, in shining dark waves. Sam had never seen it down before; it made her look younger, softer.

"You look very nice," he said, and she gave a small, tense smile.

"Thank you, Captain."

"You can call me Sam, you know."

She smiled and said nothing, and they headed out to the car, riding in silence across the city, its ruins shrouded by night, to the café on Potsdamer Platz.

As he helped Anna out of the car, they both glanced around the devastated Potsdamer Platz; half the buildings were nothing but shells. The square was busy though, even at this time of night, with what Sam realized—from the huddled figures and furtive passing back and forth—had to be black-market trade, no doubt thanks to its easy access to all four districts.

Sam glanced at a sign proclaiming "You Are Now Leaving the American Sector" and felt a sense of unreality at being in this place in time, in history, the world forever changed all around them. He wondered how Anna felt, seeing her country so commanded, and supposed she was used to it by now.

"Shall we?" he said and, still silent, Anna nodded, and they headed into the café.

It was, Sam realized almost immediately, something of a disappointment. Perhaps he'd been carried away by the descriptions of the pre-war version of Haus Vaterland that he'd read about, with its many cafés and restaurants, or perhaps just the spirit of optimism that its reopening was meant to reflect, but the reality was the restaurant was nothing more than a fairly basic café, just hard chairs and tables, many of them occupied by loud brown-uniformed Soviet soldiers. It was not the atmosphere he'd wanted, and he cursed himself for making such a mistake. A quiet restaurant in the American-occupied sector would have been far more pleasant.

"I'm sorry, I thought this would be nicer," he murmured as they were shown to their table.

Anna just shrugged. Her face was pale, her body like an arched bow, and she kept shooting looks at a particularly rowdy group of Soviet soldiers in the corner of the room, their sudden loud guffaws of laughter startling her every few minutes.

Sam had never actually seen a Soviet soldier before, and he was surprised by how relaxed and friendly the men who were meant to be the new enemy seemed, at least with each other. As he sat down, one of them met his eye and gave a smile and nod of acknowledgment; there was no cold war here, just soldiers off duty having a good time. He smiled back, a bit uncertainly.

"It must have been something, back when you were here last," he remarked to Anna, trying for some semblance of pleasant normality as they perused the limited menu. "Tell me about it. If you didn't go to the Wild West Bar, where did you visit?"

Her lips twitched as she studied the menu as if it were a fascinating piece of literature. "I went to the Heuriger, a sort of Austrian café. The whole place was much bigger, with many restaurants and cafés. A cinema, a ballroom." A shrug, dismissing it all. It was irrelevant now, in light of this new reality.

A waiter came to take their drink orders. Sam ordered a beer while Anna ordered a glass of wine. A few minutes later, the waiter returned with their drinks and they sat and drank in a thick, rather miserable silence.

"I'm sorry," Sam said at last. "I really thought this would be a nicer place. Fancier. I wanted to…" He paused, searching for the words. "Give you a treat." It sounded patronizing, but he didn't mean it that way.

She smiled faintly, inclining her head in acknowledgment of the truth of his words. "You are very kind."

"But you don't like it here," Sam stated. It was all too obvious. "Is it because of the soldiers?" The Soviets were both loud and foreign, but he knew Essen had been liberated by the Americans before being transferred to British occupation. He doubted Anna would have had much reason to ever come across a Soviet before.

"Any soldier makes me nervous."

"Even me?" he joked and she gave him a small smile.

"No, not you. Never you." But she sounded sad, and suddenly Sam couldn't bear being there another second.

"Let's leave."

"What...?"

Already he was rising from his seat, taking out his wallet to throw a couple of bills on the table. "Come with me."

Anna looked dazed as she rose from the table and followed him out of the restaurant. As they passed the rowdy group of Soviets, he put his arm around her protectively, the action instinctive, even necessary. She did not protest.

Out in the dark square, Anna moved out of his one-armed embrace with the graceful slipperiness of a seal, and Sam let her go. He had to be careful, he realized as he climbed into the car. He could not take advantage of this moment of vulnerability, his own desire. The strength of his own feeling was a warning he needed to heed.

They rode in silence back to the hotel.

In the lobby, Sam attempted to ask the concierge for a meal in his schoolboy German; the man gestured helplessly that he knew no English, and so Anna stepped in, speaking quickly and quietly.

"The restaurant is closed, but they say they can make us an omelet," she told him with a small smile. "And deliver it to the room."

"Is that all right?" Sam asked.

She shrugged her assent. "I am hungry."

Sam was starving. Yet he was aware of the uncomfortable intimacy of the situation as Anna stepped into his small hotel room, the bed, bureau, and chair all practically touching each other. He offered her the chair while he sat on the edge of the bed, feeling far too ill at ease, their knees nearly brushing.

Anna gave him a little smile of understanding and a lock of hair fell against her cheek; Sam's fingers twitched to tuck it back behind her ear.

"This is cozy," she said, her eyes glinting with humor, and he smiled in relief.

"I'm sorry. I wanted this evening to be nice and it's been a disaster."

"Not a disaster, no," Anna replied fairly. "We still have food and drink, and the heating seems to be working." She held her hand out to the measly heat of the electric radiator. "Far from a disaster."

A few minutes later, a maid brought a tray with two fluffy golden omelets, a cold sausage, and two bottles of beer.

"A picnic," Anna said as Sam opened the beers and handed her one. "*Prost.*" Gently they clinked bottles while Anna smiled gamely. He appreciated her willingness to enter into a convivial spirit, especially when he didn't think she actually felt it.

He struggled to think of something innocuous to say, when really he wanted to learn more about her. "When did you visit Berlin?" he asked and she paused, her beer bottle halfway to her lips.

"1936, for the Olympics."

He nodded. "I saw pictures of it all on a newsreel. It looked spectacular."

"Yes, it was."

"Hitler's heyday."

"Yes, I suppose that is true." She seemed bitter, while he'd been sounding inane.

"When did you realize?" he asked suddenly, and she glanced at him, a furrow between her brows.

"When did I...?"

"When did you realize he was evil?"

A shadow passed over her face and slowly she put her beer bottle back on the tray. "It was easy to think of Hitler as evil," she said slowly. "Because he was a madman. I always thought you could see it in his eyes. That... frenzy." She shook her head. "But it wasn't just him, of course. It was everyone. All the men standing by his side, all those men who had agreed with him and helped him and... *cheered.*" Her voice spiked. "They cheered him."

"Yes." He had seen enough newsreels of the frenzied Heil Hitlers that seemed to go on forever.

"It was everyone," she repeated, her voice stronger now. "All the hausfraus who complained about the dirty Jews, all the little boys who chased them down the street. All the girls who looked the other way." Her voice trembled on the last and she drew a quick breath, her gaze faraway, as if she was seeing something in her mind, watching it unspool. Then, to Sam's shock, she lifted her hands to undo the top three buttons of her blouse.

He inhaled sharply, unable to keep desire from spiraling through him at the sight of her pale skin, the frayed lace edge of her camisole. She looked intent, her brow slightly furrowed, unaware, or perhaps just impervious to his presence. He opened his mouth to say something, he wasn't sure what, when she drew a gold chain from beneath her camisole, and lifted out a small oval of burnished gold. Sam thought it was a locket at first, and then he realized it was a pocket watch.

"This is my biggest regret," she stated quietly and he gazed at her in confusion.

"What is...?"

"Look." She held the watch out, its chain still around her neck, so Sam had to lean forward to examine it, his fingers nearly brushing her neck, his face close to hers.

"Josef Baum." He read the inscription out slowly and then looked up; she was so close that it would take almost nothing to lean forward and kiss her, to brush his lips against the softness of her cheek. With his face so close to her, he could see her eyes were moss-green, flecked with gold. He forced himself to concentrate. "Who is he?"

"I never met him." Her warm breath fanned his face as she spoke. "He died before the war."

"Then…?"

"His wife and daughter." Her voice choked a little. "I failed them."

Sam stared at her, sensing the deep well of her grief, yet still not understanding it. "How?"

She shook her head, easing away from him as she tucked the watch back beneath her camisole. Her fingers fluttered by the hollow in her throat as they had earlier; he wondered if she wore the watch all the time, and what it meant. "It doesn't matter anymore," she told him.

"It matters to you."

"Yes. I suppose it always will." She looked up then, and her lips trembled, and he saw a sheen of her tears filming her eyes, making him ache with sorrow for her.

"Anna…" Slowly, Sam reached out to cup her cheek in his hand, her skin soft and cool beneath his palm.

She closed her eyes, leaning so very slightly into the caress. It was enough for him to leave his hand there, to offer her what comfort he could.

"Anna," he said again, and there was so much longing in his voice that he knew she had to hear it.

She opened her eyes and stared straight at him and Sam couldn't tell if she was asking him to kiss her, if she wanted him to. He leaned forward slightly, and just as slightly she drew back. He dropped his hand. Her gaze dropped from his.

"I'm sorry, Sam," she said quietly. It was the first time she'd called him by his Christian name.

"You don't need to be sorry." He rubbed his hands over his face, unsure whether he'd imagined that moment or not. "I don't even know what you're saying sorry for."

Anna looked up at him, resolute, resigned. "I wish I could be the woman you want me to be."

He dropped his hands to stare at her in frustrated confusion. "Maybe I just want you to be you."

She smiled, the curve of her lips touched with sadness. "Maybe you want me to be a woman who wants to be kissed."

He let out a tired laugh. "Your English is very good. It took me a few seconds to unscramble that sentence."

"Is it true?"

His laugh turned into a sigh. Suddenly he felt very tired, and very old. "I suppose it is, in a way. But you're telling me you're not?" It was not really a question.

"I want to be a woman who wants to be kissed," she answered after a moment. "Sometimes I almost feel as if I am… when I am with you." She smiled faintly, her eyes still dark and full of sorrow. "Does that make it any better?"

"I don't know." Sam reached for the crumpled packet of cigarettes in his breast pocket. He desperately needed a smoke. "Maybe."

He offered her the packet although he'd never seen her smoke, and after a second she withdrew a cigarette from it. Sam struck a match and lit hers and then his own. They smoked in silence for a few minutes; Anna held her cigarette between two straight fingers, as if it were in a holder. It looked both elegant and awkward.

"You don't smoke," he said finally, and she let out a little laugh.

"Not really." She raised her eyebrows, a smile flirting with her lips, her eyes glinting once more with humor. "But how can you tell?"

Sam let out a guffaw of laughter, and Anna's smile widened. His heart felt as if it were somersaulting in his chest. He loved her, he thought. It was absurd, because she was still such a mystery, and yet he felt—he knew—it to be true.

"Tell me about your family," he blurted. "Your parents." He'd only asked because he wanted to know more about her, but her smile slid right off her face and Sam cursed himself for a thoughtless fool. Her parents were dead. She'd told him so herself. "I'm sorry. I only…"

"Tell me about *your* family," she said. "I want to know all about them."

"Okay." Sam settled back more comfortably, as if preparing to tell a story. He wanted to tell her about himself; he wanted her to know. And so he began, talking of the brick house in Bryn Mawr where he'd grown up, its trellises climbing with roses; about his mother commandeering him at thirteen to make up a fourth for her ladies' bridge club, much to his horror; about his dad's work in Philadelphia as a doctor, and how he'd wanted Sam to go into medicine but he'd chosen teaching instead.

"Why did you?" Anna asked. She'd let her cigarette burn down to the filter before she'd stubbed it out, and she now sat leaning forward, her chin propped in one hand, her other arm wrapped around her waist.

"I'm not all that good with the sight of blood, to be honest," he admitted, and she let out a laugh.

"Yet you are a soldier."

"I never actually saw any active duty," he confessed. He could picture Major Pitt's curled lip at the admission. "To tell you the truth, a fellow broke his arm during training and that was enough to have me putting my head down between my knees." Much to his CO's disgust.

"Oh, Sam." She laughed and shook her head, her eyes sparkling. Sam loved to see her looking so vibrant, so alive.

"Pretty pathetic, isn't it?" he half-joked, conscious of his own failings, but she shook her head.

"No. It's..." She paused, blowing out a breath as she thought of the word. "Lovely," she said, and then to his utter surprise, she leaned over and kissed him.

The brush of her lips against his was a shock, welcome yet still so surprising. He reached for her, one hand grappling clumsily at her shoulder, but before he'd made any purchase, she had already moved back, giving him a rather bemused smile. He had the sense that she was as surprised as he was by the kiss, that she hadn't entirely meant to do it.

"That wasn't so bad, was it?" he half-joked, and something flashed across her face; he felt as if she'd closed herself up, like a fan snapping shut.

She rose from her chair. "I should go."

Sam reached out one hand. "Anna..."

She shook her head, her gaze sliding away. "I'm sorry."

"Don't be—"

"Even so." She turned back to him with a sudden, hard look. "We have a big day tomorrow, yes?" She tilted her chin up at a determined angle. "We are going to find the Nazi chemists."

CHAPTER NINETEEN

Berlin, June 1940

The night Otto returned with Friedy was a turning point, profound and terrible in its finality; it had changed everyone, some for better, some for far worse.

Her mother, Liesel soon saw, had become a woman of purpose. She walked out of the drawing room without looking back; it was as if her husband had become invisible to her. It wasn't until the next morning, when Liesel saw, to her surprise, her mother drinking coffee at eight o'clock in the morning, dressed and ready for the day, that she started to have an inkling of what it meant.

Last night she'd gone to Friedy's room to say goodnight, only to find him hunched in bed, his thin back to her, his pale face streaked with tears. He was asleep, felled by exhaustion. Liesel had smoothed his dark hair back from his forehead, her heart aching with love. Then she saw his *Jungvolk* uniform in the corner of the room. He'd taken his precious knife to it and cut it savagely into shreds. Her little brother was, it seemed, no longer a Nazi, and as much as that brought relief, it also, paradoxically, made her feel a little sad. His innocence had been destroyed in the worst way possible.

That morning, Ilse waited until her husband had gone to work—she had not said a word to him at the breakfast table and he'd wearily taken it as his due—before turning to Liesel with bright, hard-eyed alacrity.

"Things have changed," she stated simply. "We must act."

"How?" Liesel glanced back at the doorway to the kitchen, where Helga was washing the breakfast dishes. Friedy was still asleep upstairs, exhausted from his ordeal.

"I don't know how. I don't know what. I only know we must." Ilse's eyes were diamond-bright and just as hard as she sipped her coffee. "I've been a selfish, pathetic fool for far too long, thinking it was enough simply to feel sad." Her lip curled with self-disgust and she put her coffee cup down with a clatter. "That ends here and now, Liesel. We must *do* something to resist this madness. To *change*, and even to defeat it."

"But I don't know what we can do, Mutti." No matter how fiery her mother now seemed, Liesel still felt helpless, trapped in the gilded cage of her own existence, the bars created by her father's position. What stand could she possibly make? To not attend a party with Fritz or her father? Was that even being brave?

Ilse pressed her lips together. "Perhaps nothing, not yet. We will have to watch and wait."

But for what? They could pass the entire war simply waiting, and convince themselves they were doing enough. Then Liesel thought of Rosa.

"There might be something," she said slowly, and Ilse's gaze brightened. Liesel glanced back at the kitchen, and her mother's mouth tightened.

"Let's go upstairs."

They tiptoed upstairs like two naughty children intent on mischief. As Liesel stepped into her mother's bedroom, she saw that it already felt different; the windows were open to the fresh summer air, and the overflowing ashtrays and crystal glasses with their dregs of schnapps had disappeared. Her mother closed the door with a firm click.

"Tell me," she commanded.

"When Rosa was here… do you remember?"

Regret flashed briefly in Ilse's eyes as she recalled her own drunken behavior. "Yes."

"She said something about papers. Asking me to ask… to ask Father to help them." She would never call him Vati again. "They need help to escape when they're able to… Gerda's mother won't go, but…" She trailed off uncertainly. She realized she still had no idea what they could do that would be of any use.

"We cannot ask your father for anything." Her mother's words were final, absolute.

"No, I know that, but…" Liesel hesitated. "But we could do it, couldn't we? Somehow?"

Ilse frowned. "I don't know who even to ask, Liesel, for forged papers or safe passage. We don't know those sorts of people. I wouldn't know where to begin." And asking the wrong person could be deadly.

"Rosa or Gerda must know someone," Liesel insisted. "Jews are being smuggled out. Father even said as much to me. It just costs money."

"We have money."

"Then we could help them in that way, at least."

"Yes." Ilse pressed one hand to her middle as she let out a shaky breath. "You know what would happen to us, if we were discovered to have helped Jews to escape? If we gave them so much as a *pfennig*?"

"I expect we'd be arrested." The simply spoken words belied the terror that had hollowed out Liesel's insides.

"We wouldn't just be arrested, Liesel," her mother replied flatly. "We'd be taken to Prinz-Albrecht-Strasse. We'd be interrogated. Tortured. I saw a man released from there once—he tottered out into the street, barely looking half-human. His fingers…" She shuddered and shook her head. "And even after that, if we survived the experience, we'd most likely be deported to a camp, or killed outright. I suppose one would lead to the other. In the end we'd be dead, it's just a matter of how much pain we experienced first." She pressed her lips together to keep from saying anything more.

Liesel's legs turned watery and she sank onto the edge of her mother's bed. She found she couldn't speak, but Ilse nodded as if she had.

"Yes. Exactly."

"But you still want to do it?"

Ilse let out a trembling laugh. "*Mein Gott*, but it feels different when it's real. Do I want to do it? *No.* It terrifies me utterly. But I can't bear *not* doing anything any longer. I cannot live with myself if I keep hiding in my bedroom. I have Gerda's address. We can visit her. That is the first step, at least."

Liesel nodded slowly. "All right, then."

They stared at each other for a long moment, aware of the momentousness of their decision. It could change the course of their very lives, or even the length of them. Yet underneath the fear that shrouded her in a blind fog, Liesel felt a small but reassuring spark of excitement. Finally, *finally* they were doing something. She would no longer be passive, complicit, *guilty.*

"In the meantime," her mother said, her voice turning sharp, "you must give no reason for suspicion to anyone. Every party your father asks you to attend, every parade, every rally, every single event—you must go, and you must enjoy yourself. You must have the most fun in the world, as if you are nothing but a lighthearted girl, enjoying all the attention. Those handsome officers!" Her mouth twisted. "Do you understand?"

Liesel stared at her unhappily. She did not want to do any such thing, now more than ever. "What about you?"

Ilse shrugged. "It would look strange if I suddenly showed up after being absent for so long. People would remark on it, and wonder. And, in truth, I fear I wouldn't be able to pull it off convincingly. I could give the whole thing away… when there is something to reveal, to hide. God willing, there will be." She shook her head. "It must be you, Liesel. You must be your father's adoring daughter, the life of the party."

"I wasn't the life of the party before," Liesel protested.

Ilse took her by both shoulders. "You must be now."

Liesel was given ample opportunity to be just that a few weeks later, when her father invited her to accompany him to a party at Göring's state residence after the Field Marshal Ceremony at the Kroll Opera House, where Hitler, flush from the glorious fall of France, had awarded twelve generals the rank of Generalfeld-marschall, and Göring the newly created rank of Reichsmarschall.

"I'm so pleased you chose to attend with me," Otto remarked with a small, whimsical smile as they drove to the state residence on Leipziger Platz that Göring shared with his wife Emmy and their daughter Edda, now two years old.

Over the last few weeks, Ilse had continued to icily freeze Otto out, while Liesel had been attempting to find some sort of normality and surely failed.

So much felt uncertain, dangerous. Rosa's challenging glare when she'd gone to her cramped, shabby apartment in the Mitte district a week ago flitted through her mind. *Do you really want to help us?*

Did she really want to answer that question?

Liesel pushed the memory of the conversation out of her mind as she did her best to return her father's smile. Outside, Berliners were strolling in the balmy summer evening, the sky a rainbow of pinks and violets as the sun sank behind the old Wertheim department store where Liesel had once bought a pair of party shoes, now renamed *Allgemeine Warenhandelsgesellschaft*, or AWAG, after being sold to approved Aryans.

"Life must go on, after all," she told her father with a little shrug of her shoulders.

"Indeed." He reached over and clasped her cold hand in his. "I know this is difficult, Lieseling, but it won't be forever."

"No." She paused. "What do you suppose will happen after the war?" She realized she was genuinely curious as to where her father thought all this was going. What future did he see for himself, for their family, in the world of destruction and domination that Hitler was intent on creating? When would it end? What would that look like? She could not imagine it. She did not want to.

Otto gave her hand a reassuring squeeze. "Everything will settle down, you'll see. The fighting won't go on forever, even though I know it feels as if it must."

"And what of the Jews?" Liesel couldn't keep from asking, even though she knew it would only aggravate her father.

He sighed, just as she expected he would, and squeezed her hand again. "That is a problem that is already being solved, Liesel, whether you like the means or not. In a few years' time, there will not be many, if any, Jews left in the Greater Reich."

She stared at him in shocked alarm, sensing an import to his words that could have only been gained by knowledge. "What do you mean? How could there not be any at all?"

Otto shrugged evasively. "They'll leave, or they'll be made to leave. It's already happening." Yet Liesel sensed there was something he was not saying, and she dreaded to think what it was. "The point is," he resumed, "Germany will be the strongest, greatest country in the world, a place of peace and prosperity."

"Isn't it already the greatest?" Liesel asked, trying not to sound sharp, and her father turned to her with a smile, although his eyes looked weary. There had been, Liesel noticed, a haggard defeatism to him since he'd fetched Friedy back, visible in his stooped shoulders and lined face. No amount of wry smiles or cheerful bonhomie could disguise it.

"Indeed. And tonight we are celebrating its many victories."

Liesel didn't think she could have felt less like celebrating as she entered Göring's palatial state residence. Like the Reichsmarschall himself, the house was one of unbearable, gluttonous excess, its grand rooms crammed with absurdly opulent furniture of marble and gold, as well as priceless antiques. Paintings worthy of a museum lined the walls, gilt-framed oils by Grand Masters as well as pale-washed watercolors painted by a more delicate hand, and an enormous mosaic of a swastika had been worked into the marble floor beneath their feet. Liesel did her best to look entertained and impressed by it all when, in truth, she felt horrified to be there—and fearful that her racing thoughts would somehow be apparent on her face.

Her father was taking it all in with his usual expression of lively and alert interest, although Liesel suspected his cheerful attitude took a bit more effort these days, after what had happened with Friedy. Although he had been determined to continue to regard the episode as nothing more than an administrative error, Liesel thought she saw the bleak truth in his eyes, not that he would ever admit it.

Gazing warily around the huge room, she plucked a glass of champagne from a tray, deciding she was going to need alcohol to get through what would surely be an interminable evening. All around her, women in evening gowns and men in uniform—the gray of the Wehrmacht, the blue of the Luftwaffe, and the midnight black of the SS—circulated, chatting and laughing, high on their victories, smugly certain of their exalted place in the world.

Platters of every kind of delicacy or dessert were also circulating, making it hard to remember that in most households in Berlin, and indeed all of Germany, people were being forcefully reminded that the choice was "guns not butter," and meat was often no more than congealed rice fried in mutton fat and passed off as a chop. The average Berliner's sacrifice was his duty to the Führer, but clearly not the Reichsmarschall, who, amidst all of his guests looked to be the most extravagant of all, with rings on every finger and his chest bristling with war medals; his new uniform as Reichsmarschall included a jeweled baton.

It wasn't long before the man himself came over to greet them, his manner as obnoxiously effusive as ever, his face flushed from drink.

"Ah, Otto!" He clapped her father hard on the shoulder. "It is good to see you. I'm glad we got that little matter sorted out, eh?" He smiled indulgently while Liesel watched her father give a humble little bow, as if Göring spoke of some small and simple misunderstanding rather than the cold-hearted murder of her brother.

"Indeed, Herr Reichsmarschall. I have much to thank you for."

"Oh think nothing of it, my good man, nothing of it," Göring dismissed. Liesel thought he sounded a bit bored, as if the matter were something tedious he did not wish to discuss.

Her father fell silent, a bit chastised, as Göring's gaze, both benevolent and shrewd, rested on Liesel with the same sort of paternalistic lasciviousness he'd shown before that made her skin crawl and her stomach curdle.

"Your daughter grows more beautiful by the day. I hear my godson is half in love with you, Fraulein Scholz."

A smile stretched Liesel's lips. "Only half, Herr Reichsmarschall?" she dared to tease, and was rewarded with a booming laugh.

"Indeed, indeed! You must practice your charms with a bit more effort and alacrity, I think, Fraulein!" Another booming laugh, and Liesel kept her smile in place as Göring pinched her cheek, just as he had the last time she'd seen him.

"How is Hauptman Burkhardt, as it happens?" her father asked lightly once the Reichsmarschall had moved on; Göring had not spent nearly as much time with her father as he had at Carinhall, which was a relief, yet also made Liesel wonder. Had her feted father fallen out of favor, if just a little?

"Fine, I suppose," she answered. "I haven't seen him in a while." Fritz had received a promotion from *Oberleutnant* after the fall of France; her father was obviously aware of it, as no doubt was the Reichsmarschall. It chilled her, how much the man seemed to know, and it was a grim reminder of just how careful she needed to be.

"Oh?" Her father's voice was light as a slight frown creased his forehead. "And why is that?"

Liesel hesitated and then decided honesty, whenever possible, was the wisest, and indeed the safest, course of action for her new life of subterfuge. "He was talking of marriage and babies, and I am only eighteen, after all."

"Marriage!" Otto looked surprised, but not, Liesel noted, displeased. No doubt it would serve him very well to be father-in-law to Göring's godson. "Is that thought so unpleasant to you?" he asked teasingly and Liesel shrugged.

"I'm not in love with Fritz."

"He seems like a good man."

"Does he?" Her voice sharpened despite her efforts to sound careless and light. "I didn't think you really knew him."

"I would hardly agree for him to escort my daughter anywhere if I didn't think he was," he replied mildly.

Liesel took a sip of champagne to give her time to organize her thoughts. She did not want to pick a fight with her father about Fritz, far from it. The truth was, his absence had felt more like a relief than anything else, not that she would say as much. She needed to be careful, to keep things light, and yet since seeing Rosa, her mind had been like a rat in maze, searching for a way out. An answer, an escape.

Do you really want to help us?

"When are you next going to Schkopau, Father?" Liesel asked, hoping she sounded interested rather than desperate. "You seem to travel there so often now. Or is Poland where you will be going to now?"

"Indeed, I expect to have more business in Poland," he replied, his gaze scanning the room, no doubt looking for someone important to converse with. No one caught his gaze.

"Because of the new factory?"

"It hasn't been built yet, and I don't expect it will be until the spring."

"For Buna rubber?"

Her father's eyes narrowed as he turned to give her a probing look. "Yes—but why are you so interested, Liesel? You don't usually ask questions about my work."

"I must make small talk," Liesel answered, her voice turning truculent to hide her fear. "What else should I talk about? And sometimes people ask. What should I tell them?"

"That it is government business, not meant for discussion," he replied sharply. "Surely you know that."

"Can you not even tell your own daughter when you will be traveling?" Liesel returned with a shrug, chastened by her father's rebuke. In truth she didn't care much about Buna rubber, or where her father's new factory would be built, but she did need to know when he might be out of the house.

She thought of Rosa's hard voice, a challenge in the words, a dare, as if she expected Liesel to back down. *If you want to help us, then help our friends. Our neighbors. The people who are prepared to try to escape.*

How? The single word had slipped from her lips reluctantly, because she hadn't wanted to ask. To know. And when Rosa had told her, she'd felt as if the very ground had fallen away beneath her feet, as if she were being swept up in a churning sea of danger, the waves already closing over her head.

Will you do it?

"So will you be going to Poland again soon?" Liesel asked, trying to sound offhand and feeling she failed.

"Perhaps in the autumn." Her father nodded toward a man in a gray silk business suit. "Now I must say hello to Herr Schmidt. It will be boring business talk, I'm afraid." He glanced around the room with the air of someone hunting for a present. "Isn't there a handsome Luftwaffe officer here for you to flirt with?"

"Do you see one?" she teased with a pretend pout. Göring's party was for the Nazi elite, not young, handsome nobody pilots.

"Perhaps you could admire the artwork, then." He nodded toward one of the walls where heavy-framed canvases jostled for space.

"There is so very much of it," Liesel couldn't keep from replying, for they both knew that many, if not all, of the paintings hanging on the walls had been stolen.

Her father merely smiled, giving a mock salute with his half-drunk glass of champagne, before he headed off to work his way through the room.

Liesel wandered over toward the wall, longing only to be ignored. She wished she hadn't come, even though she knew she'd had to. Rosa's words were still emblazoned on her mind.

If you are serious, there are people you could help. If people want to leave, they have to do so by darkness.

Liesel hadn't understood at first. She'd stared blankly, and then, with a touch of both impatience and pity, Rosa had explained how there was a system to get Jews out of the city, out of the country. How they hid, going from house to house under the cover of darkness, until they were able to get to somewhere safe—Switzerland or Sweden, and then, God willing, on to England or America. Away. Anywhere, away.

"And you want me… to hide these people?" Liesel had whispered, appalled, terrified. She'd never imagined something like this. People in her house, under the beady eye of Helga, Friedy even, who, despite his new hatred of the *Jungvolk*, perhaps could still not be trusted. He was so young, after all, and his love for his Führer had been so fervent. And what of her father, who was at this moment talking to Emmy Göring? Liesel could hear his bellow of laughter from across the room.

It was impossible, she thought as she gazed unseeingly at an oil painting of a woman smiling with smug sensuality at the artist, a falcon perched on one bare shoulder. Rosa had arranged to meet her tomorrow in the Weissensee Jewish Cemetery—the only place Jews were now free to walk—on the other side of the city, to discuss the details of the endeavor, but Liesel couldn't see how any of it would be possible. She couldn't do it. She couldn't risk so much. She would have to tell Rosa no…

"Beautiful, is it not?"

Startled, Liesel turned to see a tall man in the dress uniform of the SS nod at the picture. He had close-set light blue eyes and a thin-lipped mouth, and he looked both shrewd and vaguely familiar. She was sure he must be somebody important, but in her champagne-fueled fuzziness she couldn't recall who.

"Yes, indeed it is."

"*The Falconer* by Hans Makart. A birthday present from the Führer. The Reichsmarschall is a lucky man, is he not?"

Liesel nodded, not trusting herself to say any more than she had to.

The man took a step closer to her, so his boot nudged Liesel's foot. "I have met your father a few times, but I have not yet had the pleasure of meeting your mother." He raised thin, nearly colorless eyebrows in query. "She is so often absent."

"She is often unwell," Liesel replied, trying to hide her alarm that this stranger knew precisely who she was. "And I'm afraid loud parties fatigue her."

"How unfortunate." There was far too much assessment in his narrowed eyes, and Liesel had to remind herself to breathe.

"She is a pianist, is she not? My own father was a musician and composer. I do enjoy music."

"Yes…" Her mind felt as if it were buzzing. *Who was he?*

"Perhaps I will hear her play, when she is feeling better."

"I am sure she would be delighted to play for you…" She trailed off, realizing she could not use his title, because she did not know what it was, but she suspected she should.

"I look forward to it," he replied with a cold smile, and somehow it felt like a warning.

As he moved off, Liesel turned to a nearby waiter.

"Who was that officer?" she asked in a low voice, and the waiter's eyes widened in both surprise and alarm.

"That was the Chief of Security Police," he whispered. "Reinhard Heydrich."

Liesel nearly swayed where she stood. Heydrich, the chief of police and the orchestrator of Gestapo arrests, disappearances, and torture. The man responsible for *Kristallnacht*, whom Hitler himself said had an iron heart. And he'd been chatting to her about her mother…! How could she possibly agree to help Rosa now, when Heydrich himself was aware of their family's movements?

Yet how could she not?

To think is easy, to act is hard. Liesel had never felt the truth of those words more than now, staring at the stiff, narrow lines of Heydrich's departing back.

CHAPTER TWENTY

September 1940

Liesel had been waiting for nearly two months for the first of them to arrive. Two months of jumping at every noise, her heart in her mouth, her body like ice, every nerve on high, twanging alert. It felt like an impossible way to live. Yet now the day—or rather, the night—was finally here. Her father was in Schkopau, and Helga had left for the day, clumping out of the kitchen in her heavy boots, after leaving a meal of congealed rice and cold potatoes. The source of her father's largesse, whatever it had been, seemed to have dried up.

Night had fallen, a forgiving cloak that could hide so much, including the British bombers that had been dropping their deadly cargo on Berlin for the last three weeks.

What had started out as something of a novelty—one of the first bombs that had been dropped in late August had wrecked a house in Templehof that curious Berliners had gone to view, as if it were a museum exhibit—had now become a strained and fatiguing reality.

Three or four nights a week, the sirens sent up their loathsome wail and Liesel and her family headed down to the cellar, made comfortable enough thanks to her father's earlier preparations, but still not the cozy warmth of a bedroom, with the smell of damp and the cool air. The lack of sleep along with the rat-a-tat-tat of the anti-aircraft guns and the distant thud and crackle of bombs had added to the strain of waiting for their other night-time visitors to come.

"When will they arrive?" Ilse whispered as they peered between the crack of the blackout curtains, although under a cloud-filled, moonless sky, there was nothing to see.

"I don't know. All I know is sometime tonight."

Two months ago, when Liesel had met Rosa in the Jewish cemetery, they'd arranged a system of communication. Liesel was to put a vase of flowers in the drawing-room window when her father was away. Someone would come to the door, acting as if they were collecting for Winter Relief, and give her the message if anyone was to come that night. *My mother says it is going to be a long, cold winter* was the code; Liesel's response in the affirmative was to say "My mother says the same." Liesel lived in terror that some unknowing HJ would say a similar thing simply as conversation, and she would blurt out something revealing and ruin everything.

But for two months no one had come at night except for the bombers. Then this morning, while rattling a tin box full of *pfennigs*, a young man with blond hair and an easy smile had remarked in an offhand way, "It's only September, but my mother says it's going to be a long, cold winter."

Liesel had frozen right there in the doorway, transfixed with both shock and terror, her purse clutched in her hands. He'd smiled and held out the box, and she had no idea whether to trust him or not.

"My mother says the same," she had finally managed to reply, and he'd nodded and left as soon as she'd dropped a couple of coins in the box.

She'd meant to tell Rosa she couldn't help, when she'd met her in the cemetery back in July. Now, as she stared out at the endlessly dark night, Liesel almost wished she had. She felt as if she'd aged a decade in the last few months, living in this constant state of alertness and ignorance, wonder and worry. She'd plucked out a dozen gray hairs already, and she wasn't even nineteen.

Yet somehow, in the face of Rosa's blazing determination, to refuse had felt not just cowardly, but wrong. Evil, even. She could not live with herself if she refused, and yet to accept felt as good as a death sentence. Still, she'd forced the words past her numb lips. *I'll do it.*

From behind her, her mother drew a sudden breath. "I heard something."

Liesel tensed, and then she heard it too—the clink of the latch on the gate sliding back into place. She and her mother stared at each other for a few tense seconds, and then Liesel heard a soft knock on the kitchen door. She hurried back to the kitchen, followed by Ilse; when she opened the door, she saw two people huddled there, a man and a woman, both in their thirties, shabbily dressed, gaunt-faced, and apprehensive.

"Come in, come in," Liesel whispered, although there was no one to hear. The villa was set back from its neighbors, as well as from the street; the real dangers, Liesel knew, were from the people within—Helga, Friedy, her father, who was due back in two days. Would this poor couple still be here then? She didn't know.

They didn't give names, and no one spoke as they tiptoed upstairs, past Friedy's bedroom, where he slept peacefully, to the attic rooms where no one ever slept. Liesel slipped into the bedroom farthest from the stairs, and then pried open the door that led to the shadowy space under the eaves.

She and her mother had, over the last two months, slowly transformed the dark, cobwebby space into as welcoming a room as they could. The rough planks on the floor were covered with old carpets, to muffle sound as much as provide comfort, and they'd dragged several mattresses inside from the attic bedroom, hoping no one would come upstairs to notice the empty bed frames.

They'd also begun stockpiling tins of food, a challenging proposition under Helga's watchful eye. As mistress of the kitchen, she knew exactly how much food there was at any given time, and with rationing and shortages in the shops it was difficult to procure extra of anything. Liesel hadn't seen butter, meat, beans, or rice in weeks, despite her entitlement to all four on her ration card. Even her father's treats—real coffee or the extravagant box of chocolates—had been absent in the last few months. He was so often away, and when he was in Berlin, he seemed almost to forget they were there with him, never mind that they were hungry. He moved around like a man both on a mission and in a daze, focused on something invisible, startled out of a trance. It didn't help that Ilse ignored him, and Liesel never knew what to say. Only his ten-year-old son addressed him with anything like affection.

Now, as Liesel showed the couple their new lodgings, she explained in a faltering voice, every word an apology, "If there's an air raid… we'll all go to the cellar." She'd already discussed this with her mother, and they'd both agreed they could not leave whoever was hiding up in the eaves to their fate. "You may come down with us, but you must leave before dawn, even if…" She paused guiltily. "Even if the all-clear hasn't sounded. I'm so sorry, but we can't risk it…"

The woman clutched both her hands in hers, her gaze full of both desperation and gratitude. "Yes, of course, we understand. *Danke… danke.*"

A lump forming in her throat, knowing she was offering both so much and yet so little, Liesel could only nod.

Back downstairs, Ilse poured them both glasses of schnapps before tossing hers back in a single gulp. She hadn't touched a drop since the night Friedy had come home, but Liesel knew they both needed the courage now. The couple's presence upstairs seemed to pulse through the house, as loud as a scream.

"We must be crazy," her mother muttered as she paced the sitting room. "Completely crazy."

"There's no reason for anyone to be suspicious," Liesel replied as calmly as she could. She took a sip of schnapps, wincing at the taste, and then tossed the rest down just as her mother had. "No one saw anything."

"You don't know that. How did they even get here?" Ilse lit a cigarette and inhaled deeply. "Crossing the city on their own, when Jews can't go anywhere anymore? Everyone notices everything, and the police are always asking for papers. They could have been seen. They probably were."

"If they'd been seen, we would know it by now."

"Would we?" Ilse countered as she blew out a stream of smoke. "Or would they wait? Perhaps some nosy busybody has gone to the Gestapo, told them what they saw. Perhaps they're coming right now."

Liesel's breath hitched and inadvertently they both looked to the window, nothing but a stretch of black crepe, waiting for the sound of screeching tires as a black Mercedes pulled up in front of the house. A hammering on the door…

It felt so possible, so *real*, that Liesel tensed in expectation, straining to hear the knock, the shouts, but all was silent. Then, from far above, a faint creak. Ilse's eyes widened.

"*Mein Gott,*" she whispered. "You can hear them from down here?"

"Only because it's so still," Liesel answered quickly. "We'll leave the radio on as often as we can. Or you can play the piano. Helga always makes such a racket with her pots and pans…"

Ilse shook her head, smoking frantically. "This will never work."

"It has to," Liesel insisted flatly.

"If only we could fire Helga," her mother muttered. "I never liked the old witch, anyway."

They both knew they couldn't let the housekeeper go. To fire Helga now would look far too suspicious, both to her father and anyone who might be keeping an eye on their household. Heydrich? Göring? It seemed as if far too many high-ranking officials made it their business to know the goings-on of their small household.

"We must keep our nerve, Mutti," Liesel entreated, even though she wasn't sure how much she had to begin with. "That's all we can do now."

Two days later, the couple was gone—another soft knock on the side door, and then they slipped away like shadows into the night. It had felt like the longest two days of Liesel's life, and she and her mother clasped each other in silent, exhausted solidarity after they'd gone. There had been no major mishaps, and thankfully no air raids; Helga had remained oblivious, humming in the kitchen, listening to an operetta on the radio as she dusted the sitting room. After she'd left, Liesel had crept upstairs to give the couple some supper; they'd thanked her profusely, and she'd wanted to ask them where they were going, or at least their names, but fear kept her silent. The less she knew, the better. Just in case.

Friedy caught her coming back downstairs, a look of surprised curiosity on his face as Liesel started guiltily.

"What are you doing up there?" he'd asked, wrinkling his nose, and for a few seconds Liesel's mind had blanked.

"I was looking for some extra blankets," she had said finally, doing her best to shrug the question off, as of no importance. "It's getting so cold at night now."

"There are spiders up there," Friedy had warned her, and Liesel had nodded her agreement.

"Yes, I saw a big one. It scuttled into the corner." She had pretended to shudder, and Friedy had made a face. Perhaps the threat of spiders would keep her little brother from exploring too much.

"But you haven't got any blankets," he'd remarked as she went down the hall, and Liesel had pretended not to hear him.

A week later, Liesel put the vase of flowers in the window again; the next morning, an older man with wispy white hair and kindly, tired eyes came to her door.

"My mother says it's going to be a long, cold winter," he said, and Liesel's heart sank. She'd been hoping for a reprieve, at least for a little while, as selfish as she knew that was.

"My mother says the same," she returned woodenly, and the man smiled, his eyes crinkling at the corners. Liesel smiled back, heartened by this small sign of solidarity. She wasn't in this alone.

That evening, while Ilse was upstairs with Friedy, there was another knock on the side door, and this time a young couple with two children stood there. The woman held a baby and a boy no more than three clung to his father's legs. They all stared at Liesel in wordless entreaty.

"Oh…" She could not keep the dismay from her voice. "I don't know if we can manage a baby… there is a housekeeper, you see… she can't know anything about it…"

The look of naked despair on the couple's faces had her ushering them in anyway. There was no way she could send them back out into the street when they'd come this far and risked so much. "Never mind, never mind. We'll manage."

The next morning, as Helga clumped into the kitchen, a faint cry could be heard from upstairs. Ilse threw Liesel a panicked look and then hurried to the piano. She played rousing marching songs for the better part of the morning, much to Helga's bemused pleasure.

By the time Helga left at six, her mother was exhausted and Liesel's head throbbed with tension. They ate a quiet dinner and then Ilse went to bed and Friedy to his room; Liesel had just sunk onto the sofa in the sitting room when a sharp, purposeful tap sounded at the front door and she froze in terror.

If it was the Gestapo, she told herself, they wouldn't have knocked. They'd have kicked the door in and would already be rushing into the house, voices and rubber truncheons raised. As it was, whoever was at the door simply knocked again, a bit louder this time, a bit more impatient.

With trepidation, Liesel wiped her damp hands on her skirt and went to unlock the door. She had no idea whom to expect, and her face fell almost comically when she saw who was there, determinedly dashing in his blue uniform.

"Fritz."

"You don't sound happy to see me!" He tried to laugh, but already there was a petulant cast to his handsome features, a pout on his lips. He held his cap in his hand, his blond hair ruffled by the breeze, his cheeks pinked with cold.

"No, no, of course I am pleased," Liesel said quickly. "Especially after the way we parted that day at the Strandbad Wannsee." She had not seen Fritz since that day on the lido back in June, and she hadn't really thought of him since she'd become involved with Rosa. She realized now she had been glad not to.

"Well, can I come in, then?" Fritz raised his eyebrows in the same gently arrogant way he had when she'd first met him at Carinhall. She'd been charmed then, albeit somewhat reluctantly; she wasn't now.

Liesel hesitated, not knowing how to put him off, yet most certainly not wanting him to come in. She could not think of a reason to demur, at least not one she could tell him, and she feared rousing his anger, or worse, his suspicion, if she prevaricated.

Then, before she could say anything, a faint cry filtered from above.

Fritz frowned. "Was that a baby?" he asked incredulously.

"No, it was a cat." The lie sprang to her lips with surprising ease as Liesel rolled her eyes and shook her head. "Our housekeeper is devoted to the stupid creature, but I can't stand its caterwauling. We should just put it down." Another cry, louder and more plaintive, and she gave him a playful smile. "Well come in, then, if you want to." She pulled him by the hand into the sitting room, closing the door firmly behind her. Even then she could still hear it—the baby was crying in earnest now, God help them all. She held her arms out to Fritz, giving him the approximation of a coy smile. "I'm so glad to see you. I thought you were still angry with me over that silly business about the mother's cross."

He gave her a slightly shamefaced smile. "No, no, I'm sorry about that. I shouldn't have behaved like such a boor. The truth is, I've been thinking about you all the time." He reached for her, brushing his lips with hers before the kiss suddenly turned hard, desperate and demanding, his body pushing into hers with alarming force. Shocked, Liesel stiffened against him.

"Fritz…"

"You don't know how I've needed you, Liesel…" Fritz murmured against her throat. His fingers were already at her blouse, fumbling with the buttons in a way he never had before. "I'm flying tomorrow night… to England. I've already flown four sorties since the beginning of the month. Last night, one of my closest friends was shot down. Frank Lubert. I saw it, a fireball in the sky… it's like a nightmare that never ends. You can't even imagine…" A button popped and he pushed her blouse aside. "Please… please let me…" He kissed her again, harder this time, and panic welled in Liesel's throat, tightened her chest. She could still hear crying.

"Oh, Fritz, how terrible…" she managed in a choked voice. He was kissing her all over—her lips, her throat, her breasts, as she'd never been kissed before, and certainly didn't want to be now, not by him. Fritz was like a man in the grip of fear rather than desire, kissing her with a frenzied passion that felt more like terror and provoked the same response in her. She didn't want him to touch her. *She didn't want him to hear.*

Somehow he steered her over to the sofa, or perhaps she did, away from the door and the sound of the crying that continued on insistently, shrill and desperate. They fell onto the worn velveteen in a tangle of limbs, and distantly Liesel wondered if this was the price she would have to pay, in order to keep him from hearing the baby's plaintive cries. He put one hand under her skirt.

"Fritz, please," she said with a breathless laugh as she tried to wriggle out from beneath him. "My mother is upstairs. My brother, as well. We can't…"

"Just for a little bit…" His fingers skimmed her thigh and Liesel tensed, both from the touch and the sound of crying that was most definitely still audible.

"What…" Fritz paused, frowning, raising his head as he heard it and recklessly Liesel arched toward him so his fingers went even farther. The cries were forgotten. She closed her eyes.

For a few seconds, there was nothing but the sound of Fritz's panting, the blood pounding in her temples as Liesel clenched her jaw and he pressed against her, his hand still under her skirt. She had a sudden memory of Marianne, one of the older girls in the BDM, taunting her. *You know he puts his thing right inside you?*

Surely it wouldn't come to that now. Fritz was still fully dressed, his fingers fumbling against her.

Then, after a few interminable minutes, the baby finally stopped its crying, and Liesel heaved at Fritz's chest. "Fritz… *please.*"

His expression dazed, as if he were coming to, he finally—thankfully—rolled off her. Liesel pushed her skirt down.

A faintly smirking smile curved Fritz's mouth as he lounged back against the cushions, his breath still ragged, his uniform rumpled. "You liked that, didn't you?"

Liesel could not make herself reply, and so she feigned embarrassment instead, ducking her head as she did up her blouse. Her finger trembled on the buttons.

"I should go," Fritz said as he clambered off the sofa. "Wish me luck?"

"I just did," Liesel returned, meaning to tease, but her voice came out sharp. She hated him, she realized. Perhaps she always had.

He gave her a slow smile in return. "So you did," he said, and he snuck an arm around her waist to pull her in for a thorough and lingering kiss that she forced herself to accept. "I'll try to come again soon."

That, Liesel thought, was a problem for another day.

"Stay safe," she murmured, unable to make her tone sincere, although Fritz hardly seemed to notice. A few moments later, the house thankfully silent the whole while, he was gone.

Liesel let out a shuddering breath, her body twinging in places that had her struggling not to cry from the shame of it. She pushed the memory deep into the recesses of her mind and hurried upstairs.

As she came into the attic, she saw the door to the eaves was wide open, and Friedy was sitting on the floor, playing marbles with the little boy. The mother held the baby to her chest, her eyes wide with fear.

"I'm sorry, so sorry. The baby, she was frightened…"

"Friedy…" Her brother's name escaped Liesel in a breath. "What are you doing here?"

Her brother shrugged. "I heard crying."

"But…" She glanced at the mother, who was still looking terrified; the father looked guarded, wary. The baby snuffled. "You shouldn't have come up here, Friedy."

"I won't tell, Liesel," he said, sounding far older than his ten years. "I know they're Jews."

She gave the little family what she hoped was a reassuring smile while they stared back wide-eyed, as fearful as ever.

"Come out of there, Friedy," she said firmly. "Leave them in peace." She touched the baby's head and smiled at the mother. "All right now?"

She nodded. "I'm so sorry…"

Briefly Liesel thought of Fritz, his searching hands, that smirking smile. "It's all right now," she told them. "It's going to be all right."

Downstairs, she boiled the kettle for coffee and gave Friedy a slice of bread with a thin scraping of margarine—even their father couldn't get butter anymore, and the shops simply didn't have it.

"You mustn't tell anyone, Friedy," she told him, trying to keep her tone both gentle and firm. "Not a word. Not even to Vati."

Her brother gave her a quiet, sober look. "I know, Liesel," he said. "I know that, more than anyone in this family."

She thought of his dazed look, the night their father had brought him back. How much had he seen at Schloss Hartheim? How much had he understood?

Liesel's body sagged under the weight of it all. *Why,* she wondered as she took a sip of scalding hot but mostly tasteless coffee, *is the world so evil?*

The family left the next day, once again slipping out into the night, and the day after, her father returned. It was another two weeks before Liesel could put the vase of flowers in the window once more, and another three days before someone—a woman this time—came with the Winter Relief collection.

My mother says it is going to be a long, cold winter.
My mother says the same.

As the months slipped by, people came and went, bombs fell on the city and the shops emptied out of food. Her father was home less and less; he was going to Poland more than Schkopau now, a journey of some six or seven hours, and so he was gone for days, or even a week, at a time. When Liesel dared to ask him about it, he shrugged, his gaze sliding away from hers.

"Oh, just as I said, another factory for making Buna rubber. A larger one this time."

"But why all the way in Poland?"

Her father did not look at her as he answered, "The labor is cheaper there. The Poles are desperate for work."

Liesel did not know anything about the Poles, beyond that they had been conquered, and it had been Germany's occupation of their country that had started this wretched war.

Sometimes, when her father was traveling, she and her mother "listened in to London," as many Germans did, tuning into the BBC's German Service, despite the many dangers of doing so. The penalty for listening to *Feindsender*, or enemy radio, was imprisonment, at the least. And yet many Germans wanted a source of news that was not controlled by the Ministry of Propaganda. Unfortunately, much of the German broadcasts focused on missing soldiers and the numbers of bombs falling rather than anything that was happening in Poland.

December bled into January, another new year of war. People came to stay in fits and starts and Liesel found that it was as she'd once thought—what had been hard became easy, or almost. Not quite. Not truly, for the terror still lined her stomach with its ice and she often found she was too anxious to eat, which was just as well since the food on offer was paltry at best. Still, she and her mother were able to do it—day after day, and night after night, sometimes with months in between visits, sometimes only weeks or even days.

In March, Fritz returned for another visit, and thankfully her father was present, her parents in the sitting room, listening to a concert of popular *Volksmusik*—her mother couldn't stand its sentimentality but her father seemed to like it—on the radio. At the end of the evening, Liesel fobbed him off with little more than a kiss, and tried not to remember his grasping hands.

In May, her father traveled to Poland for nearly a month, and they had two lots of visitors to the eaves. Friedy, Liesel discovered, had become adept at the process; he often begged Helga for extra food—she spoiled him, just as Ilse did—and then he spirited it upstairs. When any suspicious noises might be heard, he would play a loud game of bumping down the stairs or racing his cars in the hallway.

"He's giving me a headache," her mother would complain, but she would be smiling.

Sometimes, in the peaceful sunshine of a spring afternoon or the quiet stillness of a windless night, the anxiety that knotted Liesel's stomach would lessen, just a little. *Maybe we'll actually get away with this,* she thought, and then wished she hadn't. It felt like bad luck, an ill omen, to hope for so much. To think it could happen.

Then, in the autumn, the mood of the whole country began to change. The news of Germany's invasion of the Soviet Union in June had been met with hopeful apprehension; the Soviets might be considered subhuman, but they were many and powerful. How could the Germans possibly win a war against them? Her father seemed to think it dire news; he returned from Poland often in a grim mood.

One chilly evening in late October, after listening to the news, he turned off the radio with a vicious twist of the dial. "Hitler is a madman if he thinks he can conquer all of Russia."

Ilse's eyes widened and she shot Liesel a wary look, half apprehension, half hope. "Otto…"

"The troops are worn down. They can't sustain a siege over a Russian winter. Only a third of their motor vehicles still function."

"That's not what we just heard," Liesel said, for the report had been full of German victories, and her father gave a snort of disgust.

"Of course they won't say anything like that on the radio. But I hear things. Hitler is deploying far too much firepower to the Eastern Front, and he will lose on all the others, especially if America is drawn into the war, as they seem intent on being. Even a child playing with tin soldiers could see it." He stalked out of the room without saying another word, while Liesel and her mother exchanged a long, uncertain look. Could her father be coming out of his Nazi stupor at last? He had been in a particularly ill temper since he'd returned from Poland in September, snapping at everyone when he wasn't staring into space.

The question still lingered, when, a few days later, Liesel heard a soft knock on the kitchen door. It was not quite seven o'clock in the evening; Helga had only just left, and her parents were once again listening to the news on the radio in the sitting room while Liesel made coffee. A frisson of panic skated along her skin; unexpected visitors were never welcome these days.

She slid the bolt and cracked open the door, her heart seeming to jump into her mouth as she saw who was standing there, haggard and desperate.

"Gerda. *Rosa…* "

"Liesel," Rosa said, her voice hard and urgent, "you must help us."

CHAPTER TWENTY-ONE

Berlin, January 1946

The Berlin Document Center was housed in a white-washed building with pretty, painted green shutters that looked, from the outside, like a pleasant house in a leafy neighborhood, save for the gatehouse and guards that had been installed on the compound. On the inside, however, the building was crammed with files, the air thick with dust and cigarette smoke, the atmosphere stuffy and oppressive.

The radio was tuned to *Nordwestdeutscher Rundfunk,* or NWDR, which was broadcasting from the Nuremberg Trials. That morning, SS General Otto Ohlendorf of *Einsatzgruppe* D was giving his testimony in a modulated, cultured voice disconcertingly at odds with the crimes he was being tried for, the translator speaking over him so both voices could be heard at the same time.

"In what respects, if any, were the official duties of the Einsatz *groups concerned with Jews and Communist commissars?"*

"The instructions were that in the Russian operational areas of the Einsatzgruppen, *the Jews, as well as the Soviet political commissars, were to be liquidated."*

"And when you say 'liquidated' do you mean 'killed'?"

"Yes, I mean 'killed.'"

The second's pause after this statement passed like a visceral shudder through the central room of the building, a few seconds of silent acknowledgment before everyone continued working.

There were half a dozen CIC agents and army clerks there, sifting through the thousands of files for evidence to be used in the trials they were currently listening to. The archivist in charge of the Center stood fuming over them as they carelessly tossed files aside, riffling through papers with urgent intensity rather than the careful, deliberate documentation the archivist insisted was required for such classified and important material.

In addition to the several million NSDAP membership cards courtesy of Herr Huber, the Center held many of the SS's personnel files, as well those of the SA and Gestapo, and a million and a half items of Party correspondence. It was a huge amount of paperwork for anyone to go through.

Sam had been working there alongside Anna, quietly and consistently, for two days, combing through the NSDAP membership cards stacked in flimsy cardboard boxes, looking for those that belonged to the scientists they'd identified from the questionnaires. Sam thought he would see the pale pink cards in his sleep.

He'd been surprised by Anna's diligence as she'd worked alongside him; while she'd always been a good worker, she seemed even more intent now, sorting deliberately and determinedly through the cards, fingers flying as she cross-checked them with the *fragebogen*. Almost, he thought, as if she were looking for something—or someone—in particular.

Searching for the membership cards of the handful of scientists they had identified felt like hunting for a needle in a dozen haystacks, just as Sergeant Belmont had once so sardonically remarked. Sam had wondered yet again if he was merely being fobbed off with busy work while "real" agents got on with the business of hunting down Nazis. It was hard to know what the point of any of it was; he suspected Supreme Command didn't know, either. More and more he realized that not just Berlin, but the whole country, was in an utter shambles, and no consistent policy was being enacted anywhere.

Half of the American army seemed to want to leave the Germans to it, while the other half wanted to lock them all up, or worse. The camps housing millions of displaced persons—or DPs—that littered Germany's landscape inspired both pity and derision. General Patton himself had been known to say DPs were not even human beings, and Jews "lower than an animal."

The broadcasts of the trials in Nuremberg could fire a man's soul, but then that same man went to a bar that evening and picked up a *fraulein*, or sold a pack of cigarettes for twenty bucks. Sam couldn't make any sense of it, but he supposed he wasn't meant to. War was senseless, the aftermath even more so. Creating order out of chaos became near impossible.

The radio continued to drone on with Ohlendorf's questioning and the translator talking over him as Sam pulled another box of cards toward him.

"Will you tell the Tribunal in what way, or ways, the command officer of the 11th Army directed or supervised Einsatz Group D in carrying out its liquidation activities?"

"In Simferopol, the army command requested the Einsatzkommandos *in its area to hasten liquidations, because famine was threatening and there was a great housing shortage."*

"Do you know how many persons were liquidated by Einsatz Group D under your command?"

"In the year between June 1941 to June 1942, the Einsatzkommandos *reported ninety thousand people liquidated."*

"Did that include men, women, and children?"

"Yes."

"For the love of God." One of the agents, a cigarette dangling from his lips, looked up from his pile of papers, an expression of stunned disgust on his face. A bit of ash dropped onto the papers and he swept it away. "We've *got* to nail these bastards."

Sam glanced at Anna; she had raised her head from her work when the clerk had spoken and was sitting very still, her gaze distant and hooded. She had been working diligently for the two days they'd been there, going through files faster than he was, her eyes narrowed, her gaze assessing, almost as if she knew even more than he did what to look for.

Yesterday afternoon she'd drawn a sharp breath in and Sam had looked up blearily from his own pile of papers. "You found something?"

She'd glanced at him, her eyes blazing with a strange, savage sort of triumph. "Yes," she had said simply, and added a card to the pile they'd collected.

Now it was late afternoon, and his neck ached from bending over files. "Why don't we call it a day?" he told her.

She raised her eyebrows in query. "Call it a day?"

"Finish. We've gotten through a fair amount, haven't we?" Between the two of them, they'd located the membership cards of forty chemists, including the one Anna had found yesterday, most of them middlemen who had probably spent the whole war squinting into test tubes in some basement lab, but still. It wasn't bad for three days of ferreting through files, and right now Sam had had enough of the stuffy room, the drone of the radio, the feeling of hopelessness that fell on him like a heavy, oppressive cloak.

The other men sifting through their files looked bemused as Anna rose from her seat and went to get her coat. Sam knew they assumed he was sleeping with her; they'd given him smirking looks and several winks since they'd arrived at the Document Center, and each one had made him cringe inside.

He felt guilty for their kiss, and he didn't know why. She'd been the one to kiss him, after all. He'd wanted to ask her why she had, but somehow the words wouldn't come. Last night they'd eaten dinner at a restaurant around the corner from the hotel, a hole-in-the-wall place frequented by rowdy Americans with surprisingly decent food. It had been lovely, surprisingly comfortable, if without the compelling intimacy of that first evening in his bedroom at the hotel, when she'd told him about her biggest regret—he still didn't know what it was—and then kissed him.

They'd eaten mostly in companionable silence, and when they'd spoken, it had been about the most innocuous of subjects. Anna had asked him if he liked American films, and then she'd listened to him stiltedly recap the plot of *I'll Be Seeing You*, the last film he'd seen with his sister Nancy, a romantic drama with Ginger Rogers that he hadn't paid much attention to.

"I wish life was like that," Anna had said with a small, wistful smile. "All wrapped up neatly at the end, where everything makes sense. All the tragedy has a reason."

"I'm not sure tragedy ever makes sense," Sam had said and Anna's gaze had swept slowly over him.

"No, I suppose it doesn't. It is us who try to find meaning where perhaps there is none. Perhaps we should simply do as Goethe says, and 'Enjoy what you can. Endure what you must.'"

"You like Goethe, don't you?" Sam had remarked. "You mentioned him before, when you thought I knew *Faust*."

Anna had inclined her head in acknowledgment. "Most Germans know a bit of Goethe. My father enjoyed his work very much."

"Do you miss him?" Sam had asked, for he'd heard an ache of remembrance in her voice that made him want to comfort her. Anna's expression had hardened briefly.

"I miss the man he was," she had replied, which was not quite the answer Sam had expected.

Now, as they left the compound, the sky was a pale blue threaded with gold, wisps of mist caught on the trees like bits of cotton wool, the dark promise of dusk already in the frigid air.

"Do you want to walk for a little while?" Sam asked. They were on the edge of the large, leafy park that ran along the Schlachtensee and Krumme Lanke, two of the southernmost in Grunewald's chain of lakes.

Anan gave a brief nod and they headed into the park, the grass stiff with frost, crackling beneath their feet as they walked among the stark, bare-branched trees, shadows lengthening along the stretch of slate-blue water.

Anna, Sam saw, had started to stride with purpose; there was a focused air of decision about her, almost as if she were going somewhere certain as they made their way along the muddy path by the lake, the air cold and damp all around them, their breath coming out in frosty puffs. Sam's cheeks were stinging with cold and he had to quicken his step to keep up with her.

"You did well these last few days," he said. "You've worked hard."

She slid him a quick, blazing look. "Yes."

It was not quite the response he'd expected, and not one he knew how to answer.

"I don't know how much longer we'll stay in Berlin," he told her after a moment. He had not been given a brief from either Pitt or Lewis, and sometimes he wondered if they would happily let him molder away along with the boxes of membership cards that had almost been pulped.

"We have found enough," Anna answered, and Sam slowed his steps.

"Were you looking for something in particular?" he asked, recalling that strange moment of triumph yesterday. "Someone?"

"The chemists," Anna replied after a pause. "Just as you were."

"You know what I mean—"

"It's getting dark," Anna answered, and hurried her steps.

Frowning, Sam followed her as they emerged from beside Krumme Lanke to the path that ran northeast through the park, past the Riding Club on the shores of the Grunewaldsee, to the Berlin-Grunewald neighborhood of elegant, nineteenth-century villas, some of them flattened by bombs, yet many still preserved and now housing British or American officers.

"Are we going somewhere in particular?" Sam asked with a little laugh as Anna strode ahead, arms now swinging by her sides, seeming to be on some sort of mission.

"I just want to see," she said, and kept walking.

"See what?" Sam called after her, but she didn't answer.

They emerged from the park onto Koenigsallee, opposite the tranquil waters of the smaller Hundekehlesee; it was a gracious street lined with large villas, some positively palatial, others more modest, all designed in a variety of eclectic styles. There were Swiss chalets, Bavarian castles, angular, glass-fronted hymns to modern architecture and Greek-colonnaded temples that looked like ancient shrines to domesticity.

The variation somehow made the gaps in the street more jarring; some were nothing but foundations of rubble, others were missing merely a wall or a roof. Sam knew the neighborhood had been a gentrified district, home to artists, actors, writers, and scientists, many of them Jewish, until the Nazi top brass took possession of many of the houses in the thirties.

Anna paused at the bottom of the street that was empty of people, a chill wind blowing down it as twilight fell like a curtain drawing closed on a play. Her fingers went to her throat, touching the pocket watch that Sam knew now nestled there. Then she kept walking. After a second's pause, Sam followed.

They walked in silence for around ten minutes, past house after elegant house, until they arrived at one of the more modest villas, although still impressive with its white stucco façade, red-tiled roof, and oval portico supported by several slender pillars. It looked both undamaged and occupied, with flowers in the windows, a silver Mercedes in the drive.

Anna stood in front of the house, her fingers clutching reflexively at the pocket watch as she stared at the house in silence for a few taut minutes.

"You know who lived there?" Sam finally asked quietly, because that was the only reason he could think of for her to be looking at the house with such a ferocious mixture of longing and hatred.

"Yes." The single word was spoken with firm decision, yet her voice ached with regret.

"Who…?"

She didn't reply right away; she was staring at the house as if she wanted either to burn it down or run inside. "Everyone," she said at last, and then she turned and starting walked back toward the park.

Sam stood there for a moment, his mind ticking over as the wind ruffled his hair and he felt the damp, numbing cold seep into his bones. Then he turned and walked smartly back, catching up with Anna in a few long strides.

"You're not from Essen," he stated flatly, only just keeping himself from making it an accusation. She didn't reply. "You're from Berlin." He was an analyst, for Pete's sake, and it had taken him this long to fit the pieces together. She was cultured, she knew both Goethe and the streets of Berlin, as well as being as good as fluent in English. Of course she wasn't the daughter of a shopkeeper from Essen. Mentally, he shook his head, annoyed with himself for being so ridiculously foolish. No wonder Major Pitt thought he was a greenhorn, and Major Lewis fobbed him with off with busy work more suitable for a sixth-grader. How could he have been so blind?

Because you're in love with her.

"Anna—" He reached for her sleeve, wanting to stay her, and she whirled around, a fierce look on her face.

"Don't ask me," she said. "Not yet."

He stared at her in surprise and growing anger for a few seconds. "Why not?" he demanded roughly.

She let out a rush of breath. "What is going to happen to the scientists we've found?"

He shrugged. "I don't know. I'll pass the files on to Major Lewis, and he'll probably pass them on to someone else. They'll be the ones to decide, not me."

"Some of those chemists were party members since the twenties," she continued, her voice nearly vibrating with the force of her feeling. "They were dedicated Nazis."

"I know." One of the advantages of having the membership cards was that each recorded the date of membership; someone who joined the Party after 1936 most likely had done so because of pressure rather than conviction, and was therefore far less of a threat. The information was, Sam hoped, invaluable. "They'll have to find them first," he told her with another shrug. "I'm only involved on the paperwork side of things, as you know."

"But at least they will know who to find."

"Yes." He stared at her for a moment. "What's it to you?" But he had a feeling he already knew. "Who," he asked slowly, feeling for each word as if groping in the dark, "do you know? Who were you looking for in those files?" He thought of how assiduous she'd been, her head bent, her gaze intent as she'd searched through the endless cards as if looking for something specific. *Someone.* And that moment of triumph, the satisfaction blazing in her eyes. "Whose membership card did you find yesterday?" he demanded, and now he sounded angry. Was she trying to find someone, or trying to hide them? It would have been so easy for her to slip a card back into the box, or even into her purse. He'd trusted her, and she might have had her own private agenda all along. Who might she be trying to protect?

Because Anna Vogel had lied, he realized, about a lot of things. He'd always suspected she'd been lying about something; most

Germans were, either out of desperation or expediency. But now, as dusk fell all around them, he sensed a seething sea of deception surging beneath her seemingly placid surface, and he knew he could be swept away on it.

"Who are you?" he demanded.

Still she didn't reply.

"Anna, *tell me*."

She was silent for a long moment, her lips pursed, her gaze sliding away from his.

"I have a *right*," Sam said, his voice rising. "If you've been deceiving me, deceiving the U.S. government—"

"It's better for you not to know," she said at last. "Please. Give the files we've found to Major Lewis. Wait until he has them."

"Why?"

She shook her head, and he felt himself getting properly angry.

"Why won't you tell me? You have no right to lie to me like this. You could be in serious trouble if my superiors discover you're not who you said who you were, you know. That sort of thing doesn't go down well with the U.S. Army at *all*." His belligerent tone didn't sit well with him, and it didn't with Anna, either. Temper flared in her eyes and she whirled around, walking back toward the park, leaving Sam no choice but to follow, fuming, impotent.

"Give him the files," she said again, over her shoulder, and then did not speak all the way back to the hotel, no matter how many times Sam tried to get her to talk. By the time they passed Krumme Lanke, the lake now cloaked in indigo shadows, he gave up. He was angry, but worse, he was hurt. He thought they'd shared something— something small, yes, but still something. Obviously they hadn't. Anna—if that was even her name—had some other agenda, some secret. Many secrets, even. And Sam had no idea what they were.

Anna hurried up to her room as soon as they got back to the hotel, and Sam waited at the front desk to check for messages from Frankfurt, as he did every evening. There hadn't been one yet, but tonight the man behind the desk, balding and whey-faced, handed over a scrap of paper with a message in German scrawled on it, which, after everything he'd just experienced, infuriated Sam beyond reason.

"I can't read this," he snapped at the man, waving the paper as if it were something truly offensive. "How do you expect me to read this?"

"*Verzeihung…*" the man stammered, abject, fluttering his hands, and Sam wheeled away, more impatient with himself than the poor sod who clearly spoke no English.

"Never mind," he muttered. "I'll deal with it."

Upstairs, he rapped sharply on Anna's door; it was a good thirty seconds before she opened it, and when she did, Sam realized she must have been undressing. Her blouse was buttoned up wrong, and she was holding it together at the neck, her eyes wide, the pocket watch visible between the undone buttons.

"Captain Houghton…"

"Read this," he demanded, and thrust the paper at her.

Anna took it between slender fingers, a frown creasing the smooth paleness of her forehead. "Major Lewis wishes you to return to Frankfurt tomorrow morning," she translated slowly.

"Tomorrow." He nodded tersely. "Well, be ready to leave, then, right after breakfast." He still sounded aggressive, even angry, and Anna lowered the paper to look at him for a moment.

"I'm sorry, Sam," she said quietly.

"Sorry?" he practically sneered. "For what?" It was a challenge; he wanted her to name the reason. To tell him at last whatever it was she'd been hiding.

But she just shook her head, handing him back the scrap of paper before gently, almost apologetically, she closed the door in his face. As he stood there feeling furious, he had the unsettling sense she'd been apologizing not for what had or hadn't happened already, but for what was yet to come.

CHAPTER TWENTY-TWO

Berlin, October 1941

"Rosa…"

The name slipped from her lips as Liesel shot a frantic glance over her shoulder, although there was no one else in the kitchen. Her parents were still listening to the radio, the sound of Hitler's furious rhetoric loud enough, thankfully, to have drowned out the soft tapping at the door.

"What are you doing here?"

"Please, please help us," Gerda said, her voice a soft, urgent whisper.

Liesel swallowed dryly. "I didn't put the flowers in the window." She feared she sounded petulant, when really she was merely afraid. Utterly, overwhelmingly afraid. If her father came in… if someone had seen them… It wasn't even dark yet.

The others had never come like this, in the soft twilight, the sun still spreading over the city, turning everything to gold… and making everyone perfectly visible. What on earth had Gerda and Rosa been thinking? They had taken an extraordinary and extremely reckless risk. Liesel's throat felt as if it had closed up, her insides contracting with fear.

"Please, may we come in?" Gerda entreated quietly.

Wordlessly, Liesel nodded, not trusting herself to speak. Amidst all the fear, a white-hot flare of anger burned inside her. After all she'd done, how could they risk her life—her family's lives—like this? They surely knew better, and yet here they were.

Quietly, Liesel closed the door, while Gerda and Rose stood close together in the kitchen; their shabby overcoats, Liesel saw, had a yellow star with the word "Jew" written on it sewed onto the left shoulder. Heydrich had instituted the measure for German Jews only a few weeks ago, although Jews in Poland had had to wear them since the beginning of the war. Gerda was clutching a flimsy suitcase, and Rosa held a cardboard box. They looked exhausted.

"What has happened?" Liesel asked, and that familiar look of scorn mixed with hope flashed across Rosa's face.

"Have you not heard?" she demanded.

"No, I'm sorry."

Gerda gave her daughter an admonishing look. "The Gestapo came to the synagogue on Levetzowstrasse on Yom Kippur. The highest of our holy days." Her voice trembled and Liesel stayed silent. "Our leaders were told that all the Jews in Berlin would be resettled."

"Resettled…?"

"Who knows what it means?" Gerda lifted her shoulders in a weary shrug. "All the Jews have been put on a list, given dates when they need to come to a collection point. Our baggage can be deposited at Levetzowstrasse." She fumbled in her pocket and then handed a leaflet to Liesel. "They've even told us what we can bring."

Liesel scanned down the typed list of what was permitted—warm clothes, bedding, umbrellas and underwear, matches and medicine. All documents save for passports were to be handed in to the proper authorities, along with any cash, savings bonds, financial papers, and even jewelry. Evacuees were to compile an inventory of all household belongings that would have to be left behind.

Liesel glanced up from the sheet. From the sitting room, she could hear that the news report was ending. In a few minutes, maybe only seconds, her father would turn off the radio and call back to her. *Liesel? Coffee?* Or maybe he would come back himself, although the kitchen was hardly his domain. Still, the mere possibility made her breath catch.

"Where will you go?" she whispered as she handed the sheet back to Gerda. She tucked it away in her coat pocket. "Where is this resettlement?"

Gerda shrugged her bony shoulders in helpless ignorance. "No one knows."

"We're not going," Rosa stated, her voice rising with alarming stridency. Liesel shot a panicked glance toward the sitting room. "They can't just ship us off like… like *cattle.*"

"We can't talk here," Liesel hissed. "My father…" She glanced at Gerda. "He's changed. I don't think he'll be very sympathetic. We've been keeping what… what we're doing from him."

Gerda's face paled, but Rosa only looked mutinous, as if she wanted to march into the sitting room and take Otto by the ear. Liesel could almost picture her doing it. It seemed as if the increased injustice had magnified her anger, made her want to fight. Liesel did not feel the same; all she felt now was fear, and yet she knew she would not turn them away.

"Come upstairs," she urged. "We'll discuss this properly when we have the freedom to do so." Although she did not know when that would be; freedom was a rare commodity these days.

She led them up the back set of stairs, meant for servants, wincing as the weathered wood creaked under their steps. As they came onto the first floor, Friedy poked his head out of his bedroom, his eyes widening owlishly at the sight of the two women creeping up the stairs in their overcoats, but he said nothing. Liesel pressed her finger to her lips just in case, although, in truth, Friedy was probably the most worldly-wise of all of them.

He'd certainly handled the furtive trips up and down the stairs without turning a hair. Liesel thought it likely that she was more afraid of the possible repercussions than Friedy was.

Up in the attics, the eaves were cobwebby, the air stuffy and stale, with a lingering smell of unwashed clothing and sweat. Liesel had not been up there in several weeks, since the last time the space had been used. She preferred not to climb the stairs when she didn't have to; sometimes she could almost forget the space under the eaves existed, that it was waiting for its next residents.

"I'm sorry," she whispered as she reached for a blanket and shook it out, sending a cloud of dust into the air. "My father has been home for several weeks. I didn't think…"

"I'm sorry to inconvenience you," Gerda replied with dignity. "We had no choice."

Yes, you did, Liesel thought, but she did not say it. She knew the response was small-minded and ungenerous; she didn't even want to think it. Yet she couldn't help it; she did.

"I must return downstairs," she told them. "My father will be wondering where I am. But I'll come up later. We'll talk then."

Gerda nodded, and with a deep breath, doing her best to avoid Rosa's challenging gaze, Liesel headed back downstairs. Her mother was in the kitchen making the coffee as she came down the stairs, and she gave Liesel a sharp look of silent inquiry.

Liesel shook her head, not wanting to explain with her father so close by, and her mother remarked quietly, knowingly, "You have cobwebs in your hair."

"It's Gerda and Rosa," Liesel whispered. She swiped the cobwebs out of her hair as Ilse's eyes widened and her lips parted soundlessly.

"They're here now? But…" Her gaze slid inexorably toward the sitting room; the strains of a symphony by Beethoven had replaced Hitler's speech.

"They said they had no choice. All the Jews of Berlin are being resettled."

"Resettled?"

"I don't know what it means."

"They can't stay here." Ilse sounded panicked rather than resolute. "Your father isn't returning to Schkopau for over a week."

"I know."

For a few seconds, they simply stared at each other in silent, wide-eyed understanding; they both knew, without having to say a word, that they would not turn Gerda and her daughter from their home, no matter what the risk. It was not even to be considered, no matter what Ilse had just said.

The next hour passed with painful slowness. Ilse brought the coffee into the sitting room, and they sipped the bitter chicory and listened to Beethoven while night fell softly outside, the golds and reds leached from the sky. Ilse rose to close the blackout curtains; in recent weeks, the Soviet Union had been sending its bombers to Berlin, and many nights had been spent in the cellar, although it had quieted down in the last few days, thank goodness. If there was an air raid tonight, Liesel thought, Gerda and Rosa would have to stay in the attic and take their chances. She closed her eyes at the thought.

"Liesel? Are you well?" Liesel opened her eyes to see her father giving her a questioning smile, his forehead creased with concern, his narrowed eyes as shrewd as ever. "You seem so quiet."

"I'm merely tired."

"Perhaps a visit from Hauptmann Burkhardt would cheer you up," Otto said with a wink, and Liesel forced a smile in return. She had not seen Fritz in months, and she had no desire to see him ever again, no matter that her father seemed to wish to encourage their relationship. She did not bother to make a reply, however, for she knew anything but absolute agreement would annoy her father now.

He turned back to the radio, and as Liesel sipped her coffee, she considered how her relationship with her father had changed over recent months and years. It had been just over five years ago that he'd taken her to the Opening Ceremony of the Olympics, when she'd been so starry-eyed and silly.

Lovely though it had been, that day now felt like the start of it all, or at least of her questioning. She remembered asking him why he didn't like Hitler and how unsettled and annoyed her father had seemed by the question.

She understood so much more now; mentally, she shook her head at the thought of her naïve, fourteen-year-old self asking her father such a question while SS loitered about, and the cream of Nazi officers streamed out of the stadium. It had been incredibly imprudent, and yet her father had done his best to take it in his stride even as he'd scolded her.

She hadn't understood then, as she did now, how deeply rooted her father's ambition was, how poisonous a vine that had twined around all their lives, choking and choking them. For years he'd made justifications to her and her mother, as well as to himself, for his choices, and while at first Liesel had felt some flicker of sympathy, desperate to understand, that was soon replaced by scorn and anger.

She felt neither now. Now she felt fear—a metallic taste in her mouth, a hollowing-out of her stomach, a loosening of her bowels. It took over completely her mind and body. She knew her mother felt it too, and more alarmingly, she suspected her father knew it, as well. In the last year, the balance had somehow shifted, from her and Ilse's icy self-righteousness under which Otto had been humbled, to a cringing wariness that he now accepted as his due. She was *afraid* of her adored father, and she thought at least part of him was glad.

She saw it in the satisfied look on his face as he sipped his coffee, and how he'd deliberately mentioned Fritz, even though she'd already told him she didn't care for him that way. He was master of his domain, pulling the puppet strings of all their lives, and it seemed he liked it that way.

Liesel wondered if Ilse's coolness to him even bothered him anymore. As long as he had the illusion of domestic bliss, did he even care about its reality? Bitterness twisted her gut and she feared the effect of it was visible on her face. Had her father actually changed, or was this the man he'd been all along, the man he'd been hoping to become, when finally given the opportunity and the power?

"I think I shall go to bed," she announced when the Beethoven had ended.

Ilse lurched up at the same time. "As will I."

Otto looked bemused. "Everyone is tired tonight, it seems." There was a slight, implied rebuke to the words; normally he decided when they retired.

Liesel gathered the coffee cups and put them in the sink for Helga to deal with in the morning, while her parents headed upstairs. They slept in separate bedrooms now, and had since the night Friedrich had come home from Schloss Hartheim. Otto had taken a guest bedroom down the hall without a murmur; he'd moved his things across himself. Such self-effacement seemed at odds with the power he now wielded over them, and yet Liesel knew they would always go hand in hand. Her father would never lose his light touch, his wry manner, even as he marched determinedly on, goose-stepping to his Party's demands.

In her own bedroom, Liesel changed into her nightgown and robe and then brushed her hair out, all the while listening for the sounds of her father going to bed. She heard the turning of a tap, the flush of a toilet, a particularly loud yawn, and then the creak of bedsprings. Liesel counted to one hundred slowly as she perched on the edge of her bed, her heart thudding as she waited for her father to fall asleep.

How *did* he sleep at night? she wondered. What did he think of when he closed his eyes? Had he truly made peace with the regime he served, with the atrocities they committed? By all accounts, it seemed he had, and yet some part of her still resisted believing that. Wanting to believe the best of him, even now.

She counted to one hundred again, just to be sure, and then, as quietly as she could, she opened her bedroom door and tiptoed down the hall. As she reached the stairs that led to the attics, Friedy opened his door. He was dressed in his pajamas, but despite the late hour, his expression was alert.

"Friedy, you should be asleep," Liesel scolded in a whisper that was barely more than a breath.

"How could I sleep?"

"Go back to bed."

"No."

She shook her head, knowing they couldn't afford to have an argument in the hall, and Friedy obviously knew it, too. Together, they climbed the steps to the attic, Liesel wincing at the audible creaks their footsteps made.

As she pried open the door to the space under the eaves, she realized she hadn't brought anything to eat or drink. Guilt soured her stomach as she peered inside the dark space and saw Gerda and Rosa sitting there, hunched over, still in their coats, alert and anxious.

"I'm sorry," Liesel whispered. "I had to wait until my father was asleep. I didn't think to bring anything to eat."

"I did," Friedy said, and took some black bread wrapped in a dishcloth from his pocket. Gerda took it with a murmured thanks while Liesel blushed in shame.

"We are grateful," Gerda said after she'd broken the bread into two and handed one hunk to her daughter. "That you allowed us in here at all." She nudged her daughter. "Rosa."

Rosa's face, Liesel saw, was full of the old hostility. She hadn't seen her in over a year, and when they'd last parted it had been, if not quite as friends, then something close to it. But now Rosa was all anger and accusation: Liesel realized she could hardly blame her. Fifteen years old, and her entire world had not just been upended, but deliberately destroyed. There were no Nazis here to rage against, and so she would make do with Liesel. She would have been the same at that age, Liesel knew. The young could be fearless; anger made them strong.

"Are you going to make us leave?" Rosa demanded.

Liesel took a deep, steadying breath. "No, but I must tell you how dangerous it is. When—when people have come before, my father was away. He's never known."

"Herr Scholz is a good man," Gerda stated quietly, and Liesel bit her lip to keep from disagreeing with her. Heaven knew she wanted to believe it, as well.

"That may be so, but it is still very dangerous for you to be here," she insisted in a whisper. "There is our new housekeeper, as well, who is devoted to Hitler. And we don't know who watches the house, because of my father's work." A thought that still made her dizzy and sick with terror. She thought of Heydrich's cold smile, his remark about her mother. *Perhaps she will play for me sometime.* Heaven forbid.

Gerda stared at her for a moment, her expression barely visible in the shadowy space, but Liesel felt her fear, along with Rosa's anger. "There is nowhere else for us to go," she stated quietly, a simple fact.

"This resettlement program…" Liesel hesitated, Rosa's animosity rolling off her in silent, pulsing waves. "Could you not consider it? Perhaps, once you are out of Berlin, out of Germany, things will be easier for you. You'll have more freedoms…" Rosa let out a huff of disbelief and Liesel continued quickly, "I'm not saying it is right. Of course I'm not. It's all so dreadfully wrong." She took another swift breath. "But… considering how things are, perhaps it would be better?" This suggestion was met with a silence that felt both uncomprehending and eloquent. "I only mean…" She struggled to find the words, to make them sound reasonable. "Maybe this could be a new beginning for you both."

Rosa let out another huff and folded her arms as she looked away. Gerda stared hard at her for a moment.

"Surely you have seen how the Nazis treat us Jews," she said finally. "Why would you think it would be any better elsewhere? It is likely to be worse. Much worse."

"Besides, I've seen the transit camp in Levetzowstrasse," Rosa said. "They take everything from you, and there is nothing to sleep on but straw. If they wanted to *resettle* us, they'd allow us to keep our belongings as well as our money. We would not have to hand over our passports, our jewelry, everything."

Liesel stared at her for a moment, as her father's words filtered back through her mind. *In a few years' time, there will not be many, if any, Jews left in the Greater Reich.* He must have known about this. He understood what this resettlement might mean, and yet she knew she could not ask him.

"If you want us to go," Gerda said, straightening, "we'll go."

"Mama—"

"We cannot stay, if we are not wanted," Gerda told Rosa sharply. "It is not fair to ask Fraulein Scholz to risk her life for us, the life of her family. You cannot make such demands, Rosa."

"I don't mind, Liesel," Friedy said quietly. "I think they should stay."

Liesel blinked, feeling the terrible rebuke in Gerda's words as well as her brother's. Friedy was braver than she was. How could she be so selfish? Of course Gerda had seen through her flimsy reasons for them to accept being resettled. "No, no, you must stay," she murmured. "I only wanted to explain how it is dangerous—not just for me, but for you as well. You must understand the risks."

"Everywhere is dangerous for us," Rosa interjected. "An attic is not so bad."

Liesel looked down at her lap, entirely humbled and chastened now.

"Rosa," Gerda said softly. "Fraulein Scholz has done so much for our friends, as well as for us. Show respect."

Rosa did not reply and Liesel looked up.

"You must stay here," she said as firmly as she could. "And tomorrow I will try to discover more about this resettlement program. Perhaps—perhaps it is not as bad as it sounds." The words sounded feeble, utterly so, to her own ears, and yet she had to say them. What was the alternative? For the Baums to live in her attic forever?

"Here." Quickly, Gerda slipped a golden chain from around her neck. "Take this. It was my husband's. Perhaps you can get something for it, to pay for our board."

"That's not necessary," Liesel protested as Gerda pressed a pocket watch of deep, mellow gold into her hands. "Please—"

"I insist," Gerda said with iron in her voice. "I will be no one's debtor."

Reluctantly, Liesel slipped the watch into her pocket, the smooth oval fitting neatly into the palm of her hand. She caught Rosa's furious stare, and could only imagine how angry the girl would be at her taking such a precious heirloom, perhaps the only one they had left. As soon as she could return it, she would.

"I'll bring some breakfast tomorrow, before Helga comes," she said as she rose from where she'd been crouching, along with Friedy. "But you must be very, very quiet. And if the air raid sounds…"

"We know," Gerda said swiftly. "We understand."

Liesel nodded slowly, trying to not to be hurt by Rosa's silent glower, feeling guilty for how little she could do. How little she *wanted* to do. It was both shaming and humbling, to realize the abhorrent extent of her own selfishness. She would much rather Gerda and Rosa had never come at all, and what did that say about her?

As she crept back down the stairs with Friedy, she felt only misery mixed with that terrible, churning fear. Her little brother was far more pragmatic.

"If I practice piano after school for an hour," he told her, "they can move around for a bit and no one will hear. I do bang the keys terribly."

"Oh, Friedy." Liesel pulled him into a hug and he returned it, slightly startled, for as he'd grown older they had not had occasion to embrace in such an affectionate manner. Now, however, she felt a fierce, almost maternal love for him, all of twelve years old, resolute and even cheerful in his determination to do what was right. "You are a good boy," she said, sniffing back tears.

Friedy pulled back with a crooked grin. "Well, since I wasn't able to be useful to the Reich," he said with a hint of their father's old wryness, "at least I can be useful in this."

"You are," Liesel told him fiercely. "You *are.*"

Ilse was waiting for them outside her bedroom, her arms wrapped around the belted waist of her dressing gown. "Well?"

Liesel shrugged. "I don't know. I need to find out about this resettlement program tomorrow. Maybe…"

"Resettlement program?" Ilse repeated harshly. "The only place the Nazis want to *resettle* the Jews is in hell."

"But then what will we do? They can't stay here forever."

Her mother was quiet for a long moment, her face drawn, her eyes dark. She looked old; Liesel suspected she did as well, although she'd only be twenty in February.

"There is no 'forever' for any of us," Ilse said at last, and then she turned and went into her bedroom, closing the door softly behind her.

CHAPTER TWENTY-THREE

Berlin, October 1941

Liesel could not find out anything. When she took to the streets the next morning, having crept up the stairs after her father had gone to work and given Gerda and Rosa some water, bread, and a lump of hard cheese, she only encountered blank-faced people hurrying on their way to work, heads lowered against the chill wind off the Spree. No one wanted to talk about anything. No one wanted to know.

She was well used to the stony look most Berliners gave these days, a mixture of blank indifference and wary suspicion, the façade everyone wore to face the world. Better not to ask, not to say, not to know.

Even the usual newspapers weren't covering the deportation; she scanned the headlines of the papers at a stall and saw nothing that spoke of it, only of glorious victories in the Soviet Union— the successful siege of Odessa, the Wehrmacht's inexorable march on Moscow as the Soviet government evacuated.

Reluctantly, she paused in front of one of the red *Sturmerkasten* that held a copy of the infamously vitriolic, anti-Jewish newspaper *Der Sturmer*. Liesel had stopped so much as looking at it years ago, hating its vile caricatures and evil headlines, but now she paused as she scanned the lead article written by Julius Streicher, the newspaper's founder: *If the danger of the reproduction of that curse of God in the Jewish blood is to finally come to an end, then there is only one way—the extermination of that people whose father is the devil.*

Extermination, Liesel thought hollowly, was not resettlement, and yet she still struggled to believe in so evil a possibility. How could anyone exterminate thousands—*millions*—of people? How could it possibly be accomplished, never mind allowed? Besides, *Der Stürmer* was notoriously hate-filled; it had been spouting such vile rhetoric for over fifteen years. It didn't mean any of it was true.

Searching for more answers, she walked all the way to the synagogue on Levetzowstrasse that had been made into a transit camp, and watched from across the street as the place bustled with evacuees and bristled with Gestapo. Her heart in her mouth, Liesel could barely keep from crying out as a Gestapo ruthlessly went through an old man's possessions, letting family photographs flutter to the ground as he dumped out the single suitcase the man had brought to the collection point. Money, a savings book, a gold ring—it all went into the Gestapo's pocket as he gave the man a push toward the synagogue, now stripped of all its ornamentation, leaving nothing but an empty space for people to be packed into.

Liesel turned to a woman who was hurrying by, her head down, her face averted from the scene across the street.

"Do you know where they're going?" she asked and the only response she received was a flicker of alarm in the woman's eyes before she hurried on.

"Do *you* know where they're going?"

Liesel turned to see a man wearing a checked suit and a cynical expression gazing at her. He looked to be in his early fifties, balding, with round spectacles and a face that looked careworn and battle weary.

"To be resettled," she said, with all of her uncertainty in her voice.

"Resettled. You make it sound like a vacation. Trust me, it won't be." His German was accented, and after a second's pause, Liesel realized he had to be American.

"You're a reporter," she said in English, and his gaze cleared.

"You know English?"

"My father made me take lessons." Much use they had been. She could speak English well enough, but they would never emigrate to America now.

"Well, then let me tell you in plain English, miss. Wherever they're going, they won't be coming back."

"What do you mean?"

"What do you think I mean?" His voice held both gentleness and a faint sneer. "The Gestapo is taking everything from them, even the metal blades from their razors. Where they're going, they won't need it. Any of it."

"But…" She thought again of the vitriol she'd read in *Der Sturmer*. "Why?"

"Why do you think?"

Tired of his questions, and feeling perilously close to tears, Liesel snapped, "Just tell me what *you* think."

"I think they're going to camps," the man said quietly. "You've heard of them?"

"For…" She struggled for a moment to remember the words in English. "Political prisoners? Surely there isn't enough space."

"There is if they've been building more, and they have."

"How do you know?" she asked, startled by his matter-of-fact tone.

"I'm the bureau chief for the Associated Press." He stuck out a hand, which she shook hesitantly. "Louis Lochner. Did you come here today for a purpose?"

She swallowed, thinking of Gerda and Rosa. "I'd heard about it, and I wanted to see."

"And have you seen enough?" He nodded toward the line of slump-shouldered people being herded into the synagogue. "Do you think anything good is happening there?"

"No," Liesel whispered.

"And I think it's a lot worse than anyone is willing to say or believe." He eyed her with some sympathy, although there was a certain hardness to his features. "If you have any friends who are Jews, miss, I'd tell them to be careful. Very careful, if you get my meaning."

Liesel's face flushed as she thought again of Gerda and Rosa. "How…" The single word trailed away into nothing, because she didn't even know what to ask.

"And you should be careful too, miss," Lochner said.

A bubble of hysteria rose in her throat as she stared wildly at Lochner. If a reporter she'd never met before had been able to figure out, more or less, what she was doing here, who else could? What if she'd been followed?

"These are dangerous days, although my time's almost up in Berlin, if America joins the war."

"You think they will?" Her father had said as much, but Liesel hardly dared hope.

"I certainly hope so. If they do, Germany hasn't a snowball's chance in hell of winning." He gave her a look of undisguised pity. "It won't be easy, you know, for Germans like you then."

"No…" And yet if Germany lost the war… Hitler would no longer be in power. Jews would no longer be in danger. Berlin would be safe again. But what would happen to her father? To her? "Thank you," she whispered, and then she started toward home, walking quickly, her head down.

She'd been thinking of visiting the Reich Association of Jews in Germany on Kurfurstenstrasse to ask more questions, but now she realized it was too dangerous. She knew the bureau was overseen by Adolf Eichmann, who reported directly to Heydrich. What if he realized she was asking questions? It had been foolish even to come here, to Levetzowstrasse. The last thing she wanted to do was draw attention to herself, or to Gerda and Rosa.

Back at home, her mother hurried out of the sitting room the moment Liesel opened the front door, a gust of cold wind blowing in and rattling the windowpanes.

"Well?" she asked quietly.

Liesel shook her head. "I couldn't learn very much. But…" She paused, thinking of Louis Lochner, the Gestapo calmly and carelessly going through that poor man's possessions. "They will have to stay," she said softly. "I can see no other way."

Ilse's hands bunched on her skirt. "Liesel, you know that is impossible."

"Is it?" Liesel's mind was racing. "Why should it be? No one knows. Father's gone most of the time, anyway."

"But you know he's not leaving for another week. Besides…" she trailed off as they both listened to Helga singing the catchy marching song "*Die Hitlerleute*" in the kitchen.

"*Many Hitlerites died in the struggle for their homeland,*" she sang lustily. "*But nobody thinks about complaining, everyone wants to dare to be brave.*"

"We can dare, Mutti," Liesel said softly. "We can dare to be brave."

The next week seemed to crawl past with agonizing slowness. Every morning before Helga arrived, Liesel crept up to the eaves to give Gerda and Rose some breakfast, along with some hope. She told them about the Wehrmacht's setbacks in Moscow; although they had taken more ground, it had come at a heavy loss, and the mood in Berlin had turned bleak. The rumors that America might enter the war were also growing stronger, and she told them what Louisa Lochner had said about Germany's chances then.

"Please God it will all be finished," Gerda exclaimed fervently. "This nightmare will finally come to an end."

Rosa's anger had thankfully dissipated, replaced by a worldly weariness that made Liesel ache for her. Her childhood had been stolen, along with so much else. She did her best to give Rosa a few treats—bringing up some novels she'd enjoyed at the same age, while Friedy brought board games and cards.

"When my father goes to Schkopau," Liesel promised her and Gerda, "you'll be able to walk around more, at least in the evenings and on the weekends, when Helga isn't here."

True to his words, Friedy practiced piano for an hour every afternoon, banging mercilessly on his mother's precious instrument, while she looked on with tears of joy in her eyes, and Gerda and Rosa were able to creep out from under the eaves and stretch their legs upstairs.

"Isn't he marvelous?" her mother told Liesel. "A virtuoso he'll never be."

"No," Liesel agreed with a smile.

Friedy grinned at them and winked.

In the kitchen, Helga had started banging pots with even more force than necessary as she prepared the evening meal, the way she usually registered any discontent. It just added to the noise and made it that much safer.

Finally, her father went to Schkopau, and everyone breathed a silent sigh of relief. Helga, Liesel realized, was far easier to manage than her father, with his shrewd gaze and deceptively relaxed manner.

"Why shouldn't they come downstairs?" Friedy suggested one evening in late November. "Surely it's safe. No one comes to the door, and the blackout curtains are drawn. Besides, if someone does, they can hurry upstairs quick enough."

Ilse and Liesel exchanged uncertain looks. "It's too dangerous…" Ilse began, but then Liesel shook her head.

"It is dangerous, but it's a risk we should be willing to take, if they are. I'd go mad, if I were stuck in that tiny room for twenty-three hours out of twenty-four. Let's ask them."

Rosa responded with alacrity, Gerda slightly less so, but the next evening, they duly, albeit with some trepidation, crept downstairs to the sitting room and listened to a symphony on the radio while drinking coffee.

It was all so poignantly pleasant and companionable, so *normal*, in a way that things hadn't been normal in a long time, and afterward Gerda clasped Ilse's hands in hers and, with tears in her eyes, murmured her thanks.

After that it became something of a routine; every evening, an hour after Helga left, just to be safe, Rosa and Gerda came downstairs and they all spent a few hours together in the sitting room, listening to the radio or playing *Skat* or *Dame*, or simply sitting quietly and enjoying a rare moment of peace. Sometimes they even joked or laughed; it started to feel normal, these precious evening hours, almost as if the war didn't exist.

One night, they were all enjoying a rousing game of *Mensch ärgere Dich nicht*—Don't Get Upset, Man!—when Friedy rolled the dice and his marble landed on top of Rosa's, much to her annoyance. He burst out laughing and Gerda clapped her hands in amusement—and then a knock sounded on the door.

The room snapped into stillness as, for a single, taut moment, everyone stared at each other, Friedy's laughter lingering like an echo.

Then Liesel rose and smoothed down her skirt. "The back stairs," she said quietly, and went to the front door. Taking a deep breath, willing her expression into something both calm and pleasant, she opened it.

A slouchy, sullen-mouthed girl stood there, wearing a worn BDM uniform and rattling a tin. "*Winterhilfswerk*," she said dolefully, and Liesel couldn't keep from sagging a little in relief. She was selling badges for the Winter Relief, that was all.

"Of course, just one moment." Liesel fished a few *pfennigs* out of her purse and dropped them into the tin with a smile, while the girl handed her a little wooden badge she would never wear. "Thank you."

The girl looked at her a bit suspiciously; most people were not quite so eager to donate, especially when there might be compulsory collections several nights a week. The houses on Koenigsallee, set back from the road, did not get so many "Can Rattlers," as they were known, but once in a while, members of the HJ or BDM, the Red Cross, or even the Nazi sports or cycling associations, ventured past the garden gate and knocked at the door, asking for *pfennigs*.

Letting out a long, slow breath, Liesel slowly closed the door. When she went back into the sitting room, Friedy and her mother were playing the game with it set up only for two people. Ilse looked anxious; Friedy smiled.

"Well?" her mother asked in a tense voice.

"*Winterhilfswerk*."

Ilse nodded and pressed one hand to her chest. "My heart. It's still thudding."

"Mine too," Liesel admitted.

"I knew it had to be something like that," Friedy said.

Even though it had turned out to be nothing, the sense of danger still lingered, and Gerda and Rosa stayed upstairs every night until Otto came home two weeks later, breezing into the house on a gust of cold air, full of a bonhomie that was beginning to feel more and more forced. Liesel saw the deep crows' feet by his eyes, the rivulets running from nose to mouth. No matter how bright his smile, her father carried a burden whose weight she did not like to consider. It had become more pronounced in recent months and there had been, much to her relief, far fewer parties or parades to attend with him. She'd been too grateful to not have to go to consider the matter, but now she wondered whether it was due to the scarcity of such events as the war went on, or the scarcity of invitations.

"Well, well!" he said as he rubbed his hands together and looked around with an air of satisfaction, despite the near-frigid temperature because there was no coal for a fire. "Did you miss me?"

Liesel wondered how he could ask such a question, or how he could wait for an answer with such smiling expectancy as he shrugged off his coat and hung his hat on the stand in the hall.

"I missed you, Vati," Friedy replied, giving him a hug. Her brother's love for his father was still uncomplicated; Liesel didn't know how much he knew or understood about Otto's trip to Schloss Hartheim or the favor he'd had to call in, but she suspected, in Friedy's eyes, their father had rescued him. It was that simple, which she knew was a good thing. A boy should love his father. She did not want to take that away from Friedy… or even from her father.

"And you, Liesel?" her father asked lightly, searching her face with far too much knowledge in his gaze. He seemed to see right through her, although she told herself that could not be the case.

She shrugged, unable to look him in the eye. "Of course. But you travel so much now. I confess, I've become used to it."

"Ah, well, it won't last forever," he returned brightly. "What's been happening while I've been away?"

Had she imagined the slight pointedness of the question? Her father could not possibly know anything. Still, Liesel struggled to answer, and the ensuing silence felt like a thunderclap. Ilse had absented herself from her husband's homecoming entirely, and even Friedy had no real response, standing there with his head slightly bowed as he kicked his good foot against the brass runner on the stairs.

"Nothing, really," Liesel said at last. "At least there have been no air raids."

"Well, that's something."

Dinner was interminable; the house seeming far too quiet, so every potential scrape or creak could be heard. It was a still, clear night, which made it all the worse, and Ilse was so tense she jumped when Friedy dropped his spoon.

"My goodness," Otto remarked as he dabbed his mouth with his napkin, his gaze moving slowly over his silent family. "You do seem nervy, my dear."

Ilse did not reply. She retired to her bedroom immediately after dinner, while Liesel went to the sitting room with Friedy and her father and listened to the radio. Anything, she thought, to make things seem normal.

Yet nothing felt normal. Her father smiled faintly as they listened to the nightly news report, followed by a concert of *Volksmusik*, his narrowed gaze moving thoughtfully between Friedy and Liesel, making her heart beat all the faster. He looked as if he knew… but he *couldn't* know.

Finally, at nine o'clock, she made her excuses and went to bed, thankful only to get away. She wanted to tiptoe upstairs and check on Gerda and Rosa, but as her father remained downstairs, she didn't feel she could risk it, and so she went to bed instead, thinking she would lie there gritty-eyed and tense, but exhaustion felled her and she drifted into sleep, only to startle awake in the middle of the night at the sound of the air-raid siren.

She stumbled out of bed, fumbling for her dressing gown, her mind a fogged blur. In the hallway, she could hear her father calling to Friedy and her mother, and then he was knocking on her door.

"Liesel, Lieseling, we must go downstairs."

"Yes—" She stopped in the act of tying the sash of her robe as she remembered. Gerda. Rosa. They would have to stay upstairs for the air raid.

"Liesel—"

"I'm coming." She couldn't keep from glancing up toward the attic stairs as she followed her father down the hall, and then down the stairs all the way to the cellar. As comfortable a space as it was, it still felt claustrophobic. It felt like a tomb.

Otto tried to engage them in a game of *Skat*, but Friedy was half-asleep and Liesel felt too tense. Ilse sat in the corner, chewing her nails and deliberately ignoring her husband. Every so often, Liesel kept glancing at the reinforced door, as if it might open. What if a bomb fell near them? What if Gerda and Rosa were hurt—or discovered?

Two hours later, the crackle and thud of the bombs had started to fade, and Liesel rose from the stool where she'd been sitting, hunched over.

"Liesel—" her father began, half-rising.

"I need some air. It's passing, anyway." Without looking at him, she hurried up the stairs and opened the door to the kitchen.

She'd never been out of the shelter during a raid; she felt a strange, surreal sense of liberation as she hurried through the empty house, the reverberation from a bomb falling closer than she realized throbbing in her chest.

She ran up the attic stairs, and then stopped short. The door to the eaves was open, and so were the windows overlooking the garden. Rosa sat perched on the roof tiles, her face lifted to a sky on fire.

"*Rosa—*"

"I tried to get her not to," Gerda said anxiously as she hurried to Liesel's side. "But she wouldn't. She said no one would see her."

No one would, for trees hid the back of the house from view, and yet it was still incredibly foolhardy and dangerous. She could have been blown to pieces, or fallen right off the roof.

"I needed to breathe," Rosa said without lowering her face from the livid, reddened sky. "I needed to feel free." She looked at Liesel over her shoulder. "You could come out here, too, if you want."

Liesel hesitated, bizarrely half-tempted by the invitation, yet an innate caution keeping her feet on the floor.

"Rosa, you could have been hit by something," she said. "The bombs were quite close."

"If I was going to be hit, it would happen in there or out here. It doesn't matter." That was true, Liesel realized. If a bomb fell on the house, Rosa and Gerda would have been killed, regardless of where they sat. "Come out," Rosa urged. "Just for a moment. It's beautiful, isn't it? The sky is such a brilliant color, and all because they're bombing the Nazis. They're trying to win."

Liesel had never thought about it like that before; the idea that Rosa *wanted* the city to be bombed, wanted Germany to lose this wretched war... well, of course she did. And Liesel did as well, just as she'd thought when Louis Lochner had said as much. And yet... out there, where the bombs were falling, lives were being lost, families and houses destroyed. Was that the price of peace?

"Come out," Rosa said again, and so Liesel did.

The roof tiles were steep and slippery under her feet, and her toes curled reflexively, seeking purchase. This was insane, absolutely *mad,* and yet she was glad she was doing it. She perched on the apex of the roof next to Rosa, their knees brushing, pearly traces of smoke trailing across the wounded sky. When she breathed in, she smelled something sharp and burning, along with the smell of plaster and damp grass.

"Isn't it wonderful?" Rosa said, and Liesel did not know how to respond. The city was on fire, houses and buildings had been bombed, lives surely lost... and yet there *was* something beautiful about the lit-up sky, the traces of smoke and cloud, the exhilarating sense of freedom. Liesel almost felt as if she could fly.

"I wanted to be free," Rosa said quietly. "Even if just for a few minutes. It might be all I have."

"Don't say that, Rosa. The war will end."

"For you, maybe. But will it for me? If Hitler wins…" She let out a shaky breath and nodded toward the night sky. "That's my only hope, out there. That's why I'm happy to see the bombs fall." She glanced at Liesel, a fierce light in her eyes. "Do you think I'm cruel?"

"No, of course not. If I were you…" Liesel let out a shaky breath. "I want the war to end, too," she said.

"Yes, but do you want Hitler to lose?"

"Yes," Liesel said firmly, although once more she wondered what it would mean for her, for her family… and especially for her father. "What will you do when the war ends?" she asked. "When Hitler loses?"

Rosa glanced at her, startled, and then, as Liesel smiled her encouragement, a shy look of excitement transformed the sullen cast of her features and she tilted her face to the orange sky once more. "I'll go back to school," she stated. "And finish all my lessons. And then I want to go to university in Heidelberg. Do you know that it is the oldest university in Germany?"

"I didn't," Liesel confessed.

"No one in my family has gone to university. I want to go. I want to study medicine and become a doctor." She gave Liesel a look that was half challenge, half entreaty. "Do you think that is foolish?"

"No," Liesel answered honestly. "I think it is wonderful."

Rosa smiled, and for a second Liesel could imagine the woman she would become—confident, kind, determined, the futile anger she'd felt for so long transformed into a strength of purpose.

"You'll do all those things," she told her, longing for it to be made true. "And more."

Rosa turned back to the sky. "I hope so," she said quietly. "One day."

"I should return the pocket watch your mother gave me," Liesel said suddenly. The simple fact of the watch had bothered her since Gerda had first thrust it into her hand. "You could use it, one day. Sell it to help fund your studies, perhaps."

Rosa shook her head. "You keep it for now," she answered. "It seals the bargain between us. And when the war is over, and we're all safe and free…" She turned to Liesel with a burning look. "Give it to me then."

"Rosa, please come in," Gerda hissed from the windowsill. "The all-clear will surely sound soon. You cannot be caught out like this. You are risking too much!"

"I'm coming, Mama," Rosa called back, and she gave Liesel a fleeting smile of solidarity before she clambered back through the window, Liesel following, just as the long, lonely wail of the siren rose to an insistent pitch in the darkness.

Liesel felt a flicker of regret and even guilt as Rosa and Gerda disappeared once more under the eaves, and she shut the door after them, entombing them in their hideaway. When would Rosa breathe fresh air again? When would she finally be free?

She was still considering the questions as she came downstairs, tightening the sash of her dressing gown—and stopping short when she saw her father there, at the bottom of the steps, waiting for her.

"Hello, Liesel," he said.

For a second, Liesel couldn't speak. Couldn't think. She simply stared, her pulse beating in her throat, her gaze trapped.

"What were you doing up there at this time of night, with the bombs falling all around us?" he asked, his tone conversational, almost pleasant.

"I told you, I wanted some fresh air." Liesel tried to sound dismissive, but she knew she failed.

"I heard voices."

"I was talking to myself."

"Liesel." Her father took a step toward her, intent, menacing now, his expression so very hard and unyielding. "Don't lie to me. What were you doing up there? What have you done?"

"What have *I* done?" Liesel couldn't keep from retorting, and her father's face darkened.

"You'd blame me for the entire war if you could," he said, a savage edge to his voice. "The bombs that fell tonight were my doing, I suppose."

"No, but the ones that fall on London might be." Why was she picking a fight *now,* of all times? And yet perhaps it would distract him. With shaking fingers, Liesel knotted her sash. "I'm going back to bed."

"Liesel." She'd walked only four steps before her father stopped her with the single word, her name. "What have you done?" He spoke quietly. Wearily. As if he already knew... and even if he didn't, Liesel realized she could not keep it from him. All he would have to do was walk upstairs.

She took a deep breath and turned around. "You're a good man, Vati."

A shadow passed over his face. "Liesel." His voice was a hoarse demand. "*What have you done?*"

Liesel stared at him for a long moment, willing him to realize. To accept. Her father *was* a good man, beneath the ambition, the rhetoric, the fear. If she and her mother had been able to be brave, surely he could be, as well?

"You're a good man," she repeated, and her father's eyes narrowed.

"Why are you saying such a thing now?"

Liesel swallowed dryly. "Because Gerda and Rosa are upstairs," she whispered. It felt like flinging herself off a cliff; it felt like such a relief. Finally he knew. There need be no more secrets.

Her father stared at her for a long moment, a blank look on his face, almost as if he hadn't understood what she'd said.

"Upstairs…" He shook his head slowly. "*Mein Gott,* Liesel, how could you?"

"They had nowhere to go. The Jews are being deported, sent somewhere east—"

He wheeled around, one hand pressed to his forehead. "I *know* that, Liesel."

"Yes, of course you do," she said quietly. Her heart was hammering, and her stomach roiled. Please God, she had not made a terrible, terrible mistake. "Father, these are people who have done nothing wrong. People you've known and liked."

"Do you know this house could be watched?" he asked after a moment, his voice toneless. "That it probably is?"

"If it had been, the Gestapo would have come already. Gerda and Rose have been here for weeks, Vati. *Weeks.*"

He shook his head again, a slow back and forth that felt like defeat, or perhaps something even worse.

"Please," she whispered.

A silence followed, a dreadful, heavy silence that felt like falling into a hole.

"Vati…"

"You don't know what you've done, Liesel. It would have been better if you'd simply turned them away when they first came to the door."

"Turn them away?" she repeated, her voice cracking. "Do you know what these camps are like?"

"You don't even know where they're going."

"But *you* do."

He shook his head for the third time. "I can't risk it. None of us can."

"They have nowhere else!"

He turned around to face her. "I know that," he stated coldly.

She stared at him—the slump of his shoulders, the hardness in his eyes. "What are you going to do?" She realized, sickly, that Gerda and Rosa's fate was entirely in her father's hands.

He hesitated, not quite meeting her gaze. "I don't know. I must think on it."

"Please, Vati—"

"That's enough, Liesel. You've done enough." Slowly, like a broken old man, he walked into the bedroom.

Liesel spent the rest of the night lying in bed, staring at the ceiling, her ears straining in the silence. She told herself her father would see reason, see goodness. He was a good man, just like Gerda had said. Just like she had said. He had to be. He had to be.

It was after dawn by the time she drifted into an uneasy sleep, only to wake with a jolt at the sudden, loud knocking on the door.

As she scrambled out of bed, she watched in horrified disbelief as black-booted Gestapo, their gray-green coats flapping about them, thundered up the stairs. She shrank back against her doorway, her heart in her mouth, as they strode down the hall. And then she saw her father, his expression stony as he followed the men, straightening the cuffs of his jacket.

"They're up in the attics," he stated coolly. "Under the eaves."

CHAPTER TWENTY-FOUR

January 1946

The trip from Berlin back to Frankfurt felt endless, a slog of bumpy hours along broken roads, past marshes and fields half-covered in dirty snow. Sam and Anna did not speak; the silence between them was oppressive, the weight of their conversation—or lack of it—the previous night lying between them like some heavy, cumbersome thing neither could manage to lift.

As he gazed out the window at the depressing landscape, Sam went over in his mind everything he knew about Anna Vogel. She was really from Berlin. Had she lived in that house on Koenigsallee? It seemed most likely. Surely "*everyone*" implied all her family? But who were they? Had she lied about them, along with the details of her national service? Had her family even died? Who was the chemist she knew? A father, friend, brother, lover? If she was trying to protect him, she'd fail. Sam would make sure of that.

And yet... if she was trying to protect him, why was she so determined he give the files to Major Lewis? Did she assume the job would be done then, and no more chemists would be found? She might be right; Sam had no idea how long Operation Paperclip would remain in play. From some of the murmurings he'd been starting to hear at HQ, he didn't think it would be all that long. The U.S. Army was getting tired of managing a broken and defeated country. Soldiers wanted to go home, and the consensus was still that they would pull out of Germany by

1947, just a year away, although Sam couldn't actually see that happening.

He certainly wanted to go home. He wanted to see pretty houses and fresh flowers and cities that weren't half rubble. He wanted to go ice skating on Gustine Lake in East Fairmount Park, as he used to every Christmas, skating along with Nancy or Helen or playing ice hockey with broomsticks with his friends. He wanted to see something other than hopelessness, and feel something other than despair.

He was tired of Frankfurt, of Germany, of gaunt faces and abject expressions and Anna's cool silence. Even now he fought the urge to take her by the shoulders, to demand she be honest with him. *What are you not telling me?*

"I suppose," he said at last, breaking a five-hour silence, "I'll take the files to Major Lewis as soon as we return."

She nodded, said nothing.

"And then you'll tell me what you've been hiding."

A quick, sliding look, yet still no response. Sam had meant it as a command, but it was only after he'd said it that he realized it sounded more like a plea.

By four o'clock, they were back in Frankfurt, the afternoon dusky, already turning dark. Sam asked for Major Lewis as soon as he arrived back in the CIC operation center; Major Pitt gave him a repressive look.

"Aren't we eager?" he remarked dryly. "Have a nice time away?"

"I'm not sure what the point of it all was, to be frank, sir," Sam replied. He still felt belligerent. "Even with these files, the scientists need to be physically found." And they could be anywhere, even Argentina. He knew many Nazi industrialists, like the proverbial rats off a sinking ship, had scuttled all the way across the Atlantic even before the war had officially ended. The men whose names he held in this folder could be halfway across the world, sipping pina coladas on the Copacabana.

"That aspect of the operation is not your concern, Houghton," Pitt told him. "In any case, we need the paperwork. Prosecution can never take place without the damned paperwork." He gave him a mirthless smile. "Even if they're guilty as hell and every Tom, Dick, and Harry knows it."

"And will they be prosecuted?" Sam challenged.

Pitt's expression hardened. "They'd better be."

Back in his office, Anna was tidying up her desk; there seemed little to do so late in the day. He closed the door with a decisive click and gave her a long, level look which she returned with cool equanimity.

"So?" he asked quietly. "I've passed the files on. Are you going to tell me now who you are? What you've been hiding?"

Anna let out a little sigh, her expression turning resigned. "It won't make much difference to you, Sam."

He tried not to let the use of his first name affect him, or the implication that there wasn't enough between them for it to matter. Of course there wasn't. And yet… he remembered her smile, and how she'd told him she hadn't known what her answer would be. That brief brush of her lips against his… "Then why lie at all?"

She paused. "So I could be hired here."

He blinked, taking that in. "Why wouldn't you have been, with your real identity?"

"Why do you think?" she tossed at him, a bitter smile twisting her lips.

He was silent for a moment. "You're no Nazi," he said at last, a statement to which she did not reply. Still, he believed that; he had to believe it. Nothing about Anna suggested otherwise, and yet… did he really know anything about her at all? He'd thought he had, but now he wondered. Doubted. He didn't even know her name. "Who is Anna Vogel?" he asked abruptly.

"She is who I said she was. A girl from Essen who worked in her father's hardware store. I took her identity papers from her dead body." He couldn't keep from flinching a little at that, and she continued flatly, "I met her in Berlin. She'd come to the city to find her cousin. He was sixteen years old and he'd run off to join the *Volksturm*. You know what that is?" Her voice rang out sharp with a deeply held cynicism he'd never heard from her before.

"The national militia established during the last months of the war." He sounded as if he were reading from a textbook, and in essence he was. All his knowledge came from reports, files, newsreels. Not experience. Not like Anna.

"Yes, made up of little boys and old men. Some very…" She frowned, searching for the word. "Excited…"

"Committed to the war effort?" Sam surmised, for he'd read that too, and she nodded.

"Others… forced." A pause that felt like the breaking of glass. "Anna's cousin was the first kind."

The silence stretched between them, a shattered thing. "I still don't understand why you lied about it all."

She shrugged restively. "My father was—*is*—a Nazi. A chemist with IG Farben. I wanted to find his file. Find *him.*"

"To protect him," he stated flatly.

An incredulous sneer took over her face, curling her lip and flashing in her eyes. "*No.* To make him pay for his crimes."

As much as he wanted to believe that, he found he couldn't, at least not completely, despite the venomous certainty in her voice. "If that's true, then why not just come forward? You'd have more credibility as his daughter than some shop girl from Essen. People have been denouncing Nazis left and right."

"And not always being believed when doing so."

That was true enough; sometimes it seemed as if anyone with an axe to grind was declaring their neighbor a Nazi.

Sam sighed. "Even so, the subterfuge seems unnecessary to me." Unless she was hiding something else. Something worse.

Anna frowned. "Subter… I do not know that word."

"Subterfuge? It means deception. Trickery. *Lies.*" Now his voice was ringing out, just as cynical as hers had been, and even more hurt. He'd *trusted* her. He thought that even now he might still love her, except of course he didn't even know her. The intensity of his emotions made him feel like a fool.

She regarded him for a moment, her head tilted to one side. She seemed remarkably unruffled, considering the situation, although perhaps she was just sad. Resigned, but to what exactly? "You're angry with me," she said at last.

"I'm not *angry.*" That made him sound like a child stamping his foot. "I just want to understand."

"My father…" She paused, struggling for words. "I had to make sure he was found. That was why I came here."

Sam stared at her blankly. "You mean to Frankfurt?"

"I knew I could not work for the Counterintelligence Corps if my connection to my father was known."

"And you wanted to work for the CIC in particular?"

Anna nodded, and a fierce light came into her eyes, reminding Sam of rage. He nearly recoiled from its brightness. "Yes. I wanted to work for you, in particular. For Operation Paperclip."

"*What?*" He stared at her in incomprehension. "How did you even know of it? Or that I would be involved in it?"

Anna's lips curved humorlessly. "You soldiers like to talk in bars. I met Major Lewis before I made my application. He told me about it, how they were looking for the scientists. I came here the next day."

"What…" The word came out like an exhalation. Sam didn't know whether to feel impressed by her determination or duped by what she'd done. Had she really planned it all? "How did you know I was involved? I barely knew myself."

"I didn't," Anna said simply. "But I told Major Lewis I wanted to help. I trusted the rest to Providence."

Sam stared at her, amazed at how much she'd arranged and manipulated—and all so her father could be found? "And you found your father's membership card in Berlin," he said. "The other afternoon. Didn't you?"

She gave a brief nod. "It is in the file you gave to Major Lewis."

"Do you know where he is now? Your father?"

"No. He left Berlin in April of '45." Her mouth twisted. "Before the Soviets came."

"You were there when the city fell?"

A hesitation, then a nod. No wonder she had been agitated around the Soviet soldiers at Café Vaterland.

Slowly Sam walked over to his desk and slumped into the chair. "You've lied about everything."

"I've had to."

His mind whirled, a dervish going nowhere. Anna looked resolute, unrepentant. He had no idea what to think about any of it—her, her father, her involvement in Operation Paperclip, with him.

"And you have no idea where your father could be now?" he finally asked.

She shook her head. "I thought he might have come here to Frankfurt, after the war. We used to live here, when I was a child. But I have not found him. That is why I need you."

"You still didn't have to lie," he said.

She didn't reply, and Sam wondered whether he could blame her. Some of the CIC agents were desperate to lock up anyone with so much as a whiff of National Socialism. Considering her close connection to a dedicated Nazi, he could understand her fear. And yet he still felt duped. He felt stupid.

"I'm going to have to tell my superiors," he said after a moment, and she nodded.

"I know."

Would she be fired, or maybe even worse? Sam had no idea, and he suspected it would depend on the day, and who handled her case. Sometimes it felt as if there was no rhyme or reason as to who went free and who paid the price. A railway signalman forced into party membership might live in fear for his job; an SS officer walked. He'd seen it happen. He'd read the reports.

He rose from his desk, feeling utterly wearied by it all. He wanted to go home now more than ever, away from the endless bleakness of life here—of lies and fear and black-market cigarettes; of starving children, desperate women, and smug soldiers of any stripe.

"What is your real name, out of interest?" he asked and she hesitated, looking, for the first time, as if she were sorry for deceiving him, or perhaps that too was simply more of his wishful thinking.

"Liesel," she said softly. "Liesel Scholz."

Three days passed and Sam didn't mention Anna's deception—he couldn't yet think of her as Liesel—to Major Pitt. Major Lewis was off site, and he told himself it was he who needed to know, and so it made sense to wait until he returned. It was a poor excuse, but he held onto it, because he wasn't ready to set whatever he would in motion.

In the meantime, they were back to sorting through the endless questionnaires; it seemed his brief work with Operation Paperclip had finished, at least for now. Apparently over ten million had been filled out by desperate Germans; he only had a couple thousand in his office. The thought that he might spend the rest of his days in Berlin sorting through the forms depressed him unbearably. He'd seen the tiny black type every time he closed his eyes, and what good could he do with these endless forms anyway, when there might have been a Nazi right before his eyes?

Neither he nor Anna spoke, and the silence between them which he'd once fancied companionable now felt as cold and hard as the frozen ground outside. The mild winter had given way to a cold snap, an icy wind blowing off the Main. It suited his mood, and yet with each passing day he felt more miserable.

Then, one gray afternoon, the sky like gunmetal, Major Pitt summoned him, looking up from his desk with his usual terse expression.

"You're wanted at Camp King. Major Lewis needs you to aid in the interrogation of some chemists."

"You mean found from the files I gave him?" He spoke neutrally although his heart had skipped a beat. He felt as if he had done nothing but think of those files since Anna had told him about her father.

Major Pitt shrugged, irritated already. "How should I know? There's a car waiting." He paused. "He wants your little secretary to come along, too."

Sam felt a flicker of foreboding as he went back to tell Anna the news. He knew of Camp King, of course, although he'd never expected to go there himself. Around fifteen miles north of Frankfurt, once an educational farm, during the war it had been used for the interrogation of captured Allied pilots. At the war's end, the Americans had repurposed it as their own interrogation center for high-ranking Nazis. Grand Admiral Doenitz and Reichsmarschall Göring had both passed through its cells, as had many other Nazi officials, before they were taken to Nuremberg for prosecution.

As the car drove north under a darkening sky, Sam wondered why Major Lewis had summoned him—and Anna. She'd been tight-lipped and accepting when he'd told her she was instructed to come, and had asked no questions, even though Sam thought she must have some, just as he did. He'd given the files over already. He wasn't properly experienced in interrogation besides a brief stint during his intelligence training, and in any case he didn't speak good enough German, so he couldn't be wanted for that. So what, then?

They reached the outskirts of Oberursel after forty minutes, and soon the pretty buildings of Camp King came into view; part of it had been constructed as a model village in the thirties, complete with quaint cottages and clock tower, and the effect was disconcerting—Nazi prisoners and interrogation cells in houses with wooden shutters and flower boxes.

Major Lewis requested to see him first, while Anna cooled her heels in another room, having said not a word during their entire journey. As Sam entered the small office with its chairs and cheap wooden table, a pile of folders on top and a smell of old coffee and cigarette smoke in the air, he saluted.

"Sir."

"Well, well, well." Major Lewis leaned back in his chair as he gave Sam an uncomfortably considering look. "Isn't this quite the pickle?"

"Sir?"

"The files you gave me were very interesting, Captain Houghton. Very interesting indeed. For as it happened, we already had a couple of those men in custody. We just didn't fully appreciate their possible significance."

"I'm glad to have helped, sir."

"And you're here to help some more, Captain. One of those men is a chemist who insists his information is useful, but he's reluctant to share it with us until he has a guarantee of diplomatic immunity. The trouble is, we don't know whether to believe him. Everyone these days says their information is important."

Sam thought of Sergeant Belmont—*they'll say anything for a cigarette or a bar of soap.* "What is it you would like me to do, sir?"

"Interrogate him, naturally. Find out if it really is useful, what he says he knows."

Sam hesitated. As much as he longed to prove his mettle, he was pretty sure he wasn't qualified for this kind of job. "Sir, there must be far more qualified chemists than me to conduct such an interrogation."

"Well, there are, of course," Lewis drawled, "but they're mostly Morgenthau's boys."

Sam stared at him, uncertain, uncomprehending. "I'm not sure I follow you, sir." He knew not everyone agreed with the Secretary of the Treasury, Henry Morgenthau Junior, whose plan for the Allied occupation of Germany had severe consequences not only for Germans, but for the future of the country itself, as well as its industry and prosperity. Morgenthau wanted to disarm Germany entirely, and make it a country of potato farmers, or so his critics, including both Goebbels and Churchill, had claimed. But what did that have to do with interrogating a chemist at Camp King?

"Well, they're *Jews*," Lewis said, as if explaining arithmetic to a six-year-old. "And I rather think they have something of an axe to grind, don't you?" He lit a cigarette. "I understand, of course. What the Nazis did was pretty ugly. But we've got to move on now, haven't we?" He blew a plume of smoke toward the ceiling. "We've got the Soviets to think of. The Nazi regime is finished, after all. And many of the most senior Nazis are already dead."

As were millions of Jews, Czechs, Poles… Sam swallowed the words down.

"So you want me to interrogate him because I'm not Jewish?" He could hardly believe he was saying the words, and yet at the same time he realized he wasn't surprised at all. He'd seen this before—for every soldier's rage and horror at the sight of the death camps, there was another's bored indifference.

"Well, yes, but there's something else, as well." Major Lewis paused, letting Sam stew in the silence. "Trust me, Houghton,

I wouldn't drag you all the way out here just because you're not a Jew. You only have a BA in chemistry, after all." He let out a short laugh and leaned back, tipping the front legs of his chair, a small, knowing smile playing about his thin mouth.

Sam kept his gaze steady, even though a sense of unease was deepening inside him. Lewis looked as if he was enjoying this too much; he was playing with him, teasing him with a little information while holding back something far more significant, Sam felt sure of it. And he was afraid he knew what it was.

The answer came with Lewis' next words, dropped with deliberate casualness into the stillness of the room. "There's the matter of your secretary."

Sam's mouth was dry as he answered, "Sir?"

Lewis leaned forward, dropping the legs of his chair back onto the floor. "The chemist in question is her father."

Sam tried to school his expression into one of what—Surprise? Professionalism? He struggled to know how to react, whether to feign ignorance or not.

"I suspect you knew she wasn't telling the truth," Lewis remarked languidly. "Most of them are terrible liars, as are you, incidentally. For an agent, you really haven't got much of a poker face at all, have you? I suppose that's why you're an analyst."

"Sir?" Sam managed.

"It's obvious you knew. Did she tell you? A bit of pillow talk, perhaps?"

Sam chose not to dignify that remark with a reply.

"Well, never mind, eh?" Major Lewis paused, and Sam knew he was enjoying this little play of power. "The trouble is, Houghton, it's a bit embarrassing for us, do you see? It's one thing to have the daughter of a chemist working for us. In fact, fair dues, everyone needs to eat, and a job is a job, never mind what her father did or didn't do, and the war is over, after all." He paused, letting the seconds spin out while Sam waited, teeth gritted. "Unfortunately HQ has to take a *slightly* dimmer view when the lady in question is a dyed-in-the-wool Nazi."

The breath left him as if he'd been punched. "What…"

Major Lewis tossed some photographs across the desk. "We found these gems when we seized a cache of Heinrich Hoffmann's photographs. Hitler's personal photographer? It's proved to be an absolute treasure trove of evidence. One of the sergeants found the photos of your little secretary and recognized her. When we asked her father, he confirmed who she was. Have a look."

Slowly, stonily, Sam took the photos and went through them, his muscles contracting at the sight of each one. They were all of Anna. *Liesel.* There she was in a dark green evening gown—the same color as the dress she'd worn at Christmas—attending a party, arm in arm with a Luftwaffe officer. That must have been the man she'd spoken about, the *nice* one.

There she was again, posing with Göring himself at what looked like a rally, flags bedecking the background. Another one, chatting with Reinhard Heydrich, of all people, in front of some painting, at yet another party. Another in a huge room, leaning against the wall, looking bored.

"She got around a bit, didn't she, hobnobbing with all those fellows?" Lewis almost sounded amused. "That first one we think was taken at Carinhall, Göring's hunting lodge. He had a Luftwaffe demolition squad blow it up before the end of the war. Evacuated all the looted artwork first, of course. The last is in the Chancellery itself. A diplomatic reception, most likely. I think Hoffmann liked the look of her, don't you? He certainly had a fair few photos, and she *is* a bit of a looker."

Sam looked up from the photos. The blood was pounding in his temples, surging in his veins. "Why are you showing me these?"

"Well, like I said, it's a bit embarrassing, isn't it? The U.S. Army employed a Nazi socialite, let her have a good look at our classified files, went to our Document Center, for heaven's sake, and all without even realizing who she was. If word gets out, we'd have a bit of egg on our faces, wouldn't we?" He let the question hang in the air.

"Perhaps," Sam allowed. "But it's unlikely to get out. And what does this have to do with me interrogating Herr Scholz?"

"So you do know who he is." Lewis smiled, and Sam cursed himself for the slip. Lewis had never mentioned his name. "Well, here's the thing, Houghton. I don't want just *you* to interrogate the man. I want you to do it together. Pretty little Liesel Scholz and you." His smile widened. "You might have the chemistry know-how, but she can put on the pressure. It's in her best interest to do so, after all, isn't it? If the information is useful, she and her father can skip off to America. If it's not…" He let that unspoken possibility linger in the air. "Because if Scholz won't talk without some guarantee of immunity that I can assure you he's not going to get," he finished, "then we have a problem, don't we?"

"So you want Anna—Miss Vogel—to encourage him to talk?" Sam clarified. His stomach was sour with guilt and regret, as well as a pulsing anger. *Those photographs.* "Why would he listen to her?"

"Because apparently they were quite close, by all accounts. A few of the other men we've got in custody knew them both. And if he doesn't, well," Lewis shrugged, spreading his hands wide, "we might have to nab his daughter instead."

"But she didn't do anything," Sam protested sickly.

"Didn't she?" Major Lewis met his gaze in cool challenge. "Those photographs look pretty damning to me. A girl doesn't cozy up to the likes of Reichsmarschall Göring without knowing a thing or two. But in any case, we need to know what he knows. Then we'll decide if it's worth knowing or not."

"And if it is?"

Major Lewis spread his arms wide. "Then, like I said, he and his pretty little daughter can have a nice trip to the United

States of America, all expenses paid. A pretty house in California, perhaps, and a research job at a lab at Stanford. Who knows, maybe they'll get a dog."

Sam swallowed down the bitter words he wanted to say. "And if isn't?"

"Straight back to the internment camp for Herr Scholz." He smiled while his eyes remained hard. "Unless we decide to try him for war crimes, of course. But that's hardly your concern."

"And what about Anna?"

"That's not your concern, either, as much as you might want it to be," Lewis stated coolly.

So this was why Anna—*Liesel*—had hidden her identity. Not because she feared she wouldn't be believed, but because she was a Nazi. Sam glanced down at the photograph of her with Göring, their cheeks practically pressed together, and his stomach cramped.

"And it goes without saying you can't mess this one up," Lewis remarked rather casually. "You've already blotted your copybook once, after all, Houghton, so be careful."

CHAPTER TWENTY-FIVE

Poland, December 1943

The car crawled slowly across the border, stopping and starting every few minutes thanks to other, more important vehicles clogging the roads—government Mercedes as well as Wehrmacht Jeeps and trucks, the latter, her father pointed out mildly, made by America's Ford Motor Company.

If he'd been trying to show Liesel that the Nazis had managed to garner some support from around the world, he'd hardly need have bothered. She no longer cared; for the last two years her deep-seated grief had been cloaked in a numb indifference, even as the specter of war—and worse, defeat—crept closer, touching every aspect of their lives with its cold, bony fingers. Only a month ago, she'd heard that Fritz had been shot down over the Channel and was presumed dead. She had felt a stirring of sorrow for the boy he once was, but nothing more.

Liesel shifted in her seat by the window, uncaring of the dreary landscape of brown fields and leaden skies. Next to her, Friedy was practicing his English by reading Dickens' *Great Expectations*. He was determined, he'd told her, to emigrate to America when the war was over, because he wanted to be a cowboy. Liesel did not have the heart to tell him that Dickens had precious little to do with cowboys. In any case, despite the losses Germany continued to sustain, from Stalingrad nearly a year ago onwards, she could not imagine the war ever actually being over.

Her father was sitting by the window on the other side of the car, reading the latest edition of the *Völkischer Beobachter*, the official newspaper of the Nazi Party. Her mother sat between him and Friedy, staring sightlessly in front of her with a vacant expression. She'd accepted the latest turn of fate with the same indifference Liesel had; several weeks ago, her father had announced, with a sort of manic jollity, that they were moving to Poland for the rest of the war, so he could manage Buna Werke, the synthetic rubber factory that had been built over the last few years, directly.

"It will be better for all of us," he'd enthused. "More space, country living, and no air raids!"

Berlin had remained mostly unscathed this last year, as both British and American bombers had been targeting U-boats for a long period, but the attacks had increased disastrously in the last few weeks, with hundreds of planes dropping their deadly cargo on the city nearly every night. At the end of November, the western suburbs had been hit, and a house only two doors down from theirs on Koenigsallee had been devastated, with two children killed in the blast. It was, Otto had told them firmly, time to go.

No one had resisted the relocation, but then the resistance, Liesel thought, had been leached out of each of them slowly but surely since the Gestapo had crashed through their front door and marched upstairs on the orders of her father.

That bleak dawn, Liesel had watched in numb horror as they'd thundered up the stairs, thrown the little door open that she'd carefully closed only the night before. She'd listened to Gerda's pitiful scream and Rosa's shout and had let out a little whimper, her only pathetic objection to the whole, terrible ordeal.

The men had marched the women down the stairs; Rosa's nose was bleeding and Gerda's eye was already swelling shut. They both looked dazed, and worse, there was a terrible emptiness in their eyes that Liesel couldn't bear to see. Liesel had whimpered again, uselessly, like a puppy that had been kicked.

"Heil Hitler," one of the men had barked, glaring at them all, and her father had replied soberly, "Heil Hitler."

When they'd gone, the door slamming behind them, it had felt as if a storm had ripped through the house, leaving only devastation in its wake, even though nothing actually looked as if it had changed. The grandfather clock in the hall chimed seven o'clock. Friedy, Ilse, and Liesel had all stood there, dazed and silent, while Otto had given a little sigh, a sound almost of regret, as he'd straightened his cuffs. Then, as if she'd been suddenly startled awake, Liesel had flown at her father, pummeling him with her fists, her voice a ragged scream of impotent fury.

"How could you do it! How could you! You could have just let them go… given them a *chance*… You know what will happen to them now? Don't you?" She'd railed at him until her voice was hoarse, her body limp, and he took it all, allowing her to punch and pummel him, to scream and curse, a look of weary resignation on his face, as if she were a child having a tantrum and he, the wise father, needed simply to wait it out.

Finally, when the fight had left her, her head dropping down as her diatribe ended on a sob, he had caught her hands in his own. "Liesel, Lieseling, I had to. Please see that. Please understand."

"You *didn't*."

"They were watching the house, Liesel!" He peered urgently into her tear-streaked face. "Why do you think I came home early? Someone told me Heydrich himself had taken an interest in us. He suspected we were harboring Jews. I couldn't believe it—"

"If he knew, why didn't they come before?"

"Because he knew who I was! Because everyone gets to call in a favor, at least once. Göring himself has saved dozens of Jews, actor friends of his wife. Heydrich was allowing me the space to deal with the matter myself before he acted, which is a courtesy I am grateful for—"

"A *courtesy*," Liesel had repeated disbelievingly. She stared at him for a moment, absorbing his words, the abhorrent hypocrisy of the whole evil system. "If all that is true," she had said more quietly yet with no less vicious conviction, "why could you not have called in such a favor, and saved Gerda and Rosa? If Göring can do it, why not you?"

Her father had sagged visibly, a sigh escaping him like the stale air from a set of bellows. "Because I already called in one favor for Friedy," he'd replied heavily. "As you well know. It was enough that I received a warning. But I promise you, if I hadn't informed the Gestapo first, they would have come anyway, and we'd *all* have been marching down those stairs. I saved our lives, Liesel."

Liesel had twisted away from him. "I don't believe you," she'd spat. "If you're so important that Heydrich himself keeps away, you could have saved Gerda and Rosa, and not just us. And even if you couldn't have…" She'd turned around, holding her hands out in front of her as she gazed pleadingly at him, her anger giving way once more to despair, and worse, a wounded love she still couldn't keep herself from. "You didn't have to betray them, Father. You were just scoring points, showing what a devoted servant of the Reich you are. Feeding your ambition ever still, and at the cost of people's lives."

"Hardly their lives," her father had returned levelly. "They'll be resettled, after all." But he hadn't looked at her as he'd said it. "But what was the alternative?" he'd pressed. "Hiding them here for a year or two or more? The war is not going to be over anytime soon, Liesel, and when it is…"

"There will be no place for Jews in Hitler's new Germany?" she'd practically sneered.

"No," he had answered flatly. There was a lifeless look in his eyes that disconcerted her more than his pleading had. "There won't be."

"And if Hitler doesn't win?" Liesel had thought of the bombers over Berlin she and Rosa had watched only last night, lighting up the sky, promising hope. "What then?"

Her father had seemed to deflate, his shoulders slumping, his weathered cheeks drooping as his mouth turned down. "God help us all, then."

Liesel couldn't bear to hear anymore. She had dressed and left the house, determined to do *something,* no matter how futile. And it was futile—she went first to Levetzowstrasse but was refused entry by a clipped-voiced SS who threatened to report her, or worse; she saw no sign of either Gerda or Rosa in the huddled figures in front of the synagogue. Where were they—at one of the collection points, or in one of the cells deep in the Gestapo headquarters at Prinz-Albrecht-Strasse? Or even worse than that, already dead?

She'd paced the street, longing for answers, and then ended up following a long line of haggard-looking Jews, marching toward the freight yards at Grunewald station, to be loaded onto cattle cars, their bundles of possessions clasped in their tired arms, their faces pale with anxiety and fatigue as they were herded forward like sheep to a slaughter by indifferent masters.

It was a terrible sight—an unwilling exodus, a deliberate, dreadful deportation, watched over by smug- or bored-looking SS who would hit or trip an evacuee simply because they could, just as her mother had said all those years ago.

Here was the evidence, the ending point of the casual cruelty she'd seen on the street, with the old man and his cap. This was where it had led—to deportation, to death, to the end of all civilization as Liesel had ever understood it.

How would they be remembered, these brutal guards with their bored manner, their casual cruelty? Death was to them no more than a task to be performed, or perhaps an amusement to be enjoyed. Could anyone become so hardened, so evil, if given the time and chance? Liesel had shrunk away from the thought, and yet she feared she only had to look at her father to believe it to be true.

When she'd returned home, defeated and sick at heart, the house was quiet. Her father had gone to work, as if it were any other ordinary day. Her mother was in bed; Friedy was at school.

When she was able to bring herself to go upstairs, everything under the eaves had been tidied away, as if it had never been. That brief, blazing chapter of her life, Liesel realized, had ended. Yet what could the future possibly hold?

She had discovered that evening, when her father told her he had to attend a reception at the New Reich Chancellery, and he expected her to accompany him.

"The Chancellery?" she had goggled at him in disbelief. Just hours earlier she'd been pressed against the railings at the Grunewald freight yards, watching Jews be loaded onto trains as if they were animals, or even objects, not human beings. And now she was expected to walk right into the evil heart of Hitler's government? "I won't."

"You must, Liesel. Considering what a close call we had, it's important to show our loyalty now more than ever."

"I'm not loyal," she had retorted, and anger had flashed in his eyes.

"If you are not loyal to the Party, then at least have the kindness to pretend you are, for the sake of your family. Or would you prefer that Friedy be thrown into a camp, or given a lethal injection, all because of his foot?"

Liesel had been horrified by his cool, matter-of-fact tone, but she had gone. She'd had no choice.

The New Reich Chancellery on Vossstrasse was a large, coldly impressive building, newly built after Hitler had proclaimed the old Chancellery, the former palace of Prince Radziwill, was "fit for a soap company." Its fixtures and fittings had only just been installed, and the reception that evening would be in the main gallery, an enormous mosaic-tiled room that was a hundred and fifty meters in length.

Liesel had walked down the endless corridors to the gallery with a growing sense of unreality. Everything was enormous, absurdly oversized, so she'd felt like a doll in a giant's house. There was something ghoulishly fairy-tale-like about it all, as she'd tiptoed across the marble, the expectant and slightly fearful hush of the guests as they'd processed reminding her how dangerous it all was—and every single person knew it. No one was safe.

The reception was, her father had told her, in honor of the Grand Mufti of Jerusalem, Haj Amin al-Husseini, who was visiting Hitler to discuss his support of the war, as "the Arabs and the Germans had the same enemies."

Liesel had spent the evening sidling along the walls, trying not to be noticed. When Hitler had entered the room with the Grand Mufti, the roar of *Sieg Heils* had made her cringe, until she'd sensed someone's eyes on her and she'd seen Reinhard Heydrich from across the room, smiling coolly. Her blood had felt as if it had frozen in her veins, as if her heart had stopped beating, as she registered the knowledge in his eyes and knew she would never be safe… just as she would never be free of guilt. Every time she closed her eyes, she knew she would see Gerda's swollen eye, Rosa's burning gaze. Their capture was her fault as much as her father's. If she hadn't told him… if she hadn't gone up to check on them during the air raid, as a salve to her own conscience, if she hadn't been so reckless, so *thoughtless*… she might have been able to save them, no matter what her father said about the house being watched. Somehow. Some way.

She'd pressed her fingers to the pocket watch she now wore around her neck like a talisman, a reminder of Gerda and Rosa she would take with her everywhere. She'd forced herself to return Heydrich's smile, as if he were just another guest, before she looked away.

"Almost there," Otto said cheerfully as the car turned off the main road by a sign marked Oswiecim. "Wait till you see the house we have! Twice the size of ours back in Berlin."

No one replied, and Liesel noted the flicker of irritation in her father's eyes that he quickly suppressed. He was determined to be jolly, as he had been, with increasing effort, over the last two years, despite the strain and fatigue she saw in his eyes, the stoop of his shoulders.

Back at that reception for Amin al-Husseini, Germany had seemed on the brink of ebullient victory, with soldiers camped outside Moscow, and the imminent collapse of the Soviet Union expected by just about everyone. Then, like the shifting of tides, it had all started to change. The Americans had entered the war in December, and the battle of Moscow had been—despite the news reports determinedly declaring heroic victories—a complete disaster, and the Germans were, inch by inch, mile by painful mile, inexorably being pushed back out of the Soviet Union.

The mood in Berlin had begun to change as well, in grim increments; everything began to possess a desperate edge, from the hunger people felt as shops emptied out and rations—which had been plentiful mere months ago, thanks to all the food coming from conquered territories—now began to dry up, to the short tempers of the SS who restlessly patrolled the streets, seeming to be on the prowl for someone to abuse.

Over the course of the year, Berlin, and indeed all of Germany, emptied out of Jews; Liesel no longer saw them hurrying down the street, heads bent, the damning yellow star sewn to the shoulder of their coats. It was, in an eerie, awful way, as if they'd never even been. She had no idea what had happened to Gerda or Rosa, but she prayed, to a God she struggled to believe in any longer, that they were safe.

The car drove slowly down the narrow single-track road, and then as her mother let out a soft gasp, Friedy looked up from his book and Liesel turned to glance out the window.

"Vati," Friedy asked, "what is all that?"

They were driving by a fierce-looking fence of barbed wire that seemed to go on forever, rows and rows of single-story barracks visible behind. Liesel saw a few haggard-looking people, hurrying with their heads down, dressed in striped coats and loose trousers.

"Oh, that?" Otto gave the huge facility a quick, dismissive look. "That is where the workers in the factory sleep."

"With watchtowers, guarded by the SS?" Ilse said, her voice sounding as if it had been dipped in acid. One of the wooden towers her mother had mentioned loomed ahead of them, with two soldiers standing on guard, MG42 machine guns at the ready. Instinctively, she shrank back against the seat.

"Many of them are prisoners of war," Otto replied evenly. "It is, alas, a necessary precaution."

They continued to drive by the fenced-in camp, mile after mile of barbed wire, while her father determinedly turned his attention to his newspaper. Eventually they came to the camp's front gates and Liesel silently read the inscription wrought in iron above them. *Arbeit Macht Frei*. Work will set you free. It was a cruel mockery of the Bible verse found inscribed in many churches—*Wahrheit macht frei*. The truth will set you free.

She shuddered inwardly and glanced at her mother, but Ilse had turned away from her, and away from the window, not wanting to look. Like Liesel, she had lost the will to fight. Her occasional comments, as barbed as the wire they were driving by, were all she seemed to have left in her.

After another few minutes, they finally left the camp behind, and Liesel felt a restless sort of relief, glad not to have it in her sights, although it still lingered uncomfortably in her consciousness. There had been something a bit too glib about her father's reply, but then lately there always had been.

A few miles later, they came to another camp, just as grim, and then her father cheerfully pointed out the factory he would be managing, set behind the gates, an ugly, hulking building. The camp, he told them, was called Monowitz, and would house the laborers. No one said anything.

The house they would be living in was indeed bigger than the one on Koenigsallee—a proper little palace, with a grand front of ornate stucco and gardens that ran down to the Sola River.

"Do you like it?" Otto asked as he came into the bedroom Liesel had chosen. It was one of the smaller ones yet still grander than the one she had at home, and everything about it depressed her—the canopied bed, the velvet curtains, the chaise lounge piled high with satin pillows. Whose house had this been, and why were they not here any longer? "You can see the river from the window," he remarked with a nod toward the view.

"Yes." Liesel lifted her gaze from the icy, churning waters to the smokestacks just visible on the horizon, emitting great big bellows of black smoke that dissipated into pale vapor in the gray sky. Country living, indeed. "Who lived here before us?"

The slightly arctic pause told Liesel she'd annoyed her father, as she often seemed to do nowadays, sometimes deliberately, sometimes without meaning to. She no longer cared which it was.

"Poles," he said at last. "Obviously. Does it matter?"

Where were they now? Liesel had known for years that Poland was systematically being rid of all its inhabitants; Berlin had been flooded with cheap labor, its grand new buildings constructed by grim-faced men in coats marked with a P, while many of her neighbors had Polish cooks or charwomen. Yet it felt different standing there, in a bedroom that had clearly belonged to someone else. A silver hairbrush lay on top of the bureau, along with a mirror and comb, and it reminded her of Rosa.

"I just wondered," she said. "They must have had to leave in a hurry." The words were pointed, and she knew her father felt them.

"Can you not," he asked, his teeth gritted, "simply be happy that we are here? Can you not be thankful for just one thing?"

Liesel turned from the window. "Thankful," she repeated, not bothering to hide her incredulity. "Why should I?"

"Because I have provided for you," her father said. His voice was strident, but Liesel saw a torment in his eyes that even now aroused a tiny flicker of sympathy before she deliberately extinguished it. "Because I have kept you safe."

"Safe." She thought of the Gestapo coming up the stairs. Heydrich smiling at her from across the Chancellery. Yes, her father had kept her safe, but at what price? "I never asked to be kept safe."

"Oh, didn't you?" He let out a humorless laugh. "Forgive me for being so stupid as to think you wanted to live."

His mouth twisted and Liesel didn't reply, damned once again by her own cowardice. Yes, she wanted to live. Even now, when years of war had made her so very weary, she wanted to. Or perhaps, she acknowledged as she gazed once more out at the churning river, she simply wanted to make her death count. She had yet to discover a way to do that.

Her father left the room without saying anything more, and, desperate to escape the confines of the house that smelled of lavender polish and leather and cigar smoke—the ghostly remnants of other people's happy lives—Liesel went out into the garden, picking her way through the frost-tipped grass as she shivered under the leaden sky.

At the bottom of the garden the Sola River flowed, on toward Oswiecim before joining the mighty Vistula and then out to the Baltic Sea, six hundred miles away. Here it wasn't very wide, its ruffled surface flowing by quickly, looking gray under the cloud-filled sky.

As Liesel stepped closer, she saw the real reason for the water's color—it was filled with silt, to the point of being opaque. She crouched down to trail her fingers through the icy water, drawing back with a small gasp when she felt the sticky, gray film that clung to her fingers. *What on earth was that?*

Then her eye caught the gleam of something white amidst all the silted-up gray, caught on some twigs and leaves. Heedless of the freezing water now, driven by a deeper instinct, she plunged ankle-deep into the river and yanked the item free.

It wasn't until it was lying in the palm of her hand, the water rushing all around her, that she realized what it was. The remnant of a human jawbone.

CHAPTER TWENTY-SIX

Oswiecim, December 1944

They were losing the war. Surely, steadily, with a deeper, darker certainty that was felt with every passing day. Six months ago, the Allies had landed in France; Germany had proclaimed a glorious counterattack, but Liesel had yet to see its results. Instead she saw the fighter planes flying across the crystalline blue skies; the Buna Werke had been bombed twice since September, bringing with it plumes of smoke, and both hope and terror.

Now, sitting at the breakfast table a week before Christmas, Liesel pushed away the copy of *Völkischer Beobachter* that her father read every morning and that today declared victory in "the battle in the West." She doubted there was any victory. Papers peddled lies, now more than ever, as Germany was wrested from the clinging control of its ever more desperate leaders.

They had been living in Oswiecim for a year, a year of trying to block out the black smoke that belched to the sky, trying not to see the barbed wire that bracketed every day and bisected her dreams at night. That first day, when Liesel had realized what she'd held in her hand, she'd flung it away from her with a cry, watching as the bone was swept along in the silted current, horror clenching her insides, her mouth wide open in a silent scream. She'd waded out of the river, barely aware that her feet were soaking and entirely numb, and she had started back to the house in search of her father, only to realize he would fob her off as he always did. *Are you sure of what you saw, my Lieseling?* Or perhaps *Prisoners try to escape occasionally, my dear. I'm afraid it is an unfortunate part of life here.*

No. She would not look to her father for answers. She'd learned that lesson in the most painful of circumstances, refined in the crucible of grief and guilt. Instead, she had walked around to the front of the house and then down the road, toward the wire that ran along the sky. It took her half an hour of following the fence, her feet throbbing with cold, until she found the tall, severe gates to the camp, the brick hulk of the Buna Werke factory rising behind it like an ugly monolith. She had started forward, only to be stopped immediately by an SS guard, his MG42 at the ready.

"*Halt!*" He had strode toward her, his face thunderous, but Liesel had met him head-on, even though everything in her trembled at the anger and authority she saw in his sharp features—the hard eyes, the tight mouth, his finger already on the trigger of his gun.

"My father is Otto Scholz, the administrator of the Buna Werke factory," she had stated in her most imperious tone. "He requested that I be given a tour of the camp."

The guard's expression was almost entirely one of disbelief. "We have received no such request, *fraulein*. If you are who you say you are, then go back home."

"I want to see," she had insisted, and the guard took a step toward her.

"Go back home," he'd growled.

Liesel had the suspicion that he would happily shoot her, were it not only for the slight lingering doubt that she might actually be who she said she was. Tilting her chin at a haughty angle, she had whirled around and started back toward the road.

"Liesel, for the love of heaven, where were you?" her father had asked as soon as she came through the front door, exhausted and aching. Her feet had become so cold they now felt fiery, and she suspected she had frostbite.

"I went for a walk."

"You look chilled to the bone. Come into the drawing room, by the fire, to warm up." He had drawn her by the hand, and Liesel had let him, because it felt so wonderful to be in a warm house, with a father who cared for her, and if she just closed her eyes for long enough, life could be simple. She could let it...

But she couldn't. No matter how much she wanted to, she couldn't. And as her father had knelt and eased off her sodden shoes, Liesel had felt herself crumple inside and she began to weep, her body doubled over as the tears slipped down her face, one after the other, a silent litany of regret and grief.

"Liesel, Liesel, my little Lieseling." Her father's voice had been a tender murmur as he had held her in his arms and she had breathed in the smell of his cigarettes and aftershave, felt the rough wool of his coat against her cheek, and wept and wept.

"What has brought this on, my darling?" he had asked when the sobs wracking her body had finally ceased, although her eyes continued to leak tears, as if her body was no longer to contain what her head and heart both knew.

Liesel had shaken her head, unwilling and unable to articulate the cause of her tears. Was she crying for the inmates of that wretched camp, and the fate they surely did not deserve? Or for her father, who even now could look so concerned for her tears, while thousands—millions—suffered and perhaps even died at his hand? Or was she crying for herself, because she was so lost and so grief-stricken and she did not know what to do?

"I just want the war to be over," she had finally gasped, and her father had taken her in his arms once again.

"I know," he had murmured. "So do I."

*

She had arranged a tour of the camp a week later, while her father was at work. It had been surprisingly easy to do; she had forged his signature without a second thought, writing a letter to SS-Hauptsturmführer Heinrich Schwarz, the commandant of the labor camp, appointed only last month. She'd seen the papers on her father's desk, and she'd used them without a single scruple, writing how *"my daughter has taken an interest in the running of the camp, and how the prisoners are used most effectively. Please indulge her girlish whim to be given a tour of the entire facility."*

Sure enough, Hauptsturmführer Schwarz himself had been waiting for her as the car drove up to the gates, looking, Liesel had noted nervously, a bit annoyed; her chauffeur, a Pole who spoke no German and simply did as he was told, had not objected to driving her there, and seemed most anxious to leave as soon as possible.

"Fraulein Scholz! It is indeed my pleasure." Irritation had thinned the man's mouth as he took her hand. "If only Herr Scholz had told me himself of your interest, I could have had something more easily arranged."

"I believe he wrote a letter," Liesel had said sweetly. "I am so very interested in my father's important work."

Hauptsturmführer Schwarz had looked less than impressed. "Indeed," he'd replied. "Well, we are very busy here, Fraulein Scholz, as I am sure you can appreciate, but I will show you a few of the highlights, as a favor to your father."

Her heart had beat like a drum as the *Hauptsturmführer* had taken her through the camp himself, skirting certain sections while happily showing her others—a comfortable room with a cot, chair, and table that was, ostensibly, an example of a prisoner's accommodation; a visit to the kitchen where a nourishing soup and freshly baked bread awaited for their midday meal.

All the prisoners, the *Hauptsturmführer* assured her, were happy and well-fed. Unfortunately, Liesel could not see any individuals to judge the matter for herself, but as they had rounded one of the barracks, she glimpsed a concrete wall spattered with blood and in that moment she knew what she'd suspected was true, and everything the commandant was telling her was lies.

"I'd like to say hello to my father, before I leave," she had told the man in the same sweetly girlish voice she'd used before, and seeming both reluctant and put out, he had a guard escort her to her father's office deep in the bowels of the Buna Werke factory.

"Liesel!" Otto had risen from his desk, his face draining of color as she'd closed the door behind her with a decisive click. The room was much smaller than she'd expected for the manager of the whole factory, with a single, high window overlooking a concrete courtyard, a stack of files tottering on his battered wooden desk. "What on earth are you doing here?"

"I wanted to see it for myself," she had said quietly. "And now I know. Not all of it, of course, but enough." She had kept his gaze, willing him to say something more, but he had simply watched her warily, a hunted yet crafty look in his eyes. Suddenly Liesel was so very tired of the pretense they'd both been keeping up—the telling silences, the barbed comments, the constant edging around the stark, grim reality. "Tell me the truth, Father," she had said. "For once. Be man enough for that, if not for anything else." She had met his guarded gaze with a steely one of her own, willing to wait out his reluctant silence. "Well?"

Her father had regarded her for another moment before something in him seemed to sag and he sat back down behind his desk, raking a hand through his hair, and then gestured for her to take a seat. "What is it you want to know?"

Liesel had sat down gingerly, as if she didn't trust the wooden chair to hold her. She certainly didn't know whether to trust her father's words. "I want to know everything," she had said.

Wearily, he'd lifted one hand, palm up. "Ask a question, then."

Liesel had hesitated; she felt as if she'd been given a rare and precious treasure, this shimmering possibility of knowledge, of *truth,* and yet she sensed its terrible weight. Once she knew, there would be no not knowing.

"Is this camp just for prisoners of war?"

"No."

"Who else, then?"

"Poles, Czechs, Slavs, gypsies." A pause. "Jews."

She had thought of the barracks, the barbed wire. *"This* is where they were resettled?"

Her father had met her gaze flatly, unflinchingly. "Yes."

"Will the Nazis keep them locked away here forever?" she had asked disbelievingly.

Another pause. "No."

"Where, then, will they go?"

He didn't answer and she had pictured, quite vividly, the towering smokestacks, the jawbone she'd held in her own hand. The dreadful *Der Sturmer's* insistence on extermination. Yet even now she backed away from the idea with a horror that contracted her insides.

"*No…*"

"Ask, Liesel." Her father had lifted his chin, his eyes now blazing with a challenge of his own. "Since you wanted to know so much. *Ask.*"

She had formed the words through lips that felt numb. "What do they do," she had asked, "with the Jews? And the others?"

Otto had placed his hands flat on his desk. "Many work—in this factory, as well as performing other needed tasks. I told you before that the labor was cheap."

"And they have comfortable beds and bowls of hot soup, as Hauptsturmführer Schwarz was showing me?" The sharp ring of cynicism had sounded in her voice.

Irritation had flickered in her father's eyes. "No, of course they don't. You know that as well as I do. They are fed on starvation rations and sleep on wooden planks, and when they become too ill or weak to work, they are taken out of the camp and killed, either by a lethal injection of phenol to the heart, or in the gas chambers at Auschwitz." He had paused, his steely gaze seeming to bore into hers with something almost like satisfaction. "You wanted to know."

Liesel had stared at him, shocked into a terrible silence by the starkness of his words. She had felt as if she'd been punched, as if she were gasping for breath, even as she sat there completely still, staring at her father, the look on his face both remorseless and resigned. He was, she thought, *glad* he'd told her. Glad he'd shocked her.

"Gas chambers," she had repeated finally. "Why are there gas chambers, for just a few of the ill or weak…?"

"Why are there gas chambers? Why are there smokestacks? It's not just for an unlucky few, Liesel. You must realize that, even if you don't want to. They are there because the *kommandos* can gas and burn four thousand bodies a day, although I believe they've managed as many as eight thousand, if they're particularly efficient."

Liesel had doubled over, a retch had caught in her throat as she'd wrapped her arms around her waist and tried to breathe in deeply. She'd felt her father's gaze on her, cold and assessing. "You mean," she had managed as she stared at the floor, "that they are killing the Jews in these chambers. Murdering them, and then burning their bodies." She had thought of the jawbone, the silted water, sticky on her fingers. *Ash.* The ashes of the dead.

"Others, as well, but yes, mainly the Jews." Her father had sounded so matter-of-fact, as if he were simply reciting statistics, and slightly dull ones at that.

Liesel, still doubled over, had looked up at him, the taste of bile coating her throat. "How long have you known about this?"

"How long?" He had shrugged, tapping his knuckles lightly against his desk. "That is difficult to say. I knew of the possibility of using forced labor back when I was involved in discussions about the factory being built, in 1941, but I couldn't have imagined this. I don't think anyone could have." For a second, the mask of brisk efficiency had dropped, and Liesel saw a glimmer of the man she'd once known and loved, horrified by what he'd seen, rather than just hardened. Then it was reassembled, and her father gave her a cool smile.

"But you knew," Liesel had stated quietly. "At some point, you knew for certain. You must remember when. Surely... *surely* you remember the moment you realized. You can't have forgotten such a terrible thing, knowing it for the first time." Her voice rose in desperation, and her father had hesitated, a faraway look coming over his face as he'd rolled his fountain pen between his fingers.

"If I had to point to a particular moment," he had said heavily, "I suppose it would have been when I came to visit the building site in September of '41. They had been conducting some experiments on the use of gas to kill some Soviet prisoners. They asked for my advice."

"Your *advice?*"

"Yes, because they were using Zyklon B. It is a form of the pesticide I helped develop back in the twenties, with Abraham Stern. You remember him?" He had given a faint, sad smile of remembrance and she had nodded wordlessly. "Of course, that was a long time ago, and what we were working on was to help humankind, not destroy it. But I suppose that is the danger of discovery. Whatever you invent can be used for another's purpose, evil or not." He had let out a little sigh, as if that were beyond him now, as if it was not his concern that his discoveries were now killing thousands—millions—of people mere miles away.

Liesel had shaken her head slowly. She had felt empty inside, as if she'd been turned inside out, as if she were nothing more than a husk. Her head had throbbed and her mouth was dry and she had a desperate urge to go lie down somewhere and never get up again. "How," she had asked her father, "can you live with yourself?"

He had shrugged, a twitch of his shoulders, his face bleak yet also indifferent. "What choice do I have?"

"You could refuse, Father. All along, at *some point,* you could have refused. When you realized what they intended. What it all meant."

"You mean when they gassed those Soviet prisoners? Liesel, when I came, the men were already dead. What would have been the point of that? If I'd made some objection, they would have marched me to a wall and shot me in the head. It's as simple as that. And I would have died for what—a couple dozen dirty Cossacks? Is that what my life is worth?"

She had thought of what her mother had said. *Make it count.* And here was her father's twisted version of it, the dark side of the same terrible coin.

"Why," she had asked, everything in her aching, "is your life worth more than even one of those *dirty Cossacks*?"

Her father had stared at her for a moment before he made a dismissive note in his throat and looked away. "Don't be so sanctimonious. It doesn't suit you. And," he had continued, his voice rising primly, "I'll have you know, I have not sold my soul to the Nazis the way you seem to think I have. I do what I can to make things more bearable for the prisoners here. I allow them sick leave when they are too ill to work, and I try to give them extra rations when it is possible. I've stopped several executions, and at some risk to myself."

Liesel didn't know whether this little speech heartened her or made her feel even more wretched. "You're in charge of the whole factory," she had said. "Surely there is more that you can do."

Her father's mouth had tightened. "It's never enough for you, is it? As it happens, I am not in charge of the entire factory. I run one department."

"But…" She had stared at him, surprised, because he'd always acted as if he ran it all, as if he were so very important. She knew she had not come to that belief without reason. But looking at his small office now, and remembering Hauptsturmführer Schwarz's attitude of annoyance, she had realized the truth of it. Her father wasn't that important at all.

All that glad-handing of high-ranking Nazis, smoking cigars with Göring and weaseling invitations to Carinhall or the Chancellery… it hadn't got him very far, had it? From one hundred thousand marks from Hitler himself to a little box of an office in a rubber factory on the Polish border, halfway to becoming irrelevant.

"Well?" Otto had demanded, his voice rising once more, this time in impatience. "What do you have to say, now that you know it all?"

Liesel had simply stared at him. She had nothing to say, nothing she *could* say. Her head ached abominably and her stomach cramped. Silently she had risen from her chair and walked out of the room.

That had been a year ago. A long, lonely, terrible year of waiting, wondering, wanting only for the war to be over, while Friedy involved himself with his books and her mother, rather surprisingly, with bridge; she had the wives of other factory and camp administrators over several times a week for cocktails and cards, their laughter rising from the drawing room like the raucous cawing of crows. For someone who had never concerned herself much with such things, Ilse seemed to take to the card afternoons with an almost manic determination. Liesel supposed she needed something—anything—to stave off the boredom of life there, and worse, the fear.

Three days after she'd visited the Buna Werke factory, Liesel had gathered what extra food she could from the kitchen—while the cook, a Pole with no German, watched anxiously—parceled it up and then walked toward the wire.

She had felt empty inside, indifferent almost to both the danger and the potential benefit of her actions, as she walked along the fence until she came to a place where there were no guards, no watchtowers, no one at all to see what she was doing. Then she had dropped the parcel of food through the wire, watching it fall onto the ground. She had no idea if anyone would come across it or not, if it would help anyone at all. She only knew, for her own sake, she had to do something.

The next day, when she went to the kitchen, the cook had already wrapped the food up in a dishcloth. She had handed it to her silently, her face full of knowledge and pain. Liesel had wondered what the punishment would be for the poor woman, were she to be discovered. Beating? Death? And what about her? Her father had made it clear that they were not exempt. His position was not the protection it had once seemed. There were certainly no more favors to be called in.

When she came to the same point in the fence, the parcel of food in her arms, a young woman had hurried up to her, her hair caught back in a kerchief, her thin face prematurely lined. Liesel had pushed the parcel through the wire, and the woman took it silently, mouthing her thanks. Then Liesel had turned and gone back home.

She had continued with her journeys nearly every day of that long year, scrounging what food she could, going without as it became more scarce. One hot, dry day in the middle of summer, she had stopped in surprised to see her mother secreting a tiny slip of paper among the wrapped packages of bread and cheese.

"What are you doing!" she had exclaimed.

"What does it look like I'm doing?" Ilse had countered coolly.

The cook hovered silently, her hands twisted in her apron.

"It looks like you're sending a secret message to a prisoner," Liesel had said slowly and her mother had straightened with a smile.

"I always knew you were clever, darling."

"But…" Liesel had gaped as her mother adjusted her earring before taking out a cigarette and lighting it up.

"It's a pity that all I can get are these dreadful Junos," she had remarked as she inhaled.

"What message are you sending?" Liesel had asked, still shocked by her mother's casual act of treason.

She had shrugged. "Whatever I can." She had raised her eyebrows in delicate challenge. "Why do you think I endure those endless rounds of bridge, Liesel, if not to get information from those awful, insipid wives? You know I've never been able to abide card games."

"And you never thought to tell me?" Liesel had struggled to untangle her feelings—relief that like her, her mother was doing *something,* and fear that if she were to be discovered, they would most certainly both be killed. Delivering food was one thing; contraband intelligence another.

"It was better for you not to know."

Liesel had to agree with that sentiment; she never read the messages her mother sent, although in October she wondered, when there was an uprising of the *Sonderkommandos* in Auschwitz-Birkenau, if her mother's information had had anything to do with it. The rebellion had ended with several hundred executions, and nothing more was heard. It had put her father in an even worse mood; he barely spoke to any of them anymore, and his eyes were bloodshot, his face haggard.

"It's because the Soviets are coming," Friedy told her matter-of-factly that morning in December, after her father had strode out of the dining room, muttering under his breath. "He's worried, of course."

She and Friedy had spent much of their days together—playing *Skat*, reading books, practicing their English. In some ways Liesel felt like a child again, and it was not an unwelcome sensation. "The Soviets," she repeated. "You mean coming *here*?"

"I should think so," Friedy replied placidly. "They're already at the Vistula River, and the Americans are still only in Belgium."

Liesel glanced again at the newspaper, with its triumphant headline of the attack in the west. "How do you know where the armies are?" she demanded. The papers said nothing.

Friedy looked up from his book with a patient air. "You've got to read between the lines in the newspapers," he explained. "A 'strategic withdrawal' means a defeat. Look, I've mapped it all out." He opened the notebook he carried everywhere to show a carefully drawn map of all of Eastern Europe, the places of significant battles marked with a dark circle. Looking at those childish lines, Liesel saw with cold clarity how the Soviets were drawing closer. She'd known, of course, for it was impossible not to know, and yet she hadn't realized quite as starkly as that. "I imagine they'll be here after Christmas," Friedy told her happily.

"But, Friedy…" Liesel stared at her little brother in perplexed concern. All her life she'd been told of the dreaded evil of communism, the known savagery of the Soviet soldiers. Friedy had, as well. They were to be feared above all else. "Aren't you scared?"

Her little brother shrugged his assent. "Well, yes. I'm not *particularly* looking forward to being overrun by the Red Army, you know, Liesel." He gave her a rather supercilious look over the top of his spectacles that made Liesel smile. Her brother was fourteen, although he still looked no more than nine or ten, and he possessed an endearing combination of maturity and innocence that made her long to protect him. He'd already been through so much. "But I expect," Friedy continued with an air of knowledgeable gravity, "Father will take us back to Berlin before they come."

"Berlin…" All Liesel knew about Berlin now was that it had been bombed relentlessly since they'd left. From the scathing reports in the papers about the unconscionable Allied attacks, it seemed as if hardly a home would be standing.

"Yes, and then that will be the real question," Friedy told her, propping his chin in his hand. "Will the Soviets or the Americans get to Berlin first?"

His matter-of-fact attitude amazed her. How did he know so much? The war, to her, was a dark swirling force all around them, but to Friedy it was maps drawn on a page, chess moves on a board. "Who do you think will get there first?" she asked her brother.

"The Americans," he replied firmly. "Because I'm going to be a cowboy."

CHAPTER TWENTY-SEVEN

Camp King, January 1946

Sam walked out of Major Lewis' office in a daze, barely aware of his surroundings. All he could see were those damn photographs—Anna with Göring, with Heydrich, in Carinhall, in the Chancellery itself...

"What is it?"

As Sam looked up, he saw Anna had lurched to her feet, her wide-eyed gaze surveying him anxiously as she clutched her handbag.

"You swore," she explained. "And I have never heard you swear before. What is it?"

He hadn't even realized he'd spoken. And now that he was looking right at her, he had no idea what to say. Words crowded in his throat and tangled on his lips. He shook his head.

"Sam..." Her voice lowered, softened. "What did Major Lewis say about me?"

"What do you think he said about you?" Sam challenged. He glanced toward the room he'd just come from, and then motioned to Anna. "Let's go outside. We can't talk here."

Outside, the air was frigid, the sky the color of slate. Sam paced in front of the twee little cottage where he'd had his wretched interview, while Anna watched him, her arms folded protectively across her body.

"Sam," she said after a few moments, and there was a familiarity in her voice that once would have pleased him but now only made him feel fury, a sudden, towering rage that crashed over him and dragged him under.

He whirled around to face her, his hands already bunching into fists, his chest aching with the effort of holding back the torrent of words he knew he shouldn't say. *How could you. You're a liar. You betrayed me.*

"Your father is here," he finally said, his voice tight.

Anna's mouth dropped open soundlessly and for a second she swayed where she stood.

"*Here…*"

"He's insisting he has scientific information the U.S. will want, but he won't say what it is until he's given diplomatic immunity."

Her lips twisted and her eyes sparked. "That sounds like him."

"You lied to me, Anna. *Liesel.*" He heard the raw hurt in his voice and still he could not keep himself from it. "Major Lewis showed me the photographs."

Her forehead creased as she stared at him in confusion. "Photographs…"

"Don't pretend you don't know. There were plenty of them."

Still she stared, and he glared back at her, and slowly he saw realization penetrate, like a mist lifting—or perhaps descending. Suddenly she looked like a stranger, someone he'd never even known, as she straightened slowly, looking almost regal. "You mean official photographs," she stated quietly.

"Taken by Heinrich Hoffmann himself, or so Major Lewis told me."

Anna let out a huff of hard laughter, shaking her head slowly. "So they were."

Her admission only made him angrier. "You lied. You *are* a Nazi. A Nazi… *lover!*" The words spilled out of him, unstoppable, filled with vitriol and hurt. "You were with Heydrich… Göring… at the Chancellery, the very heart of it all, enjoying their parties, their posturing, cheek to cheek sometimes…" She didn't deny any of it, simply watched him with a level look, and he finished with a sound caught between a cry and a groan. "How could you?"

She bowed her head. "I asked myself that every day." A pause as she considered her next words. "As I told you before, my father was a chemist with IG Farben. He helped to develop Buna rubber. He was, in his own small way, something of an important man." She looked away. "Or so he thought he was, at least for a little while."

"What does that have to do with those photos?"

"He went to those events—the ones at which I was present—as part of his work."

Sam thought of her cheek pressed to Göring's. "It didn't look like work to me."

"Well, it was," she said, her tone sharpening a little. "And I hated every minute of it. If I did not attend, I was afraid it would reflect badly on my father, on me. Dangerously so. That was what I was told, at least." She drew a shuddering breath. "I do not make excuses. I only explain. It was…" She exhaled, trying to think of the words, struggling to regain control of her emotions, her voice. "It was a very frightening time."

He could hardly disagree with that, and yet still the fact of those photos lodged sourly in his gut. "Not every German had their photo taken at the Reich Chancellery, hobnobbing with Hitler himself," he said flatly. "You had a choice."

She let out a half-wild laugh as she nodded almost frantically. "You sound as I once did! That is what I told my father, many times." She took a step toward him, her eyes glittering with both ferocity and tears. "You have a *choice*. You always have a choice. To say *Sieg Heil*. To not enter a shop run by Jews. To look the other way when a man is beaten half to death for no reason. To hide a Jew." Another laugh, even wilder, as a tear trickled down her face. "To say no to all of it, any of it, even if just once, and it causes you—what?" She cocked her thumb and forefinger toward her temple. "A bullet in the head? Well, would that be so bad? I do not think so. There were many times I did not think so."

Sam stared at her, longing to take her in his arms even as he fought to remain unmoved. Those photographs told their own story, and it was one he could not ignore, even now. "And what choice did you make?"

Her eyes widened, her mouth turning down at the corners, as a breath blew through her in a gust, leaving her empty. "The wrong ones," she said quietly. "Many times."

Sam waited for more, and slowly she withdrew the slender golden chain from underneath her blouse. The pocket watch. Her biggest regret.

"Gerda Baum was our housekeeper," she said quietly. "She and her daughter Rosa came to us before the Jews in Berlin were taken to the camps. We didn't know about the camps then. No one was told the truth. But they were afraid, and I wanted to help them." She sighed deeply, a burden whose heavy weight she still bore. "We hid them in our attic. My father couldn't know. They gave me this watch to pay for their keep. I didn't want it, but Gerda—she had her pride." Another sigh, this time a shudder from the depths of her being. "I told my father that they were there. At the time… I don't know. Perhaps I felt I had no choice or perhaps… perhaps… I wanted my father to prove he was a good man. I hated lying to him. I hated thinking that I had to."

Her voice broke on the words, but she pressed her lips together and continued, "When I told him, he called the Gestapo. They came the next morning, just after dawn. I never saw Gerda or Rosa again. I think they must be dead, most likely in one of the camps." Her fingers curled around the perfect golden oval of the watch. "And it was my fault. Mine. If I hadn't told him… if I hadn't been so afraid…" Her voice broke again, and a shudder went through her, shaking her slender frame.

This time, Sam did not resist the instinct that overwhelmed him, far stronger than the fury he'd felt. He put his arms around her and she pressed her cheek against his shoulder as she wept, her body shaking with the force of her feelings.

"Oh Anna… *Liesel*…" He stroked her hair, longing to comfort her, his thoughts in a ferment. She was innocent. She was guilty. She was suffering. She was complicit. But then, he realized, perhaps they all were. It was all too easy to point to Hitler, to Heydrich, to Göring or Goebbels or any of the men who had become monsters in the public's mind, and they *were* monsters. Of course they were. But they were also men. Men who breathed and ate, slept and laughed, loved and wept. Just men. And they'd been sustained, whether through complicity or fear, by an entire population that had watched them rise to power.

And could he say he would have been any different, if he'd been there? Any better? Would he have been brave, or would he have waited, thinking surely it wouldn't get any worse? Even now, with the benefit of hindsight, he struggled to know what to do. What was right. How to help.

Eventually she lifted her tear-stained face to him. "So you are right, Sam. I *was* a Nazi. But here?" She touched her breastbone, her fingers skimming the pocket watch once more. "I was not. Though, as my mother once said, perhaps that makes it worse." She stepped back, out of the shelter of his arms as she dashed the tears from her eyes. "So now you know. I am sorry. Truly I am sorry."

"You took Anna Vogel's identity not because of your father, but because of who *you* were." He stated it without emotion, trying to process what she was telling him and all that it meant, but pain flashed across her face, and he knew he'd spoken too harshly.

"Both," she said quietly. "It is true."

"And you're here to protect your father," Sam couldn't keep from saying. "Or maybe get out on the same deal he wants."

Confusion crossed her face, creased it. "What... deal?"

"A free ride all the way to America," Sam said, and now he didn't even try to keep the bitterness from his voice. His emotions were in an impossible tangle: he was angry, he was hurt, he was aching with the pain he knew she felt. Still he forced himself to speak levelly. "That's what he's hoping for, I'm guessing, and that's what we'll give him, if his information is useful enough."

"He'll go *free*?" She looked disbelieving, as shocked as if he'd slapped her across the face.

"That's what Operation Paperclip is all about. Finding the chemists and physicists and engineers and all the rest to help us in the war against the Soviets. Never mind that they were Nazis." Until he'd said it out loud, Sam hadn't realized just how much he had come to hate the idea. How wrong it all felt. He wanted to prosecute these people, not let them go. Had he changed, since he'd first arrived in this country, unable to summon the rage Major Pitt or Sergeant Belmont had felt? He felt it now.

Anna took a few faltering steps away from him, holding her hands to the sides of her head as if she were wounded, bleeding. "This is all so they can go *free*?" she said dazedly. "So they can go to America?"

"Isn't that what you want?" Sam demanded, even though he could see very clearly now that it wasn't, and in the midst of his anger, that made him glad. "You and your father can ride off into the sunset. Settle in California, or maybe New York."

Anna turned to him as she dropped her hands from her head. "That is *not* what I want," she declared savagely.

"What, then?" he challenged.

"To see him *punished*. To pay for his crimes. I told you! I told you!" Her voice rose in a ragged cry. "To finally make him answer."

"Well, he can answer you, at least," Sam told her grimly. "You'll be interrogating him."

She blinked at him for a few seconds, stunned. "What… what do you mean?"

"Major Lewis has requested that we interview him together. I'll ask him about the chemistry, you'll put on the pressure."

"Pressure? To do what?"

"Tell us what he knows. He wants to keep his chemistry secrets to himself, until he is given a guarantee. You need to convince him that's not such a good idea. Then you'll both be able to go to America."

"But I don't want that!" she cried in frustration. "I want him to pay."

"Well," Sam answered grimly, "then you'd better hope he doesn't know as much as he claims he does."

She stared at him for a moment, her lips trembling before she pressed them together. "Do you hate me?" she asked finally, and her voice sounded small.

Sam struggled to keep his composure, his emotions still in knots. His hand bunched again at his sides, his only resistance against reaching for her another time. "Anna," he said roughly, "I've never hated you." Which would, he told himself, be as close as he allowed himself to come to telling her how he really felt.

She shook her head slowly. "I have not seen my father since he left us in Berlin, in April of 1945."

"Nine months ago."

"Is it only nine months?" She let out a little, disbelieving laugh. "It feels like a lifetime. Two lifetimes."

"What happened between now and then?" He sensed more to her story than what she'd said so far, and yet at this question, Anna just shook her head, the movement surprisingly firm.

"It doesn't matter. I can't talk to him."

"Don't you want to see him again? Even if just to make him answer, like you said?" He searched her face—her eyes the color of damp moss, her cheeks so pale, her lips blood-red as she nibbled the bottom one with fearful misery.

"I'm scared," she whispered.

"Scared of what?" Sam asked, his tone gentling. It took all his effort not to touch her—her shoulder, her cheek, a caress he kept himself from.

"Scared of still loving him," she whispered.

"Would that really be so bad?" The man was her father, after all. Sam could understand the tender feelings she still might harbor, no matter what he might have done.

Anna's expression hardened, her mouth set in an uncompromising line. "Yes, it would," she answered, "because he killed my brother."

CHAPTER TWENTY-EIGHT

January 1945

They left Monowitz as if they were fleeing a fire, and indeed they were. The SS were systematically destroying the evidence of the camps—blowing up the gas chambers, burning the looted possession of the Jews, trying to hide the overwhelming evidence of their evil. Prisoners who were well enough to walk had been formed into long, abject columns to make their way west on foot through frozen snow; any who lagged behind were shot. Everyone else was simply told to get out, by whatever means they could find.

Liesel had barely time to pack her suitcase before they were hurrying out of the house that had never been theirs, into the waiting car, the sky full of smoke and fire. Her father was driving, as there was no one on hand to act as chauffeur. The Polish servants who had cooked their meals, cleaned their clothes, and ferried them around were now being marched toward Germany with thousands of others. Those too ill or weak to move still languished in the camps, left to their fate.

"What will happen to them?" Liesel asked as they drove toward the main road that led toward Breslau and then on to Berlin.

"They might be the lucky ones," her father replied. "Who knows how long they'll make the prisoners march, and it's twenty below outside." His hands gripped the steering wheel tightly, everything in him tense and straining. He had, he'd told them, been fortunate to procure any petrol, though it most likely wouldn't be enough to see them all the way to Berlin.

There had been two more air raids on Monowitz in the last few weeks, but worse, there had been the news of Soviet victory after victory as they rolled on inexorably and ruthlessly through a devastated East Prussia, dealing brutally with anyone they encountered, if the reports in the newspapers were anything to go by.

Christmas had been a white-knuckled, unhappy affair, with absolutely nothing to celebrate. Everyone knew, even the prisoners in the camps, that it was but a matter of weeks or even days before the Soviets made it to Oswiecim, and then carried on to Germany itself.

Liesel glanced at the barbed wire fence that ran along the side of the road as they drove back toward whatever safety they could find. It seemed so strange to think of the camps being emptied, abandoned, their gates flung open to welcome the liberators, such as they were.

Even though she'd been aware of the Red Army's relentless advance, it had not felt quite real, tucked away in the house outside Oswiecim as she was, her days spent playing cards or reading books or trying to translate Goethe into English with Friedy.

The air raids had been sporadic, and not as bad as the ones in Berlin, thanks, her father had said grimly, to the fact that Stalin wanted Buna Werke and the other factories for himself. She'd stopped reading the papers because she hadn't wanted to see the grim litanies of death and defeat couched in fantasist terms of German strength and superiority. She'd isolated herself in a bubble of ignorance, thinking only that she wanted the war to be over, and one day it surely would be.

It was only now, as her father drove in grim silence toward an uncertain future, that she realized the world as she knew it was being laid to ruin, and nothing but ashes might remain.

The main road, when they finally turned on it, was clogged with people fleeing the Red Army. Almost all cars had been requisitioned by the army, but Liesel saw bicycles, wagons, handcarts, and even people on foot, carrying what they could in their arms, trying to escape. It was like a macabre circus, a terrible, unlikely parade, this stream of desperate humanity. Some people were trying to take their fine china or their precious paintings; other people had nothing but the clothes they wore, but everyone knew the Soviets wanted vengeance. Goebbels had made sure the newspapers were full of what the Red Army would do with the hapless and innocent Germans; they would rape your mother, behead your baby, gut a man like a fish. Over and over again. A tremor of terror went through Liesel at the thought. Could it possibly be true, or was it more relentless propaganda, to keep the Germans in servile thrall?

They crawled along the road, past a gray-faced woman pushing a wheelbarrow that held a couple of tow-headed toddlers, curled up like puppies among a nest of woolen blankets. Liesel wondered how they could possibly manage for more than an hour or two; it was the middle of January and well below freezing, the world cloaked in a hard, unforgiving mantle of white.

She saw an old-fashioned landau that must have been taken from the stables of a Prussian castle, pulled by men rather than horses, as well as a woman with a couple of scrawny chickens in a rusty black pram. She glanced at her father and saw he was sweating, despite the frigid temperature inside the car.

"Are they really as bad as that?" she asked in a small voice, and her father hunched his shoulders.

"Worse. Men, women, children, even babies—they don't care. They treat them all like animals. *Worse* than animals. They shoot them in the street, or toss their babies into the fire." He shook his head. "They have no humanity."

But that's what you did, Liesel thought. *What we all did. We have no moral right, no claim to having humanity ourselves.* Why, she wondered, as her father pointlessly sounded the car horn to get a man pushing a handcart out of the way, did everyone have such capacity for evil? Could they possibly have the same kind of capacity for good?

"Don't worry, Liesel," Friedy said. "It will all be over soon."

"Yes, it will." There was no question about that, but foolishly she'd imagined the war ending like the curtain closing on a play. Everyone would rise from their seats and go home, tired but happy. That had been ridiculously, childishly naïve. She realized now that the war was going to end with fire and ruin, death and destruction—far more than there had been in the five and a half years of waging it.

"Will it be any better in Berlin?" she asked, and her father just shook his head, his eyes on the road ahead, the pavement choked with desperate people.

Liesel remembered what her brother had said about the Americans. If they got to Berlin first… They *had* to, she thought with sudden, frantic desperation. She felt like a little girl, skipping the pages to the end of her storybook, desperate to make sure it turned out all right. They had to… because she did not want to imagine the alternative.

It took them nineteen hours to get back to Berlin, through the clogged stream of people heading west; they ran out of petrol sixty miles from the city, and ended up walking for some of the way through the freezing cold, before a farmer took pity on poor Friedy with his foot, and said they could all clamber onto the back of his wagon, huddled together in the dirty straw, trying not to freeze in the icy wind as the extent of the city's destruction was revealed all around them.

Houses had been levelled, streets torn apart, ruins still smoking. They gazed at it all in shocked silence as the wagon made its way ever westward, before the farmer left them outside Anhalter Bahnhof, where dazed refugees were stumbling out of the station, grim-faced and staring. Liesel heard one of them say that some of the children had frozen to death on the journey. In shocked, exhausted silence, they took the S-Bahn back to Grunewald; amazingly, despite all the chaos, it was still running.

By the time they arrived back home, Liesel barely recognized herself. She was exhausted, filthy, and half-frozen; she hadn't eaten in over twenty-four hours. All she wanted was a bath and a hot meal, but neither were to be had in the house on Koenigsallee.

As they came up to the villa, Otto hesitated in his stride, for the house looked well-lit and warm; they'd left it with curtains drawn, shutters as well, closed up for the duration. "Perhaps Helga…" he murmured, and then stopped. Helga, of course, could not possibly have known they were coming.

Liesel waited outside with her mother and Friedy, all of them shivering and ready to drop, while her father went to his own front door and rather timidly knocked. Liesel couldn't understand his nervousness until she saw a shadow darken the door, heard the sharp tone if not the words.

Just a few minutes later, Otto came back to them, looking shamefaced, although he tried to speak with dignity.

"I'm afraid the house has been requisitioned."

"Requisitioned!" Ilse's voice rose sharply in disbelief. She'd remained in a shocked silence, as they all had, during the endless journey from Monowitz, but Liesel knew that the promise of the comforts of home had been sustaining her, just as it had been for them all. "What can you mean? It's our *home*."

Otto shrugged unhappily. "Someone from the Führer's General Staff has taken it on. It was meant to be empty… We were meant to stay in Oswiecim, after all."

Ilse simply stared, and in that moment's silence, Liesel saw all her father's weaknesses, laid out like pathetic trophies for them to inspect. He was nothing but a small and shabby man, round-shouldered and gray-faced, a tiny cog in a great, ruthless piece of machinery, and no one important had any more need of him, now there was no factory to help run. All the cigars and handshakes in the world couldn't save him now.

"What shall we do?" Liesel asked out loud, and Otto shrugged again.

"We shall find somewhere."

"Where?" Ilse demanded incredulously. They had no friends in Berlin, save for the Nazi officials Otto had courted so assiduously and who now did not seem at all interested in his sorry plight. "Otto, we will freeze to death if we cannot find somewhere to stay. Surely they could at least let us have a room."

"It's not possible," he said stiffly, and Liesel was not surprised. This was the way of the Reich—a constant jostling for position, indifferent to whose fingers you stamped on. Petty wars waged amidst the huge one raging all around them. Her father was no longer important; there would be no favors called in, no kindnesses shown. At best, he would simply be forgotten.

"Surely we can go to a shelter, at least," she said. "And then we'll be assigned somewhere to stay in the morning."

As if in agreement, the air-raid siren began its long, mournful wail. As one, they hurried out into the street, stumbling all the way to the shelter at Grunewald as the siren wailed and the bombs began to drop.

They spent a miserable night huddled in a damp cellar that smelled of wet wool and stale sweat and misery, crammed with refugees from East Prussia, who, like them, had had nowhere else to go. One woman babbled her story of soldiers coming and raping her in a shed for hours while her baby cried to be fed. As she broke down into sobs, Ilse turned away, pale-faced, her eyes like dark, icy pools.

"I cannot…" she whispered to Liesel. "If it comes to that, I would rather kill myself."

Liesel supposed not everyone had had the luxury of that choice. She wondered if they would; when would that spark of instinct to live, no matter what the cost, finally be extinguished? How much would have to be endured first?

The next morning, they were allocated a three-room apartment in the working-class neighborhood of Prenzlauer Berg, in the Pankow district in northeast Berlin.

Liesel gazed around the basic rooms with their few bits of furniture, the peeling linoleum floor, and the intermittent running water and gas. The tenant across the hall, a nosy spinster who seemed to care more for preserving her last few heirlooms—a Meissen milk jug and a gold ring—than anything else, informed them the gas was usually no more than a faint blue flicker that could barely boil a potato, but at least it was on.

Ilse collapsed onto a rickety chair in the main room, looking lost. As Liesel walked slowly to the window and gazed out at the unfamiliar landscape of tall, narrow apartment buildings and the squat water tower known by locals as Fat Hermann, she realized afresh just how much absolutely everything had changed.

All during the arduous journey back to Berlin, they'd thought of the house on Koenigsallee waiting like a bright and welcoming beacon, a haven of safety. But it wasn't theirs; it had never been theirs. It had belonged to a Jewish family before they'd been evicted, and now it was their turn to endure the same. Surely that was justice, and yet it still felt shocking, to realize nothing was sacred, nothing was safe. They no longer had a house; her father, it seemed, no longer had a job. Although in the coming weeks he would sometimes don a suit and hat and go out trying to find someone important to help him, he inevitably returned home looking defeated, a shadow of the man with the gleam in his eye, the spring in his step.

The days crept past in a dreary blur of hunger and cold, punctuated by terror. Berlin was bombed several times a night, and they spent more time crowded into the building's dark cellar than in their apartment. When Liesel ventured outside, it was to see the city yet more ruined.

At the end of January, the biggest film to come out of Babelsberg, *Kolberg*, a story of a small village fighting courageously against fearsome invaders, premiered at Alexanderplatz; a few days later the cinema was a smoking ruin. In early February, the Chancellery, the Gestapo's headquarters, and the People's Court were all damaged—these symbols of Nazi power reduced to near rubble.

And yet amidst all the ruin, people still trudged to work and back again, queued for the limited rations available in near-empty shops, and waited for the war to be over, however it came.

Friedy was continuing to chart the Red Army's progress across East Prussia, along with the U.S. and British Armies coming from the west. Now fifteen years old, he still looked no older than twelve, with a scrawny chest and a serious expression, although he'd grown taller, which made him seem even skinnier. "The Soviets will take Breslau soon," he told her one evening as they pored over a map by the sputtering light of an oil lamp; the electricity was off again. "And then it will be straight to Berlin."

Liesel's heart thrummed in her chest. "And the Americans?"

Friedy shook his head sorrowfully. "Still fighting the Germans by Aachen. They've barely left Belgium."

Liesel stared at the map, the lines and names that scored it blurring before her. Despite the supposedly decisive Germany victory in Hurtgen Forest, and Hitler's insistent speech at the end of January that "Whatever our enemies may plot, whatever sufferings they may inflict on our German cities, on German landscapes, and, above all, on our people, all that cannot bear any comparison with the irreparable misery, the tragedy that would befall us if the Bolshevistic conspiracy were victorious," it seemed as if exactly that was going to happen. The Red Army would take Berlin.

As the month wore on, the mood in the city became inexorably grimmer, a fatalistic desperation punctuated by the Berliners' typical dark humor. At Christmas, the joke had been what the best present to receive was—a coffin. Now it was how LSR no longer stood for *Luftschutzraum*, or air-raid shelter, but *lernt schnell Russisch*—"Learn Russian Quickly."

Liesel understood well enough that in the face of tragedy sometimes the only response could be laughter, and yet at the same time an acidic terror lined her stomach, and she felt as if she were living in a constant state of high alert and anxiety, startling at every noise, everything in her straining all the time, barely able to eat, which was just as well since there was so little food.

Her mother was even worse. There were no cigarettes or alcohol to be found anywhere, and so she had taken to biting her nails, and then the skin around her nails, and finally her fingers whole, until they were raw and cracked and bleeding, as if she would eat away at herself until there was nothing left.

February descended into March, and the Red Army marched closer as U.S. and British planes dropped bombs both day and night and blank-eyed refugees from East Prussia streamed into the city with horror stories Liesel couldn't bear to listen to. Hitler had neither been seen nor heard from since the end of January; the newspapers were nothing but a single printed sheet of lies. Food was impossible to procure, and Liesel spent almost all of her daylight hours waiting in queues or tramping through the city streets, tracking down rumors of depots giving out bread, or a butcher who had some old offcuts of pork. What she found she gave to Friedy; he was already little more than skin or bone, and he needed it far more than she did. Her mother would not eat at all.

"Surely you can get us out of Berlin," her mother would say to her father, whenever she was startled out of her stupor. "Somewhere, Otto, anywhere. In the west of the country they are already liberated. They say the Americans will reach Frankfurt by the end of the month. We could go there, stay with your sister..."

"And how would we get there?" he demanded, his voice strained, as it had been since they'd returned to Berlin—to no job, no home, no hope. "There are no trains running. We do not have a car. And with all the fighting going on, we would likely be killed on the way."

"You could ask your old friend Göring," Ilse mocked. "He could send a car to take us to Carinhall." She gave her husband a look of such savagery that Liesel cringed to see it.

"The Reichsmarschall is staying in Berlin," Otto replied with dignity, "and so will we. Besides, I have already called in too many favors." This was said with a dark look toward Friedy that made Liesel want to cry out. Could her father possibly blame Friedy for the predicament they now found themselves in? And yet he seemed to need to blame someone, at least someone other than himself. When he wasn't despairing, he was angry, lashing out at everyone before taking to the streets again.

"He's looking for someone who recognizes him as somebody important," Ilse told Liesel once sadly. The anger her mother encased herself in dropped for a moment, to show her grief. "And of course nobody does."

As spring came in early April, Liesel was almost shocked to find nature impervious to the war being raged all around; lilacs spread their sweet perfume over the ruins of bombed-out buildings and trees burst into glorious green bud. It all felt like an insult, a mockery. Liesel would have rather it rained, for the sight of beauty hurt too much, like a brightness to the eyes, the unbearable possibility of a world where things could be appreciated again, and survival was not about scrounging through a sack of potatoes crawling with weevils, while the sky cracked in two overhead.

Then, toward the end of April, her world truly did split apart. Liesel woke one gray dawn, the air still holding the chill of night, to find her father dressing quietly in the main room. It was not quite five o'clock in the morning.

"Where are you going?" she whispered as she pulled her dressing gown on, a useless thing of silk and ribbons that felt as if it were from another life. The apartment was freezing; there had been no water or gas for two days, and a nearby blast had shattered the panes of two windows.

"Out." Her father wouldn't look at her as he put on his overcoat and then slid a wad of marks into his pocket. Disbelief nearly choked her.

"You're leaving," Liesel said in an incredulous whisper. "You're leaving us, right as the Soviets come!"

"I am going for help," he told her through gritted teeth. "I have to do something. We cannot stay in this miserable hovel and simply wait for the Red Army to trample over us." He paused, his throat working. "Liesel, many of the prisoners in the factory were Soviets. What do you think they'll do to me when they find out who I am?"

Even now, Liesel thought, her father had delusions of his own importance. Who would even know who he was or what he'd done unless he told them himself? No one in Prenzlauer Berg knew anything about them, so he couldn't even be denounced by a nosy neighbor. "What do you think they'll do to *us*?" she demanded.

"I told you, I'm going to get help. I know that the Reichsmarschall is at the Chancellery for the Führer's birthday. Perhaps he will listen to me, his old friend." He gave her a smile, a ghostly remnant of the man he'd used to be. "Did you know it's his birthday today?"

Liesel just shook her head wearily. As if she cared that it was the Führer's birthday. She thought of the huge parade six years ago, when German military pride had been out in full force. Five hours she'd stood and watched the might of the Wehrmacht on display. Where was any of it now?

"Do you actually think you'll get an audience with Göring now?" she said despairingly. Calling her father his old friend was, she feared, no more than an utter and absurd delusion. She wondered if Göring would even remember who he was, or care.

"I can try."

"And you'll be back?" She stared at him hard, for the furtiveness of his manner, the fact that he was leaving at the crack of dawn with his pockets full of money, made her wonder. Doubt.

"Of course I will, Lieseling," her father said. He held out his arms as if to hug her, but Liesel didn't move and he dropped them defeatedly to his sides. "Do you honestly think I could leave you three, the lights of my whole life? I'm going for help. You'll see, Göring will listen. It would be no trouble to him to send us a car, arrange our passage to Frankfurt, even a house there. We'll be safe." He smiled at her, but she saw how much effort it took, and she felt only despair. She wondered if her father would even get a glimpse of Göring. It seemed far more likely he'd be turned away by an SS guard well before he had such an opportunity.

A few minutes later, he was gone; and the very next day they came for Friedy.

CHAPTER TWENTY-NINE

April 1945

The Red Army were said to be just forty miles outside of the city; the sound of gunfire was like a distant thunder, and the vibrations were strong enough for pictures to fall from their hooks, and even, jarringly, to cause telephones to ring, although there was no one to answer them.

The city of Berlin had become a town of ghosts as everyone went underground to hide from the constant shelling as well as the advancing army. The air was thick and acrid with smoke, and in the east, the horizon was a deep, wounded red, as if the sky itself were bleeding.

While the other residents of the apartment building had decamped to the cellar, Liesel had stayed, along with Friedy and her mother, feeling the walls shake as bits of plaster dropped onto the floor, the howling wail of the *Katyusha* rocket launchers, nicknamed Stalin's organ, a constant, unholy symphony in the distance. They were waiting for Otto's return. He didn't come.

Liesel was not afraid for his wellbeing; the possibility that he'd been captured or killed she'd dismissed almost at once. She'd known when she'd seen him the morning before that he was running away, saving his own skin instead of his family's. She could hardly believe it of him, and yet she no longer had it in her to be surprised or even disappointed.

"For heaven's sake, let's get to the cellar," Ilse exclaimed as a nearby blast reverberated through their chests. "He's not coming back. I told him he was no husband of mine, and now he has shown that he isn't."

Her mother looked grimly determined, but Liesel could hardly bear to let go of this last desperate hope. There would be no car to Frankfurt, no shining, golden road to safety. Of course there wouldn't. She hadn't ever really believed there would be, and yet it still felt unbearable, to have that last faint flicker of hope firmly extinguished.

Safety was no more than a cramped cellar with the stench of unwashed bodies and the ragged sound of terror as they waited out the fall of Berlin—and then what? The future loomed ahead of them, impossible to know. Would they survive? Would they ever live normally again—to eat and drink, laugh and love, walk in the park or go to the cinema? It all seemed laughably, horribly out of reach. There was nothing but this—starvation and fear, shelling and gunfire, and the ever-present threat of the Red Army, for when they came. Surely now it was only a matter of days, if not hours.

"All right, we'll go," Liesel said. She was just throwing things into a suitcase to take downstairs when the knock came at the door. She and Ilse exchanged a wild-eyed look before Liesel went to the door, her heart seeming to still in her chest at the sight of two SS officers, their jackets dusty, their expressions both savage and resolute.

"We are looking for Friedrich Scholz," one of them said, and Liesel felt as if she'd been thrown back into a nightmare, when a steely-eyed doctor had said the very same words.

"What…"

"He will be sixteen next month," the other man said, consulting a paper. "He is eligible to be conscripted into the *Volkssturm*."

"The *Volkssturm*…" Liesel stared at the men in horror. She knew of the militia conscripted from old men, mere boys, and even wounded soldiers that was meant to defend Berlin from its attackers. Often they were given nothing more than obsolete rifles or a single grenade, or sometimes nothing at all. Many of them were crazed with nationalistic pride; others were simply terrified. The idea of them being able to stop the Soviet tanks from rolling in was painfully, horribly absurd. "He's only fifteen," she insisted staunchly. "And he has a crooked foot. He is not suitable to fight." Please God, his poor, twisted foot would now save him. "Look, Friedy," she called desperately. "Show them your foot."

Friedy limped slowly to the door, his shoulders thrown back, his expression almost haughty.

The SS eyed him with a cynical curl of his lip. "He looks good enough to me. And even a cripple can throw a grenade."

"No, it can't be—" Liesel exclaimed, only to be silenced by her brother's hand on her shoulder. She realized, distantly, how tall he'd grown; he was half a head taller than her now, although still skinny as a reed. In her mind's eye, he was still a precocious twelve-year-old, a dreamy-eyed boy of six, not an almost-man.

"It's all right, Liesel," he said, and she heard his man's voice, as if for the first time. When had it become so deep? He still looked so young; there wasn't a bit of fuzz above his lip or on his chin, and despite his height, his slight frame made him look years younger. They *couldn't* take him.

"This is wrong," Liesel declared wildly, and she felt her mother's hand on her shoulder. She turned to Ilse, whose face was sober, accepting in a way that terrified her all the more. "Mutti, we can't let them! The Soviets are almost here—you'd be as good as killing him!"

"We are all proud to fight for our Führer," one of the men declared. "Our youth must be willing to sacrifice themselves for their Fatherland."

"This is madness," Liesel insisted yet again, and was silenced by one of the SS slapping her hard across the face.

"Be careful you do not speak treason," he said with quiet menace, as her mother squeezed her shoulder warningly and Friedy reached for his coat.

"You can take me," he said in a calm voice, almost as if he were speaking of the weather, "but I will not fight."

The two men stared at him in something like disbelief, while Liesel pressed one hand to her throbbing cheek and her mother stood silently beside her.

"I won't fight for the *Fatherland*," Friedy continued in a clear, firm voice, "because it is not my Fatherland. Germany is no country of mine, and I despise the Führer and the evil he has wrought, the destruction he has caused our country—"

He wasn't able to get any more out for one of the men had backhanded him so hard his head whipped round, blood pouring out of his nose, while the other grabbed him by his arm.

"You know what happens to traitors?" he exclaimed, shaking Friedy like a rag doll.

Liesel opened her mouth to scream, yet no sound came out. She was transfixed with horror as Friedy didn't attempt to defend himself; instead he let himself be hustled from the doorway, out into the hallway and down to the street.

"Don't be afraid, Liesel," he called, before another punch silenced him.

"I have to get him—" she gasped, and started forward.

Ilse reached for her. "Liesel, there is nothing you can do. You must let him take his stand."

"*No.*" The word erupted from her savagely as she flew out into the hall, then clattered down the stairs and outside. She saw the SS down the street, Friedy being frogmarched between them, his twisted foot dragging pitifully behind him, and she cried out, the single word tearing at her throat, her lungs, "*Friedy!*"

They marched on.

*

It took her the better part of two days to find him. Two days of wandering broken streets, dodging shells, the sky lit up like a terrible firework, and then spending the night shivering in a strange cellar, asking anyone she could if they knew where the *Volkssturm* were fighting.

She prayed only that Friedy had seen sense and taken back his words, or perhaps the SS had thrust a rifle into his hands anyway and forced him to fight. Anything that meant he was still alive, and not taking his stand, like her mother had said. It was almost the end of the war; what good were such theatrics now?

On the afternoon of the second day, an old man with broken teeth and sunken cheeks told her he'd seen the HJ mustering on the Reichsportsfeld, by the Olympic stadium. They were hoping to defend the bridges across the Havel, when the time came.

Liesel thanked him profusely and then ran, winding her way through deserted, rubble-filled streets, sheltering in buildings that were barely standing, working her way west through a city under siege until the Olympic stadium came into view, as magnificent as ever, an ode to Greek architecture amidst a rubble-filled ruin.

She had a brief, piercing memory of skipping along this very street toward the stadium almost nine years ago, for the Olympic Opening Ceremony. She'd been so glad then, that Friedy had been forbidden to come, so she could revel in her father's benevolent attentions.

Liesel let out a choked sob as she thought of how ignorant she'd been on that day, how blessedly naïve. How silly her problems had been, and yet that had been the beginning of it all.

This is how I will make our fortune.

She raised a weary fist and shook it at the sky, as if her father could see her, as if he could hear. *Look at us now, Vati! Look at us now!*

Then she hurried across to the Reichsportsfeld, where she could see HJ and old men in various get-ups, from oversized coats to faded uniforms from the first war; it looked more like a child's costume party than a battalion of fighting men, yet that was what it was supposed to be.

She did not find Friedy anywhere, and then a young boy, no more than fourteen, with sad eyes and stooped shoulders, nodded toward the stadium.

"Perhaps," he said quietly, "you should look there."

Liesel was full of foreboding as she walked toward the stadium where she'd once sat so happily next to her father and watched all the athletes on parade, the Canadians offering the Olympic salute, the Americans taking off their straw boaters.

The stadium was not full of cheering spectators today. As planes flew overhead and gunfire boomed throughout the city, with the echo of the flak guns thudding steadily in return, Liesel walked down the Marathon steps that Hitler himself had taken nine years ago, and into the stadium itself.

A choked cry escaped her and then was cut off as the enormity of what she was looking at slammed into her. Bodies—dozens of bodies, laid out like offerings in the huge arena. Crumpled bodies of old men, and bodies of teenage boys—little more than children, curled up like babies, as if they were sleeping, but not one of them was.

Liesel walked slowly into the arena, her dazed gazes scanning the faces—the bulging eyes and clenched jaws. She realized they'd all been hanged, and then cut down and laid out here like offerings. Around the neck or pinned to the chest of each and every one was a scrawled placard—*I am a Traitor*. Liesel let out another cry as she pressed her fist to her mouth.

Please God she would not find Friedy here.

But she did. It took half an hour of staring into blank eyes and distorted faces, but she found him at the far end, near the viewing platform where Hitler had once stood so triumphantly. He was dead, of course, his hands folded on his chest. Despite the clenched jaw and bulging eyes, Liesel thought he almost looked peaceful. She wanted to believe he was, that he was free from suffering, that he was glad he'd had a chance to stand up to the evil they'd both despaired of, and that he'd taken it.

With a shudder, she ripped the placard from his chest and threw it into the wind. Friedy had not been a traitor, not to his soul. He'd been the bravest boy she'd ever known.

She crouched by him as she gently ran her fingers through his dark fringe, as unruly as ever, still soft. "Friedy… *Friedy…*"

Even looking down into his lifeless face, his eyes staring, she couldn't believe he was dead. She willed him to wake up, for the light to come back into his eyes as his mouth curved into a teasing smile. *You didn't think I'd let the Red Army get me, did you?*

But it hadn't been the Red Army. It had been the German one, the soldiers who had once sworn to protect the people of this country, who had killed a mere boy, and for what? *For what?*

The city was going to be taken in a matter of days, if not sooner; the war might be over in less than a week. The Soviets were already rolling into the east of Berlin. They might be in Prenzlauer Berg by tomorrow.

She had to get back to her mother. Liesel's insides froze with sudden realization. She'd left her mother, grieving, no doubt half out of her wits, completely alone while the Soviets marched onwards. She had to get back.

Gently, she touched Friedy's cheek and closed his eyes. His skin was strangely warm from the sun but still felt dead, like old wax. Liesel rose from where she stood and surveyed all the dead sons and fathers, grandfathers even, who would never go home. Who might never even have a grave. Her father had been part of this. He had sanctioned it, he had allowed it to happen. In her mind he was as guilty of her brother's death as if he'd made the noose himself.

"Goodbye, Friedy," she whispered, and then she started back.

*

It took until early evening to make it back to Prenzlauer Berg, dodging and sheltering as she could. There were so few landmarks to guide her way; nearly the whole center of the city had been completely flattened so it reminded Liesel of a short science-fiction film she'd seen with her father, at the start of the war, depicting a lunar landscape of eerie emptiness.

Except, unlike the film, this seemingly empty landscape was pockmarked by death; Liesel nearly tripped over the corpse of a woman who had been felled by a bomb, her head half gone, a stale loaf of bread lying next to her. Liesel took the bread and ate it as she walked, hardly able to believe she had descended so low.

The streets were empty as everyone had taken shelter from the shelling; several times, Liesel had had to duck into a building where she'd lain curled up on the floor as the shells fell all around, the thuds and blasts sounds she'd almost become numb to.

By the time she finally stumbled up to the apartment building, exhausted and filthy, the street was surprisingly quiet, and she felt nearly faint with hunger. She hadn't anything more than a few bites from the loaf she'd taken from the woman in over two days.

When she climbed up to the third floor, she found the apartment they'd called home since January empty and desolate, and downstairs, when she hammered on the cellar door, a sullen woman unlocked it after Liesel had become hoarse from shouting that she was alone and she wanted to find her mother.

"Ilse, that stuck-up piece? I don't know where she is."

"But she wouldn't have just *gone*."

"Who knows? Now either get in or out, because the Ivans are here."

Liesel's stomach cramped. "The Russians?" she said dumbly, and the woman's lip curled.

"Who else?"

Even now, with the gunfire and the smoke and death hovering all around, Liesel could hardly believe it. "Where?"

"Everywhere. See for yourself. They arrived a few hours ago." And the woman slammed the door in her face.

Liesel stood there, dazed, struggling not to collapse on the ground, as she heard the sound of the bolt being slid into place.

Slowly, she walked back upstairs and out of the building. It was a beautiful evening, the sky a deep blue softening into violet, the sun still shining. It was as if even springtime had joined the fight and was waging a war of beauty. Roses climbed a wall nearby, their blowsy fragrance overpowering, making Liesel want to retch with their sickly-sweet scent. Her stomach felt as if it were eating itself, hollowed out, desperate for sustenance. She pressed one hand to the side of her head, trying to think. Where was her mother?

Then, quite suddenly, a Soviet soldier came into view, riding a bicycle badly, a silly grin on his youthful face. Liesel only recognized him by his uniform; she'd seen it enough in the papers, the olive green, with a peaked cap, wide leather belt and trousers like pantaloons. The bicycle came to a squeaky stop and he stared at her in surprise. He looked no more than seventeen or eighteen, barely older than Friedy, with a sweet, round face and wide blue eyes. Liesel stared back, too overwhelmed and numb to think, much less speak.

"*Guten Tag*," he said, his accent making the words sound clumsy. He smiled, and Liesel had a sudden wild urge to laugh.

"*Guten Tag*," she replied.

The man stared at her for another moment, and Liesel kept staring back, and then he began to cycle again, the bicycle wobbling across the road, before he disappeared around the corner.

Liesel sank onto the steps, her head in her hands. Her heart was pounding, the aftereffect of the surreal experience. So that was the much-feared Soviet.

She sat there for a few more moments, exhaustion pulling at her bones, until she heard another noise and looked up to see a pair of soldiers coming around the corner with a swagger; one had no less than five watches on his arm.

As they caught sight of her, the one with the watches narrowed his gaze speculatively.

"*Mann*?" he asked, and Liesel blinked. Husband. He was asking her if she had a husband. She opened her mouth and realized there was no reply she could possibly make. The man slid a sideways glance at his compatriot and then they started forward. Liesel jumped and ran, the sound of the soldiers' mocking laughter echoing behind her.

She ran until she thought her lungs would burst, only to stop by the side of an apartment building, her hands on her knees, her chest and legs both burning, sweat trickling down her back and dampening her dress under her arms.

She looked up and realized she had no idea where she was. She still needed to find her mother.

She kept walking, slowly, in a daze, heedless of the Soviets who might be lurking around the corner, lying in wait. She could barely put one foot in front of another, and yet she didn't know what else to do but keep walking as the shadows lengthened around her.

"Liesel!" The sudden, urgent hiss had her straightening and looking around. "Up here!" She looked up and saw her mother peering out of a window, her face wild, her hair in a graying tangle.

Liesel let out a huff of incredulous laughter and then ran into the building.

Her mother met her in the stairwell, both of them crying and laughing as they held each other by the arms, until her mother drew back, her gaunt face drawn into even more haggard lines.

"Friedy?"

Liesel shook her head. Tears filled her mother's eyes. "They hanged him. He was so brave, Mutti."

"The bravest," she agreed hoarsely. Her body sagged, the life seeming to drain from it as she aged even more in front of Liesel's eyes. "You are well?" she finally asked, and it took a few seconds for Liesel to realize what she meant.

"I haven't… They haven't…"

Her mother nodded slowly and then glanced outside at the sun sinking behind the broken buildings. "It didn't happen until night, when they arrived yesterday. It seems they need to drink first."

Liesel let out a choked gasp. "They haven't…"

"No, not me, thank God. Last night they all went down to the cellar. I was late, waiting for you."

"Oh, Mutti—"

Ilse waved a hand. "No matter. When I went down, they'd locked the door and they wouldn't let me in, the bastards. I could hear the soldiers looting the apartments, looking for something to drink. I went through the courtyard in the back, and ended up here, hiding in the attic with a young woman no more than eighteen. We both kept safe." Her expression grew serious. "But not everyone did." She shook her head slowly. "The things some of them do. A woman was caught alone in the square. There must have been twenty men." Liesel let out a sound like a whimper and her mother drew her up the stairs, toward the attics. "Let's go where it's safe."

"The cellar—"

"They've already broken in the door. Everyone had been keeping their prized possessions down there—the finest porcelain and a full set of encyclopedias!"

Liesel let out a ragged laugh at the thought. "At least we don't have anything to care about anymore."

Upstairs, in the attics of the building, the air was breathlessly stifling, the eaves making it so Liesel had to stoop nearly double. She couldn't imagine a Soviet would venture all the way up here, but who knew?

"And here is my roommate," her mother said as if she were introducing them at a dinner party. "Fraulein Vogel. She came from Essen to find her cousin, but she's had no luck."

For a second, Liesel felt as if she had catapulted back in time. Here she was under the eaves, and a young girl with blond hair and angry eyes glared back at her.

"*Rosa…*"

"I know," her mother said quietly. "I thought the same."

The girl lifted her chin. "My name is Anna. Who are you?"

"She's my daughter," Ilse said soothingly. "Don't be afraid." She turned to Liesel. "She's been hiding here for days, poor thing. I found her when I came up here yesterday. I think we're both half-mad. We've had nothing to eat."

"I'll get something—"

"It's too dangerous."

"It isn't dark yet," Liesel insisted. She glanced at Rosa—Anna—and remembered how she'd once failed her. Her fingers fluttered toward her throat, where the pocket watch nestled. "Let me go."

Her mother shrugged and held up her hands, and Anna simply stared. They were both too starved and dazed to make any rational decisions, and even though Liesel knew she wasn't much better off herself, she turned and headed back down the narrow stairs, to creep through the empty apartments like a thief.

There was, of course, nothing. No one had any food, and if they did, they would have taken it with them down to the cellar, just as everyone did. Liesel looked in all the larder cupboards, as well as more unlikely places; the spinster across the hall, she remembered, had hidden tins of corned beef among some old blankets. She had hoped others might have done the same, but she couldn't find so much as a crumb.

Dusk was starting to fall as Liesel stood in the hallway, debating whether to leave the building and search elsewhere. She thought of what her mother had said—the woman in the square, the twenty men. She hated to take such a risk, and yet without food and water they would starve. They would die.

Taking a deep breath, she crept down the stairs to the third floor. She saw a spill of light from down the hall and heard the rumble of Russian voices. She froze for a minute until she heard a girlish laugh, tired and strained, and realized they were already being entertained. She crept down another floor.

Only a few of the apartments in the building were occupied, and they all seemed to have Soviet soldiers in them, drinking whatever alcohol they could find and chatting to women, some of it sounding remarkably friendly. They were lonely, these men, and not all of them were savages. Liesel thought of what her mother had said—*they need to drink first.*

She kept going, down the stairs, sidling along the wall, her heart beating in her throat. Out in the street, thankfully empty, it was dark enough that Liesel could just about stay in the shadows as she darted from one building to another.

Across the street, she hurried into a building that looked abandoned, its tenants dead or gone or perhaps simply still hiding. Most of the apartments had nothing but a couple of pieces of furniture, a few paltry possessions—a blanket, a single shoe, a bucket with a hole in it. It was hard to believe that at one time these apartments had been *homes,* with families and children, laughter and tables laden with food. This had been a bustling neighborhood, with shops that sold things and people stepping jauntily out into the street. It was utterly impossible to imagine any of it now, or that it would be anything like that ever again.

Liesel crept through the first apartment she came to, searching for anything she could eat and finding nothing. Then, in the bedroom, under the mattress, she came across a pot of strawberry jam. She stared at in disbelief, this unheard-of treasure, and had just turned to creep back out when she heard the thud of footsteps and then the sound of someone blundering into the next room. Even from the bedroom, she could smell the stench of schnapps.

She froze as the soldier continued to stumble around, and then as quietly as she could, she tiptoed toward the door and sidled behind it, her blood pounding in her ears, her body pressed so hard against the wall she couldn't breathe.

The soldier came into the bedroom, wide-shouldered, bleary-eyed, his face unshaven. He was close enough that Liesel could have touched him. If he turned around, he would see her.

A few seconds passed that felt like an age. The man looked slowly around the empty, darkened room, shaking his head, reminding her of a big, shaggy bear. Then he turned and lumbered out of the room. Liesel did not breathe again until she heard his thudding footsteps down the stairs.

Somehow, by the grace of God, she made it back across the street and up to the attics without encountering another soldier. Ilse let out a cry of relief as she crawled along the eaves back to them, brandishing the jam.

They shared it between the three of them, sticking their fingers into the pot and licking them greedily, until every last sticky bit was gone. Her mother, with a red ring of jam around her mouth, looked at them both and suddenly burst out of laughing.

"We are like naughty children!" she exclaimed, and suddenly Liesel was laughing as well, and Anna too, until their sides ached. It felt good to laugh, even though she knew she could just as easily start to sob. Still, the human heart had to find the humor, the joy, even in this. What point was there to living, otherwise?

Somehow the effect of eating the jam made her only feel hungrier though. Her stomach growled like an angry dog, and Ilse gave her a little smile of sympathy. "Perhaps tomorrow we will find some proper food."

"Perhaps," Liesel replied doubtfully before turning to Anna. "Tell me about yourself," she said, because she needed to be distracted from her hunger, and the girl did. She listened sleepily as she spoke about Essen, and her father's hardware store, and how her cousin, who had lived with them since he was small, had run off to join the *Volkssturm*, and her mother had begged her to find him. He was only sixteen.

"She loved him more than me," Anna said without any real bitterness. "I don't know what I will tell her, if I ever get back."

The hours passed slowly as the night woke up the sleeping beasts. They heard feminine laughter, a scream, a sob, the slam of a door, and then silence. None of them moved. Eventually Anna fell asleep, her head lolling toward her shoulder. Liesel stretched her legs out as she gazed at the moonlight filtering through the chinks in the roof tiles.

"Who would have thought we would end up like this?" her mother said softly into the silence after several hours had passed. "All those years ago? I think of you refusing to wear that wretched uniform. You were right, of course."

Liesel didn't reply as she tried to make her mother's face out in the shadows, sensing she had something more to say.

"I'm sorry," she added quietly. "I know I was hard sometimes. Love, gentleness, they take a certain sort of strength. And I was weak." She leaned back against the wall and closed her eyes. "Perhaps that is why there is so much war. People are simply not strong enough to love."

"I suppose I made it difficult for you to love me," Liesel said after a moment. "I know I was prickly."

"Oh, Liesel." Her mother opened her eyes. "I always loved you. It was simply how to show it, without being afraid. You know I lost several babies between you and Friedy…?"

"Yes." She remembered whispers conversations, having to be quiet, her mother lying so still in a bed, her face turned to the wall.

"I was scared of loving someone and having them taken away from me. Fear guided me, when love should have."

"What about Friedy?" His name caused an ache in her chest. "You were able to love him."

Ilse nodded in acknowledgement. "But that was out of fear, as well. I protected him, because I knew he would have trouble in this world, with the way he was. I couldn't bear to lose him… and yet now I have. I had to let him go." She drew a shuddering breath. "God alone knows if I did as I should. And as for you… you were always strong. You didn't need protecting. And so I let you be. Perhaps I shouldn't have. Perhaps I should have been braver, to show you the love I felt." She sighed. "I would do it all differently now, if I had the chance. Now that I know how fleeting and dangerous life can be, I would take every opportunity I had to show love, to give it, to wring every last drop of it from this world. I *would*."

"Mutti, we will get out of here." Liesel leaned forward, gazing almost sternly into her mother's face. Her hair was gray, her skin deeply scored by suffering. She looked like an old woman, and yet Liesel felt more love for her then than she ever had when her mother had been cool, remote, and beautiful.

"I hope so, my darling," she returned with a weary smile. "I pray so. But I don't know."

As dawn broke, the stuffy space under the eaves became unbearably hot. Liesel longed for water, for the jam the night before had made her even thirstier. She thought of the grocery store on the corner of the street, and wondered if it had any food left in it at all. Was life going on with any sort of semblance of normality now? Would it ever again?

"We have to go down," she told her mother and Anna. "We can't stay up here forever. We'll boil to death."

The words seemed to reverberate through them all. What, Liesel wondered, would happen? They might hide for a night or two, scrounging what food they could, but what about for the next week, month, year? What about the rest of their lives?

If the Soviets took the whole city, which they seemed more than likely to do, they would be their occupiers—just as the Poles and Czechs had had to live under Germans. How would that look? What would happen to them?

For a moment, she could picture her brother so clearly, telling her in his sensible way: *The shelling won't last forever, Liesel. Once the war ends, the Soviets will stop with their looting. They'll want to live like anyone else, and they'll make things orderly again. You'll see.*

The sledgehammer of grief slammed into her once more, and she doubled over, pressing her hot face into her knees. *Friedy... Friedy.* How could he be dead? If only their father hadn't abandoned them. If only he'd been there to protect them, or they'd gone down to the cellar sooner, or she'd done something... anything...

Liesel felt her mother's hand patting her shoulder. "It will pass," she murmured. "It will pass."

They crept downstairs when they could bear the heat no longer, and found that in a surreal, warped way, the world was indeed going on, much as before. A few soldiers sat on a stoop in the sunshine, eating hunks of black bread and looking relaxed. Another was playing marbles in the dirt with a stick-thin child, letting out big bellows of laughter when the child's marble knocked his. A woman was at the pump on the corner, filling a bucket, looking exhausted and furtive, as if she were doing something wrong, while at least twenty people waited wearily behind her for their turn. The sun shone.

Then someone shouted there was food to be had at a nearby depot, and people started racing down the street. Liesel followed the jostling crowd, her mother and Anna hurrying to keep up behind her. At the depot, a sweating, officious-looking man had appointed himself *gauleiter*, and was making sure no one took too much. Liesel found herself with a bottle of wine, a sack of potatoes, and the unbelievable bounty of an entire sausage.

They ate their feast in an empty apartment on the third floor; judging from the dust, there had been no one living there for a long time. But there was a pot for the potatoes, and a flicker of gas, and the water they'd got from the pump outside. After the meal, Liesel felt almost content. It was enough, in the moment, that they had this.

By the time they finished, it was nearly dusk; it had taken hours for the potatoes to boil.

"We should go back upstairs," Ilse whispered.

Liesel nodded, although she was reluctant to spend another night in the airless attics, hot and sweaty, thirsty and tired. Still, she knew it was better than the other possibilities.

They had just come out into the hall and were creeping up the stairs, blinking in the gloom, when Anna let out a soft gasp. Looming on the landing above them were three soldiers, and from the fumes rolling off them, they'd already been drinking heavily.

The three women froze, as trapped as rabbits in a snare. Liesel glanced down the stairwell; there was no one blocking their way, but she knew already they wouldn't be fast enough. She sensed the weary menace in the men, their drunken determination. The younger one's gaze had already moved speculatively to Anna, who was surely the youngest and prettiest of the women, and then he smiled with wolfish intent.

The one in the middle, older and grizzled, with a livid scar down one cheek, hefted his rifle. "*Drei*," he said with satisfaction, and smiled to show a mouthful of broken teeth.

Three. Three men and three women. Liesel's heart slammed against her ribs. She had a sudden, piercing realization that felt like a stab to the heart—she'd been so *spoiled* for most of the war. So stupidly cossetted and protected, worrying endlessly about what she should do, how she could help, from the safety of her sitting room, her warm kitchen. She'd never understood that standing up to evil *had* to be a necessity, an absolute mandate for being human, not even when she'd been sheltering Jews in the attic or delivering the food parcels every day across the wire. Some part of her had felt almost smug for doing what little she could, while feeling as if she'd done so much, simply because she'd done *something*.

Now, when faced with as stark a choice as she'd ever had, she realized the useless, shameful luxury of simply wringing her hands. In the moment, in the end, there was only doing, no matter what the cost.

"Run," she whispered to Anna. She glanced meaningfully at her mother. "*Run.*"

A split second of indecision crossed their faces like a shadow and then they took to their heels, half-sprinting, half-falling down the stairs as they fled the building. Liesel followed them, making sure both Ilse and Anna were in front of her, through the front door and out into the street. She whirled back around, the door at her back, as the men stood there, weary rather than furious. She knew she was simply prolonging the worst, and yet she had to. For her mother's sake. For Anna's sake. For Rosa.

"Open the door, *fraulein*," the man said in his clumsy German. She was an irritant, nothing more. Liesel lifted her chin. "Open the door, *fraulein. Jetzt.*"

The younger soldier hefted his rifle.

Liesel braced herself. Please God they'd got away by now. They were safe…

Then the older soldier grabbed her arm, pulled her roughly toward him. She didn't fight as she was half-dragged up the steps and into an empty apartment. She knew there was no point, that any resistance would likely make the ordeal even worse. One of the younger soldiers closed the door with a deliberate-sounding click. The older man shook her and then, with deliberate precision, spat in her face. She tried to wipe away the gob of spit, but he wouldn't let her.

As he threw her on the bed, Liesel closed her eyes.

CHAPTER THIRTY

Camp King, January 1946

Otto Scholz was a broken old man. Sam stood in the doorway of the interrogation room and surveyed the man who had been occupying his thoughts ever since he'd learned his name. His hair was gray and thin, his face scored with deep lines. He seemed diminished, his clothes hanging off narrow shoulders and a sunken chest.

He glanced at Sam with a mixture of curiosity and indifference, and then his eyes widened and his jaw slackened as he saw Liesel come in next to him.

"Liesel… Lieseling…"

"Hello, Father." She spoke in English, her voice low and controlled, but Sam could feel the tension vibrating through her. Her hands were clasped tightly together at her waist, the knuckles white.

Otto half-rose from his chair, holding one hand out to her in desperate appeal. "I have been hoping so much to see you again. I tried…"

"Did you?" Liesel's voice was hard and Otto collapsed back into the chair, shaking his head sorrowfully.

Sam sat down and after a second's pause Liesel did as well. The silence in the room felt thick, suffocating.

"I am here to discover what you know that might be of interest to the United States Government," Sam began, but Otto Scholz only had eyes for his daughter.

"Ilse?" he asked, and she shook her head. The old man seemed to collapse inward. "Friedy?"

"No." A pause, and then Liesel said in a voice that shook with anger, with raw feeling, "Do you want to know what happened, after you left us?"

Otto shrank back, and Sam had the distinct impression he did not want to know at all, but his daughter was going to tell him anyway.

"They came for Friedy the day after you left," she began in a level voice that still thrummed with emotion. "To be conscripted for the *Volkssturm*."

"No…"

"He refused, Father. He was so brave. He said he would not fight for the Fatherland. He would not support Hitler, no matter what the cost. He was willing to give his life, and they hanged him." Otto's eyes filled with tears. "I found him in the Olympic stadium, with dozens of others, all dead. When I came back, the Soviets had already arrived. Mother and I hid in the attics with another girl." A pause, meaningful not for her father, but, Sam realized, for him. "Her name was Anna Vogel."

"Liesel, please, I am so sorry…"

She leaned forward, her fists bunched. "How could you leave us? Even for a moment? Do you know what it was like? Do you know what the Soviets did to women alone, women without husbands and fathers to protect them?"

A tear trickled down Otto's cheek.

"Don't worry," Liesel said in a hard voice. "Mutti didn't suffer, not in that way. I kept the Soviets out while she and Anna ran into the street, and away to safety." A tremble in her voice, but she kept going. "When I finally found them two days later, they'd been killed by a shell. We thought the fighting was over, at least in that part of the city, but of course it wasn't. Still, at least it was quick. A mercy, considering."

"Liesel…"

"And then I was alone. Do you know what it is like, to be a young woman alone in Berlin, with soldiers all around?" She shook her head slowly. "I won't tell you. I won't tell you the nights I spent, the price I paid for your ambition and your folly. This is where it has led us, Father. To this."

Otto nodded slowly. "You blame me."

"Of course I blame you! We could have left Germany years ago. We could have gone to America back then. We could have been *safe*. Mutti. *Friedy*…" Her voice broke and she bowed her head, drawing in ragged breaths to keep herself under control. Sam wanted to touch her, comfort her, but he felt frozen, shocked by all she'd told her father—and him.

"Liesel," Otto pleaded, "I did try. I went to the Chancellery. I wanted to find a way out of the city for all of us…"

"Then you were a fool. Who would have bothered with you?"

"No one did," he agreed sadly. "I realized then just how unimportant I'd become. They no longer needed my chemistry. They no longer needed me." Liesel stared at him without pity. "And then the fighting… the shelling was so bad… Liesel, I could not get back."

"And yet I could go all the way to the Reichsportsfeld and back." She shook her head. "You could have returned, Father. You just didn't want to risk your own sorry skin. Again."

Otto bowed his head, an acknowledgment of his sins. Liesel stared at him coldly, and then her body sagged and the fury drained out of her.

"I loved you," she whispered. "I loved you so much."

"And I love you, my Lieseling, truly. I know you won't believe that, but it is true. I know it is all my fault. I have lived with that burden for a long time now."

"And yet you still want to save yourself and go to America." She shook her head, her features twisted with cynicism.

Otto leaned forward, his eyes alight with urgency. "No, Liesel, no, it is not like that. I want to go to America to help. To give them my knowledge for *good*."

"Even though you wouldn't before? You're not a traitor to your country now, eh, Father?" She shook her head. "But you've always been a traitor to your soul."

"Would you rather I was hanged?" Otto asked sadly. "Do you want me to die?"

Liesel pressed her lips together. "Sometimes I do. Or at least I wish I did."

Sam had been sitting there transfixed by the exchange; now, in the ensuing silence, he forced himself to take control of the conversation. "Tell us what you know," he said to Otto. "That is what you can do for yourself now, as well as for your daughter."

Liesel let out a harsh laugh. "I'll tell you what he knows. He knows how to make synthetic rubber. He helped invent it back in the twenties; he was Göring's protégé back then, but he hasn't done a damned thing since. He's a second-rate scientist who has ridden on the successes of others—of Jews—for most of his life. If you want to make Buna rubber, then he's your man. But somehow I doubt you do, since America already has neoprene." She glanced at her father. "Göring told me that, Father. Do you remember?"

Otto did not reply.

Liesel drew a shuddering breath. "I've seen you now," she said. "I dreamed of the day I'd see you, what I'd say. I've thought about how you said you wouldn't give your life for a dozen dirty Cossacks, because it wasn't worth it." She glanced at Sam, a defiant look in her eyes. "We spent a year near Auschwitz, when he managed one of the factories. He knew about the death camps. He was there even at the beginning. They asked him about how to use Zyklon B."

"Liesel…" Otto protested in a trembling voice.

Clearly the old man had wanted to keep that secret, and no wonder. Images flashed through Sam's mind from the film he'd seen, and he felt the old anger rise up. What must Liesel have felt?

"Mutti said the same," she continued, "but in a different way. She always said if I was going to take a stand, I had to make it count. 'Don't waste your life on a pointless gesture,' she said. But do you know what I've realized? There is no 'making it count.' There are no pointless gestures. There will never be a moment when you weigh your life on the scales, when anything will seem worthwhile to lose it. You can always put it off, convince yourself you can make it count *later*, for something more important. No." She straightened her shoulders. "There is only acting according to your conscience, whatever happens, whatever the cost. That is what I finally learned. What I finally did. But it was too late for Gerda and Rosa, much to my shame, and to yours." She glanced at Sam, and he saw a hardness in her face he'd never seen before. He realized she'd spoken in English all this time for his sake, so that he would know her story, so that he would understand. "I'm finished here," she said, and she rose from the table and walked out of the room.

In the silence afterward, Sam glanced at Otto. He looked even less of a man than he did at the start, everything about him sunken and defeated. "Do you know anything worthwhile?" Sam asked. "Anything that might be of scientific importance to the U.S. Army?"

Slowly, his face full of resignation, Otto shook his head.

Three hours later, his heart weighing heavily inside him, Sam went in search of Anna—*Liesel*. He would think of her as Liesel now.

He found her sitting in the same bare room as before, her hands in her lap and a faraway look on her face, but she rose swiftly as he opened the door, everything about her alert.

"Will he be able to go to America?" Sam shook his head, and she let out a long, low breath. "Will he be prosecuted?"

"Yes, I should think so. He'll stay at Camp King until his case comes to trial. What happens then, or what sentence he receives, I don't know." The sentences for men like Otto Scholz, scientists and industrialists and businessmen, would most likely be light. Germany needed these men to get back on its feet, whatever they'd believed, whatever they'd done.

She nodded slowly. "It doesn't feel the way I thought it would."

"How did you think it would feel?"

She shrugged and pursed her lips. "I don't know the word in English. As if things have been made right."

"But they haven't been?"

"I don't know. I said what I wanted to say. I suppose that is all I should have expected. It is over, now."

Sam's gut tightened, because it wasn't over. Liesel just didn't know it yet, and he was the one who had to tell her. "Liesel… the photographs taken by Hoffmann… they've been released to the newspapers."

She stared at him for a second, uncomprehending, before realization flared darkly in her eyes. "You mean… of me?" He nodded. "How?"

"I don't know." Major Lewis hadn't told him, but Sam suspected Sergeant Belmont. He was the sergeant Lewis had mentioned who had found the photos of Liesel, and he had an axe to grind, just as Major Lewis had said. And, by heaven, what an axe it was. Sam couldn't even blame him, although it felt unfair, considering what he knew of Liesel.

Liesel let out a soft huff of breath. "So I am—what is it you say? Fired?"

"Yes…"

Her eyes narrowed as she looked at him. "There is more, isn't there?"

Sam shoved his hands in his pockets as he hunched his shoulders. "The U.S. Army has been put in something of a difficult position. It looks pretty bad, to have a secretary with access to classified files having had her photo taken at the Chancellery."

"You blame me?" She sounded more disbelieving than hurt.

"*No.* Of course I don't. Not since you've explained. And I told Major Lewis how you weren't like that, how you actually hid Jews in your house. But… he didn't care."

Liesel's lips twisted. "Of course he didn't."

"He's got to look as if he's doing something," Sam explained miserably. "It doesn't really matter what the facts are."

"So what is he doing?"

"He's said you'll have to be taken to a detention camp, until they decide what to do with you. I tried to argue with him, but he's not even the one making the decision. It's out of our hands. I'm so sorry…" He trailed off, hating how helpless he felt.

Liesel stared at him for a moment before she slowly sank into a chair. "Prison," she stated almost wonderingly. "Am I to be tried?"

"They can't try you for anything," Sam assured her, although it felt like little comfort at the moment. "Only women who were actively involved, guards in camps and the like, are being tried for war crimes."

"But I could remain in a camp for months, or years," she said slowly. "You've seen how it is. I'll be forgotten."

"Surely not years," Sam said, albeit a bit weakly. He had no idea what would happen to her. The camps were overflowing, badly run, terribly disorganized. They bred disease and despair in equal measure, and Liesel would have no one in this country to be her advocate.

"I suppose it doesn't matter," Liesel said after a moment, her gaze distant and unfocused. "I don't have anywhere else to go, after all." She shrugged her shoulders in what Sam suspected was meant to be a gesture of indifference but looked to him like despair.

"There is another possibility," he said, his voice full of hesitation, his heart starting to thud. Major Lewis had said as much, in his careless, sardonic way. *If you care about her so much, Houghton, then do something about it. You'll be demobbed soon enough anyway, after this.*

Liesel looked up, her hazel eyes clear and guileless. "What is it?"

"You could…" He took a deep breath. "You could marry me."

The silence that followed this statement felt absolute, as if he'd thrown a blanket over the room, snuffed everything out.

She stared at him, her expression more opaque than ever.

Sam let out a shaky laugh. "Sometimes," he said, "just sometimes, I wish I could tell what you were thinking. Like now."

"Why would you marry *me*?" she asked quietly.

Sam felt himself flushing. "Because I love you." She simply stared and he rushed to add, "I admit, we don't know each other as well as… as well as we could. But what I've seen of you, Liesel, of your strength and kindness… your determination… what I've seen, I have loved. And I want to… to know you more. Better. To love you more." He was stumbling over the words, embarrassed by the ring of sincerity in his voice. He'd accused her only hours ago, so why should she believe him now? And yet he meant every word.

Liesel continued to stare. Her silence unnerved him; it made him feel as if he were a raw boy and she a worldly-wise woman who knew so much better, having lived so much more. And wasn't that how it really was, despite the fact he was eight years older than her?

Then, to his surprise, her eyes filled with tears and she looked down, hiding her face from him.

"Liesel…"

"I don't deserve you," she whispered. "You heard what I said to my father? About the Soviets?"

"You mean you were raped," Sam answered steadily. "Yes."

"They weren't all evil," she said after a moment. "Some of them were quite kind." She glanced up at him for a brief second, her expression veiled, the tracks of her tears visible on her cheeks. "I stayed with a lieutenant from Kiev for several weeks. To keep the others away."

Sam swallowed. "I understand."

"Do you? Sometimes I feel like a stranger to myself. I did then. As if I wasn't even living. It went on for months, every day feeling like it could be my last, as if the world was ending all around me... and then, suddenly, it was as if we were meant to be normal again. As if someone had pushed a button and it was time to go to work and to the shops and to *live* again, but I'd forgotten how. I still don't know if I can ever remember."

"I understand what you're telling me, Liesel. I know you've... you've been through so much." The words felt completely inadequate, but he didn't have any others. What could he say to that? What comfort could he possibly offer? "I want to offer you freedom, not a different kind of prison." For if she went into a detention camp, he knew, it would be as good as a prison. He paused, his throat working as he tried to form the words. "I wouldn't expect... *that* of you, not until you were ready." Even the tips of his ears were burning now.

She pursed her lips. "And if I was never ready?"

"Then I'd learn to live with that," he said staunchly.

"That is quite a sacrifice to make."

"You've made a few sacrifices yourself, Liesel."

Her lips curved faintly. "It's strange to hear you say my real name."

"I'll say it again. Marry me, Liesel." Sam's voice grew stronger with the strength of his conviction. "Marry me, and we'll make a life together. It will take time and patience and effort, but I really do believe we could learn to be happy together."

As she stared at him, her eyes filled with tears once more. "You are too good a man for me, Sam Houghton."

"I'm not," Sam insisted. "I swear I'm not."

"To tie yourself to a woman such as me?"

"I told you, I love you. I know you don't… you don't love me." He felt he had to say it. "But maybe in time…"

"You're wrong," she said quietly, and he tried not to flinch at the obvious rejection. "You're wrong," she repeated, "because I do love you… at least as much as I can love anyone, with the way that I am. You are a good man, Sam Houghton, the best man I have ever known. But…" She let out a heavy sigh and dabbed at her eyes. "You paint such a pretty picture with your words. I want to believe it could be true."

"It could be, Liesel. I swear it. I want to marry you. Marry me. Please." As he said the words, he realized how much he meant them, but he also realized what an impossible choice he was giving her. *Marry me or be sent to a camp.* It was hardly fair, and yet what other option did he have? She couldn't come to America unless she was his wife. Major Lewis had made that much clear. "I don't want to pressure you," he continued stiltedly. "If… if you really felt you couldn't… it wouldn't…"

"I can't say that," she admitted brokenly. "But I am afraid to hope. To believe. What if you felt you'd made a mistake? You might hate me one day."

"I could never hate you."

"You were angry with me before," she reminded him with a small, sad smile.

"Because I took those photographs at face value. I should have waited for you to explain. I should have trusted you."

"I don't blame you." She wiped her eyes. "I don't blame you at all."

"Perhaps you need to stop blaming yourself," Sam said quietly. "And give yourself a chance to be happy. If… if you think you could be happy, with me."

She let out a soft laugh, her eyes still full of tears. "I *want* to believe that."

"Just like you wanted to want to kiss me," Sam returned wryly.

"And I did," she reminded him. "So perhaps I could take another risk."

Sam could hardly believe she was saying what he thought she was, what he longed for so desperately. "You... could?"

"Maybe." Her eyes glinted with humor now as well as tears, and she took a step toward him. "If you really mean all you say."

"I do. I'll say it again. I want to marry you, Liesel, and make a life with you. If you want it, as well."

They stared at each other as the silence in the room stretched on, spooled into something else. Something like hope.

A faint, fragile smile teased the corners of Liesel's mouth. "And if I said yes?" she asked, and Sam felt his heart expanding like a balloon in his chest. A grin spread over his face, one he couldn't help.

"You'd make me a very happy man indeed. The happiest." A pause as she continued to stare at him, her eyes still so dark, that lovely, faint smile on her face, flickering like a promise. "Will you say it?" Sam asked.

Another pause, endless with possibility, with memory, with regret and hope and wonderful what-ifs that felt just out of his reach, but coming closer.

Her smile deepened, and a light came into her eyes. "Yes," Liesel said, and she stepped into Sam's arms.

EPILOGUE

New York, October 1948

The wind off the harbor is brisk, the trees full of autumn color. Her hair whips around her face before, with a little laugh, she tucks it under her scarf.

"It shouldn't be long now," Sam says. He puts his arm around her, gently, because it still feels fragile, this thing that has been growing between them since she first said yes.

They married in a quiet ceremony just a few weeks after his proposal, and she went to live with him in his villa in Bergen-Enkheim. It had felt so strange, drifting around those rooms, having nothing to do yet plenty to eat. The cook and the chauffeur hadn't known how to deal with her; they'd been wary at first, but in time they'd become, if not friends, then companions of a sort.

As for Sam… for those first few months they'd moved around each other like awkward and polite strangers, murmuring their apologies every time they came into contact. Sam had made a great show of sleeping in the second bedroom, assuring her she could lock her door if she needed to. She knew she didn't, but she was tempted nonetheless, just to be sure, even though she knew the sound of the bolt sliding across would surely hurt him.

Then, in March, Sam had been demobbed and they'd gone back to America. Home for him, and a world of utter otherness for her.

Sam had assured her there were plenty of Germans in Philadelphia—"The area is known for the Pennsylvania Dutch—but it's actually *Deutsch*, see? Germans!" He'd been ebullient, as excited as a little kid, which filled her with affection. Still, it didn't take long for her to realize that none of the Pennsylvania Dutch spoke with an accent like she did, and everyone else realized it, as well.

She tried not to mind their sideways, suspicious looks; at least Sam's family had been gracious, if a bit surprised, welcoming her warily and then, with time, more warmly. And Sam… Sam had been so patient, so kind, so much so that it almost hurt, like the beauty of a spring day, a sweetness that was hard to bear because she wasn't used to it.

Six months into their marriage, she had told him she was ready for them to truly be man and wife, and the look of hunger in his eyes had sent a tremor through her, of both longing and fear. She felt she owed him that much at least, but then he'd kissed her, his lips moving to her neck, her shoulder, and already she'd gone somewhere else in her mind. She was on the shore of the Baltic Sea, where they'd once gone on holiday, collecting seashells with Friedy, the sun on her face, the wind in her hair, Friedy's laugh one of pure joy…

Sam had drawn back, a bemused look on his face, pain in his eyes. "We'll try again another time, eh?" he'd said, and he'd kissed her forehead, which had made Liesel love him all the more.

It had taken another six months of gentle patience before she hadn't had to go anywhere in her mind. Sometimes, next to him, she feels about a thousand years old, as if when she looked in the mirror she'd see an old crone like in a fairy tale, with a beaky nose and gray straggly hair, warts on her chin.

Even now, she craves Sam's innocence, his simple sense of right and wrong, his joy and wonder at what the world can hold. He still believes in concepts like justice and truth, and he greets every new day like an adventure. His attitude is like an elixir of youth, injected into her very veins, reminding her that there are still good things, that hope exists, and so does love. She loves him now more than she did the day he proposed at Camp King; love, she has discovered, is something that can be nurtured, something that can grow. Something that can survive.

"Look," Sam says, and she sees it—the *S.S. Columbia*, chugging slowly and surely into the white-ruffled harbor.

She turns to him and smiles, feels it bloom in her heart and burst forth like a song on her face. *At last.*

It is another hour before the passengers begin to disembark, and she strains to see the face of each one as they come through the doors of the immigration hall. Half of them are well-heeled tourists, the other half dressed neatly in thrice-mended clothes, a look of weary, wary hope on their faces that she knows so well.

The passengers keep coming, but she doesn't recognize a single one. Hope sours into disappointment, and worse, fear.

Sam squeezes her hand. "Don't worry," he says. "More are coming."

She nods, knowing her fears are groundless. She *knows* whom she is meeting today; she has been waiting for her for years, has been hoping for and dreaming of this moment.

And then she is there—emerging from behind the swinging doors, her anxious gaze scanning the waiting crowds. Her hair is shorter now, a blonde bob that brushes her chin, and her coat cannot quite hide the angular gauntness of her body, even after all this time. She is twenty-two years old.

"*Rosa!*" Liesel calls, and she turns, her face lighting up with joy. Liesel runs toward her and they embrace, weeping and laughing, as if they are long-lost sisters, as if they are the only family the other has, and perhaps they are.

It took Sam nearly a year to track Rosa down; she'd survived Theresienstadt, although her mother had not, and she had been in a camp for displaced persons near Dresden since the end of the war. Liesel had written her a letter full of apology as well as trepidation, afraid that Rosa would hate her for her part in her father's betrayal. Yet when Rosa had written back, her letter had only held gratitude, as well as joy that Liesel had reached out to her. It had made the rest easy, even obvious. It had taken a year for Sam to arrange a visa and passage for her to come to America; she would live with them, her family now.

Liesel hugs her tightly, unable to keep the tears from streaking down her face. At last. *At last.* As Rosa's arms clasp her just as tightly, she thinks of all whom they have lost—Gerda and Ilse, dear, dear Friedy. And her father, too, in a different way.

He is still serving his prison sentence; he was prosecuted six months after she'd seen him at Camp King and in the end he was given just a year and a half. He will be released in a few months, and Liesel does not know what will happen then. Will she forgive him? She wrote to him, at least, to let him know where she was, and he has written back many times, pleading with her to forgive him, and she has not yet been able to bring herself to reply, although she thinks she might one day. She wants to, and that is, she has realized, a good thing.

She does not want to harden herself the way her father once did, inured to other people's pain and misery, justifying it out of fear or indifference. She wants to be able to forgive; she wants not to *want* to love, but to actually do it, day by day.

Because love, she has come to understand, is a choice that can be made every day, with effort, with deliberate conviction, with difficulty. It takes strength, just as her mother said.

She lifts her face to the sky, to the sun, and holding Rosa's hand, with the other she unclasps the pocket watch that she has worn around her neck for the last seven years. She presses it into Rosa's hand, and the other woman nods her understanding, tears spilling out of her eyes once more. A promise kept.

Still holding's Rosa hand, she reaches for Sam's with her other. He laces his fingers with hers and squeezes, making her smile. Then the three of them head for home.

A LETTER FROM KATE

I want to say a huge thank you for choosing to read *The Girl from Berlin*. If you enjoyed it, and want to keep up to date with all my latest releases, just sign up at the following link. Your email address will never be shared and you can unsubscribe at any time.

www.bookouture.com/kate-hewitt

This story is one I have had in my heart for many years, and I am so very glad to finally have the opportunity to tell it. I have always been fascinated and moved by the plight of ordinary Germans during the Second World War, and how extraordinary—extraordinarily brave and difficult—it must have been to stand against such a powerful and evil regime as they did.

While the Scholzes are a fictional family, Liesel's father Otto is based on the lives of several chemists who worked for IG Farben, and were involved in the development of both Buna rubber and Zyklon B, the poison gas used in Nazi extermination camps. In fact, IG Farben became known as "the devil's chemist"; it was the only German company in the Third Reich that had its own concentration camp. In 1947, twenty-four of the company directors were tried in the U.S. military courts, and eleven were acquitted. Of the remaining thirteen, none served more than eight years in prison, most much less; they almost all returned to company directorships or other positions of power afterwards.

I hope you loved *The Girl from Berlin* and if you did, I would be very grateful if you could write a review. I'd love to hear what you think, and it makes such a difference helping new readers to discover one of my books for the first time.

I love hearing from my readers—you can get in touch on my Facebook page, through Twitter, Goodreads or my website. Thanks again for reading *The Girl from Berlin*!

Thanks,
Kate

katehewittauthor

www.kate-hewitt.com

@author_kate

ACKNOWLEDGEMENTS

While I had the idea for *The Girl from Berlin* for many years, I was too daunted to write it, because I knew how much research it would require. Therefore I must thank my dear husband, Cliff, who was my very capable research assistant, and in particular helped immensely with the many details regarding the workings of IG Farben. He also cheerfully accepted a wife virtually living in Nazi Germany for several months, so much so that I actually dreamed about it!

Many books informed my research and helped me immensely with the details of everyday life in pre and post-war Germany, and I must make particular mention of Roger Moorhouse's *Berlin at War*, Frederick Taylor's *Exorcising Hitler*, Tim Heath's *Hitler's Girls: Doves Among Eagles* and the memoirs *Woman in Berlin* and *Growing up in Hitler's Germany*.

I also must thank all the wonderful team at Bookouture, including my lovely editor Isobel, who gives me so much encouragement and freedom to write the stories I do, as well as my wonderful copyeditor Jade, and the others at Bookouture, including Alexandra, Alex, Alba, Saidah, Sarah, and Kim, who all help to make my books the best they can be. Thank you!

Also thank you to my many friends who asked about the book, and then patiently listened to me go on and on about all I'd researched. And last but not least, thanks to Caroline, Ellen, Teddy, Anna, and Charlotte. This book is finally finished! I promise I won't talk about it anymore. Love, Mom

Lightning Source UK Ltd.
Milton Keynes UK
UKHW010633210721
387524UK00001B/196

9 781838 888008

BOOKS BY KATE HEWITT

A Mother's Goodbye
Secrets We Keep
Not My Daughter
No Time to Say Goodbye
A Hope for Emily
Into the Darkest Day
When You Were Mine

THE FAR HORIZONS TRILOGY
The Heart Goes On
Her Rebel Heart
This Fragile Heart

THE AMHERST ISLAND TRILOGY
The Orphan's Island
Dreams of the Island
Return to the Island

THE
GIRL
FROM
BERLIN